The Vicar of Sorrows

By the same author

The Sweets of Pimlico
Unguarded Hours
Kindly Light
The Healing Art
Who Was Oswald Fish?
Wise Virgin
Scandal
Gentlemen in England
Love Unknown
Stray
The Laird of Abbotsford
The Life of John Milton
Hilaire Belloc
How Can We Know?
Pen Friends From Porlock
Tolstoy
Incline Our Hearts
A Bottle in the Smoke
The Daughters of Albion
Jesus
The Rise and Fall of the House of Windsor

A. N. WILSON

The Vicar of Sorrows

W·W·NORTON & COMPANY
New York London

First American edition 1994
First published as a Norton paperback 1995

Printed in the United States of America

Manufacturing by the Haddon Craftsmen, Inc.

ISBN 0-393-31294-1

W. W. Norton & Company, Inc.
500 Fifth Avenue, New York, N.Y. 10110
W. W. Norton & Company Ltd.
10 Coptic Street, London WC1A 1PU

1 2 3 4 5 6 7 8 9 0

Note

Ditcham, the village where much of this story takes place, is fictitious, but from its rough general location in Berkshire the reader could discern that, if it existed, it would be in the diocese of Oxford. I should like to emphasise that all the characters in this book are wholly imaginary, and that none of them is intended as a portrait of any actual person, living or dead. This is true of the main characters, and of peripheral characters, such as the Archdeacon, the diocesan Bishop and the suffragan 'Bishop of Didcot'. These characters in my book are not intended to be portraits of any past, present or future bishops or archdeacons who might operate within the diocese of Oxford.

A. N. Wilson

Innocents

I

In the bleak mid-winter,
Lo-o-ong ago!

The words of the carol, which Griselda Kreer sang in church, three days after Christmas, suddenly set off a train of irrelevant associations. Her mind often played this trick with hymns or familiar lines of poetry. It seized the words and appropriated them for her own inner history. She thought now, not of the stable of Bethlehem but of her lover, half a century ago. The winter was the winter of 1942–3. She and her husband were living in Gerrard's Cross. Francis was a little boy. The flat in Cornwall Gardens, which had belonged to her parents, was more or less permanently empty.

She had been in love with Eric, off and on, for about three years. She could never work out in her mind whether her husband knew of this fact and bravely overlooked it, or whether, as she suspected, she had married the least sensitive man in the world. Either way, there was little that she could do about loving Eric. Everything stood in their way. The war caused periods of long separation. Eric had joined the RAF in the late summer of '39; he had not needed to be called up. He had been in the Battle of Britain; his Spitfire had been shot down, and he had written to tell her that he had been badly burned. While he was in a hospital, more than a hundred miles from Gerrard's Cross, she could hardly see him. She had thought about him all the time. Letters intensified feelings on both sides. Until they began to exchange letters, Griselda had imprisoned her feelings about Eric inside her own head. He must have guessed, from all their exchanges of 'meaningful' glances at parties, and from the fact that, even after she had admitted she was married, she still permitted – on the few occasions they had been alone together – a little 'necking'.

They had not, at that stage, been lovers. There was too much at stake: the house in Gerrard's Cross, the happiness of her husband (about which she cared), the Little Boy. She could not risk all that, for the sake of an adventure with an airman whom she did not, in reality, know very well.

Only in the letters had her feelings come tumbling out: the frustrations, the missed opportunities, the simple lust for Eric's body cascaded in her looping hand over many a blue page, guiltily and surreptitiously conveyed to the Post Office when she walked the Little Boy into the village! Strange that her husband, whose war was devoted to decoding messages and unearthing German plots, should have allowed all this to take place beneath his very gaze.

And, then, that curious set of chances, *In the bleak mid-winter, Long ago*!

Her husband had scarcely looked up from his crossword; merely removed his pipe from his mouth and said, 'You seem bored. It's a wretched life for you at the moment. I'm all right. I always have my puzzles to amuse me, either here or at Bletchley.' (He worked on ENIGMA.) 'It's not natural for you to be stuck here for months, never seeing people you care about.'

How these sentences had made her heart leap; that 'school' feeling of having been found out in a misdemeanour! But, if so, he played it very cool! He paused long enough, after the last phrase, to allow her to think of Eric, to let the emanation of Eric, the idea of him, float powerfully into the room, so that his presence there seemed stronger than her husband's. And then the husband continued, 'I mean – when did you last hear from Joan? Or Joyce, come to that? Or Gwen?'

Gwen was in the WRAF, Joyce had joined the WRNS; Joan, braving out the Blitz, was driving ambulances in London, and in her last, effusive, round-bottomed letter had insisted that she and Griselda simply *must* get together.

'Apart from anything else, you really should keep an eye on the flat,' said her husband.

This was all true: and he could not, even with all his cleverness, have foreseen what would happen. Griselda had gone up to London, leaving Little Boy with her husband and the young woman who 'helped' – hardly worthy to be called a nanny. She and Joan had enjoyed themselves for a girlish few days: fish and chips at midnight on Joan's floor, talk of boys, and of the old days; improvised little parties in friends' flats – men whom one had not expected to meet, back on surprise leave, records on the wind-up gramophone, dancing in confined rooms.

At one of these parties, wholly by chance, she had found herself face to face with Eric. Nothing could have prepared her for the shock of seeing his poor face without the bandages. For the rest of her life, Griselda felt ashamed that, for a short second, she had allowed disgust to flicker into her own face. How brave of him, to walk about with that face! It was braver than being a fighter pilot. The eyes still functioned, but they seemed so much darker and smaller, as though they were peering at the world through a purplish mask. The left of his face was a garish splash of colour. The nose had been reconstructed, rather crudely, by plastic surgeons, and the surface of chin and neck looked stretched and plasticky, like sausage-skin, presumably grafted from some other part of the body.

Dancing in the darkness, she had felt a passionate need to show him that she disregarded the face. If she had shown more control of her own expression, in the first seconds of their encounter, perhaps she would have been able to show fiercer control, later in the evening, of her passions; but a refusal to become his lover that night would have been unimaginably mean-spirited. Smooching in the dark, and gliding up and down the tiny space of carpet in someone's room to the melody of those wonderful songs, she did not, anyway, notice his face. *South of the Border*! *The Isle of Capri*! How sad they all were, these songs of separation and passion and romantic love. It would be 'goodbye on the Isle of Capri' for Eric and her; but not yet, not yet. They had not even stayed long enough at the party to find Joan to explain where they were going. You did not need to explain in those days. If you saw a chance, you took it.

The party had been somewhere in Knightsbridge. Though not

tight, they could have been soberer, and the pedestrian journey, in the black-out, had been perilous and long. They took at least two false turns. At one point, they found themselves, giggling and arm in arm, coming out into Exhibition Road and looking up towards the Albert Memorial, a brooding spire against an inky, blue-black sky.

Walks in the black-out were charged with a sense of danger and a quasi-erotic excitement. Even if they were invisible, you had this sense that there were couples, in almost any doorway or alley which you passed, coupling. In any event, Griselda had felt an overpowering desire for Eric during their dark walk. She really wanted *it*, greedily and insatiably, in a way that she never recalled wanting it with any man before. Neither of them slept much that night when, after many a twisty-turn and loss of step, they found Cornwall Gardens and blundered into the flat. For the whole of the next day, too, with the telephone off the hook, they rampaged about among her mother's furniture. Later that evening, they had replaced the receiver, and Joan had telephoned and they had all gone dancing. Joan had befriended a dreamy Sub-Lieutenant, at that point seconded to the Admiralty, and they had all had supper together at a restaurant in Soho – and then a short spell at the dance – and then back to Cornwall Gardens, the two of them. It was extraordinary that two people could have such energy, and such hunger, for one another and for *it*.

Fifty years had passed since the incident, and now the details all flooded back into her mind, in Ditcham parish church, of all unsuitable places, a few days after Christmas. Half a century! She remembered the joy of being completely naked for Eric. She had removed her clothes in her husband's presence, but she had never, properly speaking, exposed body and soul, nakedly, to the man she had married. She now saw the difference, in the story of Adam and Eve, between their innocent and absolute nakedness before the Fall, and the cringing with fig-leaves which followed it. With Eric, she had stepped back into Paradise. Stretching her arms above her head, she had enjoyed her own nakedness as well as enjoying its effect upon him. Her breasts had tautened. The tendrils of hair beneath her arms had drawn beguiling shapes against her white skin. And she had watched that poor, wounded head creeping up her legs, and exploring and adoring her body. Standing up, sitting down, squatting like doggies, on the bed, in the bath, on the kitchen table, they had given themselves, joyfully, to this rite.

After eight days, they had reached an ultimatum. Eric, of course, dear man, had said the things he knew he must say; he had probably meant them. He had asked her to leave her husband and to marry him; he would look after Little Boy; they could set up house together – somewhere. . . .

She knew that in the real world, after the war, it would be impossible. She did not know where all the thoughts and aspirations came from, which had poured out into their letters; but, after their ten days' idyll in the flat, she knew that *life* with Eric would never make her happy; nor could she make him happy. She would be 'all right' with her husband. Perhaps the cunning old devil, with his pipe and his crossword, had known this? Perhaps that was why he had let her go up to London for ten days?

For years after the war, she had tormented herself with the knowledge that snobbery had, at that precise moment on the bed with Eric, saved her marriage. At least, it was not like the momentary expression of disgust at his physical appearance, which had brought her defences down. At least, he could never have guessed. After all, he probably thought that he 'spoke BBC', and that, therefore, one would not notice any great difference between himself, and the world she knew. But there was something shaming about this knowledge, and it did cause her pain.

Their idyll ended, they had sat in the flat in Cornwall Gardens and cried themselves silly. They agreed that they must never meet again, that it was all too strong, and that neither of them would ever be able to summon up the willpower to part for a second time. They more or less kept this vow. She did know his address, and, some time in the late 1950s, he had sent her a change of address card and reported his marriage – news which was five years stale. Later, in the '60s, another change of address card had come. He had moved further into Kent, somewhere near Deal.

Griselda Kreer was a widow by the time she received this intelligence. She had long since sold the house in Gerrard's Cross. After a couple of improvident investments, she had begun to 'dip' into capital. She lived in her mother's flat. The old lady had survived until 1970. They weren't happy sharing and, when her mother died, Griselda had sold the choicer china and furniture, just to make ends meet. Life would have been easier had Little Boy (Francis) chosen a more lucrative profession.

Her voice, though eighty years old, was still melodious as she trilled:

What can I give him
Poor as I am?
If I were a shepherd,
I could bring a lamb.

At the other end of the church, resplendent in his white and gold, Little Boy said, 'Our Father, which art in Heaven.'

Afterwards, most of the congregation – there were only about fifteen of them on that icy day – had been asked back for drinks by Wing-Commander and Mrs Maxwell-Lee.

2

The Maxwell-Lees' was not the largest house in the village: that was the Old Vicarage, now occupied by a businessman, thought to be Roman Catholic (if anything), who never came to church. The conversion of the blacksmith's forge had been the delighted invention of some minor Arts and Crafts architect in the time of the Boer War. Brick paths led to an eclectic blend of craftsy front-door (note the latch and lock, all somewhat Voysey), latticed windows, diamond panes. The long drawing-room, once the forge, was lightened by a pale green carpet and a light, flowery paper, and cream paintwork. Mrs Kreer thought contemptuously that the covers and cushions were all a bit John Lewisy, but she knew she must guard herself at this hour of morning. The tummy emptied, and irrational bursts of rage or uncharity could take possession of the mind.

If the *Iliad* began with the wrath of Achilles, this story could be said to begin with the wrath of Mrs Kreer. In fact, hovering about the pristine drawing-room of the Maxwell-Lees, some strange furies or divinities might almost have been said to take possession of those present. For during the party, which lasted about an hour, several persons there made decisions which would materially change the destiny of the others. These decisions all had a fateful strength, though none present knew what passed through the others' minds.

'No', said the Wing-Commander, 'I knew a lot of the splendid chaps who *were* involved' – they spoke of the Battle of Britain – 'but you see, I'm *just* too young. Joined up in '44, well, the very end of '43, but not really active until '44.'

He was a spare man, slight in build, with a very thin moustache over his upper lip and his very yellow teeth. He drank a pinkish liquid which, Mrs Kreer thought, looked more promising than the South African sherry which had been given to her and the other guests. He spoke with a slight stammer, and seemed wholly unbelligerent in bearing. Horticulture, and local history, and an amateurish love of Latin poetry occupied his mind more than the war.

'I think,' said Griselda Kreer, 'that this country owes more to the Battle of Britain heroes than to anyone.'

The Wing-Commander saw a pretty woman say these words. Snowy hair framed a baby-doll face. Perfect Kensington manners. Her voice was somehow redolent of parties before the war, parties more exotic than the one she was now attending.

Little Boy, still beautiful, but now grey and slightly balding, was leaning decoratively against the small mantelpiece at the far end of the room, listening with a vacant expression to Mr Pimm, a farmer (and the largest landowner in the village), and Mrs Renton, a retired gentlewoman, living in a surprisingly small house on the Green.

'When one *thinks*,' said Mrs Kreer emphatically, 'what they endured.'

'Oh, quite,' said the Wing-Co. Qs caused him slight difficulty so that the word 'quite' almost came as a little song. Mrs Kreer desperately wanted a Twiglet. She could see that a plate was 'circulating', but it was beyond her reach. Her stomach was gurgling and she could feel herself becoming over-heated.

'I mean,' she said, 'I am sure you would agree, because you have been in the Air Force. There is something so heroic about being prepared to fight in the air. Is it by Walter de la Mare, that lovely poem about the airman who foresees his death?'

Habits of inaccuracy, which the Wing-Commander regarded as typically feminine, embarrassed him. He could not have named the author of this famous anthology-piece without seeming to put his guest 'down'. And she was only here for a few days from London. 'Ah,' he said, 'I must do my duty. Empty glasses that need filling. Gerald – perhaps you can entertain Mrs Kreer.'

It seemed on the face of things improbable.

'Mrs Kreer, this is Mr Gerald S—'

'Spittle' – that gentleman had a habit, which enraged the Wing-Commander, of finishing his sentences for him.

Griselda Kreer gave a darting, imploring look to the Wing-Commander. She did not wish to be left alone with Mr Spittle, but her host had gone into the mêlée with, 'Alison, my dear! Drink up!'

You could hardly stay in the vicarage for four days, as Griselda had just done, without hearing of the Spittles. They had moved into the village a few years ago, not to retire, but with a view to retirement. Jessica, Griselda's only grandchild, did a rather cruel imitation of this last phrase. Little Boy squeezed his hands and closed his eyes and used euphemisms. He said that the Spittles were a slight pity; that it was a shame, in a small community, particularly in a rural community, when two people, so glaringly failed to – he hardly knew how to express it – to *fit in*. Griselda slightly despised Little Boy when he did not have the courage to say what he meant.

'Well,' said Gerald Spittle, 'this is all most agreeable.'

Mrs Kreer found charm in the rustic burr in Mr Spittle's voice. He seemed to 'fit in' to a village, or at any rate to her idea of a village, much better than did Little Boy. He wore a lovat-coloured suit, a knitted ochre tie and a rather smart crimson waistcoat. The face of a ploughman, though he in fact, as everyone knew, was something in central heating. White hair.

'I was just saying to the Wing-Commander,' said Mrs Kreer,

'that this country owes more to the heroes of the Battle of Britain than to any other group or person.'

'You should try telling that to your son,' said Mr Spittle. 'He gave us some real pacifist talk at Remembrance Day. Now, don't get me wrong. I'm not criticising. Not at all.'

There were innumerable examples, in all the Spittle-sagas which beguiled meal-times at the vicarage, of the fact that both Spittles disliked Little Boy's way of running the parish. Mrs Kreer, who did not understand Church, had never listened to the finer points of these disputes. She did not have the stomach for theology and its tendency to make people acrimonious. Let parsons do their job and, if we dislike it, let us shop elsewhere: this was her attitude. Professional churchgoers, like the Spittles, who took an interest in which form of service was used, were freaks. But here was something different, an altogether different reason for the hostility between Little Boy and the Spittles. It had never occurred to Griselda that Little Boy was one of those Greenham Common types of clergyman, who favoured lesbianism and Ban the Bomb. Services at the Little Boy's church had always seemed, to his mother, traditional enough.

'Oh yes,' said Mr Spittle. 'Now, in my line of country; I'm, as you may know, in heating components. Well, that's a difficult way of talking. Let's say,' he smiled patronisingly, in deference to Mrs Kreer's sex and good looks, 'let's say I have quite a lot to do with the twiddly bits of radiators. Now, I yield to no one in my admiration for the way the Germans have taken hold of themselves, and rebuilt their industry. And they are the top nation of Europe, there's no doubt about that. But your son – well, I think we neglect the past at our peril. That's my view, mind.'

'You don't mean to say,' said Mrs Kreer, 'that Francis was saying we should not have fought the war?'

'To be absolutely honest, Mrs Kreer, I don't remember the details,' said Gerald Spittle. 'And I wouldn't want to misrepresent him. I remember there was a deal about Bach and what was the other one? Oh, the author who sold his soul – Forster, was it?'

'I always think *Faust* is a typical German story,' said Mrs Kreer, parroting something she had once heard her husband say in the war. 'He seems so clever, but he puts all his cleverness at the disposal of evil; and, having worshipped power, he then becomes its slave.'

One of those surges of anger – more and more a feature of her old age – was now bubbling its way to the surface. She could do nothing about it, though a Twiglet would, she knew, have helped. She almost contained all outward composure, but she was looking across the room towards her son. Mr Spittle's mouth was still moving, but she did not listen to his words. It was just *silly* having parties with too many people, all of them bores, and where many people, particularly the elderly, couldn't really hear properly. Little Boy, by the fireplace, looked so *effete*. What had *he* ever done for his country? What risks had *he* ever taken? And he had the face, the cheek, to get up in the pulpit on Armistice Day and start praising German culture! She shook at the thought of it, and she resolved at that moment that, as soon as she returned to London, she would telephone her solicitor.

Francis Kreer, quite unaware that his destiny was changing at that second, stood between Robin Pimm and Mrs Renton (who wasn't a man, though Mrs Kreer, at a distance of twenty feet, had mistaken her for one).

'You see,' said Mrs Renton, her jowl shaking, and her very pop-eyes staring from a face which was pure Colonel Blimp, 'they are layabouts. Until you face up to what the problem is, you can't hope to solve it. We never had people living in cardboard boxes when I was a young girl in London – and, don't forget, I knew about poverty. I was secretary to a very busy parish office in Holborn. But people did a job of work in those days. We never had vagrants.'

'Oh, I'm not so sure,' said Robin Pimm, a very thin man, with a strangely pale face for a farmer. 'We always had the odd tramp. Towns – well, never having lived in a town, thank the Powers, I wouldn't know, and I'd bow to Mrs Renton. But what makes my blood run cold is these hippies. These convoys.'

'There's one very near here, you know,' said Francis. 'They've encamped for the winter at Pixton Heath. People petition the Chief Constable to move them on. But people have to live *somewhere*.'

'Don't forget,' said Mrs Renton, 'that, if you tolerate their funny behaviour, you seem to encourage them. Here we have young mothers bringing up children in the most filthy conditions. And, don't forget, I've worked with Mothers' Unions in Holborn and Hackney, I've known Mums in tenement buildings. But these women are little better – and then there are the young men. Let's face it, they are *layabouts*.'

Alison Bill, a more contemplative member of Francis Kreer's congregation, overheard this outburst and remembered the fervour with which, during the service of Christmas morning, Mrs Renton had sung the praises of a young mother giving birth in the insanitary conditions of a stable.

Miss Bill passed on – awkwardly large for a gathering such as this – in search of someone else to speak to, wondering whether to address Jessica Kreer (Francis's daughter), or whether to give the child a tactfully wide berth.

'Well, I don't honestly feel I know enough about' – Mr Pimm groped for a word, and screwed up his face at its unsatisfactoriness when he came forth with, 'hippies. But what I fear is them coming and spoiling my land. Now, supposing I've sown a field with barley and they take it into their heads to come up this way in the spring. That's what I fear. Or supposing they camp at the top of the village, Potter's Field. It's Common Land. The police couldn't stop 'em camping there, if they knew their rights.'

'We should have to organise something.'

Francis Kreer lifted his hand to shoulder height in a manner which many, particularly men, had found socially confusing. He patted Mrs Renton's shoulder.

'If it happens, if it happens. Don't get excited until it does. One step enough for me!'

'Oh,' said Farmer Pimm, 'we've got to be prepared. I agree with Mrs Renton.'

'Well done,' said Miss Bill when the conversation had broken up and the priest momentarily found himself standing in the middle of the room with no one but this lady to address.

'You handled that very well,' Miss Bill added.

'Did I?'

If Francis Kreer had a besetting sin, it was vanity. He had not noticed that his views about the 'hippies' had been shocking to Mrs Renton and to Robin Pimm. He preferred to accept the judgement of Miss Bill, even though, for the most part, he was prepared to accept hostile judgements of that lady's character. There were some days when Francis wondered how any woman could bear the burden of such plainness through life. It was impossible to know whether Miss Bill meditated upon her appearance with the same severity. She had a thick page-boy fringe, heavy lenses in her spectacles – so heavy that her eyes were like marbles at some angles – and an oval, ruddy face. A slight moustache sprouted on her upper lip. She was not yet fifty.

Miss Bill was a teacher at the private school attended by Francis's daughter, Jessica. It was a source of embarrassment that one of Jessica's teachers should live so near, and be such a faithful member of the congregation; and Francis had not made sufficient effort to resist seeing Miss Bill through the malicious eyes of her schoolgirl charges. Her intensity, her desire, both physically and in spiritual terms, to come too close, were defects of nature which led him into coarse exaggerations. He had often heard himself agree with Jessica when she said that Miss Bill was mad. But, when Miss Bill came to praise his own diplomatic and conversational powers, it was a different story. Francis smiled, even giggled slightly, revealing the one feature of his appearance which was not conventionally beautiful, the uneven teeth. An unkind person had once applied to them the epithet 'rabbity', and his nickname at school, never disclosed to a soul since, had been 'Bunny'. 'There are very big questions here,' he opined. 'It's not merely the young people themselves, often being a nuisance, no doubt. It is the whole problem of homelessness which we have to tackle. And I'm afraid the Church has all too often . . .'

From where he stood with the Vicar's mother, Gerald Spittle looked across the room and watched the priest conceitedly breaking loose from conversation with Miss Bill and fluttering across to join another group of parishioners, which contained Gerald's wife Lindie. Mr Spittle was unaware that his imperfect recollection of the Remembrance Sunday sermon was having such a powerful effect on the Vicar's mother. Malice, however, has an almost magical power of infecting its hearers, and Mr Spittle felt a profound hatred for Francis Kreer.

When they had lived in one of the more genteel suburbs

of Bagshot, Mr and Mrs Spittle had been cherished members of the church's life. Gerald was a lay reader in all but name, according to their Pastor, Terry Widger, and he had even been asked to preach at Immanuel. But then, as Lindie and Gerald had told everyone at Ditcham, Terry Widger had his finger on the pulse. Unlike some priests whom the Spittles were too polite to mention, Widger was a man of tireless energies. In those days, the Spittles had been almost run off their feet by the Church. Indeed, church membership was a full-time occupation! When Lindie was not assisting with the Sunday School, she had been organising coffee mornings, or helping with the pram services on weekday mornings in the narthex, friendly occasions on which every member of the congregation had been encouraged to read, or to lead the others in prayer. The hymns at Immanuel had been of a lively and up-to-date character, of relevance to the young; and this got results!

Mr Spittle knew, as a man of business, that, if you were marketing a product, you simply had to target your buyers. It was no use running the Church like a glorified Antiques Roadshow. It was a phrase which Gerald had used when asked to address the congregation of Immanuel from the pulpit. When they had left Immanuel, Terry had delivered the Spittles a magnificent tribute. He had said that Immanuel's loss would be Ditcham's gain.

It had been a great disappointment to find that, in Ditcham, their services were barely required. True, Kreer asked Gerald to read the lessons occasionally; Lindie started a Sunday School – there wasn't one until she suggested it! They had fought their way on to the Parochial Church Council, and Lindie had cut swathes through the flower rota. But there was no real *life* in this church, no youth fellowship, no house meetings, no Bible study organised for new members, no new members. The services were, to be candid, a one-man band. Lindie had surely put her finger on it when she said that they were little more than an ego-trip.

The Spittles had been three years in the village. The firm of central heating engineers who employed Gerald had moved him to their Reading office. He had tried to represent this change as a promotion, but at best it was 'a move sideways' and, in these hard times, redundancy threatened. 'Gleneagles', the 1950s house with three quarters of an acre of garden, was in every way a perfect retirement home. Its metal-framed windows had superb views across the Downs while allowing in no draught. Very little had needed 'doing' to the house. The Spittles had much energy which had been put at the disposal of the Church. They felt they deserved better than to be placed on flower rotas and asked to make coffee.

Both the Spittles were agreed that there was something 'funny' about their Vicar. When Francis went away, or took his wife and daughter on holiday, he had a friend who came in from Reading to take the services. This friend liked to be called 'Father': Father Wells. He made Gerald Spittle's flesh creep. When they first heard Father Wells use the word 'Mass', the Spittles had considered writing a letter to the Bishop. And you read such things nowadays about that type of clergyman. There had been a case in the *News of the World* only the week before Christmas: KINKY CANON IN VICE RING had been the headline. Lindie said there must be something 'funny' about a man who could befriend a clergyman such as Father Wells. You would never have got Terry Widger asking a creature like that to preach in Immanuel. Gerald bitterly thought of these things as he watched the Vicar make a bee-line for Mrs Maxwell-Lee; just because she gave herself airs and thought herself a lady.

The Spittles' imputation of snobbery was just, though Francis Kreer was only a snob of the mildest kind. He felt instinctively that it would be rather a shame if people such as the Spittles were to 'take over' the church. When he had been trained for the priesthood, as a fellow-seminarian of Father Wells, Francis Kreer had entertained Victorian fantasies about his ministry to the lower orders. One of his heroes had been the hymn writer, John Keble, who rose at dawn in winter months to sweep the snow from the church path so that his parishioners could hobble to Morning Prayer. All this made a powerful emotional appeal. The commuter folk who lived in Ditcham (it was, really, little better than a suburb of London and Reading as far as its population went) were, by comparison, somewhat dull.

In order to reach Mrs Maxwell-Lee, his hostess, Francis Kreer could have done one of two things. He could either have stood beside Mrs Spittle and Miss Norbury, waited for a moment of small-talk and then, when they drifted off to speak to someone else, he could have sidled over to his hostess; or he could have squeezed behind them, edging his body gingerly between Mrs Spittle's bottom and the back of a sofa. In a cowardly moment, he chose the latter course.

The truth was, he could think of nothing to say to either of these ladies, and he was painfully aware (an awareness increased by his third glass of South African amontillado) that Mrs Spittle disliked him. Mingled with her dislike, no doubt, there were some complicated sexual feelings. He had not been a clergyman for twenty years without becoming aware that a high proportion of churchgoers nurse feelings of that sort for priests.

Being very slightly inebriated, he had misjudged the distance between Mrs Spittle's bottom and the sofa; either that, or she had moved back slightly as she spoke to Miss Norbury. Having entered the gap, there was nothing he could do but press on, but the pressing involved at least one bottom.

'Terry Widger used to say,' said Lindie Spittle, 'if mums and toddlers don't come to church, then we are cutting off the church's lifeline. That is the church of the future. Sometimes Terry Widger would hold up a toddler in the pulpit. "Do you want to see the church of the twenty-first century?" he would ask. "Here it is!" '

Miss Norbury sipped her orange squash in silence. She and her mother came as close as possible to Francis's fantasy of Victorian hobblers down the wintry snow-swept path. As loyal as the parishioners of John Keble, they would not have dreamed of questioning their Vicar's manner of conducting parochial affairs.

While in the midst of lauding Terry Widger, Lindie Spittle felt, quite unmistakably, a pair of human hands on her buttocks. She had hardly expected this sort of thing at the Wing-Commander's sherry party. Turning, she saw the Vicar, smiling.

'Just squeezing past – don't let me interrupt,' he said. He was gone, without further courtesies, advancing upon Mrs Maxwell-Lee with, 'Dorothy! A *marvellous* party! And how was your Christmas?'

Mrs Spittle continued to tell Miss Norbury about the Immanuel

Church. Miss Norbury, short and mousy and obedient, looked impassive.

'You see,' said Lindie, 'as soon as Terry heard from the surveyors that the narthex extension would mean a complete rethink of the church heating system, he said: "This is an answer to prayer. We have Gerald! On the spot!" That was Terry all over. He involved people; he used to say, "We bring all our gifts to church; we can serve God by our engineering skills, as well as by preaching the Word." '

But, though she continued to speak of these uplifting matters, Lindie felt herself going all hot and cold; she had, without any question, felt that man's hands in a certain place.

Francis Kreer's wife, Sally, stood by Mrs Pimm, the farmer's wife, and a group of other women.

'My husband says' – it was Mrs Pimm who spoke – 'that them as travels in such a way should be whipped, taking kiddies about in caravans and Dormobiles, with absolutely no hygiene, and no schooling either.'

'Sometimes,' said Sally, 'they have moved out of very unhygienic places in the towns; or they simply don't have anywhere else to live. I saw a programme once on television about . . .'

'Robin says that, if they come on our land by one foot's length, we'll take the law into our *own* hands.'

'It is difficult for everyone.' Sally sighed. Yet another case of the sad old world and its problems. 'We're pretty lucky, aren't we, when you come to think of it?'

If her husband was a cat, Sally Kreer was a dog. When he preened himself, and arched his back and closed his eyes, Sally bounded up to people, hoping to be liked. She had large spaniel eyes which was why, some twenty years ago, he had fallen in love with her. Her slow sympathetic voice was marred, in her husband's ears, by her uncertain grasp of syntax and her unfortunate choice of vocabulary. These were not defects held against her by the grateful Samaritans clients who rang her once each week. (And this was only one of her good works.)

Sally Kreer was still a handsome woman, so much so that it was odd she did not make more of her appearance. She economized by doing her own hair with a 'Teasy-weasy' electrical device, and she seemed not to have noticed that back-combing had gone out of fashion a year or two after she had got married. She had high cheek-bones, and a taut, nervous little mouth, surrounded by premature lines which she emphasized by anxious twitches of the lips when she felt people judging her. It was not easy to be a vicar's wife.

Just within earshot of Sally, Francis hoped that she was being diplomatic about the Travellers. He himself had put Robin Pimm at his ease. He did not want his works of diplomacy spoilt by some gaffe of his wife's. One did not wish to appear unChristian, but one did not need to believe everything one read in the liberal newspapers; nor, in such a gathering as this, to allude to the fact that one even read such newspapers. These people were property owners. They were entitled to fear for their property if a band of Travellers were on the road nearby.

Mrs Wing-Co, as he playfully thought of Dorothy Maxwell-Lee, caught the drift of what the women were saying, and barked out: 'If they come *near* this village, I shall get Ronald to ring up the Chief Constable. If they tried coming here, we'd have to move them on!'

'Miss Bill was telling me,' said Sally, 'that Potter's Field has been Common Land since would it be the Black Death?'

'I don't care if it's been Common Land since the time of Nebuchadnezzar,' said Mrs Pimm, 'we don't want people like that in Ditcham.'

'Hear, hear,' said Mrs Wing-Co.

'Of course, you are right,' said Francis. 'What we are looking at here is essentially a social problem which Ditcham is not equipped to solve.'

'Still,' said Sally, putting, as her husband felt, her silly foot in it, 'if they did come, we could hardly set the dogs on them.'

'Why ever not?' 'Just what they deserve!' 'I'd set dogs on 'em with no hesitation.' A chorus of agreement.

'Not with kids' – Sally wrinkled her nose and opened her mouth to put everyone on her side. 'I don't know if the Mothers' Union shouldn't be thinking of ways we could help out there.'

'I'm afraid,' said Dorothy Maxwell-Lee, 'that they don't deserve helping out. They get themselves into this pickle and we all know why. It's largely through drugs.'

'Is it really?' Sally's spaniel eyes opened even wider than usual. She felt her arguments crumbling.

Francis Kreer looked at his wife and – this was another moment of profound significance – he hated her. A more sophisticated person than Sally would never have allowed herself to be drawn into a controversy about the Travellers. And, anyway, what was the point of having this discussion? The ragamuffin band might never come to the village. But it was not this he minded. It was Sally's revealed *silliness*.

How could she not know that young people, leading a peripatetic life, often took illegal drugs? It was a fact which could be found in any newspaper story about Travellers. It was one of the reasons that the police found no difficulty in making raids on the encampments of the Travellers. Whatever the ragamuffins' right to be on a particular piece of land, they would almost certainly justify a dawn raid by the Drug Squad.

Francis became aware, in the way that married people do, of what his wife was going to say next. A terrible inward game began to play itself inside his brain. If he foresaw a particularly fatuous remark, he silently condemned Sally to 'punishments'. 'Say that, and I shall forget your birthday,' would be a mild sentence, but, for more foolish utterances, stiffer penalties were required: 'Say that, and I shall invite to the house people who I know make you feel shy and awkward.' These gushes of inward malice were involuntary, and he was not proud of them. At this second, a far stronger spurt of hatred darted through his system. A thought which had never before crossed his mind formed itself into one of these secret threats: 'I do not love you. If you say, "All kids have problems," then I shall desert you, and try to humiliate you in public.' The strength and ugliness of the malediction shocked Francis, into whose mind it had crept. No one in the room could possibly know that he had had such a thought, but he felt himself blushing. It seemed as though the whole room had fallen under a curse, and as though everyone present was in a sense a witness to the descent of this dark cloud.

'All kids have problems, of course,' said Sally. 'But *that* sort of problem . . .' Words failed her. It was as if she had no function in the created order, at that specific moment, than to utter words which, like a spell, would unleash the powers of Hell.

'It's the pushers I blame,' said Mrs Maxwell-Lee, who had lost the secret supply of gin with which she and her husband had been refreshing themselves, and had now moved on to the sherry. This admixture of stimulants left her in no doubt about the solution to the world's narcotic problems. 'I should have no hesitation in hanging all pushers. I should be only too happy to pull the trap door myself on any such little vermin.'

With which the company all appeared to agree. Sally, who hated alcohol and had made her first glass 'last', was wide-eyed at such strong talk. Mrs Pimm had moved on to suggest that it would be no bad thing, in the effort to stamp out 'crack', if the habit of the public execution was revived. A gallows in every shopping mall!

Sally suddenly felt one of her mild panic attacks coming on. With a sudden sweat, she thought she might be going to faint. The idea of drugs made her shudder. The mere mention of the word terrified her, and it sometimes appalled her to know that she and Francis had brought into the world a child who would be made aware of such ugliness. But the talk of hanging was, if anything, even more alarming, even more physically repulsive. It was surely time for them all to stop drinking, and go home for some lunch. She tried to catch her husband's eye, but a strange, owlish look of concentration had come into his features, so that, although he was looking in her direction, he was not seeing her. Probably thinking of the Ancient Romans, his hobby! Men were a scream sometimes at parties! But, oh! oh! If she *were* to have a panic attack, there was only one thing which would alleviate it, and it was hard to know how she could do so with lunch to prepare, and three other people 'about' in the house. . . . It was certainly time that she assembled her party. Having failed to catch her husband's eye, Sally waved her wrist, the one with the watch on it, to alert the attention of her mother-in-law, and that of Jessica who, poor thing, had got caught with Lindie Spittle.

Jessica Kreer, nervously making her glass of lemonade warm, and clouding it with moist palms, was pleased to have been asked to a grown-up party; but she was finding it hard going.

'It must be very interesting,' said Lindie Spittle, 'with all those subjects. What was the last one you said?'

Everyone at the party had asked her what she did at school, and because she was a bit tall for her age (twelve) they all assumed she was doing GCSE – or O-levels as all but the Wing-Commander called them. (He called them School Cert.) Jessica, who derived many of her opinions from her father, considered Mrs Spittle a derisory figure: the neat little face, whose texture, slightly downy, had been smothered with an orangey foundation and dabbed with powder which emphasized the down; the very thin lips which she had coloured deep red; the slightly bad breath.

'Human biology,' said Jessica. Knowing the next question – she had been asked it five times that morning – concerned her possible choice of career, she volunteered, 'I haven't decided what I want to do yet when I leave school, but I might be a vet.'

'I was just going to ask you! So, you like animals?' said Mrs Spittle.

'Yes.' Hesitantly. (Doesn't everyone?) There was Mummy, waving her watch. Thank goodness; it would spare Jessica the necessity of listing all her Christmas presents, as she had done for Mrs Pimm, Mr Spittle, Mrs Norbury and others. At least, she had avoided speaking to the Old Bill. While Mrs Spittle moved into Christmas present mode, Jessica could overhear her grandmother repeating herself. All three spoke at once:

'Mummy's saying we should go now.'

'I expect you had some nice Christmas presents?'

'I think this country owes more to the heroes of the Battle of Britain than to *anyone*.'

Jessica was a pallid, toothy child whose dark eyes did not reveal much of what she thought of the world. She had not enjoyed the party, but she had felt humiliated by her mother so publicly calling them to order. It felt as though she was being treated like a child, instead of someone who had been asked to a grown-up party. She also disliked the condescension of the Wing-Commander who made a silly joke while he helped her on with her coat: 'Hope you can walk home, Jessica! Glad you're not driving, or you might be breathalysed!'

'I was drinking lemonade,' she said seriously. 'It is others who might have been breathalysed.'

Her mother, her father, her grandmother were all a little tipsy, or so it seemed as they emerged into the lunch-time, frosty air with their 'Lovely party!', their 'It's as much a part of the season as mince-pies – where should we be without the Maxwell-Lees' party?' on their lips.

The Old Forge House lay on the brow of the hill at the top of the village. The (modern) vicarage lay about halfway down the hill, nearer the church. It was a walk of some six or seven minutes. Puddles lay on the surface of the road like splintered glass. Stiff and hoar-frosted, the trees were magically beautiful; hedges and fields were white. Their breath came out like dragon's smoke. Above them brooded a yellowish-pink sky. Already, at twenty past one, the light was fading.

The two Mrs Kreers, mother-in-law and daughter-in-law, teetered along. Griselda, in her bootees, was fearful of a fall. Sally, who prided herself on being good with the old (as she so often said, you got enough practice, being a vicar's wife!), was annoying her mother-in-law by her displays of solicitude.

'I hope you didn't get tired, standing so long?'

'I enjoyed myself. I enjoyed meeting the Wing-Commander.'

'Only, I know with your vertigo. It is such a disability. Then, if you ever did feel a bit woozy, people would get the wrong idea!'

This attempt at jauntiness inspired another surge of ill-temper to course through Sally's mother-in-law. The full ghastliness of Little Boy, her only son, having preached a Ban the Bomb sermon came back to infuriate her; and now, Sally's soup-kitchen act.

'I can manage,' said the older Mrs Kreer. A fierce look of distaste was cast down at the gloved hand clutching her fur-clad elbow. When Sally refused to release her hold, Griselda repeated, 'I can *manage*.'

Behind them, cheerfully arm-in-arm, followed the father and the daughter.

'I wonder what Granny was talking about to the Old Bill.'

'Don't flatter yourself. There are other subjects in the world apart from yourself.'

'It's so embarrassing when the Bill goes on about school things at a party,' said the sophisticate. After they had clip-clopped over the frosty tarmacadam for a few more yards, she added, 'I really hate those Spittles.' She did quite a plausible imitation of Lindie. 'Why didn't your dad *ask* if he was having trouble with the church boiler? I mean, if it's heating, ask Gerrie!'

'Stop.'

'Now, at the Immanuel church, Terry Widger . . .'

'Stop!'

UnChristian laughter overtook them both. Then, like a stab of pain, he remembered his strange vow at the party. Just ahead of him, his mother, at about the same time, remembered Eric, and the Battle of Britain and her son's perfidious sermon.

The yellow sky above them contained no gods but, had the anger of Achilles called out to Thetis, there could have been no greater intensity of pain for a small group of people, than when Mrs Kreer arbitrarily decided to change her will, and Francis decided that, if the opportunity ever arose, he would leave his wife. These angry thoughts flew from them like prayers, to evaporate in the impassible winter air. Jessica, possessive as a lover, took her father's arm and nuzzled against his shoulder with her hair.

3

Some three weeks later, Francis Kreer sat on the sofa in his study. Beside him sat Ronald Maxwell-Lee, who held a glass of malt whisky in one hand while looking at the small volume open on his knee. Outside, it was still bitterly cold. Inside the study, they had a good fug, with two bars of an electric fire supplementing the heat from the radiators. It was a room which was not by the highest standards beautiful, but which pleasantly reflected the enthusiasms of its inhabitant. One wall was lined with books, which were mainly devoted to Latin and Greek literature, and Ancient History, though with the English poets well-represented. On the wall over the low mantelpiece, there were some Ackerman prints of Oxford – the Sheldonian Theatre, Tom Tower and Francis's old college, Lincoln. There were also photographs in frames – his mother when young, his father, and Jessica at various stages of her development. There were no photographs of Sally in the room; but there was a group photograph of Francis and other ordinands at his theological college – Mirfield – in which Damian Wells, thin in those days, could be seen looking out from the back row.

Ronald Maxwell-Lee came to the vicarage once a week to read Latin poetry. It was an idea which the two men had hit upon more or less simultaneously. The Wing-Commander was an enthusiastic amateur whose Latin was perpetually rusty; Francis, who had only just missed a First in Greats, was a competent and enthusiastic Latinist, who always had some Latin reading on the go; usually some Greek as well. At present, he and the Wing-Commander were reading the Georgics of Virgil.

'*Nec tibi tam prudens quisquam persuadeat auctor* – well, it's, "Don't let any authority" . . .'

'Or you could have adviser, counsellor,' said Francis.

'Wait a minute, hang on. However prudent, wise he may be, don't let him persuade you to turn over the topsoil when the north wind blows. . . .'

'*Rigidam*, don't forget – to stir the stiff soil. That's good.' They read to the end of the paragraph: advice against gardening in winter; and the lovely description of spring, which is the best time to plant out a vine – one of Francis's favourite passages in all Virgil. The Wing-Commander had 'done' two or three books of the *Aeneid* at school, but there were many riches in this strange writer – including the fourth *Eclogue* with its apparent prophecies of Christ – which he had enjoyed discovering with his vicar. And they both agreed that it was better to meet *à deux*. Poor Alison Bill, when she heard what they did, had been anxious to muscle in on the act; and in fact, without telling Ronald Maxwell-Lee, Francis was reading through Saint Augustine's *Confessions* with her. The sessions with Miss Bill took place at her house, and instant coffee was consumed. They were altogether less pleasant occasions, not least because Francis found Saint Augustine so uncongenial – quite possibly the least congenial writer he had ever read.

'Furthermore, or moreover–'

'Either.'

'Hold on, *virgulta*.'

'Cuttings. Whatever cuttings you plant out, be sure to spread them well with dung. Goodness, is that the time already?'

'Well, my dear – d-delightful as always,' said the Wing-Commander.

'I'll put the cough mixture back in its place,' said Francis. Neither man knew why they had developed the fantasy that the whisky had to be concealed; Sally did not disapprove of alcohol, and neither she nor Jessica was very likely to steal the drink; nevertheless, at the end of each Latin lesson, Francis hid the whisky bottle – which was supplied by the Wing-Commander – at the back of his bookshelf, behind the larger lexicons and dictionaries.

Jessica, from her bedroom, and Sally, from hers, heard the men's voices in the hall. It was about half-past eight or nine in the evening.

'Same time next week?'

'Of course.'

'Oh, and I rang that bloke about the church stove. You were quite right, and Gerald Spittle was quite wrong. He said, this b-b-bloke, that it'll last another ten years at least.'

Sally, upstairs, was feeling a little bit stronger, because she had just had one of her very private sessions; but now the wardrobe door was shut firmly upon her secret and she knew that she must face the world for another twelve hours without the comforts which that wardrobe contained. She did not hear every word, but she heard the easy tone of her husband's voice as he talked to Ronald Maxwell-Lee, and large tears filled her eyes as she tried to remember when he had last spoken to her in even comparably affectionate terms.

In the bedroom at the end of the corridor, Jessica had just finished writing an inaccurate précis of the experiment which she and Sarah Mackintosh had done that day in Chemistry. Rummaging among the heaps of rubbish on her floor, she tried to find her Chemistry text-book and look up the spelling of the word 'glycerine'. An extraordinary profusion of objects had accumulated on that floor – underwear, sports skirt, apple cores, paperbacks, cassettes, magazines, half-finished mugs of herbal infusion. It really annoyed Jessica the way her mother kept on nagging her about that room. She knew it was a mess, she knew it; but she didn't want to be hassled about it.

Sometimes Jessica felt really *pressured* by the atmosphere of that house. She was chiefly annoyed by her mother, but her father annoyed her too – by failing to *notice* Mummy, by being really crass. Of course, Mummy was irritating, but he need not show it quite so blatantly.

Jessica's current obsession at the moment was twofold – first, whether Miss Bill knew of Jessica's crush on a girl called Emily Prout; and second, if the Old Bill did know about it, whether she had grassed and told Francis. Jessica would not have put such an act of treachery past the Old Bill. Her love for Emily Prout was making her really, really unhappy at the moment, and she lay on her bed for a great part of each day, just thinking about her. She felt that this love lifted her up, and purified her. It had become a bit of a joke at school, and when Jessica just happened to find herself sitting near or next to Emily on the school bus every day for a whole week, she had been teased. That was at the beginning of an Old Bill lesson, and the Old Bill had come into the room just as Sarah Mackintosh and Henrietta had been shrieking out, really loud, 'Jess is *so* in love with Emily.' The Bill *must* have heard. It was really embarrassing to think that she might have gone blabbing to Jessica's father, with whom she enjoyed such an annoyingly close relationship.

When the Wing-Commander had gone, Sally came to her bedroom door, thinking to offer Ovaltine all round. But, by the time she got to the landing, Jessica had tripped lightly out of her bedroom, and was in the hall, offering to boil a kettle.

'Anyone like Ovaltine?' called Sally, brightly, from above.

'Jessica's making me a pot of tea. We're getting on quite well with our chess, aren't we, Jessica?'

And, before long, father and daughter were closeted together, and Sally could hear their voices from the study door, a low murmur.

Both Jessica and Francis were rather rough chess players. She was better than he was, by a small margin, but only when she was well ahead of the game did she venture any conversation.

'Sarah Mackintosh and me had a *really* funny double Chemistry'

– and the narrative poured out, interspersed with giggles.

'And how about Miss Bill?' asked her father, who always rather savoured his daughter's malice in this quarter. Jessica looked up at him sharply. So he *did* know? Or not? 'She seemed to like that Laurie Lee essay you wrote.'

'She really sucks up to people. Do you know what she said to Henrietta this morning? "Oh, Henrietta – you're my little genius" – wasn't that embarrassing – everyone creased up.'

Upstairs, excluded by the laughter, Sally sat on the floor by the wardrobe, weeping quietly. She did not dare to open the wardrobe door again this evening, in case she was found out, but she muttered through it quietly – 'Help me! Help me to be brave! You're not crying, so why should I? But oh, Mr Frumpy, they never, *never*, giggle like that when I'm around. What's wrong with me, what's so bloody wrong with me? Am I a leper or something? Oh, you'll be my friend, won't you?'

Silent within, and mysterious as a divinity, Mr Frumpy sat still.

Thirty-five miles to the south-east, in the Royal Borough of Kensington and Chelsea, Griselda Kreer was also lifting up her voice in prayer.

She looked at the photograph of Eric, which she had taken out of its secret hiding-place and framed in the silver frame which used to contain her father. He looked so handsome, poor pet, before the Luftwaffe shot down his plane.

She was ready for sleep. The laborious business of going to bed, which seemed to take longer and longer these days, was complete. She had been – she hoped – to the lavatory for the last time, but, with these wretched water pills for her heart, you could never be sure of that; her teeth were peaceful in their Steradent; a volume of Mrs David was by her bedside – so comforting to read about French Provincial Cooking before one went to sleep. But, before she read, she gave her mind to prayer.

She remembered that silly song that she and Eric kept singing during their idyll in this flat – 'Bless 'em all! Bless 'em all! The long and the short and the tall!' That was what she prayed now to God. 'Bless Eric, and make him know that I shall always love him; and bless Francis and Jessica and poor little Sally. Bless them all!'

Her mind turned to the bouillabaisse enjoyed by the inhabitants of Marseilles, and it drifted eventually into oblivion. But, a few hours later, she awoke. She had a pain in her chest, and she was not sure, now she thought about it, that she had remembered to take her pill. The bedside light was still on. She turned to Eric's young face, and she suddenly thought of Little Boy.

'Of course, Mrs Kreer, you can dispose of your estate as you choose, but have you *really* thought of all the implications of making a will of this kind?'

It was Mr Sandiman, the solicitor, who had issued this warning. She had not heeded it. She had insisted that he draw up a new will, and she had signed it on the previous day. But now she was not so sure. Mr Sandiman was right; it *would* cause pain to Little Boy, quite needless pain; and Eric would never have expected such an extravagant gesture! It might even cause *him* distress. Perhaps he had never told his wife about Griselda. In which case, how could he explain a sudden legacy on that scale? No, Mr Sandiman was right, she had been foolish.

Griselda swung her legs awkwardly off the side of the bed. She saw them by the light of the bedside lamp and was appalled by them – their texture, their scaliness, and by the discoloration of her left shin. And then at the end of these extensions (they *couldn't* be her lovely legs, could they?) there were those awful feet. In that very room, half a century earlier, Eric had stroked those toes and said 'Pretty feet', and he had been right. Now, three of the toes had turned dark purple; the nails were a sort of filthy orange, and could only be reached by a chiropodist. Why were the feet so misshapen? Someone's idea of a joke?

'Thanks!' she said to the Almighty.

By the time she was on her feet – and this was *always* happening – she had completely forgotten why she had bothered to undertake this extremely laborious and complicated operation, known as getting up. Loo? Kitchen? Tea? She had not really thought of doing any of these things but one could, she supposed, always stagger along to the loo, now one was up, and give that a whirl.

While that activity was in progress, she remembered the thought which had woken her. Mr Sandiman. The will. All she needed to do was to cancel a codicil, and she could revert to her *old* will, leaving everything to Little Boy. Bless him. She had been wrong to feel so cross with him, just because that common little man had told her about the sermon. Little Boy was probably not really Ban the Bomb – and anyway, now, what did it matter? The war had been over for nearly fifty years. Bless 'em all, bless 'em all, the long and the short and the tall!

But, as she stood to press the flush handle, she lost her balance, and her head came crashing down on to the hard-tiled bathroom floor.

4

As Francis Kreer set off to church at a quarter past seven the next morning, he was oppressed by a feeling of strong self-dislike. He had learned to protect himself by cynicism; but sometimes, especially, for no apparent reason, in the early mornings, the carapace of cynicism wore thin and he felt raw with the knowledge of his own fraudulence. A married man, for nearly twenty years, he did not love his wife. A priest of the Church of England, he did not believe in God.

There had been a time when neither of these statements was completely true. During this quite lengthy period, of about ten ambiguous years, he certainly found his wife annoying, but he would allow himself sentimental moments of thinking that 'dear old Sally' was, indeed, quite dear. And, in those days, there had been a notional attempt to maintain their sexual relations. In an analogous fashion, in those days, he would sometimes forget the fact that he no longer believed in God. Some phrase from a hymn or the old Prayer Book would move him so intensely that he would experience a great gush of sentiment and he would speak once more to God in prayer, only to find a complete emptiness.

He had outgrown this period. He did not love Sally; he was not even particularly fond of her. There were so many people of whom he was much fonder. Cynicism saved the situation, since he did not take his wife even remotely seriously. He considered her to be a fool, and he automatically disregarded everything she said or thought. It was, in fact, easier to live with Sally since he had ceased trying to like her, than in the days when his dislike of her was mingled with love and sexual attraction. Equally, it was easier to function as a priest since he had made up his mind that there was no truth whatsoever in any religious statement. The Church of England was a bizarre historical oddity, and there was nothing harmful in wishing to preserve it. He did not particularly regret being ordained, and finding himself in the historical tradition of parsons such as George Herbert, or Sydney Smith or John Keble, different as they all were. To be a clergyman was to be linked with England's past in a very appealing way. Also, Francis was quite a good clergyman. He was punctilious in his exercise of priestly functions. He was kind to the old and the sick. He made regular visits to the Berkshire Royal Hospital in Reading, and to one or two old folk's homes where former parishioners had washed up. He was faithful in taking sick communion to those villagers who wanted it. He was a judicious custodian of the village church, which was a building he loved. And he loved the village, and its place on the edge of the Berkshire Downs.

Only sometimes, on occasions such as this morning, he felt a fraud. He felt that if a man lives his life being consciously false to what he believes, he will die spiritually; and enough remained in Francis of the religious temperament for him to believe that it was possible for a man to gain the whole world and lose his own soul. This is what, in his present way of life, he knew himself capable of doing.

He could see Miss Bill's little Vauxhall Astra parked expectantly outside the lych-gate of the church, though it was still only eighteen minutes past seven. What would John Keble have made of her? The thought was enough to relieve his sudden pang of self-hatred. Alison Bill was tactfully waiting at the wheel of her car until Francis had unlocked the church and got things ready for the service.

She watched him, in his black cassock, pass through the lych-gate and walk to the porch in the south aisle. It is a fine church, St Birinus, Ditcham. Visitors will know it for the squat Saxon tower, possibly the oldest in Berkshire. Builders and craftsmen of later ages have added to the place. The nave was built at about the time that Henry V was fighting his French wars.

The pulpit dates from the time of Archbishop Laud. The reredos and the rood-screen were added by some presumably rather high incumbent at about the time Mr Gladstone was fighting to get his first Irish Home Rule Bill through the House of Commons. The 'awful' east window – depicting the Good Shepherd – was erected in memory of the last squire of the village, who had been killed at the Battle of the Somme. Riddel posts and English altar in the Lady Chapel dated from the 1930s, as did the remnants of the 'Children's Corner', with its Margaret Tarrant depiction of Jesus Blessing the Little Children. Francis loved every stitch and stone of it, even the hassocks, adorned by the Mothers' Union with a garish gros-point. It was, he thought, surely worth keeping all this going, even if every word of Christian theology was untrue?

Miss Bill was his only congregation, and she sat discreetly a few chairs from the back of the Lady Chapel. He could just hear her quietly well-modulated responses during his swift reading of Mattins. The office over, he scuttled back into the vestry and emerged in an alb and chasuble, vested for the altar.

He celebrated the service of Holy Communion with meticulous correctness, exactly as he had learned to do it at Mirfield twenty years earlier. To an expert in these matters, he would have seemed a trifle old-fashioned. He still wore the stole crosswise, rather than letting it hang straight. He wore a maniple. After the consecration he still held thumb and forefinger together until all the sacred elements had been consumed. While he did so, he thought of the morning chores which stretched ahead: he had promised Sally that he would take the car to be serviced, so he might as well drive Jess to school. He loved these little jaunts to his daughter's school, and several times each week he would pick her up from the school gates in the afternoon. Then there was a visit to an old people's home. Damian Wells, his friend in Reading, had mentioned the possibility of a pub lunch and a walk. At some stage, he must go over the accounts for the next meeting of the PCC; the parish was badly behind in its quota, and the Spittles had suggested a sponsored bicycle ride through the village and its environs to raise money. Needless to say, a sponsored bike ride was something which they had once had at the Immanuel Church.

These thoughts and impressions swam in and out of Francis

Kreer's mind as he said the familiar words of the Mass. He also thought of Christianity: how it had been there, time out of mind; and how, since the Dark Ages at least (Francis had no taste for the Early Christians), it had been a force for civilization and learning and kindness in a world often hostile to these values. Without the monks of St Benedict we should, in all likelihood, have no Tacitus, no Ovid, no Virgil. For this reason alone, it was worth getting up early on a winter morning to stand at the Holy Table mouthing words which, however beautiful, were untrue.

At the back of the church Alison Bill knelt alone, absorbed in a mystical union with Jesus Christ in the most holy sacrament of the altar. She watched Francis Kreer perform the familiar rituals of the Eucharist and, in these words and actions, she felt all the benign purposes of eternity had been focused, momentarily, in this spot, this altar of sacrifice. The Word had been made Flesh once more and, almost more miraculous than this, her will, and the will of all those who assisted at the Eucharist, was gathered together into the will of Perfect Love and Eternal Love, so that prayer could indeed be valid, and we could speak to one another in the Beloved, and be heard in the Heavenly Places: that prayer could, in short, be answered.

It mattered to her not a jot who the priest was. Francis was a nice enough man, but for Miss Bill at that moment he was merely a vessel by whom the Divine could make His mysterious matutinal invasion of the formerly unredeemed, but now sanctified, world of matter. In this time of consecration, Miss Bill lifted up those whom she loved, and her pupils, and those in need. In particular, she had made it her intention to pray for the homeless. On her way to Reading, she had seen the sad little encampments of the Travellers, who looked so bedraggled and so vulnerable in the snow. She prayed that they might find peace, through the name of Him who, when He walked this earth, had Nowhere to Lay His Head.

'And dost assure us thereby,' said Francis Kreer, 'of Thy favour and goodness towards us and that we are very members incorporate of the mystical body of Thy son, which is the blessed company of all faithful people.'

Afterwards, Francis took a while to remove his vestments, in order to give time for Alison Bill to leave the church, without 'hovering' to catch him, as she had a slight tendency to do.

It was probably getting on for half-past eight by the time he had tidied up the vestry. It was too late, probably, to drive Jessica to school. She would have gone in by bus. But as he entered the house, by the side door, through the garage, he could see her school bag on the kitchen table. The child was still here.

'You'll be late for school!' he called out. Sally, the idiot, was standing there in her nightdress, on the telephone. She was crying. And Jessica, too – oh, his poor darling, she was crying too.

'Oh, darling! What is it?'

But no words could express the horrible news. With a sort of imploring look of misery, Jessica stared up at her father through her tears and then flung herself, sobbing, into his arms.

5

The eyes of Damian Wells darted about the sitting-room of Griselda's flat, in search of an object upon which it was safe to settle without complete contempt. He inwardly conceded that, had he liked davenports, this one was acceptable. It had been kept in good condition. It even looked as if someone had rubbed it lately with wax, rather than squirting with the dreaded Pledge. If he was trying to be charitable, he would admit that he quite liked the Chinese lamp on the Pembroke table, but why, why had she ever imagined that it went with those chintz curtains? There was a surprisingly good Regency looking-glass, but it sorely cried out to be re-gilded and the eagle at the top had a wobbly wing, imperfectly mended. For the rest – rugs, chairs, the little glass chandelier, the photograph frames – well, it was deplorable.

'I know a man who wants a nice cuppa,' said Sally Kreer, advancing on Damian with a Wedgwood cup and saucer – their Kutane Crane pattern – containing a teak-coloured liquid. Damian seldom drank tea and, when he did, it was the weakest Earl Grey. Momentarily, he wondered who the man was who wanted the proffered refreshment.

'Lucky for you,' he said. Gin and tonic would have been more the thing.

'I know Francis will have said this to you already,' she said, 'but you took that service beautifully.'

He simpered self-deprecation.

'No, you were lovely.' Sally very much liked Damian, not least because the mere fact of knowing him at all made her feel raffish. She saw herself as very 'tolerant' of other human beings, regardless of their emotional preferences. 'But I was interested, because Francis said that you would probably have chosen a more modern service if you had been deciding these things. Thanks for being unselfish. I know it's what Griselda would have wanted.'

It was beyond comprehension why Francis had not wanted a Requiem Mass for his mother, just as it was beyond Damian's comprehension why everyone did not want to use Missa Normativa. But Francis was an old friend and his mother had apparently shared his own unaccountable fondness for the Book of Common Prayer.

'It's important on such an occasion to give people the funeral they would have wanted. Providing it's Christian. Which BCP is – just about.'

'But you'd rather have a more modern service?'

There was really no point in explaining why he used the Roman rite. She was baring her teeth, in a desire to be theologically accommodating, and saying, 'They do say that having modern language services would attract more young people.'

They looked at their feet in silence.

Then Sally resumed, 'And all her lovely things! All her treasures! It breaks your heart, really, doesn't it?'

It occurred to Damian that Sally was accepting the death of her mother-in-law with some composure, and that to have inherited the old lady's things, and money, and flat, must have assuaged the pangs of grief.

After the cremation at Kensal Green, which was not well-attended, a handful of distant relatives had been invited back to the flat in Cornwall Gardens.

'Well,' said Damian, 'I've told Francis. Any time. He has only to pick up the telephone, and I'm there. If he wants to talk, or if he wants me to do anything. Or if he just wants to get out of the parish for a week or two, I can always look after Ditcham. Truly.'

Damian Wells had experienced ups and downs in his professional life. Now more or less back on the straight and narrow, he had not yet been given a parish of his own. He had an administrative job in the diocese and was loosely attached to a high church in Reading. He and Francis met every few weeks, and they spoke on the telephone. They had a shared interest in ecclesiastical gossip, and would sometimes converse for hours, each on the end of a telephone with *Crockford* open in front of them for points of reference. They differed over liturgical matters. Behind Francis's back, Damian would say, 'She's so protestant, but in the nicest possible way!'

Damian was a stocky man who well filled his black suit. His face was round and red. Very closely shaven, he smelt of a lotion called Xeryus de Givenchy. His thick, crinkly hair resembled a wig, but wasn't.

'Where's Jessica?' he asked.

'Oh, she's too young,' said Sally.

'Yes,' drawled Damian, meaning 'no'. He was strongly of the view that children had as much right as adults to see off the dead, and that they were just as well equipped as adults to deal with the disturbing fact of our mortality.

'I see you've been looking at Griselda's water-colours. Aren't they smashing?'

'So, what will you do? Keep this flat as a pied-à-terre, or sell it?'

This question cheered her up, because you could see that she believed either would be nice. It occurred to Damian that they might let him use it sometimes – to stay the night, or just for the occasional afternoon.

6

Mr Sandiman, in his office in Lincoln's Inn Fields, rubbed his spectacles out of embarrassment more than because he considered them dirty.

'Were you not aware then that you were not your mother's sole beneficiary?'

'No,' said Francis, 'I was not.'

Francis Kreer was in such pain that he could not distinguish which hurt more: the shock of her death, or the extraordinary contents of the will. He had vaguely assumed that, after she had left small sums to godchildren and favourite charities, she would leave everything to him. He *was* her Little Boy! It made him feel slighted and unloved. It made him think of early days in Gerrard's Cross, when Daddy and he had waited for her to come home for lunch, and she had never come; but burst in, giggly and effervescent at four in the afternoon, to say that she had met a friend and been up to town for shopping and lunch at Harrods.

'Between ourselves, Mr Kreer, I tried to talk your mother out of making this will,' said Mr Sandiman. 'As you can see, she made it recently, and I foresaw complications.'

'I'm sure it can be worked out satisfactorily,' he said.

('We had a pork pie, Little Boy and I' – Daddy had said mournfully. 'But you might have told us you weren't going to be back.')

Griselda Kreer had left the flat in Cornwall Gardens and all its contents at the time of her death jointly to her son Francis, and to Mr Eric Gadney of the Sunnymede Garden Centre, near Deal, Kent. The residual legatee was her grand-daughter, Jessica. This meant that all the monies, stocks, shares and other benefits went to the little girl, to be held in trust until she was twenty-one. In cash terms, it broke down as follows. Jessica inherited about £52,500. The trustee was Mr Sandiman. The money could, at his discretion, be spent on the child's education, or other needs, but she would be unable to squander it until she grew up.

'Your mother took the view that your wife would probably in the end have some money of her own, and that this would mitigate any disappointment which you might feel in not inheriting the whole flat.'

'There's really no need to apologise.'

Sally was not an heiress. They would be lucky if she inherited more than £50,000 by the time everything had been shared out among her siblings. Francis had assumed that the flat would provide them with a retirement home; they could either live there or sell it, in exchange for a house in the country. It was probably worth in the region of £200,000. Of course, they could find a perfectly habitable cottage for half this value, when everything had been shared out with Mr Gadney; but he had set his heart on something larger. He now had to await the desires of Mr Gadney.

'Mr Gadney,' said the lawyer, 'has written to me, which is why I asked you to come in and see me. He says, where are we, yes, "Blah, blah, blah . . . I am very touched blah, blah, my old friend Mrs Kreer" . . . and looks forward to meeting Mrs Kreer's son, with whom he is sure an acceptable arrangement can be made.'

'You are not saying that Mr Gadney proposes to live in the flat?'

'I am not sure. You will have to arrange that between yourselves. I should not advise your attempting to share the place. It would be much better to put it on the market and share out the proceeds when it has been sold. I can organise that for you, if you would like.'

'Mr Sandiman – do you realise that I have no idea who Mr Gadney is? Could you enlighten me?'

'I did not ask your mother. We must assume that he was – very close to her.'

'I never heard her mention his name. I am forty-five years old and I never once heard my mother name a Mr Gadney. She didn't know anyone in Kent.'

He returned to the flat in Cornwall Gardens, dizzy with unhappiness. He climbed the stairs, opened the door, wandered from room to room of the flat like an automaton, scarcely aware of what he was doing. He went into her bedroom, and stared out across the twiggy tree-tops and the winter sky, realising with something like panic that he had lived in the world for nearly half-a-century without experiencing real pain. He had not felt like this when Daddy died, much as he had loved him. Pain now came upon him, great stabs of it. He could never have predicted how horrified, and surprised, he would be by his mother's death; and the pain which it now occasioned was, he realised, only the beginning of a long cycle of agony. Phrases such as the indifference of the fates, the cruelty of the universe, which had earlier been to him no more than words, now matched his mood entirely. The grey sky, the trees, the buildings – there the Albert Memorial, boxed in for cleaning like a coffin, there the Albert Hall – further away to the left, the roof-garden of Derry and Toms – they were all completely indifferent to his agony. The world went on being cruelly the same, even though, each day, some death caused another human being pain such as he suffered now. The densely-populated London scene which stretched around him outside the window suddenly seemed like a laboratory full of squealing animals in which mad scientists were practising their tortures on rats and mice. There was not a house or a block of flats in view which had not once contained someone feeling as he felt now: raw and vulnerable and searingly sad. In every dwelling, there was someone who was compelled to confront their own mortality, perhaps a painful death by cancer or a debilitating old age. And when the horrible process had been consummated and the journey to the crematorium had been made, there would be this, for someone left behind: this scalding pain, this terrible pain which could not be controlled, and which was worse than anyone had ever warned him!

He had 'counselled' many bereaved people himself. He had watched their eyes fill and refill with tears every time they tried to stammer out their feelings. He had seen the pain, but he had never appreciated how bad it could be. How could they be so brave – all these people in the parish whom he had seen arriving at funerals in hired cars with their dull, unhappy faces? He tried to reason with himself. His mother was eighty years old. She was bound to die, sooner or later. Not since early childhood had he ever lived with her, for he had always been away – at boarding school, at university or at theological college. By no rational computation should he have been caused such pain by her (apparently painless) death. He felt weak with the pain and anguish which this death had caused. He felt as though great holes had been gouged in his head, his body; as though some fiend had hacked a hole in the back of his head, and another in his breast, and as though a cold wind were blowing through his body. He felt cold. And so very, very tired. And exposed. Still, he continued to stare at the indifferent sky and the heartless trees which blew gently in the gathering darkness. And this, he thought, is the universe which they tell us was created by and for Love!

He had forgotten that his wife was going to come to the flat and meet him there. They had even spoken, that morning, of sorting through some of his mother's things. That was when they both assumed that Francis was the sole heir to his mother's estate.

Sally's 'Coo-ee!' was the first he was aware of her arrival. He had seen her jollying people along: old people who could not walk properly; children who had just failed exams; the sick and the bereaved in the parish. He realised with disgust that she was going to practise some of her kindness on him.

'You're all in the dark!' she said, switching on his mother's bedroom light.

'I wanted to be in the dark.'

Together, they looked about – the photographs on his mother's bedside table; the water-colours of the South of France on the walls; the heavy Edwardian wardrobe in the corner; the bakelite wireless set; the lace curtains. Oh, how vividly it summoned her up. It even still smelt of her scent. He could not imaginatively accept that she was gone.

'You look like a man who wants a nice cuppa.'

'Sally, I think perhaps I'd better be alone. Just for a bit.'

'Doesn't do to be morbid, does it, lovey?' There was something bouncy in her voice. She was positively cheerful. 'I stopped in the Gloucester Road on my way up,' she said, 'I bought some bin bags. If you can bear it, love' – here there was a sudden change of gear, and she switched on her 'concerned' or 'caring' voice – 'it gets worse if you leave it, so if you can face it, I think we should do the clothes. I'll do it if you can't face it.'

'What do you mean – do the clothes?'

'Well, you don't want to keep her clothes. Then if we just pop them in the bin-bags we can take them off to Oxfam. I might keep the fur coats: what do you think? People are funny about fur nowadays. There might be a few things Jess wants for dressing-up.'

'Sally, please.' He was not looking at his wife. Though it was now quite dark outside he continued to look out of the window, and at all the lighted windows. 'I do not want to touch my mother's clothes.'

'But, lovey.' She sighed. 'How 'bout old Sally makes us a nice cuppa?' She sang, she actually trilled, as she clattered about in his Mummy's kitchen. When she came back, with the tray, he said, 'I do not want tea.'

He had told her in the past that he did not like the word 'natter'; but she had failed to heed his words.

'It always helps,' she said, 'to have a good old natter. That's why I thought dear old Damian was such a brick at the funeral. He told me, you know, if Francis ever wants a natter. When you're hurting, it's something you have to do, lovey; otherwise all the horrid bits get sort of gunged up inside you, unless you let them out.'

Her words made him weep, but he continued to look out of the window, hoping that she wouldn't see his tears. If she did she would probably want to come over and hug him or comfort him. She was wandering around the room as she spoke, and had found the photographs.

'Ah! Look at this one of you. You're still just as beautiful. Do you remember how she called you Little Boy?'

This stopped him crying because it made him so angry. He wanted to reply, 'Oh, no. I'd forgotten, actually, what my own mother, who died a week ago, used to call me. Funny that. Thanks very much for reminding me.' But he remained silent. It infuriated him to hear, and to sense (for he did not turn), how she was fingering all the framed photographs.

'And there's your dad.'

He turned and saw her holding a photograph in a silver frame; she held it out towards him.

'Handsome devil, wasn't he, your dad,' she said.

'That isn't Daddy. Daddy was never in the RAF.'

'Well, well! She was a dark horse. Who do you think it is?'

'I have no idea,' said Francis. 'Absolutely no idea at all.'

He kept the news of the will until later that evening. While they were in the flat, it was as much as he could do to stop himself from weeping. Sally's cooing, sympathetic voice, and her breeziness, greatly added to the pain which he already felt. At least this misery communicated itself, and prevented her from making the promised raid on the wardrobe with her bin bags. After that, it was a drive back down the M4 through evening traffic, and a sad, sullen hour of sitting in his study before he was able to find her – she was in the bedroom with a chair against the door! – and tell her about the disposal of Mrs Kreer's estate.

The cooing, caring tone vanished soon enough from Sally's voice when the implications had sunk in. She followed him downstairs into the kitchen where Jessica was drinking a mug of tea, but she ignored the child as she barked out, 'You'll have to contest it.'

'Why? What would be the point?'

'People are always contesting wills.'

'Are you two talking about Granny's will?'

'Francis, you can say that the balance of her mind was disturbed, you can say she didn't know what she was doing. . . .'

'Where's our evidence for that? She didn't have to leave her estate to me. . . .'

'Oh, I think you're both *horrid*, talking about Granny's will!'

Francis closed his eyes, trying hard to suppress the tears which came so freely. After half a minute's pause, he managed, 'It sounds horrid, Jess darling, I agree.'

'Oh! darling!' Sally was sympathetic again, because Francis's tears had made Jessica start to cry.

'You know, neither of you would thank me for saying so, but this is all very good – it's letting it all out!' she said. Her words were received in a silence broken only by sniffs. 'And actually, you know, Jess, this is an important lesson to learn – about your granny's will. I mean, it's an awful thought, but imagine if anything were to happen to me or to Dad.'

Sally belonged to that large group of English-speakers who regarded 'anything happening' as synonymous with death.

'Nothing is going to happen,' said Francis. 'Why say upsetting things?'

'No, what I'm saying, love, is, if it did.'

'I think you're both talking like ghouls!'

Jessica, of course, did not know how much she stood to gain from her grandmother's will. Both parents had agreed instinctively that it would be a mistake to tell the young heiress of her good fortune until she was 'much older'.

'Since you have raised the matter,' said Jessica, 'Granny was allowed to leave her money how she liked.'

Both parents squirmed. It would take a clever lawyer to controvert this obvious fact.

'I think it's horrible, pretending that she wasn't of sound mind. She was of perfectly sound mind when she came for Christmas and that was only three weeks ago.'

Francis sat in a kitchen chair. This time it was Jessica who went to comfort him.

'Oh, Daddy, poor Daddy!' And she stroked his hand and planted kisses on the top of his head.

'All I'm saying is that you should write to Sandiman,' said Sally. 'It can't do any harm to write.'

'Oh, shut up, Mummy! Just shut up!' said Jessica sharply. Francis did not upbraid his daughter for speaking to Sally in this way. It was a comfort to be petted by the child. He allowed Jess to make him some tea, and after twenty minutes of nose-blowing the will was dismissed from the conversation, and from the surface of his mind. They even played a very careless game of chess. In spite of their turning in early, Francis found that there was no light coming from the door of the marital bedroom. He had thought, as he approached the door, that he heard Sally talking to herself. He slept in the spare room that night.

With the passage of a week, ten days, there was time to change his mind innumerable times about his wife's suggestion. Perhaps he *should* contest his mother's will? Sandiman himself had said that he had advised Mrs Kreer against making it. But it was hard to see any logical reason why he should contest the will, beyond the obvious one that he had hoped for more money when the old lady died. It was hardly seemly to come out with this so baldly, particularly unseemly for a clergyman.

Then came the letter in that quavery hand from Deal. The printed heading on the square page, was in blue. SUNNYMEDE GARDEN CENTRE. Underneath, printed in much smaller letters, lower case, and in black, it read: 'Proprietors, Eric and Ena

Gadney. Plants, seeds, shrubs and garden equipment. Sheds a speciality.'

Mr Gadney said how touched he was by the legacy – overwhelmed – and hoped that he and Mr Kreer could meet in the near future. The letter contained the sentences: *Probably all the legal stuff should be dealt with by our solicitors, but it would be great to meet. You were in the proverbial short trousers when I last heard of you from dear Griselda.* The letter supplied the name and address of his solicitor, and it said that he would call, 'on the off chance', at Cornwall Gardens, next Wednesday afternoon. There would no doubt be other opportunities to meet but, if Mr Kreer were free, that would be 'very nice'.

It was a strange mixture of coarseness and old-world courtesy, this letter, and Francis did not mention it to his wife. Clearly, Mr Gadney did not know much about Francis. On the envelope, his name appeared as 'Mr Francis Kreer' – no 'Reverend', and the address had been filled in by one of Mr Sandiman's clerks. Nevertheless, as Wednesday approached, Francis knew that he would go up to his mother's flat in London and keep the appointment with his co-legatee.

7

It was two days before Francis was due to meet Eric Gadney that the first communication arrived for Jessica. It came by second post, after the child had left for school. Francis was, as it happened, in his study, sitting and staring into space, which was all he felt able to do these days, much of the time. Sally, flushed with over-excitement, called him into the hall.

'Post!'

This word was repeated several times in an agitated voice before he opened the study door.

'Couldn't you have brought it in?' he asked her.

'Look!'

Had the parcel been oozing blood, Sally could not have pointed at it with more horror.

'It's that writing!' she added.

'I can see that.'

The same quavery hand, and a Deal postmark.

'What do you think's in it?'

'It's not addressed to us,' he pointed out.

Sally, clutching her habitual mug of instant coffee, vacillated between extreme measures. At first she was all for ripping the parcel open immediately – a course of action which Francis forbade. Then she decided that it should only be opened in the presence of their solicitors. Surely it compromised them, to receive presents from – that man.

'We don't even know who he is yet,' said Francis. And, when he stared at the handwriting, he caught some of his wife's sense of the parcel as a sinister object. Inwardly, he said to Eric – 'You took my mother, and now you want to take my daughter. Why don't you just leave us *alone*?'

'You must ring up Sandiman.' Sally said this to him at regular intervals. When he did so, the lawyer said that Francis could by all means tell him what was in the parcel, but it could hardly be said to constitute a *bribe*. After all, Mr Gadney was a co-legatee – unless Mr Kreer considered disputing his mother's will: and surely he was not going to do that? Francis hung up.

Jessica came out of the school gates at ten to four. Francis had been waiting there for some half-an-hour in the Maestro, still in that condition of stunned pain where he did not notice much. It was lovely, as always, when Jessica climbed into the front seat beside him, but she found her father distant and odd. He hardly listened at all while she told him what Amanda Cunningham-Hogg had done in double Drama.

The parcel which was waiting, tactfully placed on the hall table by the silver salver and the great church key, was eagerly snatched up, and conveyed to her bedroom.

Jessica certainly did not want to feel her parents' eyes on her as she unwrapped the brown paper. Since it was not her birthday, and it was not Christmas, it was really, really exciting to receive such a thing through the post. Her parents had been so odd. They had said that they insisted on seeing what the parcel contained. When she had tried to laugh off this nosiness, Daddy had said – 'No, Jessica, this could be very important.'

It was very carefully wrapped. Beneath the brown paper was some corrugated cardboard, to which was appended an envelope, written in the same slightly collapsed hand as the label on the parcel itself.

> Dear Jessica, Hello! We have never met. I am an old friend of your granny. Your Auntie Ena and I were hoping that you would accept the enclosed, with our love? I don't know how much Mum and Dad will have told you about the complicated stuff which lawyers have to do. But we should so like to be your friend. Yours, Eric Gadney.
>
> PS. The lawyer gave us your name and address. Your Auntie Ena says she hopes you haven't got this!

Jessica stared at the letter and re-read it several times. At the top of the page, it said Eric and Ena Gadney, etc. Sheds a speciality. Sadly, the child had a dawning awareness that this phrase is not one of which every family would have been proud, but surely not even her parents, snobbish as they were, would have suppressed the very existence of an aunt and uncle simply on such grounds?

'Jess! Are you all right, lamb?' Her mother was calling up the stairs. She could hear Daddy mumbling, probably telling Mummy to shut up.

'I'm coming!' she yelled back furiously, because tea had been mentioned.

Instinct made her feel that she should not communicate the contents of the parcel to her parents, whatever it was. Greedy fingers tore at Sellotape and corrugated cardboard. It was a crushing disappointment to discover that it was a Famous Five book which she had read at least three years earlier, and which she already possessed. It looked cheap and modern, this edition, whereas her copy was a nice old one which had been found by Daddy in one of his jaunts with Damian or the Wing-Co to secondhand bookshops.

She squashed the paper, and the corrugated card, and the book under her bed, and made a decision. They would keep asking what the parcel contained, but she did not see why she should tell them, unless they told her why they had said *nothing* all these years about Auntie Ena.

8

Damian Wells had telephoned several times, meaning to be kind. He had even offered to accompany Francis to London for his meeting, or confrontation, with Eric Gadney. On each occasion, Francis had turned down these offers of kindness, and on each occasion he had regretted it the moment the receiver had been replaced. He dreaded meeting Mr Gadney, and Damian's presence would have been a help. What a mistake people made in assuming that those with Damian's proclivities were weak or effete. In his sergeant-major manner, Damian could be the fiercest person Francis knew. It would have helped to have such a friend by his side.

Returning to the flat, and surveying its contents once more, he knew that he could not tolerate the idea of a stranger coming and claiming half these things as his own. Some of the things, like the lovely water-colours of the South of France, had belonged to his grandmother. The grandfather clock, similarly, was an heirloom, going back at least three generations in his family. How could Mummy have left the flat, *and its contents*, jointly to her only son and this, this – stranger?

Francis did not really want to know who Gadney was. If he had been her mother's secret lover, then Francis was not sure that he had the strength to absorb such information now. If he had *not* been his mother's lover . . . None of it made any sense at all. He had always known that his mother lacked commonsense, but this supreme muddle was almost literally maddening. Francis felt himself dizzy with it. If the old lady had wished to make a legacy, even a substantial one, even one which equalled the value of her flat (if she should turn out to be that rich) then she could have done so. But this *share*, foisted upon him by her whim, this share with a man whom he did not know and did not wish to know, it was intolerable.

When Francis got to the door of the flat – two flights up

– he found himself drained of all energy. Again, this had not happened when his father had died; but he now found himself perpetually tired. Not since student days had he ever felt these physical sensations: it was like the feeling you got the afternoon after staying up too late (or even all night) for a party. Weakness in the throat, and the knees, and the breathing; a disturbed pattern of hunger and non-hunger. Always too tired to sleep, when he went to bed; and too tired to stay awake when he was up. Being bereaved was like jet-lag.

As he turned the key in the lock of the flat, he remembered with sick dread that he had forgotten to cancel his arrangements for that morning. Why, when Damian had rung, had Francis not asked his friend to stand in for him? There was a hospital visit – a sister of Robin Pimm's, who had cancer and to whom Francis had promised a visit; and there were two sick communions in the village. (Miss Norbury had telephoned Sally and said that her mother was 'bad' again.) And there was a man coming that afternoon to give an estimate for replacing or reforming the heating system in the vestry and the Lady Chapel. Those wall-mounted electric fires would not last many more winters.

And all these things punctilious Francis had forgotten. Before his mother died, it would have been unthinkable that he should be so absent-minded. As soon as he entered the flat, he telephoned Damian, and only got his answerphone.

'Damian,' he said, 'I'm in my mother's flat. Could you ring me – I'll just give you the number,' which he did. Then he added, 'It's to ask if you could take Holy Communion to two of my parishioners.'

He paused. It was difficult to talk into one of these recording machines.

After this, he telephoned Sally, and tried to explain to her about the electric fires.

'No, no, NO!' he heard himself saying crossly. 'Not the ones up the chancel; we're talking about the one with the broken element, or filament or whatever you call it, in the vestry and the one on the . . .'

'Hang on, I'll get a pencil.'

'Oh, look, it's so easy. All you have to say . . .'

But the conversation did not reassure him. The last person he wished to involve was Gerald Spittle; but he was a practical man, and he would never get into the sort of muddle which would be bound to engulf Sally. With a heavy heart, Francis lifted the receiver: 'Gerald? Oh. When will he be back? Is that you, Lindie? Listen, I've had to come up to London on business and I never got the chance to postpone my meeting with Mr O'Rorke.'

By the time these unsatisfactory arrangements had been made, Francis felt drained of energy. The terrible sadness which kept hitting him with renewed waves was at its worst when he was most tired. He had not guessed that it was possible to be so sad, so debilitatingly sad that he could not *do* anything: he could not read, or do the crossword. He could not concentrate. He was just – sad. Time moved oddly. He could have been sitting there for ten minutes or for two hours (he would not have been able to tell the difference) when the doorbell rang to announce Eric Gadney's arrival.

Francis, like a wild animal threatened by a predator, froze. He had planned to make various speeches to Mr Gadney. He had planned to be pleasant, but firm. Over the matter of the things, for example, he had decided that he would appeal to Mr Gadney's better nature: all these objects had sentimental importance to Francis which they could not have for Mr Gadney. . . .

But these sentences flew away into feelings of pure fear when the bell rang. Francis immediately asked himself if Mr Gadney could have guessed, by surveying the front of the building, which windows were those of this particular flat. He decided that Mr Gadney could not have guessed, and that, if he switched off all the lights and lay low, the man would simply go away. On his hands and knees, Francis crept around to sockets and switches and turned the flat into darkness.

When the ring at the doorbell was repeated, this time more vigorously, Francis found an imprecation coming to his lips. It would not have been possible to determine whether he addressed his forsaken God, or his unwelcome guest, or whether the words were just a generalised expression of agony, a longing for the cup to pass from his lips: 'Oh, not yet, not yet,' he murmured tearfully. 'Please not yet.'

Passiontide

I

And the stars in their courses, and the earth on its axis turned. And the earth, which had been dark and dead and cold, began to show its habitual renewal. Clusters of snowdrops appeared in the woods at the edge of Ditcham. Then the crocuses began to flower on the Wing-Commander's lawn, and in Lindie Spittle's window-boxes, and in Mrs Norbury's small flower-pots beside her back door. And the daffodils then came to bud in the churchyard. And the dark twigs of the trees and hedges became sticky. And lambs were heard bleating in Robin Pimm's fields. And the days became longer. And everyone in the village sensed the coming of spring.

April Fool's Day came (a difficult day in the classroom for Miss Bill), and, four days later, Palm Sunday. At about twenty to eleven in the morning of Palm Sunday, a battered old Morris van, pulling a caravan, groaned its way up the hill past the Rising Sun, the village pub. It was followed by two other cars, equally dilapidated, which also towed caravans. Behind these caravans, there came a Volkswagen Dormobile, which had been crudely painted with black paint and adorned with floral patterns owing something to the primitive technique of canal-barge decorations. Behind this there was a gipsy caravan, pulled by a sad old horse called William. Behind this was an open truck. At the wheel of the truck was a bearded man of about thirty who wore a thick Icelandic jumper and three delicate rings in his left ear. His thin, handsome face carried three days' growth of beard, and his eyes were somewhat bloodshot. His tousled, slightly oily dark hair was swept back from a smudgy brow. The passenger seat of his truck was empty.

Behind him, exposed to the open air, sat a young woman.

She wore a black PVC mackintosh, black jeans and Doc Marten boots. Her mittened fingers held a cigarette which she had rolled herself, and her left arm was enfolded about the neck of a mongrel – one of whose ancestors must have been a sheepdog – whose name was Leila. The young woman's name was Jay Dunbar. Her face was distinguished by its extraordinarily bright green eyes, which were now slightly terrified and stared into the middle distance, and by the lips, which were very full but slightly irregular. Her straw-coloured hair was plaited and shoulder-length. She had a short, straight nose; her wind-blown skin was clear, except for the chin which had two or three barely perceptible pink spots. While the convoy winds its way up the village street, it might be a good moment to introduce the reader to a little of Jay's history.

She was the child of two schoolteachers from the genteel suburb of Bramhall, not far from Manchester. Her father taught history at Macclesfield, her mother, who was Norwegian, taught in a primary school nearer home. When Jay was six years old, her father had committed suicide, though this was a fact of which she still knew very little. She had tender memories of her father, who had read to her and played with her, and been her friend. At the time of his death, her mother had only been able to tell her that 'Daddy has gone away'. Only a few weeks afterwards had she been able to admit to Jay that her father was dead. Jay was eighteen before her mother explained, very briefly, that he had thrown himself under a train just outside Stockport. Although Jay had been sympathetic and intensely curious to know the circumstances of her father's death, her mother had seemed incapable of talking about it. Jay accepted this fact but she felt excluded by it, and realised, not long afterwards, that she was not 'close' to her mother at all, not as other children of her acquaintance were close to their mothers.

Her mother habitually annoyed Jay by wondering where she had 'got' her outstanding musical ability, as though all our merits come not through luck or our own efforts, but *gratis* from our families. Wherever she 'got' such abilities, Jay, from an early age, had a finely-tuned musical ear and an early mastery, first of the piano and then of the violin. Had she practised the piano in the last twelve months, she would have been still an accomplished player. As a violinist, she had been quite unusually brilliant and, with the encouragement of a sympathetic teacher, she had gained a place at the Guildhall School of Music in London.

Even when she had received the news of this great accolade, at the age of just eighteen, Jay had read anxiety in her mother's face and known the reason for it. Mrs Dunbar did not entertain a 'provincial' fear of London. The capital was no more dangerous a place for young women than Manchester. Since her teens, Jay had been accustomed to go out in the evenings, to have boyfriends, and to attend discos and parties. Her delicate musical intelligence did not spoil her enjoyment of the sort of music which her friends enjoyed in clubs. Mrs Dunbar was, by many standards, an indulgent parent. What Jay read in her mother's face, however, was a fear that if she left home, she might never return.

There was a great distance between her mother and herself, an absence of love. All her life, Jay had dreamed of running away: not because she believed herself to be very unhappy, not really for any reason which she could discern, but because images of escape appealed to her irrationally. Stories or songs – in which boys ran away to sea, or girls ran away to join the gipsies – had always exercised a powerful imaginative allure. She remembered as a small child in the playground of her primary school – the same school where her mother was a teacher – first hearing chanted out that rhyme:

My mother said
I never should
Play with the gipsies
In the wood.
If I did,
She would say,
'Naughty girl to disobey!'

Something seized her – it was an almost physical sensation in her chest – as she joined in the words with the other children. She knew that she wanted to play with the gipsies, and that she wanted to run away. She loved outdoors, and the open road. She joined the Brownies chiefly in order to go on their camp, but she was a resourceful child and won many badges. Later, she joined the Guides. She also loved going on Outward Bound courses, and in her early teens she won a Bronze Medal in the Duke of Edinburgh's Award scheme. Agile and well-made, she was a nimble rock-climber, sailor, camper. Mrs Dunbar grew used to the expression of sullen disappointment on her daughter's face when she returned after these expeditions.

There was absence of love between mother and daughter, but no violent dislike. Neither played much part in the other's inner life, but they lived together quite peacefully. Mrs Dunbar could not bring herself to be interested in any of her daughter's range of interests, nor in her friends. She contented herself with clothing the child, keeping her clean and protecting her from the knowledge of the great sadness which lay in her own heart.

When Jay's childhood came to an end, they both realised that this could be the end of their relationship. Jay went up to the Guildhall. She telephoned her mother a few times during her first few weeks at the college, but there was nothing she could tell her. What was the point of rehearsing the names of friends whom her mother would never meet, or of speaking about music – an art in which her mother seemed to take no interest whatsoever? When she went home for Christmas at the end of her first term, her mother had coyly alluded to a new 'friend' who had come into her own life. He was called Knut. He ate his Christmas dinner with them. Like Mrs Dunbar, he was a Norwegian, and they occasionally broke into that language over the meal table, even though Jay only had a smattering of it, and did not easily understand what they were saying.

Knut, who was embarrassingly quite a lot younger than her mother, asked Jay all the polite questions about her new life at college. Had her mother been alone with her, and had it been Mrs Dunbar who asked the questions, perhaps Jay would have been able to give more truthful answers. She said that she had made many friends at the Guildhall, that the teaching was excellent, and that she was most enthralled by her course of study. The truth was, however, that she had found the Guildhall a grave disappointment.

She knew that the fault for this lay neither in the Guildhall nor in herself. Rather, she had discovered that, while music continued to be one of the things she most cared about, she did not wish to be studying it in an institutional way. She would like, she thought, to play one day in a small chamber group, but she had no real desire to earn her living as a member of an orchestra; and she began to realise that she had largely negative feelings about becoming a professional musician. What she wanted to do instead, she had no very clear idea. She did not feel very close to any of the students in the Hall of Residence. She described them as 'her friends' when talking to Knut, but they were not real friends. Nor did she have a lover.

Gregory, her boyfriend from Manchester days, had visited her once or twice, but they had agreed that whatever had once existed between them during her last year in the sixth form had fizzled out. She had moved out of her Hall of Residence after Christmas and shared a flat, not with friends, but with some students who had advertised for a spare person to make up the numbers in their flat. Two of them were musicians like herself, and two were medical students. They all found Jay something of an enigma. Her stand-offishness, as they saw it, could only be explained by her having a secret love life. This was not the case. Love had never meant very much to Jay, though she had occasionally enjoyed sex. Somewhere at the back of her mind was always that thought that she would run away and have an adventure. She imagined, perhaps, that a man would ask her to run away to Cornwall. She even knew what he would look like: rugged, weather-beaten, older than herself, and wearing a thick fisherman's jumper and baggy trousers. He would be a potter or a poet and would keep a small sailing-boat moored to the landing-stage outside his cottage. There would be rock pools at the bottom of the garden, where she would fish for crabs and shrimps and starfish. If such a fantasy-figure ever materialised, Jay imagined that she might be happy. London, with its confined, messy flats, its dusty streets, its noise and smell and traffic, possessed no romance for her and, during that student year, she explored almost none of it. She never visited an art gallery or a museum, and she was too poor to attend many concerts.

Some of the students made extra money by busking and, when funds ran low, Jay did the same. She stood by a corner of the underpass at Tottenham Court Road tube station, playing minuets by Haydn, and making surprisingly large sums. She was not vain enough to ask herself why this should be. That people should love Haydn needed no explanation, and she knew that she played very well. But she had never quite acknowledged to herself that she had the sort of overpowering beauty which enchanted both sexes and which went far beyond sexual attraction. Everyone who passed and saw this figure in a coat and jeans was haunted by her face, and by the long pale hands which held the violin and bow. Many of those who caught her eye were almost embarrassed by the brightness and attractiveness of her eyes.

Fifty yards away, round a corner and down one flight of stairs near the trains, a youth was playing a very different sort of music on a guitar. Though he was only eighteen, he seemed to favour music which had been popular with his parents' generation – Bob Dylan songs and early Rolling Stones numbers – though he varied the repertoire with renditions of 'Dirty Old Town'. He played very badly, and his voice irritated Jay because he sang out of tune.

One day when the boy had finished playing, he came and stood beside her, staring in that manner in which, since she was fourteen years old, Jay had been accustomed to men and women staring at her.

'That's really beautiful,' he had said in a Birmingham accent. 'What is it?'

'It's a Haydn minuet.'

She discerned that he had not heard of Haydn and did not know what a minuet was. He proposed buying her a cup of coffee, and she accepted. This boy was called Tim. He had a plaited rat's tail at the back of his neck, but the rest of his mousy hair was cut very short. He wore a blue denim top, and blue denim jeans. Jay considered him quite pretty, though rather short. Bored, pliable, she laughed at his jokes and allowed herself to be 'picked up'.

Tim lived in a squat in North London – Leverton Road, Kentish Town. He had come down from Birmingham some six months earlier, and had lived from hand to mouth ever since. Jay found him quite good company, and was perfectly willing to be taken back to his lair to meet his friends. Like the students with whom she shared a flat, these friends of Tim's bored her at first; but they bored her marginally less than the students. They were more self-consciously raffish. Though they did not *say* much which was interesting, they endeavoured, some of them, to make their appearance amusing. They took drugs, though not in dangerous quantities; they did very little; all of them drew Social Security. A couple of them shared Jay's interest in Buddhism.

Jay used this word rather loosely. She had never known any Asiatic Buddhists, but she had read a few paperbacks on the subject and she found herself in sympathy with the Buddhist way of life. She practised vegetarianism largely for reasons of taste and she did not find it difficult to cultivate an attitude of detachment from the passing world of emotion and pain. She also practised simple forms of meditation. She distrusted the anthropocentric view of the universe which Christianity propagated and she had never believed in Christian mythology. She nevertheless entertained a vague sense that the 'spiritual' side to human nature was important and that the modern world had gone wrong largely because of its neglect of this 'spiritual' faculty.

After a few weeks of hanging around with Tim, she gradually decided to leave the Guildhall. After a row with her flatmates concerning the fair division of a telephone bill (Jay argued that, since she did not use the telephone, it was unfair to ask her to make a contribution), she moved into Tim's squat. She even wondered whether she might not be falling in love with Tim. She accepted his invitation to go for a week with some friends of his to the West Country. It turned out that these friends were Travellers who had joined a small convoy and were heading for North Wales in search of minerals.

During this week, everything had gone well except her relations with Tim. The weather had been wonderful – clear and bright and sunny. She had woken early in the caravan which they shared together (they were not lovers and slept in separate sleeping bags), and had crept out, barefooted, into the dawn. Birdsong and solitude, dew on the meadow-grass, a distant view of hills, trees in leaf, had worked a potent magic. There was nothing, after this week, which made her want to return to London. Like a principal boy in *Dick Whittington*, she had most of her belongings in a small knapsack – though not quite a spotted handkerchief tied on the end of a stick: a few changes of clothes, a transistor. And she had a violin.

In the company of the Travellers, Tim changed, or perhaps Jay's perception of him changed. He treated her as if he was showing her off, as if she was his possession. It was true that she liked him almost entirely for his looks, but it was irritating that he liked her for the same reason. When the week came to an end, she told him that she did not want to come back to London with him. Tim returned to London, and she stayed on in the caravan.

The Travellers made her feel quite welcome and, since she had her cards with her, and a cheque book, she was able to go to a nearby Social Security office and make preliminary investigations about changing her status from student to unemployed person.

Those weeks were very cheerful. She was a Jolly Miller:

I care for nobody, no, not I
And nobody cares for me!

This was a happy condition in Jay's way of seeing things. But the weather was turning, and the trees were becoming golden, and the Travellers were beginning to wonder where to spend the winter. It was at this point that Jay met Mo.

He was a loner, who had been travelling in the opposite direction from the convoy in an old Renault truck, with a two-seater cabin and an open space behind, which could be covered with canvas. He had travelled from Wales, where he had found an abundance of minerals – porphyry, quartz, silver, even gold. He travelled backwards and forwards between North Wales and London, selling these specimens to stall-holders on Camden Market before seeing some friends, having some fun and taking once more to the open road and hills.

Mo was not the bearded potter in the fisherman's jersey, but he was the closest thing to it which Jay had ever met. She also found him very beautiful. He was much older than her, perhaps ten years older, but everyone in that group seemed very vague about age. 'Mo', she discovered, was short for Eamonn. When she found out that he was Irish (by parentage, though he grew up in England), Jay was not surprised to discover that Mo could not tolerate the idea of being disliked. This was such a pronounced feature of his character that he became almost wild, like a frisky dog, whenever he met any new person whom he hoped to charm. The idea that he had not made a good impression would make him churlish. Had she known this before meeting him, Jay might have been slightly less bowled over by his charm when their paths first crossed. It was obvious, not only that he was charmed by her looks, but that he was enraptured by them; as was she by his. He laughed with her, or expressed deep interest in everything she said. She found out, when she knew him better, that his musical knowledge, for example, was rudimentary, but he had nodded so sagely when she told him about the Guildhall, and why she had left, that she had supposed him to know exactly what she was talking about. He did at least know the names of some composers and some of the more famous pieces of music, and, had she been less ready to be impressed, she would have considered some of his tastes a bit flamboyant.

'*Eroica* – it blows your mind' – a remark which he had made when she had confided in him her passion, her obsessive love, for Beethoven. She had been touched (a) because she had met a Traveller who had *heard* of Beethoven; and (b) because he pronounced the word 'Erro-eeka', which made her sure that he had read it, but not moved in a circle where such words were ever spoken.

Had she not been ready to fall in love, she might have been less impressed by Mo's saying that the other two 'classical greats' which he admired were Mahler's Second Symphony and *Madame Butterfly*. What charmed her, in these initial conversations about music, was his willingness to put himself out for her, to stretch out and find where she was. Nearly all people she had met to date – perhaps this was something to do with Mo's age – had expected her to reach out towards them. They made no concessions. Once he had *said* the words, Erro-eeka, Mahler and Butterfly, it was somehow acceptable that he should admit himself to be more a man for the Smiths and the Pogues, and then to tell a slightly boastful anecdote which let fall that one of the Pogues was a friend of his; well, an acquaintance; well, someone he once met in a pub.

All this made her laugh; and she also filled in hidden depths behind Mo's surfaces. Because he was self-confessedly conceited, she imagined that this concealed modesty. Because he seemed quite knowledgeable about minerals, she decided that he was in truth very knowledgeable; perhaps almost a man who could have held a Chair of Geology and Mineralogy at a university had his circumstances been different. Things changed when she had seen him drunk or stoned about ten times, and realised that the same little stock of mineral-lore got repeated, like a record, every time the subject occurred to his intoxicated mind.

In the initial week, he had seemed to her a very funny man – light, almost a thing of air, like one of the fairies in Shakespeare, mischievous and physically nimble. He taught her to play pool (to flatter his vanity yet further, she pretended she was a poor little girl from t'North who had never played, whereas in fact she had done so quite often in Manchester pubs); and he had shown himself to be a supremely skilful player. Here at least was something where no trace of the second-rate hung about him. His brilliance at the game had first been revealed when he had taken her into a small pub in the village near their encampment and challenged two local toughs to a game. Not just for the fun of it, for winnings. This terrified Jay, because she knew they did not have any money, and the two boys (more or less unreconstituted skinheads of a 1978 vintage – strange how fashions in the remote provinces could be frozen, and linger on) did not look as if they would be friendly if they thought themselves being duped. But Mo had been sure of himself, and the two 'bovver boys' ended up buying them drinks for the rest of the evening.

Another aspect of his nature which had impressed her very much (a pity, because it was an aspect which she later found not to exist) was his interest in her 'spiritual' side. He had nodded sagely when she talked about the Wisdom of the East. Later, she decided that he would probably have believed her had she announced that *lobha*, *dos* and *moha* were three of her great-aunts. He had even given her the impression, while not actually stating as much, that he was a vegetarian. She changed her mind, one day towards the end of the first week, when she heard one of the children in the convoy wailing aloud that Mo had stolen a sausage from its plate.

She knew, then, that she had fallen in love with Mo; even as she heard the upraised voices of those involved in the dispute.

'He st-o-o-o-o-o-o-le my sausage!'

'I honestly did not steal Zeb's sausage.'

'You shouldn't have been giving a kid sausages in any case [another voice]; do you realise what butchers put in those things?'

'It was a vegetarian sausage.'

'I thought you said you hadn't eaten it, Mo.'

'It was a joke, a joke.'

Versions of this conversation were to be replayed over and over during the next six months; only instead of her being an observer on the sidelines, hardly able to suppress the giggles, he managed to transform her into the one who was screaming. On the day she fell in love, or recognised that she was already, helplessly, in love, she had found the 'blarney' delicious and endearing. She found his unstatic qualities at first attractive, and then alarming. No one was less still than Mo. He seemed to have no fixed occupation, abode or – though this would become clear to her much more slowly – identity. He was fluid, chameleon.

His friends in Wales, the ones with whom he went on explorations for minerals, had apparently offered him a cottage for the winter, and Jay eagerly accepted his invitation to live with him there. This cottage became a dream-house to her: literally so, since she found, when waking, that she had been thinking about it in her sleep. She began to form resolutions about it. She would practise her violin there so many hours each day; she would learn to bake bread; she would live a peaceful life, at one with herself, at one with Nature, at one with Mo. The three fires of greed, hatred and illusion would be extinguished by their way of life. It had been a tremendous shock, some ten days later, when she had made some allusion to the cottage, Mo had laughed and said it had 'only been an idea'. In fact, they drifted back to London. If she complained to Mo – and, within two weeks of knowing him, she had heard herself turning into a 'nagging wife' – he told her not to be heav-ee. It was easier being in London, anyway, for the winter months. Once spring dawned, she'd see, they'd be on the road again.

True, Mo took her on various visits to friends. They went to stay with some people whom Jay disliked very much indeed, in Devon, and when the truck broke down they had an acrimonious week of hitch-hiking in Kent. But they always hurried back to London to collect Mo's Giro cheques. Mo had three separate identities, as far as the Department of Social Security was concerned. He signed on in three different offices – one in Camden, one in Bermondsey and one in Tower Hamlets; he had three different names, three different personal histories, and three different cheques. It was a full-time occupation, keeping this swindle in operation, and it sometimes required the help of his friends when he was ill. Jay found herself going to the Camden office on Mo's behalf on more than one occasion, stating, which was one of the few things which was true about him, that he was ill.

She had loved him so much at first that it had seemed exciting that he used 'smack'. She herself had never experimented with heroin. Of course, over the years, since her mid-teens, she had consumed amphetamines or puffed at blow when these were offered to her at parties. She had even, now and then, dropped acid. But she had never tried cocaine or heroin. When she first asked Mo about it, he had vigorously denied being addicted, and he had become loudly abusive when she suggested that he might have a 'problem'. When she first found a syringe in their shared room in the squat, he had said that he did not know how it got there, that he had never, ever injected himself; he had asked whether she was so ignorant that she did not know you could *smoke* 'H'. Only when she burst in accidentally and found him with a needle actually sticking in his arm, did he admit that, 'now and again', he 'mainlined'.

Jay did not particularly mind the injecting: we have all got to die somehow. She minded the lying, and from that moment, though caught up with Mo and still in love with him, she no longer believed in him. In no bit of him did she believe, forcing her to wonder what she meant by 'loving' him. If there was nothing there to love, what made it so difficult, in fact impossible, to break loose? He was not her man in a jersey, her poet/potter. He was a rather tiresome dependant for whom, during the worst of times, she felt responsible. It was like having a child. Life with him had become, within the eight months of their relationship, an absolute denial of all that she believed in. Although her 'Buddhism' made her wish to practise detachment and the conquest of desire, she found herself trapped instead on a wheel of yearning for Mo to be other than he was. She was also the prisoner of all his lack of discipline, all his sloppiness, all his slavery to bodily needs and cravings.

The day before the Travellers' convoy (which Mo and Jay had recently rejoined) struggled up the hill into Ditcham, Jay had found out that Mo had slept with Rosie – a sluttish whey-faced girl, who lived in the smaller of the two Dormobiles with a couple of children and a whippet.

Jay should never have taxed Mo with this, she knew. It had emerged as a joke. For once, they were getting on quite well in conversation. They had just had some good(ish) sex and she, giggling and prodding him in the stomach, had said that she bet he fancied many of the other girls in the convoy.

'I bet you've fucked Rosie,' she had said.

'And what if I have?' – passing her his joint. She noticed at once the edge of defensiveness in his tone and a sinking stomach made her realise that he *had* done so. And she had only meant it as a joke! And, like a jealous suburban spouse, she had found herself taxing him with it, questioning, railing: when, how many times – did this mean that his relationship with her meant nothing? No need to answer – she knew the answer! One of their rows was soon underway, in which she found herself losing control and hating herself, hating Mo, hating everything. He would get angry very fast – cuff her sometimes, or in any event swear at her – but he would then wish to cut loose from the fray. Either he would try to laugh her out of her anger, or he would just walk away, leave her alone to work out her rage.

This was the condition in which they found themselves as the convoy rumbled into Ditcham. Jay had spent the previous night sharing a caravan with a bearded mystic called Compton, a dog, and two children who might or might not have been related to Compton. Compton (his religious position could perhaps best have been described as quietist) really did seem to have broken loose from the chain of desire and being, so that even Mo at his most furious would not have suspected Jay of sleeping with the man. He said little, Compton, though he chanted a certain amount, and mumbled mantras to himself while consuming his strictly vegan diet.

Only for the purpose of the journey had Mo persuaded Jay to communicate with him at all, and as she and the dog Leila hugged one another, partly from affection, partly to avoid being thrown about in the back of the truck, Jay had some very negative thoughts. She hated Mo. It was as simple as that. In hating him, she also hated all the other Travellers. And one of the things she hated about them was that she no longer felt able to break free. She had thought that, by running away and taking to the open road, she would be liberated but, in fact, this reckless action had limited her options, just as much as staying at college would have done, or taking a job and a mortgage. If she left this group of Travellers, she felt that she could not resume her studies; she could not go home. She doubted whether her mother was even there; if the Knut thing had caught fire, quite possibly her mother had returned to Norway. So, Jay's only option would be to run away to another squat or to another encampment of wanderers and malcontents; and where would be the point in that? Life's limitedness can only fail to make us miserable if we accept it; and the limitations of life with Mo and the Travellers were not ones which Jay could accept; so, with her chin in Leila's fur and her tear-filled eyes staring down the valley over budding treetops and brown, ploughed fields, Jay was miserable. Having passed through some countryside which felt remarkably remote, despite its proximity to Reading (even London was only thirty miles away), Didcot suburban-ness asserted itself. She felt the shades of her Bramhall childhood as they came to the outskirts of Ditcham. First the very neat Council estate. Then a modern house in which someone had planted a hedge of cypress trees (how ugly they always looked) and named jauntily 'Gleneagles'. Then nondescript bungalows and cottages, some of them quite old, before the Rising Sun, and some 'olde-worlde' cottages. Somehow, though it all *looked* rustic, you could sniff that stockbrokers and travelling salesmen, rather than ploughmen, would eat the ploughman's lunch at the Rising Sun. On their left a church, a yew hedge, and a lot of parked cars. But now the convoy was coming to a halt. Mo had leaned out of the window, the cigarette-paper of his joint stuck to chapped lips, and said, as he fairly often did, 'Jesus Christ'. It did not seem so inappropriate an exclamation as it often did, for, coming down towards them from the brow of the hill, was a figure on a donkey, heralded with uplifted palms and the cries of 'Hosanna!'

2

The donkey had been Lindie Spittle's idea: something to engage the kiddies. Attempts by other members of the PCC to belittle the efforts she made with that Sunday School would not deflect her from her purpose. Several of them – the Wing-Commander, Miss Bill, all the 'inner ring', as Lindie saw them, of Francis Kreer's cronies – had 'made difficulties': suggested that a donkey could bite, kick, throw the child impersonating Jesus off its back or – a completely unnecessary suggestion, Lindie thought, from the Wing-Commander – relieve itself in an awkward place. Lindie knew that men would not indulge in that sort of lavatory talk with a woman unless they had 'problems' with her; and she knew that many men had impure thoughts about her which 'came out in other ways'.

Take the Vicar. While there were those who said that allowances must be made for a man when he was suffering a bereavement (and was it *natural* for a man to be so upset when his mum passed away?), Lindie did think that it was possible to go too far in one's indulgence. Terry Widger would never have neglected his parish duties, forgotten to visit the sick, or lost his place in a sermon, as Francis had done several times lately. Nor would Terry Widger say really sarky, bad-tempered things to valued helpers such as the Spittles.

Lindie had fought tooth and nail to get her Sunday School (now numbering an impressive nine pupils) involved with the Palm Sunday procession. Francis had wanted what he had always had: a procession around the inside of the church if the weather was poor; and, if the weather allowed, a procession outdoors, from the top of the hill where Potter's Field stretches towards the Ridgeway, down the road to the lych-gate.

When the PCC had conceded that Lindie should be allowed to lead a child on a donkey, there had then been the question of palms. Francis had been strangely prim and rigid (Gerald said it had to do with being High Church) about the palms. Terry Widger would have leapt at the idea of the kiddies making their own palms out of bright green crêpe paper.

'I would prefer to use the more traditional palm crosses,' Francis had said – really sniffily – 'but if you prefer.'

Lindie had been sure that he was losing his temper, but she had not realised until his final outburst that all that smouldering anger really meant something else. Francis had said that, as always, they would sing the processional hymn, 'All glory, laud and honour': an old-fashioned hymn which was one of those 'dirges' so much disliked by Terry Widger.

Francis would like that one, with all the lords and 'lauds' in his life. (Both the Spittles believed, without any evidence, that Francis's mild snobbery meant that he had a large number of 'aristocratic' friends.)

Why not, Gerrie had supplied, 'Sing hosanna'? That was something which all kids knew these days, and what could be more appropriate as little Jason Harper rode into Ditcham on a donkey?

And it was at this point that Francis had completely lost his temper and told Lindie that he did not care if they all followed the donkey singing 'Eskimo Nell'.

The Vicar had immediately apologised to her and – a gesture which could scarcely have gone unnoticed – called round the next day with some daffodils. Lindie had never heard the song (or hymn) 'Eskimo Nell', and when she asked Gerald about it, he had gone red and said, 'Whoever put that in your head?'

She had replied – 'Francis said it. He said that if we didn't have "All glory, laud and honour", we could have "Eskimo Nell". I'm sure it was called that.'

'That man,' said Gerald through gritted teeth, 'ought to be locked up.'

There was no persuading Gerald to tell her what was in this mysterious song. She asked several people until Mrs Pimm told her that it was bawdry, 'such as men sing after rugby matches and that'. Still, the sex theme – she only had to get near the Vicar and he *breathed* sex.

And now they processed behind the figure on the donkey, a

moment of solemn strangeness in the liturgical year which even Lindie and her paper palms had not been able to destroy. Behind the donkey, making sure that he did not fall off, was Jason's mum, Kate Harper, who had never been to church until Lindie started the Sunday School; then Lindie herself, and then the Vicar, in a scarlet cope. He was accompanied by two servers in surplices, and they were followed by the Wing-Commander and Miss Bill, churchwardens, who carried their staffs of office in place of palms. And then the congregation followed – the same crowd who had attended the Wing-Commander's Christmas party, with a dozen or so more, whose presence could be explained by the children, singing in tinny, tuneless voices:

Sing Hosanna! Sing Hosanna!
Sing Hosanna to the King of Kings!

To the Vicar's ears, the tune had a jauntiness which made it inappropriate for adults to sing, not least in Passiontide. He knew that they trilled this ditty all the time nowadays in primary schools; but, since a high proportion of those following the donkey had not been to school for over half a century, the rhythms and tune were quite unfamiliar.

Next year, if there was a next year, they would revert to 'All glory, laud and honour'! If there was a next year! Francis's sense of time had changed. This took the form of making it almost impossible to imagine a future. If he received an invitation, or the notice of a meeting at some future date, he sometimes found it impossible to write down in his engagement diary: merely to turn its pages was hard; and to suppose that he would be able, or in a mood, to do anything in such months as May or June was too hard for the mind to grasp. The other way in which time-perception had changed was that he hardly noticed time passing any more. Five minutes and three hours seemed indistinguishable. Sometimes he was so bored by someone's conversation or a church service that it felt as if it had been going on for hours, whereas only minutes had elapsed. On other occasions, he would look at a clock and find that he had been sitting in a chair for three hours without sleeping, but without noticing the minutes pass.

He had enough pastoral experience to know that he was suffering from severe depression. Just enough of himself was still sufficiently sane to grasp this, and to realise that he should have sought help: either from a doctor or from some other counsellor. But he had continued to rebut Damian Wells's offer of help, and he *would* not go to the doctor. This was because Sally had begged him to do so, and she was a repetitive bore on the subject. Francis knew that she had been talking to the doctor because one day, with artificial casualness, the plump young man, Dr Bernard, had encountered Francis in the village street and asked him, with soupy-sentimental gentleness, how he was.

Francis saw no reason to tell this man how he was. How could he begin to explain how he was? He was in Hell. Punctilious Francis, who used to know how every minute of the day would be mapped out, had turned into a vague creature with no more grasp of detail than an alcoholic. Many villagers were beginning to suspect that he was drinking, which he was not. Church services were late, and Sally's face had become drawn and sad.

Francis sometimes glimpsed their puzzled, concerned expressions as they looked at him and knew that he had become a 'case'. He was quite determined, however, that he must suffer: that there was nothing in this case to do, except to suffer. You could not go to a doctor or a counsellor and say, 'Please, my mother is dead, stop me minding about it.' It was natural to mind, natural to be devastated. The only two puzzles which tormented him were – first, why he had not been through all this when his father died; and secondly, why, after more than twenty years in the priesthood, he had never *quite* guessed the extent of ruinous pain which bereavement caused. He must have conducted hundreds of funerals, and counselled hundreds of the bereaved. He had watched their faces pucker and their eyes fill with tears, and he had stroked their hands and he had been kind. But never had he guessed that pain like this could be borne in the world of nature. When he was at his first boarding school, the Second World War was still a recent memory, and many dormitory hours were devoted to whether or how you would respond to torture if taken prisoner by the Nazis or the Japanese. Francis had been profoundly interested in this question, between the ages of seven and ten, always comforting himself with the thought that, if pain became unendurable, human beings fainted.

'Bunny' – a voice in the blackened dorm.

'What?'

'Would you tell the Gestapo secrets if they took out all your fingernails, one by one, very *very* slowly?'

'You'd pass out long before they'd finished,' he would confidently opine.

Since, he had discovered that the universe is not constructed as benignly as the Gestapo's torture-chamber. You don't pass out through unendurable pain. You go on feeling it: on and on, even when you are asleep; it deprives you of all powers of concentration and reasoning, so there can be no rest from it, no distraction even in doing something as innocent as listening to the radio or turning the pages of a newspaper.

The children sang:

Give me joy in my heart,
Keep me praising!

For Francis, the very existence of pain – the unjust suffering of animals, of the starving multitudes of the world, of sick children – had long made it impossible to believe in a Personal Creator. Long before he himself tasted how terrible pain could be, he was aware that it could not co-exist with Omnipotent Love. The only types of god in which it would be intelligent to believe in this bleeding, crucified world would be the Homeric deities, who were, by turns, indifferent to human fate, and by turns involved with individual destinies, for reasons of sadism or malice or caprice. Francis was perfectly able to 'believe' in such divine activity while he was reading the *Iliad*, and perfectly prepared to describe the world in terms of classical mythology, for this world-picture made as good imaginative sense as any other. But he could not really pray to Zeus, or Apollo, nor to Aphrodite, as he had prayed to the Triune God in the days of his faith. Strangely enough, however, he found that since the removal from his life of God, and the removal from his mind of any of the time-wasting clutter which used to constitute his 'thoughts' about God, he felt much more receptive to the power of the Christian story. Even in his present state of dejection and desolation, there did not seem to him anything better that he could be doing with himself on Palm Sunday than recalling the entry of Jesus into Jerusalem on a donkey; in recalling the mental anguish, and the bodily torture and the death of Christ. Stripped of all mythology, this terrible story seemed all the more strong. If all that remained of the story was the Agony in the Garden and the Crucifixion, with no miraculous Rising Again, no Happy Ending, no magic antidote to death – could not this still be the best way to confront our own Gethsemanes and Calvaries – to re-enact the solemnity as best we may?

Such were the thoughts of the godless priest as he processed with his people to church, his mind so churning with his own internal agony that he was unobservant of the passing scene.

His wife and daughter followed at a discreet distance, allowing about ten people to stand between themselves and the back of Francis's cope. They were in a better position, towards the back of the procession, to witness the point at which the people at the front met the Travellers.

The unhappiness of Francis Kreer had seeped into both Sally and Jessica. In Sally's case, it had led to a deterioration in her relations with Francis. A cruel outside observer might have said that things between Francis and Sally could not get worse, but this was by no means true. Although she had felt increasingly excluded from her husband's love, in a gradual process lasting several years, this latest experience had lowered a veil between them which he showed no sign of lifting. It was as if he had gone away, and been replaced by his own ghost. She was sure – or so she *kept* telling her comforters and friends in the wardrobe – that he could not help being so cruel; but cruel it was, to shut her out like this. If she asked him the simplest thing about his mother's flat, about the will, about Mr Gadney, about all the arrangements which would so materially affect their lives, Francis refused to answer. He simply would not speak about these things any more. She had tried being sharp with him and telling him he must, and she had tried cooing sympathetically, and the effect was the same.

His inability to speak about his mother, and his bereavement, seemed to infect all discourse; meals had become increasingly silent. The most harmless inquiries – 'Are you going to be back for tea?' – were now met by silence.

Sally tried to sing the jaunty little tune, but everyone was out of time, and by the time the children at the front had started on 'Give me joy in my heart, keep me praising' for the third time, the people at the back were still Hosanna-ing. Sally found that Church had gone totally dead on her – it was not that she could not believe; she simply could not focus on it. All her religious emotion was directed towards her secret friends in the wardrobe. Without them, she was not sure that she would have survived the last month, what with Francis being so odd, and Jessica joining in.

Jessica did not quite know how to manage life while sharing a house with two people who got on as badly as her parents, and so she had spent more and more time watching television, or – a new solace to which neither of the grown-ups appeared to object as much as other people's parents – on the telephone to her friends. They had still not told her that she had inherited a substantial part of her grandmother's fortune. When she overheard her mother talking (too openly, Jessica believed) about these intimate affairs to All and Sundry (the Old Bill, of all people!), she had caught the impression that they had been ruined, more or less, by the terms of Granny's will.

Meanwhile, the letters, and the little gifts, had continued to arrive. Francis had told her that she must not reply to Mr Gadney; that it might put them all in a very difficult position with the lawyers, but what sort of difficulty could that be? She had acknowledged the Enid Blyton, the battered box of Cadbury's Milk Tray, and the colouring book. It would have been discourteous not to. One day, she presumed, they would meet, and then he and 'Auntie Ena' would discover that she was not aged about six. Either, in that event, the present-giving would cease, or they would attempt to give her something more 'her own age'.

Sing Hosanna, sing Hosanna,
Sing Hosanna to the King!

Jessica hated this hymn. They had it sometimes at school assemblies, and it was a favourite with the stupider teachers (the ones who really liked to talk down to you), and those physical or emotional defectives who went in for the Christian Union. It was childish, and Jessica had reached the stage of life when she was completely bored by childhood, could not wait for the next stage to begin.

But now her attention was diverted by a strange sight. Little Jason on the donkey had come to a halt. Lindie Spittle was lifting him down. For the nose of the old Morris van which was towing the first of the caravans had crept round the corner by the Rising Sun and come face to face with the religious tableau.

It was difficult, Jessica felt, not to feel a lightening of the spirits at the confrontation. The entertaining possibility presented itself that things were to go badly wrong.

Voices were interrupting the divine praises.

'If you could be c-courteous enough to pause for a moment, we are having a re-religious procession. We shall all be in ch-church in three minutes.' The Wing-Co, trying to take command.

The hooting of horns by those further back in the convoy provided a snarling answer to this. Far, far back, Mo had looked in his driving-mirror and seen non-convoy traffic collecting behind him.

Stentorian and far less genteel, much more rustic when his voice was raised, Gerald Spittle bellowed, 'You shouldn't be here at all.'

'Well, bugger me, if it isn't the tinkers,' was a sentence instantly countered with his wife's, 'You watch your tongue, Robin Pimm.'

Giggly, a schoolgirl again, Miss Bill had turned to no one in particular – anyone behind her in the queue – and said, 'If we could just get a move on. . . .'

Ineffectual in this sort of situation, Francis had raised his voice. Gesturing limply with his large palm, he intoned, 'If we all keep to the right hand side of the road, and make our way as quickly as possible to the lych-gate. Then we shall assemble there, sing one more verse of the – one more verse – ' he could not quite bring himself to call it a hymn – 'and process into church.'

But many in the congregation did not hear these sensible instructions. Like the sheep when the shepherd was smitten, they scattered – some flattening themselves against banks and hedges, others causing chaos by trying to force themselves down towards the church and the convoy. This was because the donkey, alarmed by the motor-horns and the bossy human braying, had doubled back on its tracks. Lindie's rough tugging at its rein and bridle did nothing to persuade it to come to church that day. With a sharp toss of its head, it broke into a trot and, as Miss Norbury complained afterwards, it very nearly trod on her old mother's foot.

The confrontation between the Travellers and the worshippers, which had reached apparent *impasse*, was resolved by the jerky movements of the donkey. Some people dropped their palms; others clutched them. All made a hasty descent to the lych-gate of the church.

In order to do so, they had to squeeze past the first three or four vehicles of the convoy. Each group eyed up the other like opposing armies. Certainly, there was an observable contrast between the Ditcham folk in their Sunday best, and the Travellers, some of whom had descended from their caravans, and were wandering in the road, or looking about them with puzzlement.

Dogs barked, and pulled at their ropes. Some of the travelling children shouted out a wish to join the village children and the hope that they would be given paper palms. When Lindie hurried her Sunday School charges to the safety of the churchyard, Miss Bill strode forward and exchanged remarks with the strange, ragged urchins who had clambered from the caravans. Nor did she seem any less enchanted by these children when one of them said to her, 'If you don't mind your bum, Chris can't get his caravan through.'

It was inevitable that, before they processed into church, the thirty or so worshippers should have stood in the graveyard and watched as the Travellers juddered past in their miscellaneous collection of vehicles. The donkey was leading them at a cracking pace towards Potter's Field.

Francis Kreer, his hair and vestments blown by a cold wind,

watched passively. He could foretell that the arrival of these people in Ditcham would bring trouble. Already, local men and women had hatched plans for the actions they would take to speed the Travellers on their way. The details of these plans, which the Wing-Commander had explained at some length, had not lodged in the Vicar's brain. He stood now, rather, watching the Travellers with fascination. Though such a modern phenomenon in Britain, they did not seem to Francis's eyes as though they belonged to the present age. Although they drove cars and vans, their matted hair and smock-like shirts and blanket-mantles gave them the appearance of medieval pilgrims. He knew that the received line of Gerald Spittle and the Wing-Co and Robin Pimm was that these people were semi-criminal; but they looked attractive to Francis. He found himself looking upon them not with scorn, but with envy. They were embodiments of the fact that even in a genteel village in Southern England towards the close of the century you could still confront that impulse which had led solitaries into desert places, in all civilizations. They had escaped the prison of home and the comforts of affection. This lent them beauty in his eyes. But some of them were beautiful in themselves. He could see, for instance, why Miss Bill had been beguiled by the Blakean ragamuffins who had jumped out of the gipsy caravan. Others, male and female, passed before his gaze, making him quite forget that he and his congregation had gathered together to commemorate the passion of Christ.

As the final truck in the convoy passed the church gate, Francis could only see the outline of Mo's profile, dark in the driving-seat. But the priest stared at Jay, and the dog Leila, as they careered on up the hill. It seemed to him as if she was the most beautiful being on which he had ever set eyes. And she was staring at him! They stared and stared, the two of them, until the truck which contained her turned a corner and was lost from sight.

3

On the Saturday before Easter, the postman brought to the vicarage a letter from the solicitor, and a parcel for Jessica, containing an Easter egg.

Francis read the solicitor's letter when he was on his own in the study.

Dear Mr Kreer,

<u>The will of your mother, the late Mrs Griselda Kreer</u>

You will be pleased to know that probate is more or less complete on your mother's estate. The Royal Life Insurance have accepted your valuation of the furniture, pictures and other effects in your mother's flat, and we should be able to proceed quite quickly now with clearing up the final details. I assume that you will wish, as you agreed on our meeting of 18th January, to sell the flat and its contents and to divide the proceeds equally between yourself and Mr Eric Gadney. Mr Gadney has indicated to me that he will have no objection at all to your having the 'first refusal' on all objects of a sentimental value to yourself, but his solicitor has told me that it would be helpful if we could have a 'gentleman's agreement' that none of these items should in itself exceed £50 in value. If you do wish to have any item in the flat which is valued at more than £50, then you should buy it when the contents are offered for sale.

Mr Gadney tells me that he has been trying to get in touch with you, but without success. I know that you must be very busy, but it would make things run much more smoothly if you could agree to meet Mr Gadney, preferably at 56 Cornwall Gardens, and agree the terms of the sale, the choice of estate agents, and other such details.

It would also be helpful to me if we could have a word about the setting up of the trust for your daughter. The sum held in trust will be quite considerable, and I should feel much happier if you were involved in discussing its disposal and organisation with me, even though you are not of course a trustee.

I look forward to hearing from you.

Yours sincerely, Squiggle.

Beneath the squiggle were the words, *pp. R. M. Sandiman. Dictated by Mr Sandiman and signed in his absence.*

With a quiet but impassioned violence, Francis read this letter twice and then screwed it into a ball.

Jessica opened her egg in her bedroom. It was quite a spaz egg, just a cheap thing with chocolate buttons inside. Some baby bunnies frolicked about on the box it came in.

She had a card which showed more bunnies, and inside there were the words:

Dear Jessica,

This is a little Easter egg from your Auntie Ena and myself. I hope that you enjoy eating it, and that you enjoy Easter too! We so much want to *meet* you. Why not get your Dad to bring you down to the flat in town, and we could all meet up then? With love from your Uncle Eric.

While these two letters were being read, Sally was in her bedroom. Jessica and she had just had the following exchange in the kitchen.

'That's nice, lovey.'

'What is?'

'Someone sent you an Easter egg?'

'Mummy, you know they have.'

Long pause.

'Aren't you going to tell me who it's from?'

Silence.

So, Sally had tried some banter, and said, 'Go on, be a sport. Tell your old mum who the egg's from.'

'Mummy, you know perfectly well who sent me this egg; and it's my business who it's from; and if you have nothing better to do with your time than to sit around watching other people open parcels . . .'

With this unfinished sentence in the air, Jessica had left the room. And Sally had repaired to her own room, taut and wounded by the exchange. She knew that she did not have anything very much to do. It was a cruel taunt. She felt herself coming out in a hot flush and she knew that one of her panic attacks was about to descend. When this happened, only her wardrobe friends could console her.

Alison Bill had tried; Sally had been really touched by her sympathy the other day when she had gone round to deliver a pile of parish newsletters to the schoolmistress. They had had a coffee and a natter, and Sally had found out that Alison had been through many of the same symptoms herself about three years before.

Sally had made Alison laugh by saying, 'Francis? Sympathetic? I don't think he even knows what the menopause *is*.' It had surprised Sally that Alison Bill, so devout, had been prepared to laugh at the priest. But though Alison had been kind – so kind that Sally had cried – she had really only been able to talk about her symptoms: not about the rest; not about the dreadful sense of aloneness which she felt at home; and this frightening sense she had, when she quarrelled with Jess, that she had already lost the affection of both her husband and her daughter; and the feeling of hopelessness which it brought with it. These feelings of near-despair could only be helped by communing with her oldest friends in the world. And she would have been ashamed to admit to an intellectual woman like Alison Bill that she still needed those friends. She had always needed them.

She did not dare to get them out today, but she could open the wardrobe door and talk to them: the Dog Frumpy, Teddy, of course, the rag dolls Lettuce and Carrot; Golly, with his striped trousers. They were her best friends, and they let her say all the silly things which made Francis wince. She was too silly to see why they should make anyone wince, but she was intelligent enough to see the wincing. 'Do you have to say "natter"? What's wrong with the word *talk*?' or 'Talking about "a coffee" rather than "some coffee" implies that we are in an hotel.' And '"Vegetables", please! Not "veggies".' So, now, when she spoke to them –

and how they laughed, particularly Golly and Carrot who were the real pranksters of the nursery – she said some really naughty words almost out loud.

'A coffee. A coffee and a natter. Veggies, veggies.'

Then Teddy, who always was the naughty one, spoilt it all by saying a *really* naughty word, instead of just a word that Francis Said Was Naughty. Teddy said, 'Poo, poo'. They could not stop themselves. They could not help having a bit of a giggle about that.

4

Now encamped with the other travellers, Jay Dunbar's spirits had lifted. She loved Potter's Field – the way it swooped away, unfenced and unhedged until it reached a high windy plateau, whence, by a broad path, you could reach the Ridgeway. Walking there, beneath the vast, cold sky, she allowed her anger, and her self-regard, to lift away from her. Beneath her boots, shoots of grass appeared in the clay. She loved the feeling of life coming back to the earth. She loved the freedom which all this space gave her, these huge vistas, dotted by villages and fields and, to the north, by the coolers of a huge electric power station, but still essentially wild in feeling. Her solitary walks brought healing, but she was not always alone. Sometimes she walked with Mo, whose quick eye found out flint arrow-heads, and fossils in the rough clay. Sometimes they walked as a threesome, Mo and his young friend Dave. (Mo was happier with a sycophantic younger admirer.)

'And you see, like from here, right, where we stand,' said Mo, 'we're on a ley-line.'

'What exactly is a ley-line?' (Only Dave said, 'Worrizackly izza lie-line?')

'They are the first tracks of the human race in England,' said Mo, 'and they connect up all the ancient sites, the places of sacrifices, the big camps, the churches, like, in this network of straight lines. Only they're not like old roads, you see, always.' He laughed, becoming muddled in his own explanation. 'Hell, they're straight lines, but you have to be pissed out of your mind to see them.'

Dave had laughed, but Jay could see that the boy was more seriously interested in the matter, and when they had one of their walks *à deux*, Dave had reverted to the matter.

'Do you believe in ley-lines, Jay?'

'Yes, yes I do.'

'Connecting up all the churches in a perfectly straight line, is that it?'

'There's a harmony in things,' she said quietly, 'and we sometimes need to stand apart before we hear it. And there is a symmetry but we sometimes need to come out and look for it.'

Dave gingerly took her hand when she said this. She did not mind. Mo had been his usual charming, selfish-bastard self all week, laughing with Rosie, telling everyone how much he admired Irma's tits. Why shouldn't Jay hold Dave's hand?

He was a bit like Tim, the busker-boy, who had first introduced her to this way of life. Dave had more of the Artful Dodger to him than Tim, a fact which he emphasised by wearing a battered bowler hat, and a spotted kerchief round his neck, so that he could, at first glance, have been a costermonger or even a chimney-sweep's boy in nineteenth-century London. He was not from London, as it happened, but from Liverpool.

'So what's Mo been up to in Reading?' he asked her, coaxingly, as they had this walk together towards the Ridgeway in the high wind of the afternoon.

'I don't know. I don't always want to know what Mo's been up to.'

'Is it true he's using a lorra smack?'

'Some. So?'

'Eh, hey, girl! You want to watch him, you don't want to get mixed up with that stuff.'

It was not exactly surprising that Mo had been going into Reading for the purposes of buying heroin, nor that he had found a supplier. Jay did not quite know where the money was coming from, to pay for this expensive indulgence. In a way, this was the least of her worries. She just had that old sinking feeling of being let down, which Mo's companionship repeatedly brought to her. She knew that if she challenged Mo with having gone to Reading, he'd say – So, he had, what of it; so, he'd been to this pub, met this bloke, bought this grass. If she suggested that he had bought anything stronger than grass, he would laugh or become abusive.

It was at times like this that she valued the other Travellers, and she felt grateful to Dave for being her friend. By evening, when they were all together in a circle, her mood had changed. Mo was being funny and charming, and she forgot that this probably simply meant that his latest craving for heroin had been satisfied. Rosie, with one of her kids sucking at her breast, sat there, and Jay hardly bothered to be jealous. It was not exactly a formal act of group meditation, still less an occasion of communal worship, but they somehow found themselves, all the circle, falling silent; all but Compton, the mystic with the long hair, long beard and woolly hat, who hummed, and la-laed and swayed from side to side. As he did so, Jay ignored the flicker of sadness in Dave the Artful Dodger's face, and she kissed fickle Mo on the ear.

5

Jay's attitude to crime was uncomplicated until she had met Mo. She had never needed, nor felt tempted, to steal. She believed it was wrong for others to steal, though she could understand that they might often have motives for doing so. Mo stole to pay for drugs; but he also stole for kicks, and it was hard, since she was in love with Mo, not to be thrilled by this sometimes. It had frightened her to discover how much she was thrilled by aspects of his nature, such as his potential for violence, which she most deplored.

One evening, sitting in Rosie's caravan, the company saw Mo in benign mood. Jay and he had made love together that afternoon, and it had been pleasurable (this was not always the case). She had come to believe that her very slight flirtation with Dave made Mo treat her with a little more respect. Everyone who was squashed in the caravan shared in Mo's benignity, and Mo's joint, which was passed from person to person like a pipe of peace – from Jay, to Dave, to Rosie, to Compton.

It had been raining. The caravan smelt very damp, a bitter smell of mould and sweet and sodden cloth. To these odours was added the smell of dogs and children. The windows of the caravan were steamed up. A spirit-lamp dangled precariously above their heads, lighting their faces with a lurid glare.

'Shush, will you, shush,' Rosie said to a little child who had jumped out of the caravan to piss and stepped on a clump of nettles. But little Seth, whose three-year-old feet were now covered with nettle-stings and mud, could not stop himself hollering. 'You'll wake Semele.'

But he already had, and his baby sister was joining the roar with all the power of her lungs.

Jay looked anxiously at Mo. She knew that he couldn't stand kids, though he sometimes pretended otherwise, for the purposes of charming their mothers. In some moods, he could be terrifying on the subject. She never knew how much was meant by his bad taste jokes about bashing kids' heads, but that was the way he talked, sometimes. But he laughed tonight. When Mo laughed, in this particular light, his mouth looked weird. You could see every particle of whisker lit up (he appeared to be growing a beard), and his teeth seemed much blacker than by light of day.

'Hey, smoke,' he said to Dave, who was already far gone.

Dave, who still had the battered bowler on the back of his head – he seldom took it off except to sleep – drew deeply on the joint and stared watery-eyed and sentimental at Jay.

'You look fantastic with all your hair off.'

'Yeah,' said Mo, as though the remark had been addressed to himself.

Jay had decided to trim her pony-tail that morning. By lunch-time, carried away, she had cropped her hair as short as a boy's. It had been a restful occupation, sitting in the caravan, for a wet day. And it was true, with short hair she looked, if anything, more beautiful than before.

Sensing a bit of hostility from Mo, Dave reverted to boring the company with a narrative which most of them had known already, even before Dave had repeated it twice.

'Anyway, me and Mo, didn't we, Mo, me and Mo went into Reading. It's fantastic, Reading.'

Jay felt this took the gilt off his compliment to her.

'Anyway, we went in this pub, didn't we, Mo.'

'Martyn told us about it,' said Mo. Martyn was one of his more alarming London friends of whom Jay felt particularly afraid. 'He was too bloody expensive, that bender.'

'I think he really fancied me,' said Dave.

Everyone giggled, even Compton, who had looked so vacant that you would not have guessed he was listening to the conversation of the others.

Jay found that marijuana had quite a strong effect on her, certainly stronger than alcohol. Had she been having this conversation sober, she would have become bored and begun to hate her company. Her head floated with dope, she thought that Mo and Dave were very, very funny.

6

Had Francis been at home on the night of the burglary, the rest of this story might have been very different. If two people are destined to fall in love, much depends on timing, and Jay had not met Francis yet.

He had gone to London, yet again, supposedly to sort through his mother's belongings. In fact, as nearly always happened since his mother's death, he did nothing there. The place reduced him to an anguished inactivity. He could only wander from room to room, suffering.

Miss Bill had noticed how often, at church, Francis's large blue eyes would fill with tears these days. He himself found that he was moved to tears with an almost absurd ease. His theological beliefs were unchanged, but he spent more and more time in church, finding consolation in the recitation of the services. Often, a phrase in the liturgies choked him, not because it was of any particular relevance to his sorrowful condition but just because it was so beautiful. 'To pass our time in rest in quietness . . . who hast taught us to make prayers and supplications and to give thanks for all men . . . O God who alone canst order the unruly wills and affections of sinful men . . . whose service is perfect freedom.' All these phrases were so familiar to him that he had barely noticed them for years; now he could find himself stumbling as he recited them, so moved that he could no longer speak.

Everything could move him – some trivial radio play, a piece of music, particularly hymns, and Jessica playing the piano. It was not just that he missed his mother, though he did so most painfully. (During her lifetime, he had found her telephone conversations boring. Now he believed that he would have done almost anything to be able to hear her voice again, or to see her handwriting on an envelope as it plopped through the vicarage door.)

As well as missing her, he found that her death had knocked his life to pieces. He could explain to strangers, or to colleagues in the ruri-decanal chapter, that his mother had enjoyed a full, and comparatively healthy, life up to the end; that he had much to be grateful for. . . . And yet her death was not only the worst thing which had ever happened *to him*. It felt, objectively, like the worst thing that had ever happened in the world. Indeed, the world itself had been changed by it. Before Mrs Kreer had died, the world was, doubtless, a vale of sorrow, but it was also a vale of soul-making in which human beings could be expected to *get through*. Now, the world was a torture chamber, in which it was not really possible to see how we endured the knowledge of our own pitiful condition. For most of the human race, crawling over the surface of the earth in ever-increasing multitudes, life could hold no joy, and no meaning. It was simply a scramble for survival: a scramble which earthquakes, famines, plagues, wicked governments, or a combination of them all made scarcely endurable. One only had to turn on the news to see snapshots of the world as it actually was for human beings: stick infants with distended bellies, their tormented faces crawling with flies as their starving mothers wept in the refugee camps and the settlements; wounded bodies lying in the dust in Beirut, in Sarajevo, in Johannesburg, in Bangkok. For Westerners, the plight was different. The actual circumstances of life were different. We are not all confined to one bowl of rice a day as we crowd into the refugee camp. But that does not mean that we are happy; it simply means that we are in a different torture chamber in the same crazily-organised concentration camp, a concentration camp with no kommandant, but from which there is no hope of escape except through death.

Here we have time to think about the pointlessness of our beginning and the sure unhappiness of our end.

He knew, when he had such thoughts, that he was lost to them completely, and they would descend on him in the most inappropriate settings.

'You poor darling, Daddy, don't be so sad,' Jessica had said at that parents' evening at the beginning of her school term. Her pudgy, slightly moist hand, still touchingly the hand of a child, had come up to stroke his face. And then, inevitably, the tears.

He would have been surprised to discover how sympathetically his parishioners regarded him, but, imprisoned in the torture-chamber of his imagination, he could not see this.

'*Hanc olim ueteres vitam coluere Sabini*! I say, that's so awfully good,' said the Wing-Co during one of their recent sessions. But Francis could no longer share the old man's delight in the poem, nor his rather innocent identification between himself, as a retired airman living in the South of England in the late twentieth century, and Virgil and his rustics. Over the whisky, the Wing-Co wanted to tell Francis that he had been through something of the sort when his first wife died, but that the amazing thing about the human spirit was its resilience: people survived; they survived even the Nazi death-camps, or the most agonising and humiliating medical treatment. These words of kindness died on the old man's lips. All he had said was, 'Well – same time, same place? Let's see if we can't advance into Book III next week.' And now it was next week. And Francis had not warned the Wing-Co that he would not be there for their weekly Latin lesson, but had taken himself off to London on impulse.

Finding himself on the doorstep, and talking to Sally (not the easiest of women), Ronald Maxwell-Lee said, 'Is he any better?'

'It takes a *long* time,' Sally said sagely, nodding her head. 'I just wish he would get some of it off his chest. Having a natter makes *such* a difference.'

'Sometimes . . .' his voice strayed away at the word 'difficult'. He did not wish to be discussing the vicar with Sally. It was one thing to wish that he could be of help to Francis; quite another to enter the strange waters of another man's marriage.

As perhaps the Maxwell-Lees were not alone in intuiting,

there had been a widening distance between Francis and Sally since Griselda's death. The alliance between Francis and Jessica increased in its intensity, and the cold-shouldering of Sally became more absolute.

Now that school term had started again, Francis found himself, more days than not, driving into Reading directly after lunch and wandering in the dingier parts of the town. On one such occasion, he glimpsed Jay and Mo coming out of a pub, though he only registered who they were when he had left them several paces behind.

The near-encounter recalled the morning of their arrival in the village, a couple of weeks earlier, and the strange stirring of interest which these Travellers had awoken in him. They in turn were fed into his inner, and highly untranquil, thoughts as he paced the streets. When he saw them, he felt envy. Here were people, at least, who were not trying to cushion the consciousness with fitted carpets, and television and barbecues and mortgages and 'nice' neighbours. They were closer to the raw condition of the poor unaccommodated thing that Man is. They were also extremely erotic. His little glimpse of the Travellers around the village excited him sexually, as did his near-encounter with Mo and Jay in Reading.

Francis was not a man with a high sex-drive. When he compared his own life with that of, say, Damian Wells, he felt that it was extraordinary how little time or thought he devoted to sex. But, in the midst of the bereavement, this had begun to change. On some days, erotic thoughts invaded his melancholy, not to bring any sense of delight, but merely to add to his torment. To his generalised awareness of the infinite painfulness of the human condition, was merely added a gross vision of desire. In his own case, the desire – which was sometimes so overwhelming as to blot out other thoughts – was accompanied by the thought of all the infinitude of couplings to which the human race was driven. He thought less of satisfied lovers, happy in one another's arms, than of millions of sexual beings tortured by a quest which could bring no emotional fulfilment. Sex was another trick to torture us, and guaranteeing that in all our pitiful suffering we could not even be dignified. He thought of the three-quarters starved people in Stalin's labour camps, smelly, skinny, infinitely undesirable, rutting like farm animals. He thought of whores plying their trade, of lonely men in alleys, public lavatories, pornographic film shows.

An habitual country-dweller, Francis found that town walks brought out such thoughts more fiercely. Pacing the uglier parts of Reading, there was no temptation to pretend that 'nature' was consoling. Here 'nature' led pot-bellied men to kerb-crawl in the seedy streets near the station; it led acne'd adolescents to pore over filthy magazines in the newsagents, and neglected wives to betray their husbands with window-cleaners. He did not, in such moods and reveries, think of sex as giving anyone any pleasure. It just seemed like a burden from which only luck could release us.

He had developed the capacity to pace the pavements, past nondescript houses, shops and pubs without any consciousness of his surroundings. Hence the preference he felt these days for urban walks. If he walked out of the village towards the stupendous Downs, then the great skies, and the trees on the brow of the hill now coming into leaf and the rolling vistas beyond, all cried out to be noticed. He did not wish to *notice*. He wished that he could blot out thought, since all thought was painful. Better to walk and walk until it was time to fetch Jessica from the school gate.

Notionally, Francis's daughter still went to and from school by bus. He never actually told her that he would be coming, and there were some days when work made it impossible for him to be there. But she always looked pleased to see him if she came out of the school and saw his car parked there. Sometimes she would ask him to give a lift to one of her friends. The prattle of girlish talk in the back of the car would sometimes be enough to drag his consciousness back to the point where he was able, for a few hours, to inhabit the comforting world of everyday.

Sometimes, Jessica would be on her own, and her narratives would begin almost before she had got into the car.

'Miss Bill took assembly this morning, she read this poem by George Herbert, and before she'd even started to read it, one of the fourth formers – Susannah Cole – I know this sounds really stupid, Daddy, but she blurted out – well, she didn't blurt it, but the whole school could hear her saying it, she said, "Good old Bert." I know it doesn't sound funny, but the whole school just *collapsed*. And there was Miss Bill on the stage . . .'

'Poor Miss Bill.'

'. . . going redder and redder, and she read this poem all about love, honestly, Daddy, I mean the Old Bill, she must be about ninety. Oh, and I forgot to tell you, Anne Rockshaw and I are getting on really well at the moment and we're sharing for Chemistry, and this morning we did this experiment, well, you know sulphuric acid . . .'

By the time they reached home, shared conversations of this kind strengthened the conspiracy of love which united father and daughter, providing him with one slender thread which gave him a lifeline to existence. Without this, he would have no reason to live.

At supper, perhaps Francis might make some allusion to their talk in the car.

'You know that poem which Miss Bill was reading . . .'

While he began to think of something about George Herbert, Sally might pipe up with, 'Has Miss Bill written a poem?' Quick as a flash, Jessica would answer, 'It doesn't matter.'

It was childish not to explain such allusions to his wife, but Francis did not want to do so. She would pick up the wrong end of the stick, or say something which would make him, or Jessica, angry. Poor Sally. Better to leave her to watch television, while he and Jessica had one of their games of chess.

But, sometimes, it was not enough to repose on this minor treachery, and he had to be alone in the full blackness of his own despair; and that was when he drove to Didcot and took the train to London, and sat for hours in his mother's flat, and sometimes slept the night there. And this he did on the night when the vicarage happened to be burgled.

7

The police made their first visit to Potter's Field about a fortnight after the Travellers had settled there. Many local people had telephoned to complain about the Travellers. These complaints ranged from suggestions that the Travellers were guilty of trespass, to fears that they practised child abuse, or took illegal narcotics. No one who made such complaints to the police was prepared to substantiate his or her allegations, so it was not possible for any action to be taken, but a car containing two uniformed officers did pull up at the side of the field one day to make 'routine inquiries'.

Jay had just had a quarrel with Mo when this police car drove up. In the sober light of day, her head unaffected by marijuana, it struck her as very wicked to finance Mo's drug habit with acts of petty larceny. He was so amusing when he described, with his beguiling little shrugs, that he had done a little shop-lifting here, a bit of bag-snatching there that, when she herself was stoned, Jay considered it daring to live in this way. Now she had become frightened and, for the quarter of an hour that the police were in Potter's Field, she had felt stirrings of fear and uneasiness.

Confronted by the officers in their uniform, Jay reverted to middle-class type; she was cringingly polite to them, and she considered the offhand manner which Dave and Mo cultivated towards these young constables was simply reckless and rude. Eventually, as Jay knew, the police would find some reason for moving the Travellers on. It would be a pity – and very hard on all those innocent Travellers like Rosie and Compton – if there were good grounds for supposing the convoy to be a nest of crime.

At the end of their visit, one of the constables said to Mo, 'Oh, one other thing, sir.'

'What's that then?' said Mo.

'Mo, for God's *sake*!' said Jay. Turning to the PC, she said, 'Take no notice.'

'There have been a number of thefts lately in the vicinity, sir, and we should just like to warn you to take very special care of your property: any valuables you might have, electrical goods and so forth.'

'What property have we got here, you stupid fucker?' asked Dave, who seemed to have missed the menace in the policeman's voice.

'Smoke much, do you, sir?'

'What's that to do with you?' (Mo again.)

'Very expensive habit, sir. And not very good for you.'

When the police car left, Jay felt it was simply a matter of time before the police returned to arrest Mo. When she thought of the trouble he was getting himself into, she almost wished that they would. Then, maybe, he'd get the help he needed. Until the police took him, Mo would be Jay's responsibility: seemingly cool, laid-back, but actually incapable of getting through a week without causing trouble of some kind, usually to himself and to others.

In worrying about Mo, Jay discovered the vestiges of her old love for him. He had been flirting badly with one of the large-breasted Scandinavian girls, Irma, and this had made her determined not to lose him to the other woman, as she had momentarily lost him to Rosie.

In many moods, she was bored to distraction by her fellow-travellers; at other times, she realised that Rosie, and Dave, and Compton and Leila the dog, and the others, had provided her with some of the best companionship of her life. Sometimes, she wished that one of them could understand how much she missed her music. On such days, waking in the dark, and seeing at her side Mo's thick mane of Byronic hair, spread out on the quilted anorak which she used as a pillow, Jay would fill her head with music. It was as if she had a personal stereo playing inside her head when she thought of music. Whole Haydn Symphonies and Masses; the Beethoven Violin Concerto; orchestral works by Brahms and Wagner would flood her head sometimes. She would become so lost in a musical reverie that it was painful to return to 'real life'. She still played her fiddle, but she had no sheet-music with her and the practice which she did only reminded her of how much more she needed.

'That's a nice tune,' Dave would say to her, sometimes, and there was no harm in the remark. Mozart and Haydn and Boccherini did write 'nice tunes'. But the unsophistication of his remark would give her a pang of nostalgia for her Guildhall days, and she would think of the flat, and her flatmates who had bored her at the time. Now she remembered the quality of their talk. They had talked of concerts, and of operas, and of books they had read. How freely she had walked away from all that, and how deadly boring life was without it!

'Hey – what are you thinking about?' Mo asked her. And she had been thinking of all these things – his vulnerability, his drug problem, the police, her London days, music. . . .

'Oh, nothing.' And they had just made love, and what she said was true. She had watched his head move up and down on her chest and felt neither pleasure, nor pain; mere distraction.

Later, when the 'thieves' kitchen' had been reconstituted and Dave had come round to share a joint, she was able to look at Mo more dispassionately and to realise that it was possible to love someone, and to find them beautiful without, at that particular moment, having very strong sexual feelings for them. A puff of Dave's blow put her in a more cheerful frame of mind than all Mo's gymnastics.

'What about this pub, then, the Engineer's Whosit?' asked Dave.

'What about it?' – Mo.

'Well, are we going there or aren't we?'

'Not tonight.'

'Why ever not?'

'Because it's ten past fucking eleven already and the place closed ten minutes ago.'

'So what are we going to do for the rest of the evening if we can't go and buy nice goodies at the – what is the name of that pub? Because, you know, when Mo took me in and we met this bloke, he was a real bender, and . . .'

'He really fancied you,' said Jay. 'You've said.'

'So what are we going to do?'

'Praps go and collect a little bit more loot for our expensive habits.'

'I don't think you should go,' said Jay. 'Mo, I really don't think you should go.'

'Why ever not?'

'Because you'll get caught one of these days – that's why not. And because it's wrong.'

'Wrong, is it? What makes you so sure you've got a right to judge me?'

When Mo smoked, the timbre of his voice changed completely, sinking to a rumbling bass on some syllables and rising to falsetto on others.

'Mo, please don't go.'

'We're only going on a recce,' said Dave. 'Isn't that right, Mo?'

'Yeah. Maybe do a bit of rape tonight and save the pillage for later, eh, man?'

'Unless you come and stop us,' said Dave.

'You shouldn't go,' said Jay. 'Where are you thinking of burgling first?'

'Like Dave said, it's a reconnaissance exercise. We won't take anything very serious tonight.'

'Mo, the police have been here. They aren't stupid. . . .'

'No?'

'Do you want to be arrested, do you want to go to prison. . . ?'

'Hey!' interrupted Dave, who gave her a patronising little cuddle. 'Come along! It'll be a laff. And you can keep an eye-out for the filth while Mo and me does our recce, right?'

'That's right,' Mo agreed enthusiastically. 'If you're so worried about our getting caught, you come and keep guard for us.'

It was scarcely believable to Jay, even while it was happening, that she should have been inveigled by the two boys into accompanying them on their expedition. The Girl Guide in her, nevertheless, could not help being impressed by the seriousness and efficiency with which Mo checked through their equipment before setting forth: two stoutly-made sacks, some wire for picking locks, a couple of chisels, and some torches. Dave, as he had once before explained, had become an expert in picking locks at the children's home where he had been brought up. Jay conceded that it was a wonderful skill to possess. There was almost no car, or flat, or house which was closed to Dave if he had a few bits of wire in his pocket.

A real sense of adventure, a *Swallows and Amazons* sensation, mingled with her consciousness of wrong-doing as they set off from Potter's Field in the dark. Mo strode ahead of them, leader of the pack. Dave followed, holding Jay's hand in the darkness, a supportive as well as a furtive gesture. She felt very frightened; choked with fear when they paused by a large-ish modern house near the church.

'Why not try in here?'

Mo had no sooner made this suggestion than Jay had an involuntary memory of her mother's house in Bramhall, a functional 'family' house built in the 1960s: a carriage lamp by the front door, a garage built on to the side of the house, no lights on. Their torch lit up the words on the side of the house – 'The Vicarage'.

'C'mon,' whispered Mo. 'No car in the garage.'

(Mo said *garij*, Jay said *garahj*.)

'What if they come back?'

'Whassa time?'

'Twenty to one.'

'Let's go for it.'

The shelves at the back of the garage, when lit up by torchlight, did not appear to contain anything very exciting. Some tins of paint; some boxes of Miracle-Gro, and Gro-More, where the 'w's had presumably got lost in the manufacturers' desire to stimulate the excesses of nature; some slug death; a length of hose-pipe hanging on a nail. The torch revealed that at the back of the garage, on the right, there was a door, evidently leading into the house.

'You wait here. Call if you hear anything. *Anything*, right?' Mo the Company Commander.

Dave did not need instruction to sink to his knees. Jay was so over-excited, so wound up with emotions, that she would have been ready to believe that this sudden gesture was prompted either by the need for prayer or for oral sex. In fact, Dave was inserting a piece of wire into the lock, while Mo held the torch. Jay noticed that the light of the torch was not steady on the lock, but quivered uneasily.

'Fuck it, fuck it,' Dave muttered to himself under his breath.

'Just leave it,' urged Jay. 'Let's go and leave it.'

'Are you nearly there?' asked Mo.

'Hey?' Jay could see Dave's silly, impish grin as an idea occurred to him. 'Let's break this bastard, eh?'

Before either Jay or Mo could comment on the absurdity of this idea, Dave had used a chisel-handle to smash the smallest pane nearest the door handle. They paused for a while to see if they had woken a dog. There was silence.

Upstairs in her bedroom, Jessica dreamed of being kissed, passionately, by Sarah Mackintosh. They were in a swimming-bath together, with no clothes. In the middle of their embrace, Jessica looked up and saw the Old Bill. Jessica realised that they were looking at the Old Bill through a sea of glass, which increased her resemblance to a fish in an aquarium. Only, the Bill was outside the tank. It was she and Sarah who were being kept in a tank, like a Koi carp or goldfish. They hammered on the side of the glass, and, when it smashed, there was a great gush of water.

In a nearby bedroom, Sally also thought of Miss Bill, and of that lady's maddening habit of saying things to Francis which excluded the rest of her company. Last Sunday, coming out of church, Miss Bill had not been content to say that she had liked the sermon; she had to say, 'Augustine would have liked that sermon.' What did people in Ditcham know of Augustine? It wasn't fair. Sally felt sure Miss Bill said things like that specifically to make *her* feel small.

She felt that her husband had strayed away from her to the point where he could almost never be called back. He had more in common with the parishioners than he did with her. Sally wished that, when Griselda died, she had been able to *pretend* to mind. She sensed that Francis was terribly angry with her for not being able to enter into his grief. But surely there was something very unnatural about grieving so much for an old woman? She had never seen him so distressed. He had become so snarly lately, and also so sarky, that she was almost glad when he was out of the house. When he had told her that, if he was very late in London, he would stay the night in Cornwall Gardens, she had felt half relief, half fear.

Fear that she might be losing her husband. Relief from his gloom and his anger, and his seeming to blame her all the time.

And relief that she could for a change share the bed with someone who really loved her.

The Dog Frumpy had been quite happy to sleep in the wardrobe as usual. But, when Teddy had been tucked up next to Sally in the bed, Frumpy had really barked his head off! And then, of course, the others had joined in – Carrot and Golly positively clamouring to be allowed into her bed. They all loved her too much, that was the trouble. There was not much room for her, now that they were all crowded in between the sheets, but it was nice that they were there, and she fingered Golly's stiff little arm, and kissed the top of his woolly head to stop herself feeling too mopey.

And then she heard the glass break in the back door.

Her first thought was that Francis had decided to come home after all, and she had better stuff the dolls back into the wardrobe before he saw them. And then, with absolute horror, she realised that she and her daughter were in danger of being raped. One read such awful things. There was that vicarage case where the burglars raped the man's daughter and then clubbed the clergyman with a cricket bat.

Sally froze with fear. Her mind raced. Francis had told her – 'Whatever else you do while I'm away, remember to lock the garage door, won't you?'

This would emerge at the inquest. He would give her that withering look of his: that look which said, 'I know that you are in the wrong; you know it too; but I am *above* spelling out your fault.' For the rest of their lives, he would hold her responsible for the fact that Jessica had been raped, perhaps murdered.

'Oh, Frumpy,' she whispered. 'What *am* I to do?'

In the kitchen, Mo and Dave moved swiftly, lowering the occasional trophy into their sack. Sally's purse, containing about £25, some credit cards, a library ticket, and some stamps; a small transistor on which the Kreers normally listened to the news while having breakfast; some bottles – an unopened bottle of Sainsbury's sherry, some Bulgarian Cabernet Sauvignon, and some mineral water which, in the dark, Dave mistook for vodka. The bottles clinked in the sack. Jay could hear the clinking sound from where she stood, twenty yards away, in the garage. She wished they would just come out of the house, but she felt that the two idiots were pressing on, further and further in. A quick recce, that was what they had promised. Now they were scuttling about the ground floor, and making their way into the lounge.

'Look, there's a video,' said Dave.

'Keep your fucking voice down,' said Mo.

'And a hi-fi.'

'Sh. Whassat?'

'What?'

'Shh.'

'I didn't hear anything.'

'Will you be quiet? Listen!'

They listened, and, quite distinctly, they heard a man's voice. They could not quite make out what he was saying, but they were not very interested to find out.

'Jesus, let's get the shit outta here,' said Mo.

Running from the drawing-room, they upset an occasional table, and sent a lamp flying.

'Quick, they've woken up!' they gasped to Jay.

They did not stop running until they had returned to Potter's Field. Once they sensed they were out of danger, Mo and Dave laughed, but Jay felt a sense of fear which did not leave her for days, and she also felt tainted, unable to lose the feeling that, having participated in this botched raid on the vicarage, she had somehow lost her right to take herself seriously as a moral being.

It had been the Dog Frumpy's idea to turn on the World Service of the BBC to drown Sally's voice while she phoned the police. Well done, Frumpy! The other dolls and animals were really jealous of Frumpy for his good idea, because Sally could not help showing him favours, for a long time after the burglary.

When she had whispered her 999 call Sally had crept out of bed and listened at her door. There were some men in the drawing-room. She could hear them, smashing the place up, throwing furniture. She knew that she must leave her bedroom and place herself outside Jessica's door. She *must* stop them raping Jessica. Her poor little Jessica! They must not be allowed to touch the little girl. If necessary, Sally would let them rape *her*, or kill her, but not Jessica. But fear made it impossible for Sally to leave her room. She stood there, shaking, so paralysed with horror that she could not bring herself to put one foot on the landing.

'Jesus!' she heard one of the men say. (Oh, they were evil, *evil*!)

'Where's Jay?'

'Let's get the shit out of here!'

Oh, in her house, they were saying these things! In their lovely house! Sally was crying as she listened to the silence which followed; a long silence. And then a screech of car brakes, and a rattling at the door, but she could not go down, she just couldn't. And a ringing at the bell. Oh, Frumpy – was it such a good idea after all to have disturbed them?

She gasped when a torch shone in her face.

'Are you all right, dear?'

She could not reply, only whimper.

'Put a light on.'

'Mummy, what is it?' Jessica had come out of her room.

'It's all right, dear, you are all right.'

'What are the police doing here, Mummy?'

When she looked up and saw the policeman, she was still frightened, but also overwhelmed with relief, and she began to gabble.

'I woke up and I heard these voices, these voices downstairs, and I knew that there were men in the house and I couldn't do anything, there were these men, and my husband's had to go up to London, and Jessica, oh, Jessica. . . .'

'She's in shock,' said one of the policeman.

'What's happened?' Jessica asked.

'Oh, darling, we've been burgled.'

'Oh, no!'

And now Jess was in tears.

The policemen, two young men of barely twenty years old, calmed them. With notebooks out, they made their little inventory.

'So there was a radio, and some bottles. How about money?'

'Oh, my bag! They've taken my handbag!'

'Any credit cards in the bag, dear? We ought to ring up and cancel those.'

'Oh, it's the thought of them here. Here! In our house! And do you know,' Sally sniffed, and her nostrils took in musty, sweaty-cloth aroma – 'I can smell them still!'

Ascension

I

Ronald Maxwell-Lee did not remember a more beautiful spring. He was seventy years old, and he had just had three treats in a row: sexual intercourse with his wife; a huge mug of very strong tea; and a cold shower. Now at seven a.m. he had a hose-pipe in his hand and was watering the garden, a scene, he confidently envisaged, which Virgil would have enjoyed: the vine by the back door, coming into leaf; the wisteria making its abundant ascent up the back of the house, great splashes of pale purple; laburnum in its blossom, and lilac, and the horse chestnuts full of pink or white candles. Lovingly, Ronald watered the beds – some of the rambling roses already in bud, likewise the peonies, the hollyhocks, the foxgloves. Stocks were already in flower – astonishing for such a date! Clumps of lilies had never looked more vigorous. And, at the edge of the beds, aubretia spread its thick violet carpet, meeting the vivid green of the lawn. He never remembered the lawn or the leaves to be so green – and beyond the lawn, and the little fence, the rolling hills, and the valley gentle in the mist. Birds sang. He found that he was getting on faster with his Latin now, and being able to remember chunks of it. He recalled the lines in the third book of the Georgics where Virgil says that every race on earth, man and beast, the tribes of the sea, the cattle and the birds, rush into the fires of passion; *amor omnibus idem*.

With a little smile, he thought that the Mantuan poet was saying the same as Cole Porter – 'the pekineses in the Ritz do it – let's do it – let's fall in love.' There was almost a little dance in his step as the Wing-Commander watered the lupins and the hydrangeas.

He was a happy man. When he switched off his hose-pipe and returned to the house, he could smell bacon frying, and hear the burble of the news programme on the radio. Before going indoors, he turned once more to take in the beauty of the morning. It made him glad that he and his wife would be going to church at half-past nine. Not that he really believed. He often thought this Bishop chap talked a lot of sense, the one who said it was all a metaphor; but you felt on a day like this that you wanted to say thank you – if only to the great immensities and mysteries of Nature itself, which could sometimes smile so benignly on the race of men.

2

It was Ascension Day. On Prayer Book feasts, Francis Kreer celebrated Holy Communion at half-past nine in the morning instead of the usual half-past seven. Some members of the congregation, most notably Miss Bill, disliked this practice because it prevented them from attending before they set off to work. There were moves from other quarters to change the celebration to half-past seven in the evening. Francis resisted this idea.

Though now an out-and-out unbeliever he was still *au fond* an old-fashioned 'Prayer Book Catholic', who deplored the new ways. He remembered an old priest who had said to him, in the days of his piety, that evening celebrations of the Holy Communion 'smacked of chapel'. Francis still believed this, even though the Pope apparently thought otherwise. Besides, almost no one came to the early morning celebrations, whereas he got quite a respectable little crowd of the retired people in the village at half-past nine.

At his Mass for the Ascension, there were the following communicants: Mrs Norbury, Miss Norbury, Mrs Renton, Mr and Mrs Wing-Co and the Spittles. In his mind, Francis thought of these 9.30 celebrations as 'Norbury Masses', since they were so obviously convenient for Mrs Norbury and her like. After the Mass, it was customary for the congregation to stay behind and to clean the church, while Mrs Renton, the only villager high enough to make use of this privilege, made her confession.

This was the scene on the morning of Ascension Day when

Jay Dunbar stepped into the church. She had just lived through a week in which she had become increasingly bored and disillusioned by the other members of the convoy. She had begun the day with Mo, rather smelly, wriggling into her sleeping bag for an erotic experience which she had not wanted, and which had in any case failed to materialise. She had tried to play her violin and Dave had come up and begun asking her to play 'tunes'. Now she wanted to be alone, and she half had it in mind to sit in a corner of the churchyard to play.

Ditcham churchyard, as she walked into it, was a splash of vivid green and bright sunlight, like the background of Arthur Hughes's painting *Home from Sea*, a reproduction of which had once been given to Jay as a birthday card, and which she had long kept as a bookmark, vaguely identifying with the abject figure in his sailor's suit, shedding tears into the sward. The vividness of the colours that day, of trees and stones, was quite as dazzling as in the Victorian painting. Around the churchyard, cow parsley and may were abundant, and thick grass sprouted around the older graves. A light breeze rustled the foliage of the copper beech. It was not oppressively hot, but quite warm enough to be dressed as she was – a white shirt and loose black trousers. Having had moments of regret for her hair, she was now glad that it was so short, and that she could feel bristles on the back of her neck, and the cool of the wind on her brow.

She was not one of those who is interested in churches as works of art; she did not know about architecture or dates; but curiosity prompted her to push open the church door and to look inside. The contrast between the heat and light outside and the cool darkness within could not have been stronger. For a time, after she entered, she had to blink to get her eyes into focus. There was a pleasant smell – a combination of flowers and furniture polish and newly-extinguished candles. A huge spray of scented stocks stood in a vase at the foot of the font. Realising with embarrassment that the place was occupied, Jay decided to slip out again quietly. And she would have done so had it not been for the guilty conscience which now oppressed her almost continuously since Mo had forced her to be involved in the burglary. To creep away from the place because there were people inside would imply guilt: it would imply that she had only come there in order to nick something. In fact, she had, in part, entered the place to see if she could soak up some of its spiritual calm.

'A bit more to the right!' called out Ronald Maxwell-Lee.

'Right you are!'

The Wing-Commander and Gerald Spittle were moving a carpet. Mrs Norbury and her daughter were smothering the brass eagle-lectern in Brasso. An air of jolly activity possessed the congregation of St Birinus. Sunlight streamed through the East Window which depicted the Risen Christ saying to Mary Magdalene: 'Touch me not, for I am not yet ascended to my Father.'

'A bit more your way!' called Gerald Spittle.

'That does it!' said the Wing-Co.

'Darling!' – Dorothy Maxwell-Lee boomed across the church. She was polishing some pew-ends with Lindie.

'What?'

'Come and look at this – I think it's loose.'

'Sounds like one for Gerrie!'

Jay sat down in a pew at the back of the church. The two old men had moved their carpet, and now moved over to join the two old ladies. It was somehow almost immediately obvious that there was nothing 'loose', and nothing which required the attention of the old gents. They had been summoned for a Council of War. One of the old women had seen Jay come into the church. It was embarrassing to sit there and feel herself being looked at. Each member of the Council of War at different moments cast looks in her direction. Then they put their heads together and began to mutter in voices which were much quieter than those used to call for more dusters and spray polish.

This little drama caused Jay not to notice immediately that the priest was still in church, sitting in a Glastonbury chair in the North Aisle with a strip of purple cloth round his neck. An old lady was kneeling at his feet. After a period in which they seemed to be whispering to one another, the priest leaned forward and made jerky little gestures with his right hand over Mrs Renton's head. Then he got up, and removed the strip of purple cloth from his neck and shoulders, kissed it and put it on the back of the chair. He appeared not to have noticed Jay. He glided across the church to join the Council of War; Jay saw one of his hands flying out to touch one of the old biddies on the bottom.

There was some more muttering, and then he spoke aloud.

'No, that's splendid! Splendid! No, don't worry, I'll lock up. You needn't hang about. Honestly.'

Jay saw that this was the moment to beat a tactful retreat from the church. She had no experience of the clergy and she did not relish the thought of questions which the priest might pose. But it was too late. She had made the mistake of looking up to see him *fluttering* down the aisle. His eyes met hers.

She saw a tall bony man, almost an old man. His head was balding. He had a high complexion and his hair, once it started above the Shakespearean brow, had some of the consistency of wire wool. But his eyes were beautifully blue, and his mouth was delicate and womanly. He wore a black cassock of a light textured linen which was very becoming.

Francis had barely finished giving Mrs Renton absolution before Gerald Spittle had come over to the confessional and made frantic hand signals in Jay's direction.

'Francis' – in a loud stage whisper – 'not to bother you, only one of them's got in the church.'

More dismay could scarcely have been suggested if the church had been invaded by termites or the Khmer Rouge.

'Keep calm, Gerald.'

It was not fair on Mrs Renton, this intrusion. She looked up with an 'is that all?' expression on her face. Francis noticed that while she was rehearsing her (completely trivial) faults, this overweight woman of nearly seventy had the facial expression of a child. By barging in like this, Gerald was being like one of those grown-ups who distracted Mummy's attention just when you thought you had her to yourself. The thought provoked in Francis the torture excited these days by the mere word *Mummy*.

He managed a smile. He knew what Gerald meant by saying that 'one of them' had got into the church. Various village people had become obsessed, in the last few weeks, by the Travellers. Robin Pimm had a right to be furious that some people – presumably Travellers – had trampled the edge of his barley fields when the young corn was green. There had also been an undeniable increase in petty crime in the village lately, but no one could prove that some of the minor, but nasty, incidents, such as the burglary at the vicarage, were the Travellers' responsibility. Francis, whenever he had seen one of the Travellers in the village, had known a revival of the surprising sexual feelings which had been provoked by his very first sighting of the convoy on Palm Sunday. Even the filthiest of the ragamuffins looked, in his eyes, beautiful and free.

So, he scurried down the aisle at some pace to reach the 'hippy' before Gerald Spittle did so. He wondered whether it would be the hippy he had been unable not to notice in the Post Office, the young man with the thick dark hair swept back from his forehead a little like Lord Byron, and the impudent smile on his lips.

Thinking of Mo (though he did not know his name), Francis himself smiled. It was the first time he had done so spontaneously since his mother's death; it was the first smile which burst from him, rather than being switched on. By the time he was halfway down the aisle, his mouth had almost formed itself into a grin, as he looked through the darkened church to identify the youth.

The church was a cave of darkened shadows, lit up here and there by shafts of light streaming through the Victorian glass. One such shaft, scattering multi-coloured rays, fell on the young person who sat in the back pew; so that, momentarily, Francis supposed that, in the way of young people, Jay had dyed her hair, clothes and skin a multitude of different colours – patches of bright green and purplish pink in the hair, more green down the sides of her face and a great gash of crimson across her chest. But she moved, and the light moved, and he recognised his optical mistake. Coming closer, he encountered a face of absolute pallor, divided by large green eyes, and a snub nose and strange, uneven lips, curled – whether in satire or sensuality it was hard to determine. About five paces away from the young person, who had short cropped yellow hair, and who was extremely beautiful, Francis decided it was a girl. His first irrational thought was of the story of Pope Gregory, coming upon the little English slave-boys in the Roman marketplace: not Angles, but Angels.

As he approached her and saw how disconcertingly beautiful

she was, he found himself grinning, an idiot grin born of embarrassment. So shocked was he by her beauty – knocked out by it – that he assumed an air of familiarity which was quite unlike his usual diffidence.

'Hall-*o*' – with great emphasis on the final syllable.

'Hallo.' Her greeting was quieter and more clipped. She smiled though – friendly, semi-amused, perhaps by the effect she was creating; but he thought that he saw a great sadness in her eyes.

And, while he was thinking this of her, she was thinking of him, 'What a sad, beautiful face.'

This they told one another many weeks later. They had reverted, with great frequency in their talk, to this first meeting. Francis always maintained that he had fallen in love at first sight. Jay said, with equal truthfulness, that she had not fallen in love with Francis at once. Perhaps neither quite told the truth about this meeting which both, almost immediately, mythologised and turned into a piece of narrative inside their heads. But both knew that a change had occurred in life.

'Jehovah is a false god,' Francis used to say in later life, 'but there are other gods, of whom I knew nothing until that Ascension Day.'

Continuing his zany and idiotic smile, he said – more in a tone of flirtation than of reproach – 'You've just missed the service.'

'Oh, good.'

'Only a few of us come to it.'

'I did not wish to be rude. By "oh, good", I meant that I am glad I did not barge in and disturb you.'

'You would certainly not have done that. Not so much to see in the church.' A guided-tour prattle now came to his lips. 'Royal Coat of Arms over the door there – Queen Anne – used to hang over the chancel arch, of course, in the old days; font's worth a look, actually, behind the good ladies' flower arrangement.'

Jay hated that 'good ladies'.

'I hadn't come for the architecture . . .' Then seeing his crestfallen expression – 'not that it isn't very nice.'

'Is that a violin?'

'It's not a rifle if that was what you were afraid of.'

She loved his laugh, and she liked him for showing a lot of goofy teeth.

'I'm up with the caravans at the top of the village. As if you couldn't have guessed.'

'Really?'

'I've been on the road a few months now.'

'With your violin?'

'With my little friend.' She hugged the violin case fondly. 'Not that I've had much chance to play. I stupidly brought no music with me.'

'What sort of thing do you play?' He knew nothing of these things: would she be able to play 'pop' music on a fiddle? Or 'folk'? That would be it.

'Most things. Many things.' She shrugged and smiled. 'I really want to do chamber music – late eighteenth-, early nineteenth-century.'

When she said these words, Jay felt an extraordinary burden lifting within her. Afterwards, she would say that it had been seven or eight months since she had met anyone with whom she could converse intelligently, with whom she could use even a phrase as simple as 'early nineteenth-century', without the burden of being thought snooty, or, worse, the temptation to patronise her audience by explaining what she was talking about. Talk suddenly flowed. She gabbled to the clergyman – about her music course, why she had given it up, about her favourite composers, above all Beethoven, her distaste for formalised study, her rash decision to cut loose and to follow the road, at least for a while. From this account of things, she noticed, even as her narrative was in progress, that she excised any reference to Mo, or to male companions. Her pursuit of the convoy was represented purely as a pursuit of an 'alternative' lifestyle.

'What people now do not always realise,' said Francis airily, 'is that there have always been wanderers. Nineteenth-century Russia, for example, was full of them. People called them the holy idiots – they would come to your kitchen window for a bit of bread and you received special blessings if you fed them. Then, think of the Middle Ages in this country: all sorts of people took to the roads in those days, as we read in Chaucer.'

Jay said, quite spontaneously, *'So priketh hem Nature in hir corages.'*

It was possible that, if she had not retrieved this line from a school textbook which she had 'done' for 'O' level, Francis Kreer might have looked back on their encounter as a purely flirtatious one: a taste of spring, a blessed token that all in life was not misery, that he would in time recover from the blinding grief which he felt for his mother. But her words seemed, in this time and mood and place and context, like a grand statement, and when she had said them, he felt as if he were being caught up in the great, irresistible flood of Nature itself. He felt that he had been excluded from the world of Nature until now; what followed, he felt, could no more be resisted than the horse chestnuts outside could have resisted coming into their extravagant flower and leaf; no more could the birds, which sang outside the church windows, have resisted coming out of their eggs. Months later, Jay said, 'You looked so surprised! You did not think a person like me had ever read a book.'

This had been the case, but he always denied it.

At the chancel end of the church, the cleaners and polishers were completing their work. Mrs Renton, having said her penance, had joined Miss Norbury, and was helping to burnish the eagle.

'You had better go and rescue him,' said Lindie Spittle, who had not taken her eyes off the young intruder since Jay had come into the church.

'Do you think she's trying to touch him for some money?' said the Wing-Commander.

'Touch him? Touch him?' Lindie's voice was sharp.

Sensing that combination of anger and indefinable excitement which often afflicted his wife when the Vicar was discussed, Gerald Spittle said, 'Leave this to me.'

'We are just about to lock up, you know,' he said to the girl, over the Vicar's shoulder.

'I'm not staying,' said Jay. 'I don't want to intrude.'

Gerald, who was a little surprised by the fact that she spoke with an educated voice (though North Country in its inflexion), said, 'We have to keep the place locked because of vandals.'

'I can lock up, Gerald,' said the Vicar quietly. 'You go.'

Afterwards, in his account of the matter to Lindie, Gerald said, 'He did not take his eyes off that young woman, not to speak to me, not ever. I tell you, he did not take his eyes off her.' He failed, in telling this to Lindie, to notice the effect of shock and disgust which it caused in his wife.

The faithful band of cleaners did, eventually, disperse, though it seemed to Francis that they were hovering longer than usual that morning, to see what would happen: it was not every day that a 'hippy' came into St Birinus's church!

Jay, who had stood up and lingered, herself unwilling to leave, said to the Vicar, 'It seems sad about the vandals. Sad that people can't come into a place like this. I was hoping . . .' Quickly, he said, 'Of course! You were hoping to play your violin.'

'Oh, not necessarily.'

'But, please! I want you to.'

'Not while everyone is still here.'

They waited, then, for Mrs Renton, and the Spittles and the Maxwell-Lees and the Norburys to depart into the bright morning.

'Bye, Ronald! Bye, Gerald! Bye, Lindie!'

No one noticed the expression, something like terror, on Lindie Spittle's face as she accepted this valediction from her priest.

When they were alone together, Francis said to Jay, 'Now. Please play.'

'I should be embarrassed now.'

'I beg.'

'I haven't played for weeks. I was looking for somewhere to practise, not to perform. I do not yet know whether I want to play again.'

'Nonsense. You were only telling me ten minutes ago that you would like to play in a chamber group.'

'This isn't an appropriate place.'

'I do not see why not.'

'I'm *shy*.' But she had become a coquette as she said it, a schoolgirl laughing.

'I shan't sit here, embarrassing you. There are various jobs which I have to do before I lock the church. You won't know I'm here.'

'I should.'

'How, if you can't see me?'

'I should feel you. Sort of.' Again, the nervous giggle.

'I am going to retreat into the shadows.'

Francis scuttled off towards the vestry. He locked the back door of the church and he checked that the faithful band had performed, as they always did, their various tasks. Brasso and Johnson's Wax and dusters had all been put back in their appropriate cupboard. Mrs Renton had laundered his alb and purificator and these were neatly laid on the vestment chest ready for the next celebration – the early service on Sunday morning. Francis stood silently, waiting. The silence was very long, or it seemed so. Then, he heard the violin being tuned. Then another long silence, during which he felt nervous. It was rather like being the parent of a child at a school concert and hoping that one's child would acquit herself with credit. He so wanted Jay's playing to be good!

But, before he had had time to mull over this wish, he was suddenly arrested by a burst of joyful sound coming from the church, confident and sharp. It was the Fifth Violin Sonata ('Spring'). Without its familiar piano accompaniment, the violin parts of the Allegro movement seemed to alternate with violence between joy and sorrow until they fused in a poignant sound where it was no longer meaningful to distinguish between the two.

Francis, who was transported by the sounds, said to himself, 'I do not believe in God, but I no longer feel ashamed of this fact. I believe in something after all, and I never knew that I did!' He was not framing thoughts into a metaphysical speculation. He was responding to the sound on some instinctual level. He felt that the hated old God in whom he first believed and then disbelieved had at last been banished. He had been hovering about Francis from the cradle. And now he was gone! With a gulp of tearful gratitude, Francis lost himself in the music and felt that the sound of the violin, and the light which streamed through the window and the smell of the summer flowers, and the heaviness of the thick foliage which soughed and swayed outside in the churchyard in all the heavy fullness of a summer morning – all this was *enough*! It was like a moment of mysticism, only it was a release from mysticism. All the time in his life which he had wasted – believing in this, not believing in that, and quietly drying up in consequence. Now, he felt refreshed. Beethoven – the sunshine – this girl, this beautiful girl; the three all seemed part of the same phenomenon, a sort of Trinity of love which released him from imprisonment in himself.

For a moment after the music stopped, he stood in awe-struck silence, astonished that five minutes of sound could have such an effect upon his spirits. It was as if he had never been happy, never been sad, never been alive until that moment. The awful gnawing grief for his mother had not been thrust from him but it seemed part of those sorrowful strains in the music just as the sunshine, and the thought of the girl's smile seemed part of its joyfulness.

So priketh hem Nature in hir corages.

Only after a significant pause did he dare to advance through the darkness of the church and to call out to her, 'That was absolutely beautiful!' He said it in such uncompromising tones that he might have easily said, 'You are absolutely beautiful!'

He peered through the shafts of sunlight and into the pools of darkness which surrounded them. She had moved from the pew where she had been sitting.

'Hallo!' he called to the blackness.

A light breeze blew the church door which she had left on the latch, and when the door blew completely open sunlight scorched cruelly on to the old font. She had gone. She had vanished like a phantom, the girl with no name.

3

'Miss Bill is right to remind us that Francis has been under a lot of strain,' said Wing-Commander Maxwell-Lee. 'I remember when my m-m-mum died, how cut up I was.'

'Oh, I'm not denying that, Ronald,' said Gerald Spittle. 'Don't think I'm being unsympathetic.'

Both Ronald Maxwell-Lee and Alison Bill did think this, but they did not say so. The Wing-Co did not mind being called by his Christian name: it was a universal habit nowadays; all the same, he thought Spittle should have asked.

'It would have been nice to be warned, that's all. Lindie

and I have got to drive into Reading later, and it would have been nice to be warned if an extraordinary meeting of the PCC was to be cancelled at the last minute. Not even cancelled. Just didn't happen, because the Vicar failed to turn up.'

Both Ronald Maxwell-Lee and Alison Bill silently counted to five inside their heads, knowing what Lindie would say next.

'I don't think I ever knew Terry Widger to miss a church meeting,' she said.

These four had been formed into a committee to supervise the arrangements for the parish fête, due to be fired off on the Feast of St Bartholomew, 24 August. They had all arranged to meet in the vestry on that Saturday for a coffee-and-sandwiches lunch. Unaccountably, the vicar had failed to turn up for this meeting. To allay the feeling of anti-climax, Ronald Maxwell-Lee had taken them all to the Rising Sun for a drink at one of the tables out in their pretty beer garden.

All four – the Spittles, Miss Bill and the Wing-Commander – were disturbed by the Vicar's pattern of behaviour over the last months. The Wing-Commander felt particular distress, because the young man (as he thought of Francis) seemed so remote; you could not reach out and help him. He had even forgotten their Latin lessons – so many of these evening dates had been forgotten or curtailed that now Ronald Maxwell-Lee was struggling along with the *Georgics* alone. It was not the same, without the young man.

Miss Bill had her own reasons for feeling strongly about the Vicar's whereabouts, and about his demeanour. They were varied and strong, these reasons, but she nursed them in secret. Other considerations apart, she worried for the parish; it was a terrible thing to have to admit, that the Spittles had a point. Francis, who was normally so faithful in his parish duties, was beginning to fail the people who needed him the most. Promised visits did not happen; now – a forgotten meeting.

In the beer garden, where the sun shone on the pots of garish geraniums, the Wing-Commander fanned himself with his panama before sipping his shandy. Then he said, 'At least one good bit of news. I've had a word with the Chief Constable, and I think we shan't be seeing too much of our f-friends up the way.'

'The tinkers?' asked Lindie Spittle sharply. 'You know, one of them came in the shop this morning! The smell! And the state of that kiddie, it can't be right, because she had a kiddie with her. This high.' (She made a gesture indicating height, not smell.) 'I mean, I was saying to Gerald, wasn't I, Gerald?'

'How they live like that,' said Gerald shaking his head. 'Their feet filthy. Did you see that woman's toe-nails?'

'So, Ronald,' said Lindie, 'you think you've pulled some strings?'

'No names, no p-p-'

'Pack-drill,' supplied Gerald.

'Pack-drill,' insisted the Wing-Commander. 'But the Chief Constable doesn't think it should be difficult to move them on.'

Robin Pimm, who had come over to stand beside their table with a pint of beer in his hand, overheard the Wing-Commander's remarks and said,'Not before time.'

'They do have certain rights under the law,' said Miss Bill, going rather red.

'That's perfectly true,' said the Wing-Commander.

Lindie Spittle had noticed the Wing-Commander's conversational cowardice. He wouldn't stand up for his point of view. He always seemed to agree with what had just been said, particularly, she noted with bitterness, if a woman had just said it.

'Rights under the law?' asked Robin Pimm. 'Rights to trample my barley, causing hundreds of pounds' worth of damage, quite possibly? Rights to break into people's houses? The Vicar's wife seems positively shaken up by that.'

Miss Bill went even redder.

'You know when they'd been in that shop,' said Lindie, 'you could smell them afterwards, you really could.'

'Same as Sally Kreer says,' confirmed the farmer, 'she said that the vicarage stank when they'd been in there.'

'Of course we don't know it was the h-hippies who burgled the vicarage,' said the Wing-Commander, 'or the Campbells', or stole the Watsons' car. These could be unrelated incidents.'

'Funny coincidence,' said Pimm, 'these layabouts come and park themselves in the village and you start having a mini crimewave.'

'I think we should try to be tolerant,' said Miss Bill, rising to her feet. 'Now, I've got to dash. I've got marking to do.'

And she waddled, then strode across the lawn towards the carpark, swinging her right arm in a marching rhythm.

'That woman is cracked,' said Robin Pimm, 'quite definitely cracked.'

'Well, we all know why,' said Gerald Spittle.

'Oh, why is that?' asked the Wing-Co.

'Bad case of spinster in love with the Vicar,' said Gerald, with a malicious sneer as he looked down into his beer, unaware perhaps of quite how much pain this barb caused in the hearts of the Wing-Commander and Lindie. Having silenced his two companions, Gerald continued to air his views. 'It was a great mistake to speak to that young hippy who came in the church the other day. I honestly thought we might have had a lesbian riot on our hands.'

'That's putting it rather strongly,' said the Wing-Commander who, since the departure of Alison, was beginning to dislike his company.

'Cropped hair like that – and dyed, I expect. I don't know if she was one of the ones with kiddies. . . .'

'Did you see her boots? She's a lesbian that one,' said Gerald informatively.

'I think,' said the Wing-Commander, allowing his voice to sink to a gentle murmur, 'that we have company.'

At a table more or less within earshot, a group of Travellers had taken up residence: Mo, Dave, Rosie, Leila the dog and Irma, the Scandinavian.

'What's she *doing* in Reading?' Rosie persisted. She enjoyed Mo's discomfort. Everyone had heard him quarrelling with Jay, who had merely said that she was going into Reading on her own, and refused to elaborate on the fact.

All the women on the convoy regarded Jay with an uneasy mixture of jealousy and awe, a fact of which Jay was entirely unaware; she knew of the effect which her beauty had on men, but she did not expect it to colour her sisterly feelings of friendship with other women.

'She could have brought us some stuff, eh?' laughed Dave, who also knew that Mo and Jay had quarrelled, but did not take it particularly seriously. 'Hey, you know Chris said . . .'

(Chris was the man who sold them drugs; they had met him at a pub near the station in Reading.)

'Keep your voice down,' drawled Mo. He was withdrawn and angry. His supplies of heroin were running low, and it worried him. He would have liked to go into Reading with Jay so as to buy some more. He assumed that it was because she did not want him to buy any more that she had said that she was going alone. But, also, he disliked her having secrets. He had secrets from her: indeed, his whole life was a secret. But he expected her to be open with him. He dimly wondered whether she was having a rendezvous with a man, but who could it be?

These things had given their recent quarrel a particular edge. Jay had even thrown a boot at his head. It had missed, and smashed the kerosene lamp, dangling from the roof of Rosie's caravan, where they had been sitting, supposedly baby-sitting while she went shopping. Now that the quarrel was over, and Jay had gone, and not told him why she had to be alone, Mo felt crushed, foolish. It was so uncool to mind, and even less cool to show that he minded where she had gone. It was like they were married or something horrible!

'I really want to get E next time. You get really, really, bored with dope,' said Dave.

'We'll go in later,' growled Mo.

Leila, who was the only member of the party in a good humour, put a paw on Dave's knee, and the boy let her drink some of his beer from the glass. He could hear one of the old bags at the next table saying, 'I don't think they should let those people in here, I don't really. Not with a dog, it isn't healthy.'

But the really old geezer, with the little, like, military moustache, was waving in an affectionate way to Leila. And, even as the bag was complaining, Leila hopped away from Dave and went to accept a potato crisp from the Wing-Commander's long, rather delicate old bony hand.

4

'More goosegogs?'

'No thanks, Mum.'

Jessica spoke impassively, but she thought that she would lose her temper if her mother said 'Righty-ho!' in the event of the conversation lagging, or 'Penny for them?'

'Old Mrs Maxwell-Lee said she'd do the cake stall again,' said Sally. 'Aren't people marvellous? I said to her, "Dorothy, after all you've suffered with your osteoporosis," but she said she insisted. I think old people are marvellous.'

Jessica wished that her father had not had to go to the silly meeting in church about the summer fête. 'Family meals' were not, these days, very happy occasions, but she missed her father's non-committal facial expressions as her mother prattled forth her condescending remarks about the older parishioners. Jessica felt her father drifting further and further away from her into his own private grief. They were not friends in the way that they used to be, and she could not quite understand why. She too had suffered when Granny died; neither of her parents appeared to consider that. They had not even allowed her to go to the funeral – they had treated her like a tiny kid!

With as much speed as she could, she spooned up the gooseberries and cream and shovelled them into her mouth.

'Penny for them?'

'Nothing, Mum.'

'You're a funny one!'

Jessica cleared the table. She put her own plate and her mother's in the washing-up machine.

'Can I make you some coffee?' asked Sally.

'I don't want coffee.'

'Righty-ho.'

Having slammed the door and run upstairs to her room, Jessica re-read the letter she had received that morning.

'. . . Why not get your Dad to bring you up to town one day? We could meet in the flat and then have some fun, go to a show. You would like that, wouldn't you? With love from your Uncle Eric.'

5

Francis Kreer and Jay Dunbar had met twice since their first strange encounter in the church. The first time had been by accident – Francis was pacing along towards the Ridgeway and he had come upon the young woman, walking her dog. The second time, when they had covered the same terrain, had been by arrangement. In their two meetings, they had spent no more than three hours in one another's company, but they had talked much. Jay found in him what she very much needed at that moment: a sympathetic listener. She had rehearsed her history to him, told him about her father's suicide, about her mother (a slightly edited version, omitting Knut), and about the Guildhall. She was in a dilemma. Life in the convoy had come to bore her considerably, and she really wanted to escape it; but there would be no possibility of returning to the world of music unless she practised, and practised long.

She found him a charming and a sympathetic listener. At first, she had misinterpreted his shrugging gestures, his womanish way of pouting with his lips, his tendency to wave his hands about while speaking, to understand that he preferred his own sex. On their second meeting, when they had talked some more, she had asked him if he was married, and he had said, 'Yes . . . yes, I'm married.'

She had been shocked to discover how much this information grieved her. She sensed that he was unhappily married, but she could not bring herself to ask about it. For her part, she had omitted all mention of her emotional history in her account of herself. She had told him nothing of Mo and his problems. Fearful that this should seem dishonest, she sometimes intruded the word 'we' into the conversation – 'we nearly got a dog', 'we hoped to take a cottage in Wales but we ended up spending the winter in London' – but none of these sentences declared ambiguously that she had a special attachment. The 'we' in these sentences could almost always have been, if one chose to interpret them thus, a reference to the Travellers as a whole. This was how Francis chose to interpret them. He did not want to think of her having a boyfriend.

His own account of the friendship would have differed from hers. Since her first appearance in church after the Norbury Mass on Ascension Day, Francis Kreer had been bewitched. Jay filled his consciousness night and day. When he closed his eyes in sleep, her eyes shone in his mind like stars. He recalled, ravenously, every detail of her physical appearance. Even imperfections, such as the very shiny, waxy quality of her nose, or the faint smell of sweat which she gave off (which would normally have offended the over-fastidious Francis), were wholly alluring to him. People spoke about falling madly in love. Francis now feared for his own sanity. All other considerations, including his grief for his mother, were now subsumed, and understood and contained in the light of this greater feeling, which was larger than lust. True, he thought obsessively about her body. He thought of her bony collar-bones sticking through her shirt; he thought of her firm, round breasts, unsupported by underwear; he thought of her boy-like hips and her beautiful ankles above the Doc Marten boots. He tried a number of absurdly inadequate phrases to describe the nature of her beauty – *gamine*, a cabin boy, *Swallows and Amazons* – but no phrase could explain her attraction. He had lost control completely, which was what made him afraid that he might actually be going mad. All sense of time was lost, and all appetite. It was days since he had been able to do more than toy with food.

He wanted to confide in someone, but he could think of no one suitable. His friendship with Damian Wells had never involved much sharing of confidences about their emotional or sexual lives. This was largely because, although he was very fond of Damian, he did not wish to know how that strange man fulfilled himself sexually. He was happier not to know such details. It was unthinkable that he could tell Alison Bill or Ronald Maxwell-Lee, so Francis suffered alone. He was anyway afraid of what had come upon him. Nothing of this kind had ever happened before. He felt as if the tranquillity of life, which had been so disturbed by his mother's death, was now irreparably destroyed. Final sentences – 'My marriage is over. My life has changed' – were frightening to utter, even silently, inside his head. But this is what he would have to say if he were telling the truth. This was no mere infatuation, of the sort which had often made Francis's heart flutter in the past. It was a great emotional hurricane which he was powerless to do anything about.

After their second walk, he had said, 'Look! I'm going into Reading on Saturday. Why don't I meet you at the crossroads at the end of the village? I could give you a lift. Perhaps we could have lunch in a pub or something.'

Smiling, and acquiescent, she had said, 'That would be lovely.'

She had not questioned his desire to see her again. She had accepted the peculiar terms of the meeting: the rendezvous by the crossroads.

('If you aren't there by 11.45, I shall just go into Reading alone.')

She came at midday, apologetic for her lateness, and found him still waiting there in the car.

Conversation in the car had been stiff, not as spontaneous as when they walked under the open sky with Leila. Jay had regretted coming with him. What was there to see or do in Reading? She had always despised Mo's fondness for the place.

But she had gradually begun to speak again.

'You'll probably be very shocked, but – I'm not a Christian,' she had felt obliged to say.

'Why should I be shocked?'

'For obvious reasons. Because you are a priest. But I do meditate, even though I can't pray exactly. No one has ever taught me how to pray. I do not know who I'd be praying to.'

'I know how you might feel.' Even with his beloved, Francis hated and was embarrassed by conversations about religion. And yet he felt that if this girl had said she belonged to the Salvation Army or the Whirling Dervishes he would have wished to share her faith and say to her, 'Thy people shall be my people, and thy God, my God.'

She talked about religion most of the way into Reading.

She was one of those who believe that religion is of great importance in people's lives, only Christianity is too difficult to swallow. Francis had decided, after twenty years as a parish priest, that religion is very unimportant in most human lives; in fact, that most people do not think about it at all, but he did not wish to spoil the romantic moment by saying so.

'Where are we going?' she asked at length.

'Oh, I thought we'd go to a pub.'

She realised, somewhat to her dismay, that he wanted to find a 'discreet' venue; that, as the vicar of a parish and as a married man, he could not, for example, take her into the Rising Sun. This somehow spoilt things. After cruising the dismal streets, they at length found a pub on the edge of a modern housing estate. Outside, young men with no shirts were drinking lager. The pub was a modern one, devoid of charm. Jay felt a little self-conscious going there with him. They sat indoors, which – on account of the bright weather – was almost uninhabited, save for a few old men.

'You know you told me about your mother – and your father.'

'Yes,' she said.

'I was grateful for that, grateful for your trust.'

'I wanted a shoulder to cry on, I suppose.' The cliché was not literally meant, but it made tears start to Francis's own, very bright blue eyes, and he said, 'My mother is dead. She died a few months ago.'

Until this point, she had been grateful to him for his sympathy, and for being someone sufficiently well-informed to know who Beethoven was. But she had seen no chink in his armour; always the same nonchalant and vaguely cynical exterior. Now these tears, which made her feel a rush of tenderness towards him. As he told her the story – only of his mother's death, but not of her will – the tears continued to stream down his face.

'I'm so sorry.'

'There's no need to be.'

'Embarrassing.'

'You're not. Honestly.' Very gently, she stroked his hand. Then she said, 'I thought you were the one who was listening to all my sorrows. It's good we should share our problems.'

'Is it?'

'Of course, if we are to be friends.'

This was a deadly thing to say, and it made him cry even more. Sorrow surged and splattered out of him, rolling down his cheeks, dribbling down the corners of his mouth, and shaking his chest.

She allowed him to cry like this for some time, doing nothing except to stroke his hands.

One of the old men, shuffling by on his way to the gents, said to Jay, 'Are you all right, love?'

'Oh, I'm sorry,' sniffed Francis.

'You poor man! Don't be sorry. Crying is good for you! It releases feelings which you have to get rid of if you are to rise above them.'

This seemed to stop him crying. He clutched the hand which stroked his own, so that they sat opposite one another in that pub, holding hands across the table.

'I haven't had anyone . . . I could talk to,' said Francis.

'What about . . .' She could not quite bring herself to say the obvious words, 'your wife'. She added, 'Isn't there anyone at home?'

'Sorry.' He sniffed again.

'Don't keep saying you're sorry. I've told you my problems, or some of them. You've told me yours, some of them. Maybe we'll solve some of them together.'

She had not quite intended this to sound like a proposal, but he stared at her with *spaniel* devotion after the words had been uttered.

They had another drink, and this time she consented to have some vodka in her orange juice, which formerly she had been drinking unadorned.

There is a guilefulness about those who are about to fall in love. Like people at war, they plan the next area of advance. Francis was anxious not to frighten Jay off, but at the same time he wished to acknowledge that they were in some senses together; they must therefore plan another 'date' together. It was the obvious thing to do.

'One gets so tired,' he said, 'apart from anything else. I

mean, I'm constantly on the London train, because I have to sort through all Mother's things in the flat. It's an easy journey, of course. Twenty-five minutes from Didcot, half an hour from Reading, and what – ten minutes when you get to Paddington?'

'I do know London.'

This was their first smile together.

'I'm sorry. Of course, you know London.'

She saw that he was hovering, cowardly, between making his suggestion and not making it. She wanted him to make it, so she helped him out.

'It must be nice having a London flat – all to yourself,' she said.

He agreed. This was decidedly not the moment to tell her about the mysterious Eric Gadney.

'I say!' said Francis. 'I've just had the most extraordinary idea. You could sometimes come with me to my mother's flat. I mean, I have a lot of boring work to do there – clearing cupboards and so forth. It would make an admirable place in which to practise the violin.'

'Wouldn't the neighbours complain?'

'Of course not! Say you'll consider it.'

'I'll be okay, Francis, really I will.'

Having liked the idea of the flat, she suddenly disliked it.

Once they were out of the pub, they knew they must be getting back. She tactfully said nothing about his wife waiting for him, but she guessed that was at the back of his mind. She leaned forward and kissed his cheek.

'Thank you for my drinks.'

'Oh, my dear!'

'Come on, come on!'

And, when he cried again, she hugged him, and rocked him like a baby.

'Remember we're in a built-up area. I hate you driving when you've been drinking. Ronald is practically an alcoholic. Did you see how much shandy he was putting away? I just had a half-pint of beer and made it last, but he must have had, oh, two pints of shandy, I should say. Oh, Gerald, do slow down. You could cut through Alexandra Road.'

'That's what I was going to do,' said Gerald Spittle. 'Only if there *is* traffic, this does avoid that nasty snarl-up from the Bagshot road.'

'I hope this wretched shop will have the attachment we need.'

'We can but try.'

The Spittles had been trying for some time to find a particular type of hose-sprinkler attachment. None of the gardening shops or nurseries which they had approached had so far yielded what they were looking for.

'Gerald!'

'What?'

'Did you see that?'

'Well, I'll be blowed.'

'On the pavement,' said Lindie, as though this made it even worse. 'Turn round, Gerrie, and let's get a better look.'

'They'll see us!'

'They won't see anyone.'

'I must say,' said Gerald Spittle as he circled the block, 'I thought it was him.' Left at Alfred Street, Arnold Crescent and back into Willow Drive. This time, Gerald Spittle drove slowly, purposefully. His wife, like a sniper or a reconnaissance officer, peered intently.

'Oh, Gerald, don't slow down or they really will see us.'

'Well, there's no doubt that's him,' said Gerald. And he moved into third and took the Rover 2000 to the top of the road. His wife stared ahead of her. She could not look back. She had just seen Francis Kreer locked in passionate embrace with a woman. Lindie was lost for words, and stared through the windscreen, numb with the shock of it.

6

'He's taking the piss.'

'I'm not taking the piss.'

'So don't, like, pressure me, OK?'

'I'm not.'

'There you go.'

The two speakers were Dave and Mo. Dave had been showing the older man his collection of fossils and geological specimens. He had quite a collection of them by now, which he kept in a loose, blue cloth bag, and he had spread them out for inspection on the grass.

Every now and then, Dave and Mo took off to London, where some friends had a squat. Sometimes they would help these friends by minding their stall in Camden Market. Such items as fossils and stones always sold well, as did some of the other curios which Mo found on his travels. The current dispute concerned the age and provenance of some pieces of coloured glass which Dave had found when walking across one of Robin Pimm's fields. Dave believed the glass to be Roman. Mo guessed they were fragments of a beer bottle, possibly of 1989 or 1990 vintage.

'You believe too much, kiddo.'

'And don't call me fucking kiddo.'

'Shut up, you two! It gets really boring, listening to you going on all day long. No wonder Jay can't take it sometimes.'

The third speaker was Rosie. She yelled above the roar of Meth's shrieks.

'Stand still, will you?' she added, addressing young Methuselah himself. She was examining the spots and blemishes on the child's skin. It was not entirely easy to see the boy's skin, since, in the eighteen months of his life, Methuselah had very seldom had a bath, but some of the red blemishes on his buttocks and shoulders and chest shone through the grimy surfaces of his little limbs.

'I think Meth might be developing a rash or something. I hope it's not measles,' said Rosie.

'So, do you think we could sell this lot?'

'Maybe, kiddo, maybe.'

Sharing women had its excitements. When it worked. The two young men (if Dave could properly speaking be called a man at his tender age) felt a closer kinship to one another. Rather than making them rivals, they felt like blood brothers. They had both made love to Rosie, at some stage, and they both 'fancied' Jay. Neither of them felt very close to the women concerned as a result of these shared feelings, but the sense of male camaraderie was confirmed.

Rivalry could flare in other ways, though. Large-breasted Scandinavian Irma, for example, was really the girlfriend of a largely silent Compton, the bearded smiling man who sat with them now as they had their acrimonious talk. Irma had shown no interest either in Mo or in Dave, which put them in a bad mood with one another. Compton, dreaming his grass-induced dreams, had seemed to be above noticing the rather crude attempts by Mo and Dave to get into Irma's bed. None of these facts contributed to the atmosphere of peace and harmony which some of the Travellers had hoped to find in their nomadic way of life.

'You two wouldn't care if Meth had bubonic plague,' said Rosie. She said the words to be provoking, but by uttering them she realised that they were true. It made her furious. Having assumed that they both fancied her, that all men fancied her, Rosie now knew that she was one of their discarded enthusiasms, on a slightly lower level of emotional importance to these men than pool or mineralogy.

'You wouldn't care if my baby died,' she repeated. 'Oh, shut *up*, will you, Meth.' Pulling at his arm made the little boy shriek even louder.

With the detachment of a mystic on the bank of the old Ganges, Compton smiled, and closed his eyes and made a low murmuring noise, like, 'Boo,bm,boo,boo,bm,bm,boo.'

'OK, so my arrow-heads don't impress you today,' said Dave with high irony. A grin spread over his face which was pure Artful Dodger. He thrust a heavily tattooed forearm into the further depths of the bag.

'Jesus,' said Mo.

'Course it's Jesus,' said Dave as he held aloft the delicate ivory crucifix. 'Who else got crucified?'

'Hundreds of people,' said Mo. 'Did you never see the film of *Spartacus*?'

'What's *Spartacus*, grand-dad?'

'No, but fucking hell, where did you, like . . . ?'

'You remember Jay said she'd been in the church, right? Well, I went in one day myself, and it was empty, man, 'cept for these two old bags down one end, muttering away, doing their magic spells, right, and there's like these hundreds of things, right, like fucking candlesticks, fucking great brass candlesticks.' Dave was now laughing enthusiastically. An Elizabethan privateer could not have laughed more lustily at the prospect of Spanish gold.

'You really wouldn't care, would you? Either of you?' She turned to Compton and said, 'Compton, do you think this is a measles rash?'

Compton's pot-noodled brain was not perhaps the best instrument for effecting a detailed medical diagnosis.

'Boo,bm,bm,boo,boo,boo.'

'Compton, I *said* . . .'

Compton had heard. He stretched out his hand towards Methuselah. Compton's hand was brown, becoming earthy and blackened at the fingertips. His voice, so seldom heard, had the rolling depths, rising to occasional yelps, of the habitual dope-smoker.

'Heh, Methuselah, don't be sad.'

This remark coincided with a brief pause in Meth's yelling. It made Rosie say later that Compton was the only man in the whole fucking convoy who like cared to talk to Meth where he was at, as a person, right.

'And is there any silver in the church?' Mo asked. All desire to needle Dave had passed. He was alert, upright, interested.

'Ask Jay,' shouted Rosie.

It was well-known that Rosie hated Jay. In Mo's experience, most women hated one another; it was only guys who really liked people. Even so, the malice of Rosie's interjection was unmistakeable.

'What's that supposed to mean?' asked Dave.

'Yeah,' said Mo. 'What the fucking hell's that supposed to mean?'

'This is a daisy, Meth,' said Compton, holding out a dandelion to the little boy.

'Well,' said Rosie in an arch imitation of high irony, 'she's the one's who's made friends with the Vicar.'

'She's fucking what?'

Mo's face darkened, and for a moment he looked not just angry, but murderous.

7

'It's a lovely flat,' said Jay. 'Look! Is that the Albert Memorial? What have they done to it since I was last in London?'

'Isn't it extraordinary – in that sort of coffin?'

They stood in the room where Griselda Kreer had died, five months before.

'Is it awfully sad for you, coming here?'

'I'd be sadder not to come,' he said. 'I wanted you to see it. Now you have come here, it is not a sad place.'

Francis had decided, in his fantasy, that he and Jay would now live together in his mother's flat. He had ignored all the letters from the lawyer and he had told Jessica not to answer any of Mr Gadney's impertinent presents and notes. He and Jay would be here. In this place, they would lead a new life. In this room, perhaps, they would make love.

It was some years since Francis had had any kind of sexual experience, and he viewed the mechanical side of his new relationship with some alarm. In almost equal measures, he was afraid of disappointing Jay, and afraid of humiliation. He knew it would be all right *in the end*, as he vaguely put it to himself, but he was worried, and wished that their first essay in physical love was in the past. He loved her with an all-pervading, obsessive, religious love. He worshipped her physically, and when she was near he felt physical arousal, but these were all reasons for dreading the sexual act itself. Would she be calm and kind, or would she reject him if he was not a good lover, and would all that they had together be lost in one angry scene? These were the worst paintings of his fear. It would be best if, suddenly and impulsively, they simply *got on with it*. That was partly why he had wanted her to see the flat.

Jay, thinking of Francis and his sadness about his mother, raised a hand to his shoulders. She wished, almost physically, to stem the flow of compliments which came from his lips. She wished he would talk to her *properly*, rather than saying really stupid things, such as that her very presence stopped the flat being sad. Why had he asked her here, why had she come? With most men, the answer would not have been very difficult to find. It was the middle of the day. Here was a bed.

With this man, though, nothing seemed so simple. Jay thought that he might well just want her to see the place where his mother lived. On the train, he had gabbled out wild phrases; a whole scheme in which Jay left the convoy and lived in this flat for a while until she found her feet. She did not like this idea. She disliked the idea of Francis managing her. She felt he was a grown-up, treating her like an unruly child, and that she hated. On the other hand, it was hard not to be beguiled by his strange flutter of adoration, and she found herself, against her better judgment, developing a taste for it. What a change from Mo! She loved Francis's good manners, and his quiet voice. She was surprised that he did not want to talk to her about religion. There were various 'Buddhist' ideas which she would have liked to throw at him, but he seemed too self-absorbed to be interested. She thought he would be so shocked when she said she did not believe in a personal God, but the information failed to engage, still less disconcert, him.

'When Mummy died, I found all these letters,' said Francis. He had opened the small bureau in the corner of his mother's bedroom.

'Who from?'

'That's just it. I thought Mummy and I were quite close and here was this whole, important part of her life one knew nothing about.'

Francis had not told Jay about Mr Gadney inheriting half the flat. It had not seemed right, somehow, to speak of such mundane facts with the woman he loved. But this was a different thing, this related to the world of the heart.

'None of them are good letters, in a literary sense, but – they reflect such anguish, such shared joy, such *love*.'

'And this was a love affair your mother had.'

On earlier occasions, she had been confused by Francis's habit of plunging into a new subject without quite explaining where the conversation was leading.

'It does make a difference to one's perception of one's parents. I mean, one thinks of them . . .'

'I try not to think of mine.'

'Really?' Again the disapproving adult, he inquired, 'When did you last write to your mother?'

'We never write. I told you that day we went to Reading, we are complete strangers, Mum and I.'

These words were beyond comprehension for him. The two most important relationships in his life had been those with his mother and his daughter. He could not imagine being indifferent to a parent. He wanted to say this, but he was frightened of seeming to preach; and instinct made him fear revealing the extent of his passion for his daughter.

The photograph of Eric Gadney when young smiled at them benignly from its silver frame: blond hair swept back from a handsome, youthful face; short back and sides; RAF uniform.

'Let's open a bottle of Soave,' said Francis as he followed her around the flat on their tour of the rooms. Jay had never seen a flat quite like it. Compared with the flat which she had shared last year with students, this was a palace. At the same time, she found herself alienated by the clutter, pretty as some of it was: the chintz sofa, the little button-backed Victorian chairs, the china cabinet with its display of Worcester, the early twentieth-century watercolours on the walls. Little silver items – dishes, cigarette boxes, small candlesticks, snuff-boxes – littered the mantelpiece and the surface of the wine-tables which stood beside each chair.

'So, you see,' said Francis, 'you could come here and practise the violin whenever you liked!'

His smile was idiotic; the scheme was wild. Why should she spend £10 on a rail-ticket in order to heave her violin up to London, so as to be able to play it in the flat of the deceased mother of a clergyman whom she had met a handful of times? The proposal was almost a threat. She sensed a takeover.

Wounded by her failure to reply, he said brightly, 'Now, I'm going to leave you for ten minutes, because I want to go to Gloucester Road to get some food.'

'But,' she said, as she fingered her glass of white wine, 'I could come with you.'

'I'll only buy picnic food; but you could lay the table.'

'All right.'

He looked at her puzzled, not-angles-but-angels face.

'I shan't be long. Do you mind being left alone?'

'Of course not.'

'Drink as much Soave as you can.'

'I don't want to get drunk!'

A little joke, a nervous, shared giggle between them. When he was gone, she stood at the window and peered down, just able to glimpse him trotting along the pavement of Cornwall Gardens, somehow no less clerical in his 'mufti' – a pale blue-and-white striped seersucker jacket, beige trousers and socks, sandals. She began to ask herself why she had come there: crossness with Mo, boredom, a desire for something new – none of these explanations quite fitted. She did not have long to devote to these speculations, since the bell went. There were two receivers in the hall. The line was dead on the telephone, so she lifted the other – the speaker which connected to the front door bell – assuming that Francis had come back for his keys, his money, his shopping-bag.

'Hullo!'

'Who's that?'

'Is that, um, er . . . is that Jessica?'

'No, it's Jay.' She gave her name instinctively but regretted doing so almost at once. What if he were a murderer?

'Jay, I'm *sorry*.' There was something almost predatory in the voice. It seemed to be of the old world: the accent was quite 'posh', and there was a studied courtesy to its inflections. At the same time it was persistent. She would not be released by it.

'Jay, mind if I step up, I've come to see . . .' There was a crackle, or the noise of a passing car and she did not hear the end of this sentence.

'Francis isn't here just at the moment,' she said. 'But he'll be back very soon.'

'If you could just let me in for a minute. I don't want to bother you. . . .'

'Who is it?'

'Your Uncle Eric.'

'But you don't understand. I really think you'd better wait until. . . .'

A sudden need to be polite had seized her. She knew that

the man talking into the microphone at the front door might be a predator or a lunatic; but what if Francis had been expecting his Uncle Eric to call? She would feel foolish to have kept him on the doorstep.

With impulsiveness, she pressed the button which opened the front door, and listened. After all, if he were a murderer, she did not have to open the door of the flat to him; she could leave him on the landing until Francis returned.

The ascent of the mysterious 'Uncle Eric' was slow. Gingerly, Jay stepped out on to the landing to watch it from above: an old man in a tweed cap and a white mackintosh was staggering up the two flights, pausing on every third or fourth step to catch his breath. Feeling it would be more polite not to watch his progress to the end, she retreated to the flat before his face came into view.

'Well! Made it at last!' He held out a hand gnarled by arthritis. The stretched mask beneath the cap was frightening and pitiable in equal measure.

'You must be careful!' Over-solicitous. 'You sound out of breath! Come and sit down.'

'Please, Jay! I'm not as old as all that! But what a kind, kind thought!'

Smiling with the triumph of a conqueror, Eric Gadney entered his domain.

'Well, who should have thought it! Back here after all these years!'

'When were you last here?'

'Long before you were even born. Fantastic, isn't it! And, more important than that, I've met *you*!'

Removing the tweed cap, he bowed with a theatrical little flourish.

'I've got your age so hopelessly wrong. Easter eggs! Enid Blyton! You must have thought I was completely mad.'

Jay dismissed any thought that he might be insane, but in fact she did not know what he was talking about. Her murmured replies were not heard by him; his insensitive smile was a useful adjunct to partial deafness.

'Can I take your coat?'

'And it's such a charming flat! Haven't got my bearings yet. Well, well.'

He had a strange gait, a slight slouching of one shoulder and arm (the result of a very minor stroke some years ago). Cheap shoes of a moccasin design. The sort of white jacket you might wear for bowls.

'And you're here with Dad?'

'I'm not Francis's daughter.'

'Jolly good! Going to see a show, perhaps?'

'We thought we'd just . . .'

Whatever plans either Francis or Jay had for the afternoon were clearly to be revised.

'I'm back!' Francis's cheerful voice in the hall, as he pushed open the door and entered, bearing a brown paper bag of luncheon foods. He carried it gently, like a babe in arms, and peered over the bulging receptacle flirtatiously at first, then with surprise.

'Eric Gadney,' said their guest. 'I can't apologise enough for blowing in just when you are about to eat. I simply thought . . .'

Francis took in the old, scorched blemish which had painted a streak of dark red across the eyes and down one cheek, and felt himself being sized up by the dark little eyes beneath the skin graft.

Here was his joint heir, and here was the moment which Francis had been dreading ever since he heard about his mother's will. Here was Mr Eric Gadney, of the Sunnymede Garden Centre, near Deal, Kent. Francis had assumed that, when he came face to face with Mr Gadney, All would somehow be Explained. Now, he felt more puzzled than ever; and the Face, at least for the first half-hour, changed his feelings about everything. At least one of the speeches which he had prepared for this moment of confrontation had, immediately, to be discarded. (The one which said, 'I do not know who you are; I do not know what your claim on my mother might have been; but this flat belongs to *me*, and if you wish to establish your claim over it, you must fight me for it.' That speech was driven out of court before it was uttered, simply because of Mr Gadney's face.)

The courtly manners which were in fact a mere device for

intruding himself further, a mere show for Mr Gadney's foot-in-the-door, took some getting used to at first, and this was another reason why Francis found himself capitulating, in all small things, before Eric Gadney's advance. A third knife, a third fork, a third spoon were fetched from the sideboard.

'But please! I hate to butt in!'

And Jay was all solicitude. Francis could almost believe that she was *glad* of Mr Gadney's intrusion. She passed olives, bottled mayonnaise, slices of smoked chicken, cheese, chutney with smiling eagerness towards the unwanted guest. At table, with his shoulders slightly hunched, Mr Gadney could almost have been some legendary sub-species of Germanic folk-tale: a troll or a dwarf, as thirsty for white wine as he was greedy for their picnic-food.

'Never guessed I'd be fed, but it's all very nice. The missus and I generally have something cold at lunchtime. A slice of pie usually goes down very well.' He smiled at the word pie, and smacked his very wet lips on the Soave. 'Oh thanks!' (this as Francis refilled). 'Of course, on a busy day, we don't have time for more than a snack. We have staff of course, but' – a certain pomposity of tone overtook him, as though great men could hardly expect such as Francis and Jay to understand what it meant to have power, and employees under them.

Francis remembered that sheds were a speciality.

'We'd never have thought it, the missus and I. I just thought – well, as you can see, I got pretty badly burnt – the war, you know.'

'Were you in an accident?' Jay's naive question embarrassed Francis, made it even less possible, in this setting, to confront Mr Gadney with the sheer injustice of his being there at all.

'Oh,' – he had the heroic shrug to perfection – 'Battle of Britain.'

For differing reasons, Francis and Jay were both silenced by this: Jay because Battle and War were so beyond her experience, Francis because he now saw any hope of regaining the flat slipping from his grasp; and because he hated Mr Gadney for having interrupted whatever it was that he would have done with Jay that afternoon.

'But as I say,' said Mr Gadney, seeming too big a man to

dwell on past heroism, 'when the war ended and I set up a little nursery garden business, I'd never have thought . . . Now!' An expansive gesture of the right hand suggested that sheds were much in demand in Kent.

'Everybody needs a garden,' said Jay earnestly. 'It's the most basic way we can get in touch with the earth, and we all need to touch the earth, we literally need to hold earth in our hands and say – this is something I'm at one with, it isn't a stranger to me.'

'That's right' – the Soave made the old man agreeable, and he was charmed, as all men were, by Jay.

'I think that's right' – Francis was anxious to show that he could, if necessary be 'greener' than the nurseryman. 'We have reached a stage of the twentieth century where we are so out of touch (literally!) with the soil. . . .'

Jay's presence ensured that everything Francis did was for her. Instead of asking basic questions of Mr Gadney – who was he, what possible reason had Griselda for remembering him in her will, what right had he to dispossess the Kreers? – Francis discoursed about the importance of horticulture. It was a prettily-turned disquisition. Virgil's *Georgics* were invoked; the importance of the garden in the Middle Ages, the Renaissance; the strange fact that anthropomorphic mythology – making us believe that human beings were the masters of the planet – made us destroy our heritage; now we returned to Mother Nature in penitence – no longer the unblemished Adam and Eve, expelled from the Garden, but sensing that only in the garden can we relearn our natural place in the scheme of things. . . .

'Anyway,' Eric Gadney had said in reply, 'you wouldn't believe the number of sheds we shifted last summer, and this year it looks as if it's going to be the same, recession or no recession. . . .'

'Do you have a lot of staff?' asked Jay.

'Oh!' a lordly pursing of the lips. 'As you'd probably guess, in our line of business, we vary. I mean, in the winter, the missus and I manage more or less on our own, but there's a very good little woman who helps us with the plants. I mean, in one of those plant-houses we've probably got over a thousand geraniums, pelargoniums, calceolarias, but by March it's a very different story. Then we have a staff of three or four "casuals".

There's too much heaving and watering and carrying for just me and the missus. . . .'

Jay showed more interest in the garden centre than Francis quite liked. She asked, with great intentness, what exactly these casual labourers did; did they require horticultural training? She seemed strangely cheered by the fact that Mr and Mrs Gadney, when in need of further assistance at the Sunnymede nursery, merely advertised in the local 'job centre'.

'You hardly need a degree in horticulture to water some petunias,' said the plantsman.

Only when leaving, as he at last did, was Mr Gadney able to seize Francis's elbow and say, 'I know we'll settle all this very amicably, dear boy.' The pseudo pre-war slang, by embarrassing Francis, made him even less powerful somehow to say any of the things which he felt.

'I am sure we shall work something out,' said the priest.

'I never said – how very sorry – your dear mother.' This was on the landing, at the stage when Mr Gadney was replacing his tweed cap, bowing, clutching the banister.

'Well, of course it has all been the most terrible shock.'

'At least you've got Jay,' said Mr Gadney. 'A lovely girl. Super to have met her, absolutely super.'

When he returned to the room, and found Jay neatly clearing away the lunch things, Francis felt almost angry with her for having been so 'good' with Mr Gadney. If she had loved Francis as he loved her, the intrusion of a stranger would be intolerable. Today was meant to have been a holiday together, a little respite, a precious time in which Love was their Lord and King; it had not been intended that lunch should have been a threesome, and conversation so prosaic.

'I'm dreading going back,' he said suddenly over the washing-up.

'Oh, poor Francis!' (Had she ever used his Christian name before? He could not remember.) There was such solicitude in the voice, but in the breezy smile he felt there was too much of kindness and not enough of involvement. 'Are all the old ladies annoying you? They must love you really.'

'They are all expecting me to organise the summer fête, and all squabbling about who will run which cake stall.'

'Can't your wife sort them out?' She had not meant the question to sound as sharp as in fact it did. He responded by looking at his fingernails. It was, she had noticed, an habitual gesture with him when nettled.

After a sufficient pause, in which his wife, as a subject, could be allowed to sink to the bottom of the pond once more, he dredged up a new subject with, 'The other ghastly thing is that we've had a robbery.'

'In your house?'

'That as well. But the church has been robbed. As it happens, it's rather valuable, the thing they stole.'

'They?'

'They – he – she. . . .'

Jay did not know Francis well enough to interpret his languid sadness as he said these words. The mere discussion of parish business, even so dramatic a piece of parish business as the theft of the crucifix, yanked him unwillingly back into the world which he so earnestly wished to escape. In her company, he was dizzy with the pain and the joy of love, at once tortured and delighted by her smiling eyes. Of a sudden, he was thinking of all the kerfuffle the theft had caused: the visits from the police; the interviews with the insurance company; and the inevitable ensuing quarrels among the congregation.

Jay interpreted his air of boredom very differently. Like a startled gazelle, she began to wonder if he had only asked her to the flat in order to quiz her about the theft. Did he in fact know that she had been a party to the burglary at the vicarage? He had wanted to be alone with her, and vanity had made her interpret this fact in only one way; he had been clearly disconcerted by the arrival of the old man with the burnt face – to whom he had not so much as properly introduced her. Now his real purpose emerged. She had not quite reached the position of feeling that all these fears were true, but they rushed upon her as he spoke.

'Why should you want to hear about it? The bore is, it belonged to Edith Renton's mother, who left it to the church in her will! Wills! The trouble we have had with them!' (Since he had not explained his difficulties with his mother's will, this remark was impenetrable to Jay.) 'Understandably, Edith Renton is very upset indeed about the loss of this crucifix. It is valuable – sixteenth-century Spanish work – but far more than the material value, of course, is the fact that it came from her mother. She got it in turn from an old priest who used to be her spiritual director—' He wondered if it was necessary to explain what this meant. Having decided that it was *so* necessary that Jay would not have the first idea what a spiritual director was, he sped on with the annal of the parish. 'It isn't easy being a parish priest at the best of times. You can't please everyone. I've always counted as among my real friends in the congregation Ronald Maxwell-Lee, Edith Renton . . . I think I've told you about the Spittles.' Already, in their short acquaintanceship, he had not been able to keep silence about this subject; Jay had an idea of them, though less grasp than Francis realised. 'It sounds paranoid to say that this theft has had the effect of sending Edith and Ronald over to the enemy camp, but that is what it feels like. Ronald comes over every now and then to read Latin poetry with me. I know, since Mother died, that I have not been able to do this as regularly as I used to. . . . But this week, it was he who cancelled.'

'That might have nothing to do with the robbery.'

'You're right. But he asked me in such a – oh, I don't know, such a fussy, accusing way, quite unlike Ronald, if I had heard from the insurance company. You see we really shouldn't have had the wretched thing out, and this is something Edith had warned me about. She actually asked me, some weeks ago, to keep it in a safe except for high days and Holy days – and I just took no notice.'

'It isn't your fault the cross has been stolen.'

'I know that the Spittles say it is. They have managed to hit a left and a right in this. On the one hand they disapproved of the crucifix anyway – an extravagant thing to possess and too Romish; on the other hand, they blame me for the thing having disappeared. The police say it could be anywhere by now; absolutely anywhere. They take such stuff to Holland or even to America.'

'They?' she asked again.

'Villains,' he said, seizing the word from police dramas seen on television.

This took them to the end of the washing-up. Nerves on

both sides were failing. Mr Gadney had mysteriously changed the whole nature of their tryst. A glance at the kitchen clock – 2.45 – gave them the option of a dash to Paddington or a more leisurely way of spending the afternoon.

'Jay–'

She looked at him quizzically, and said, 'Perhaps we should be getting back.'

He had not mentioned that, if the train reached Reading before half-past three, he might yet meet his daughter from school.

'You'll think about coming here, won't you – using the flat for your playing?'

'It might be lovely,' she said.

They did not walk to the tube in Gloucester Road. Nervously, they walked further, retracing, if they could only have known it, steps taken fifty years earlier, in the dark of the black-out, by Eric Gadney and Griselda Kreer.

'I thought he was a really sweet old man,' said Jay, who had expressed the need, before going back to the train, for some fresh air. With the eagerness of a bee in quest of pollen, she led him on towards Kensington Gardens.

8

Adjusting his trouser-zip by the profusion of the forsythia bush, Damian Wells glanced this way and that. It did not do to be seen coming out of a toilet, any more than it did to be seen going in. His experience within the cubicle had been brief, but in its way satisfactory, and now he needed to make a brisk escape before his companion of two minutes ago tried to follow him. A walk across the park, and two or three cigarettes, should be enough to settle himself down.

Damian did not discuss sex with his friend Francis Kreer. It always amused him to hear straight men (such was Damian's estimate of Francis's preferences) trying to be knowing about – a favourite phrase of Damian's – 'Nature's cruel jokes'. They tried to be so bloody understanding. Francis had once said to him how sad it was to live in a society where 'our homosexuals' – why 'our'? We're not yours, thanks all the same, had been Damian's unspoken response – were driven almost literally underground. There was something tragic, pathetic, Francis had opined, about men doing it in toilets.

Little did he know! The thrill! Often for two or three hours before he set out to a cottage, Damian would feel the blood racing, the adrenalin flowing. The sheer excitement of the expeditions often outmatched the satisfactions to be found in these venues; but this was not always the case, and it was Damian's quiet little secret, which helped him through even the darkest days of his débâcle (the Magistrates' Court, the article in the newspaper, the letter of resignation to the Bishop) that the most wonderful sensual experience of his life had been enjoyed in a little house marked GENTLEMEN. He did not need Francis's pity or the condescending 'sympathy' of liberal straights, telling him he'd be happier with a live-in lover and right-on views, and 'accepted' by society. He was much happier on his own, from a domestic point of view; but life would certainly be duller without these occasional escapades in London.

A very brisk pace, almost a run, took him from that particular toilet to the middle of Hyde Park, where he paused and lit a cigarette, and changed subject in his mind.

When not preoccupied with sex, Damian's mind, as befitted that of a clergyman, teemed, churned with theology. Just as the water-butts in Ronald Maxwell-Lee's garden refilled with the rain, so Damian Wells's mind, if left to itself, replenished itself with Catholic theology. His difficulty was quite a simple one. In belief he was a Roman Catholic, but for various emotional and biographical reasons he found himself as a priest of the Church of England. He believed in the Infallibility of the Pope. He believed in the Assumption of the Blessed Virgin Mary. He believed that the Anglican priesthood had not been separated, in any but a political sense, from its Catholic parent-stem in the sixteenth century. For this reason Damian prayed with the Roman Breviary and the Roman Missal, and he regarded nearly all manifestations of the Church of England's independence from Rome as at best a joke and at worst a blasphemy.

Francis Kreer's antiquated love of 1662, of Mrs Cranmer's little bit of nonsense, struck Damian as just a camp joke, rather sweet really. He was perfectly happy, when Francis went away, to go over to Ditcham and dress up in a surplice and scarf and call those old dears his 'Dearly Beloved Brethren'.

It was when the Church of England started getting above itself and making *de iure* decisions which flew in the face of the Catholic faith that Damian's blood grew hot. The idea of women priests made him shake with rage. He had had to stop himself, on more than one occasion, at dinner parties, from being really rude to people who casually expressed the view that if you could have a woman judge and a woman doctor, why not a woman minister? They seemed to think that priests were something *we* made, rather than something God made! Damian was of the view that you could not ordain a woman: not that it was unlawful, but that it was impossible – no more could you ordain a dog. If the unthinkable happened, and the Holy Father were to allow Catholic bishops to ordain women, then the impossible would become possible; but that was the Holy Father's prerogative, not the General Fucking Synod of the Church of England's.

It was comforting that his mind had settled back into this dear old groove. Quarter of an hour from Paddington Station. Sometimes, before hopping aboard the train, he gave half an hour to the underground toilets on Platform One, but he did not think he would do so today. One never knew quite who one might *meet* at Paddington! The thought allowed him first to parody and then to assume the deportment of an old-fashioned High churchman returning to his parish after a day at the Athenaeum Club. His pace was slower now, and he looked about him, not with the agitation of a queen on the cruise so much as with the benign air of a man who had enjoyed himself for the day. This did not prevent him from wondering, from behind his dark glasses, whether some of the men he passed were cruising, or simply looking. But the larger view took in dogs, old ladies, couples. Funny that boys and girls could lie on the grass with one another, hold hands, kiss, whereas if two blokes did it. . . . But what they *missed*, these straights, being *allowed* to do it. Good post-lapsarian Catholic Damian knew that the highest pleasures were, by definition, *verboten*.

He stood by Watts' equestrian statue, *Physical Energy*, enjoying the thighs and the great feet of the young man astride the horse, and thought how odd they looked, the straights: those two, lying on the grass, practically eating one another; the oldies on the bench, sharing a thermos; the incredibly plain, flabby girl in shorts, whose man was nibbling her ear. How they contrasted with the delicious, almost Henry Tuke, scene which had caught Damian's attention beneath the tree, at a distance of fifty yards. An old queen – *older* at any rate – was sitting timidly beside this beautiful boy, this beautiful blond boy, simply dressed in loose black trousers and a clean white shirt. They were looking into one another's eyes, or so it would seem to Damian, who could only see the grey, slightly balding back of the old queen's head, and the pretty boy eagerly looking up at him. And there seemed to Damian in that vignette more of true love than in any of the couplings which surrounded him, near at hand, on the grass.

By a single turn of the 'old queen's' head, Damian realised that it was Francis Kreer! And, when the boy eased himself from a kneeling to a standing position, Damian saw that it was a girl. In his confused embarrassment, Damian turned away and, instead of making his way direct to the station, walked towards Speaker's Corner, confused in his mind. He was shocked. They had not been touching one another, but they did not need to. So much had Damian Wells read into Jay's face as she smiled and repeated to Francis things Mr Gadney had said about hardy annuals.

9

'And did you just *see* the way she smiled at you when you handed back that essay?'

'I *know*!' Jessica agreed. 'It's really creepy!' Then in her (quite passable) 'Miss Bill' imitation, 'Jessica, that was a really *lovely* interpretation.'

(The children had been asked to write a poem to stick in the tree and be read by the idiot hero of *To Kill a Mockingbird*.)

'Did you read that poem Caroline wrote?'

This was too much, and both girls spluttered at the thought of it. In their wildest moments of fantasy, they actually spoke as if Caroline might have handed the poem in.

'Here comes Old Bill
Doing the splits–'

Sarah had started to recite it again, causing convulsions, fits of mirth in Jessica.

'Fell on her bum and . . .' But it was too funny to finish. Crude as they were, the little girls had developed a surer nose for the sort of area in which, for emotional preference, Miss Bill might shop around. It amused Jessica, and the other girls, when people spoke about the Old Bill as being in love with Daddy!

'Is your Dad fetching you again today?'

Jessica and Sarah had paused by the school gate.

'I don't know if Daddy's coming.'

'Can I have a lift if he does come?'

'Course.'

'He doesn't come as often as he used to.'

'So!' Jessica flared up. 'I'm not a baby, I don't need lifts from my parents every day.'

Discomposed by this explosion of temper, Sarah kicked a discarded 7-Up tin which had made its way, apparently of its own accord, towards their feet. After a few moments of not saying anything, Sarah came out with, 'Perhaps I'll get the bus after all.'

'Do then.' Jessica wanted to be conciliatory but she found that she was still in a bad temper with Sarah.

'See you, then, Jess.'

'OK.' And then, even crosser, 'OK, OK.'

Jessica watched her friend join a gaggle of other girls at the bus stop on the other side of the road from the school gate. Within a few minutes, they were giggling, and, it seemed to Jessica, casting furtive glances in her direction.

Let them laugh. This was Jessica's view. Sarah Mackintosh did not have to say that Daddy was not seen so often these days. Sarah Flipping Mackintosh did not even have a proper

Daddy. Sarah Stinkbottom had a 'businessman' – car salesman, Daddy said – who was divorced from Mrs Mackintosh and only visited Sarah at weekends; so what did *she* know about Daddy? Anyway, Daddy said that people like the Mackintoshes did not go to schools like theirs a generation or two ago. Daddy had said that Mr Mackintosh was really quite a 'surprising' person, and Mummy had upbraided Daddy for being so snobbish, but he wasn't being snobbish, just accurate, and Sarah Mackintosh just made Jessica sick, sick, sick.

Pursuing the errant 7-Up can, Jessica kicked it hard. She still thought as a matter of fact, that Sarah would be proved wrong and that Daddy would turn up to give her a lift home. She wished he would, certainly. The school bus had pulled up opposite and her friends were all climbing aboard. So, Daddy had jolly well *better* come.

Sarah had touched a very raw nerve. Jessica minded very acutely the fact that her father had been in a sort of daze, ever since Granny died. He had said this morning that he *might* pick her up in the car; in the old days, this would certainly have meant that he would be there. Now, it was difficult to rely on Daddy. He seemed to live in a sad dream world; and although, some of the time, Jessica remembered to be sorry for him, she also felt excluded by his sorrow. This hurt.

'Jessica! You've missed the bus.'

'I'm waiting for my father.'

'Well, it's twenty past four. Do you really think he will come now?'

It was Miss Bill, who had rolled down the window of her generously-filled Astra.

'He might come.'

'He wouldn't want you hanging around the school gate when all the others have gone home.'

This was true, and, very reluctantly, Jessica accepted her teacher's offer of a lift back to Ditcham. She hoped that it would be possible to complete the twenty-minute journey either without conversation, or at least without embarrassment. But at the first set of traffic lights, the Old Bill put on that really 'concerned' voice of hers and said, 'Are you happy, Jessica?'

Jessica felt herself blushing absolutely crimson. In the lane alongside them, the school bus had drawn up. From the passenger seat, Jessica looked across Miss Bill's fleshy profile to a bus window full of schoolgirls, pointing, waving, laughing.

10

The day after he had been to London with Jay and met Mr Gadney, Francis decided to capitulate in the matter of the flat. He wrote to his solicitor enclosing some keys to the flat, and instructed him to authorise an estate agent as soon as possible. When the sale had gone through, he and Eric Gadney would be able to discuss the division of the pictures and furniture.

This decision brought a surprising degree of relief. He knew that he did not possess the inner energy sufficient for a dispute with Mr Gadney concerning the will. Nor could he contemplate showing his mother's flat to potential purchasers. He now just wanted to be shot of the whole thing. In the initial shock of discovering that his mother had chosen to leave half her flat to Mr Gadney, he had been tormented by an acquisitive rage that a stranger might lay claim to much-loved things – many of which he associated with his childhood: the little davenport where Mummy had sat to write her letters; those two watercolours of Arles which used to hang in her bedroom at Gerrard's Cross, and which he associated with childhood illnesses, when he would be allowed to sit in his mother's bed and read Beatrix Potter. His mood had swung in an absolutely opposite direction. He now wanted to blot out the past. He would not worry – or so he felt – if every picture, cushion, chair, bed, mirror and teapot were sold. He reckoned that when the sale went through, he would possess about £90,000. With this sum of money be believed that he would easily be able to retreat – perhaps to a small house by the seaside, a refuge for the future which stretched into crazed imaginings of his new life.

This new life, his *vita nuova* as he self-consciously dubbed it, revolved around his incurable obsession with Jay. Their visit to London, and their journey home together, had in reality been marked by considerable stiltedness. They had paused in the park, and she had spoken kindly of poor Gadney and his wretched 'garden centre'. Francis knew that she had done this because she was under the impression that Gadney was some kind of relation to Francis. She was simply trying to be polite. He was unable, somehow, to explain that he had no idea who the old man was and this was chiefly because he had been afraid of revealing to her how much he minded – or had once minded – about his mother's will. With her scant possessions, and her willingness to live rough, Jay had what seemed to the priest an almost Franciscan detachment from material greed. He yearned to enter into her view of the world; and, having projected onto her so many fantasies, he wanted to be changed into a creature who was worthy of these fantasies. He was afraid that Jay could not love a middle-aged, middle-class man who cared about a small matter of £90,000. He would prefer, if necessary, to live in a tent if that was the way to her heart.

Their silence and shyness with one another, he put down entirely to his own feelings. He was unable to guess quite what her feelings were for him, but he assumed that, since she must have guessed how much he loved her, she was beginning to love him in return. He had driven her back to the village, and she chose to get out of the car at the crossroads which had been their first rendezvous. They had not kissed on parting, nor had they arranged to meet again. He was sure that they would now meet so often, and on so regular a basis, that there was nothing worrying about this fact.

When, however, two, three days, and then a week went by, in which he did not see Jay, he began to find that he could concentrate on nothing else. His distractedness was now, if such a thing were possible, even more marked than in the first weeks after his mother's death. He thought of her night and day. She occupied, in fact, very much the position in his life which had once been occupied by God. When, as a young man preparing for the priesthood, Francis had devoutly believed in God, he had believed himself to advance quite far in the spiritual life. He had spent at least an hour each day in concentrated mental prayer, and even when he was not consciously praying, he had, as the spiritual writers put it, practised the presence of God, and turned towards his maker with complete naturalness in his inward self. Such habits of thought and prayer had first grown desiccated and then been discarded; but perhaps the years in which he had practised them prepared him especially for the manner in which he was able to 'practise' Jay's presence even when she was not there. He addressed his thoughts to her. He felt himself to be her servant, even though he had almost no consciousness of what she was like. He pursued the most detailed inner 'investigations' into her history. These were not actual pieces of detective work, and were much more like the meditations which he had been accustomed to practise when he used Bible stories as a vehicle for prayer. For example, she had told him that she was born and brought up in the suburb of Bramhall. Francis had his large atlas open in his study at the north of England. He had peered for hours at Greater Manchester, and identified the place where Jay had lived in her infancy. He also had a road map open at the appropriate page, and had circled the word Bramhall in red ink. A devout Moslem could hardly have thought with more tenderness of the holy cities of Mecca and Medina.

So absorbed was he in such activities, and in the long walks where he supposed it was inevitable that he would find her once more, pacing along one of the footpaths at the top of the village, that Francis paid no attention to anything else. At meals, when he remembered to attend them, he sat vacantly, eating little or nothing, and unable to listen to Jessica's prattle about school. His work, too, which before his mother's death had been discharged so efficiently, had been neglected. Letters lay scattered on his desk, some of them not even opened, and none of them answered. He had forgotten a funeral. It was really rather an 'important' funeral in the life of the parish, being that of Mrs Norbury, who had died in the hospital in Reading. Miss Norbury had made timid visits to the vicarage and asked Francis to visit her mother in hospital. In normal circumstances, this was the sort of thing Francis did most conscientiously. He had simply forgotten about Mrs Norbury's illness the moment her daughter left. That had been some weeks ago. Now the old lady, who had attended St Birinus's so faithfully for over eighty years, had died, and the undertakers had brought her coffin to the church. The undertakers, and Ronald Maxwell-Lee as Vicar's warden, and some cousin of Mrs Norbury's had all checked the time of the funeral with Francis and he had written it down in the large desk-diary in his study. The congregation had assembled in the church. It was a large assembly – very nearly a hundred people. When they had been waiting for twenty minutes, and there was still no sign of the vicar, Gerald Spittle had gone over to the vicarage in person. He had found Francis, sitting in his shirt sleeves in the study, and staring intently at the *AA Book of the Road*.

As soon as he realised his mistake, Francis had been covered in confusion. He had tried to pretend that a matter of overriding importance had accounted for his lateness, but he saw in Gerald Spittle's eyes that the man knew he had simply forgotten the funeral. He had hurried into his cassock and surplice and run over to the church. People remarked that the Vicar had seemed flustered during the service, and that he stumbled over several prayers.

A few days after this, Francis forgot the Norbury Mass – as perhaps it should no longer be called. This time, it was Lindie Spittle who came over to the vicarage to remind him of his mistake.

Whereas Gerald's entry into the vicarage had been brisk but avuncular, Lindie stepped over the threshold timidly as one who was half in search of an adventure.

'Hi, Lindie!' Sally Kreer had said. 'Can I get you a coffee?'

'What's happened to Francis? He's supposed to be taking the service!'

'Oh, goodness! Not again!'

That woman – Lindie's way of describing Sally in her own mind – seemed positively daft. She had sent Lindie into the study to fetch Francis. When he arose from his desk, Lindie saw that the buttons of his trousers were undone. As it happened, this was completely inadvertent; Francis had been to the lavatory and forgotten to button himself up, but when Lindie's eyes strayed to this part of the vicar's anatomy she started back.

'Francis – I think you've forgotten something.'

'Oh, hallo, Lindie!'

He smiled at her his goofiest of smiles. She had not seen him smile for weeks.

'It's just that we were wondering if you were coming over to church,' she said. There was no humour and no kindness in her voice. She was angry with this man, and also frightened of him. He for his part felt threatened by her, and tried to make up for this by being especially polite and flattering.

'How nice you look, Lindie.'

'I beg your pardon?'

'I just thought you looked very nice. . . .' He realised as he said it that this was a stupid thing to say. So he added, 'Look here, I'm most awfully sorry. I'll get changed, and . . . I'll just get these things off – change. I'll . . .'

'Well, are we to expect a service or not?' she asked, edging backwards towards the door.

'My dear Lindie . . .'

He suddenly wanted to speak to this woman, who he knew disliked him. He wanted to say to her: 'Please do not judge a fellow human being harshly. It is very negligent of me to have forgotten two church services; and I know that you dislike me; but please deal kindly with me, please realise that I am a soul in torment, confused and unable to think about anything except love.' None of these words would come, but he wanted to say them, partly out of self-justification, but also out of an almost missionary zeal; for he was beginning to believe that Love was the only thing which raised human beings above the level of slime.

'What is it?' she asked cautiously.

'Lindie – do you remember when you first met Gerrie and – well, you must have been in love.'

Her lips tautened, as she saw this strange man, staring at her, with his trousers more than half undone.

'Are you coming to church, then?' she asked.

'Ten minutes,' said Francis. 'And I am very sorry.'

It was a day or two after this strange little interlude that Francis received a telephone call from Ronald Maxwell-Lee.

'You've rather n-neglected me, dear Francis, but I've been getting on q-q-quite well on my own. In fact, I've resolved to read through the *Aeneid* entire. How about a preliminary meeting to start me off?'

Francis dreaded company at the moment and he was particularly shy of regular communicants after his blundering forgetfulness over the two church services; but the Wing-Co was insistent, and he duly came that evening. Once the whisky had been poured out, and their two volumes of Virgil were open on their knees, the old man began the familiar lines: arms and the man I sing.

He read the invocation to the Muse: 'Tell me, O Muse, the reasons for which the Queen of the Gods – thwarted in her will, or enraged – drove a man of celebrated virtue to undergo so many hardships, so much suffering. . . . Can there be so much anger in the hearts of the Gods? . . .' The Wing-Co paused, and sipped his whisky. Then he said, 'As a matter of f-fact, Francis, I've c-come to have a word in your ear.'

Francis looked at the Wing-Commander with an expression of trapped panic. He felt such a welter of strange emotions – raw love for Jay, churned about in the presence of his old friend, with feelings of shame and simple embarrassment. He had been afraid that some sort of 'confrontation' would occur; he had been frightened that Miss Bill would want to have a heart-to-heart talk with him, or that his wife would somehow persuade the doctor to see him. He had not imagined that it would be old Ronald Maxwell-Lee who would use the excuse of a Virgil-session to intrude into his suffering.

'If it's about forgetting the services this week, Ronald, I'm sorry. I do not think that such a thing will happen again.'

'Francis, it's difficult for me to say this.' The old man had got his pipe out of his pocket and was fiddling about with it. To show himself a man among men, Francis too filled a pipe which always lay on the surface of his desk but which he did not much smoke.

'You see,' said the Wing-Commander, when his sweet-smelling aromatic Dutch tobacco was alight, 'I'm awfully fond of you, and so is Dorothy.'

Francis felt tears starting to his eyes at these words. It was cruel of the Wing-Co to adopt such a technique for upbraiding him; or so he believed. He had absolutely no idea that the words just spoken by Ronald Maxwell-Lee were simply true. Both Maxwell-Lees counted themselves very lucky to have a vicar who was well-spoken, well-educated and liturgically conservative; but, in the ten years or so of knowing Francis, this approval of what he was and what he stood for had deepened into affection. The Wing-Commander loved Francis Kreer – not in the passionate way in which a man might love a woman, but nevertheless with a warmth that exceeded casual feelings of good neighbourliness. Never having had children, the Wing-Commander did not know if it was true that Francis was 'the son he never had', as he had sometimes sentimentally told himself. Lately, since the Vicar had lost his mother, the Wing-Commander had been hurt by Francis's abstracted air of misery. He had hoped that Francis would treat him as a friend. There was, therefore, mingled with his genuine concern for Francis's well-being, an element of anger, and he was not sure, now that the conversation had got underway, whether he would find himself upbraiding the priest for his neglect of parish duties.

'We're here to help, you know,' he said.

'Ronald, I know you are trying to be kind, but I don't need help.'

'I'm afraid that's where you are wrong,' said the old man, and breathed out smoke ominously. 'I've come here tonight to give you a bit of a warning.'

'What?'

The impertinence of the Wing-Co's manner prompted the edgy anger of Francis's tone.

'I've got to tell you, Francis . . .'

Both men smoked for a while. Ronald Maxwell-Lee seemed momentarily unable to find the right words.

'Gerrie Spittle,' he eventually said abruptly. 'Admirable man, Gerrie, in his way, but I dare say we both have our reservations about him.'

'What about Gerrie?'

'Well, the th-thing is, Francis, Gerrie has written a letter to the Archdeacon about you.'

This extraordinary news once again plunged the room into silence. All the cosiness which normally accompanied their Virgil evenings had frozen into an atmosphere of excited tension, and

Francis felt a stab of fear: a school feeling, as though he was going to be beaten by the prefects.

'He's shown it to me, and I have asked him not to post it. I'm sure it is all based on some sort of misunderstanding, but . . . I hate to say this, my dear.'

'What on earth has that man been saying?'

'He's drawn up this great catalogue of things you are supposed to have done wrong.'

'All right – look! I admit it, I forgot Mrs Norbury's funeral. It was a terrible thing to do. I feel ashamed of it—' his voice quivered as he said it.

'Well, it's not just that, as a matter of fact.'

'And I forgot to take the service yesterday.'

'Well, they seem to think you've neglected quite a lot of duties. I've told them, you've been under a lot of strain. I know what it's like losing a m-m-m–'

'Please, Ronald . . .' Francis felt himself crying at the mention of his mother.

Thinking it best to ignore the tears which started to the eyes of 'the poor boy' (as Ronald Maxwell-Lee thought of him), he produced a piece of paper from his pocket.

'I haven't brought Gerald's letter. Thought it was better not to, but I've made a list of the main heads. Of course, they have drawn attention to the fact that ever since Christmas you have been increasingly forgetful and distracted. . . .'

'But don't they understand, don't they know what it's like? . . .'

'I know, my dear, I know. But there are some other things apart from the various services and hospital visits you've forgotten. There's, let me see.' He looked down at his notes. 'Well, there is a silly paragraph about the church heating; claims that those wall-mounted electric fires are a hazard, absolute nonsense; also claims that we need a new church boiler, which we don't. I don't think we need to worry ourselves about those complaints. They also go into a lot of boring detail about the type of service we have at church; well, quite honestly, I don't think we need worry about that. If they don't like d-dear old 1662, they can go back to Friend Widger's conventicle.'

Francis rather loved the Wing-Commander for this.

'They feel you haven't involved the congregation enough. Absolute nonsense, of course.'

'I don't mind if they do send this letter to the Bishop,' said Francis defiantly. 'Let them. I'm quite prepared to defend myself. . . .'

'Well, you see, old thing, the really awkward part of the letter is . . . I really don't know how to put this. Gerald Spittle has got it into his head that you've sometimes gone off the rails, as it were.'

'I've said, I am sure I shall never forget to take another funeral. I feel so . . .'

'No, it isn't the little oversights like that. I'm afraid he's talking about . . .'

'What about?'

'S-s-s-s-s–'

'What?'

'S-s-sex' was the word which the Wing-Commander eventually managed to say.

Francis poured himself more whisky, without offering some to the Wing-Commander. As he did so, his hand shook and a few drops splashed on to the page where the Latin poet spoke of the fury of the goddess Juno.

'They've dug up some very rum stuff about Damian Wells,' said the Wing-Commander. 'I don't know how much of it is true. They say the reason he hasn't got a proper parish of his own is that he's been in trouble with the police. Making a nuisance of himself in some l-l-loo.'

'That's all behind him,' said Francis. 'It's none of their business. As it happens the Bishop knows all about it, and I think there's every chance that Damian will find another parish.'

'You don't mean it's true? Good God, Francis, I do think you should have told me.' The Wing-Commander had become testy.

'I didn't see any reason . . .'

'No reason to tell me that this chap who's been taking s-services in St B-b-b, in our church, has been had up for indecency? Oh, really, Francis! Imagine what Dorothy would think – or Edith Renton.'

'There's no need for them to *know*,' said Francis. He too had become angry. It was outrageous that these bourgeois, petty-minded people should claim a right to sit in judgment on his friend Damian Wells. 'Anyway,' he said, 'I know about Damian, and I have every belief in him. I'm sure he's given up all that sort of silliness. We don't know what sort of temptations a man like that, I mean – we just don't.'

'It isn't just about Damian they are complaining. It's about you,' said the Wing-Commander. All sympathy between the two men had now evaporated and they sat confronting one another like enemies. Ronald Maxwell-Lee found the notion of homosexuality absolutely repugnant. It was bad enough in anyone, but in a clergyman he thought it inexcusable. He was very much shocked that Francis appeared to take such a casual view of things.

'Are you saying that they are accusing me – accusing *me* of . . . I don't believe that this conversation is taking place!' He struck his forehead in a melodramatic gesture of fury. 'I hope they *do* send this vile letter. And I'd sue them, I'd sue them for libel.'

'They are not accusing you of being mixed up with Damian Wells in that way, though they do, in a manner, hint at that. They think by not p-p-putting us in the p-p-p- by not telling us about it, you have in a way colluded. And they seem to think you've got some difficulties of your own. Apparently, you haven't been very wise with L-Lindie.'

Francis was so astonished by this suggestion that he made a splutter which was midway between a laugh and a yelp of surprise.

'Well, since we've got this far,' said the Wing-Commander, whose kindness and sympathy had completely evaporated and been replaced by the clipped fierceness he might have adopted at a court martial, 'I'd better tell you what they say.'

'Do!'

'They say you made a pass at Lindie during my Christmas party – to be absolutely frank, that you squeezed her bottom; and that you have done this on a number of occasions since. Only yesterday, when she came to find you and ask why you weren't in church, she found you with your flies undone, and when she came into this room, you told her that you were in love with her and that you wanted to get undressed.'

'What?'

'There is also a most extraordinary thing which I thought must be the product of her fevered imagination, but now I'm not so sure. Did you tell her to sing the words of "E-Eskimo N-n-nell"?'

'All this is the purest fantasy,' said Francis.

'So you never touched her?'

'I might have done, but not . . .'

'Well, did you, or didn't you?'

'Look, the idea that I find Lindie Spittle attractive is just ridiculous.'

'And you never mentioned "Eskimo Nell" to her?'

'Oh, I remember now,' he sighed. 'It was when she was nagging me about the hymns for Palm Sunday. . . .' Francis felt his mouth becoming dry with fear as he justified himself. His voice faltered. He felt the Wing-Commander disbelieving him. 'I did tell her she could sing anything, sing "Eskimo Nell" if she liked.'

'Hardly a very nice thing to say. Again, imagine Edith Renton hearing the words of that song.'

'But I wasn't going to sing – oh, what's the point in answering all these *stupid* accusations?'

'Because, if they do write to the Archdeacon, you will have to answer these points. And I am afraid the last point is much more serious,' said the old man.

'You mean, there's *more* of this filth? What are they trying to do, destroy me?'

'Francis, do you remember that day – oh, about four weeks ago, when one of the tinkers got into the church?'

This question was wholly unexpected, and the fear which Francis had felt was now intensified to the point where he thought himself almost incapable of coherent speech. How could these horrible people know about his love for Jay? It was evil, the malignity of the Spittles, and he now sensed that it was directed not merely against himself but against his beloved, his adored Jay, the light of his being, the God of his inner life. His only desire now was to protect her. He hated Maxwell-Lee for referring to her as 'one of the tinkers', and he hated the Day of Days, the sacred day when she had come into the church, and played that sublime Beethoven sonata, being an occasion of which his hated parishioners had any consciousness. The very thought of Jay being inside their filthy heads disgusted Francis.

'I'm bound to say that I dismissed all these accusations of the Spittles as some appalling mistake,' said the Wing-Commander. 'It never even occurred to me that Mr Wells was . . . or that you even knew the words of "Es-Eskimo—"'

'Oh, for God's sake stop talking about "Eskimo Nell".'

'Well, you will anyway recall that one of those layabouts from the camp got into the church. . . .'

'I'd rather not talk about this any more, Ronald.'

'The Spittles are making some very serious allegations. I'm sorry, Francis, but they will have to be answered. They say that they saw you kissing this girl in some side-street in Reading. Is that true?'

'They disgust me!'

'Is it true, Francis? I think you'd better tell me.'

'I refuse to talk about this.'

'I take that as an admission that you have been carrying on some bloody silly thing with this girl.'

'You've no right to . . . they're – oh, how dare you?'

'Look, Francis, a very valuable crucifix has been stolen from the church, and as you know – or as you would know if you were your normal, sane self – it is also of very great emotional value to Edith Renton.'

'We are all upset that the cross has been stolen,' said Francis.

'The Spittles believe that it was stolen by the hippies. It seems a reasonable deduction. We n-never had things pinched from the church before they arrived.'

'I think we should stop this conversation,' said Francis.

The Wing-Commander sighed. 'You're making such a fool of yourself,' he said. 'I came here hoping to help.'

'I don't want help.'

'Evidently. Look, can't you see that she's the obvious thief?'

'Go!'

There was such anger, and such authority, in Francis as he

issued this command that the Wing-Commander was silenced by it. After a pause, he rose to his feet and murmured, 'All right. I will. You realise what you are saying?'

'I've had enough of this conversation. I've told you that before.'

'You are not denying any of it? It's one thing to g-go off the rails with a woman – but you're colluding in the theft of church property.'

'Please leave me.'

'I'll see myself out.'

Francis heard the Wing-Commander slamming his front door. He returned to his desk, and made himself drunk with a fourth tumbler of whisky.

Upstairs, in their separate rooms, his wife and his daughter wept. Sally wept, clutching the Dog Frumpy, who had been unable to console her for her loneliness and wretchedness. Jessica, however, wept like a woman betrayed by her lover, although she was only twelve years old. For the hundredth time, she read the letter she had received three days earlier from Mr Gadney:

> Dear J! You must forgive me! You must have thought I was completely potty, sending you Easter eggs, and kids' books. I do not know what fixed it in my head that you were only a child. It was such a pleasure to meet you and your Dad the other day. Thank you for the delicious lunch. Just between ourselves, it was the first time I've eaten olives in ages. (Your Auntie gives me good plain fare for my grub!!) Now we have met, I hope we can make friends. You must come down and see us in Deal. Tell your Dad, I'm very glad to have met him too. With all good wishes from Eric Gadney.

St John the Baptist

I

With the approach of midsummer, there arose divisions among the Travellers in Potter's Field. Many of them were in favour of joining up with some of the bigger convoys who now trekked about southern England, making their way down towards Stonehenge, or westward, to take in pop festivals and spontaneous 'gatherings' of those whom the newspapers called 'New Age Travellers' or 'Ravers'. Other people took the view that the joy of their group was its smallness.

'These great big assemblies –' said one speaker ' – it's not surprising you get the local people complaining about them; I mean, they're noisy; and inevitably with a big crowd you get some who are not so honest, and there's crime and that. Whereas with us – it's different. We aren't any harm to no one.'

Jay heard this testimony with a certain embarrassment. She had not yet taxed Mo with the stolen crucifix, but she felt perfectly certain that he was the thief. They sat beside one another in a group of about a dozen, in the middle of a bright June morning. It had rained in the night, and the grass had been refreshed, and the air was clear, and there was a smell of sweetness. Jay had risen early and washed her face in dew. She looked clean, though her short hair was slightly greasy. Mo, by contrast, did not look as if he had been living in the open air for weeks. He more had the demeanour of a man who had been up late in clubs five nights on a trot. His pale face had almost begun to turn grey and there were dark rings under his eyes.

If the convoy were to break up, Jay had decided that she and Mo would part company. If he went to Stonehenge with the Ravers, she would stay behind with the quiet remnant. If he went to Wales, she might go to Stonehenge. She saw this disruption of the group as a natural way of disengaging herself from Mo. On days such as this, however, when he sat beside her on the grass and held her hand in his, and seemed weak and unhappy, she knew that it would not be such an easy decision to make. She was weary with him, and disappointed with herself for having chosen such an inappropriate companion. But she was still engaged with his fortunes, even though she could no longer find it in her heart to love him. She felt 'responsible' for him, even though she clearly saw, and believed, that Mo's troubles were of his own making.

'What do you think, Mo?' Dave asked his mentor, his hero.

'Don't ask him – what's his view count for anything?' interrupted Rosie. 'He and Jay were never with us in the hard times, they just come here and join us for a summer holiday. What's it to Mo where we move to?'

'I reckon it'd be good to split,' drawled Mo. 'Maybe Stonehenge, maybe Glastonbury – fuck it!' His nonchalant air, his way of swaying his head slightly from side to side, implied that he thought he was amusing his company. Less than a year ago, Jay could remember thinking this man 'witty'. Now his commonplace words and slurred diction seemed merely pathetic.

'We don't have to decide anything in a hurry,' said another voice, perhaps anxious to smooth over any controversy.

But then something quite unwonted occurred. Compton, with his long beard and matted hair, stood up in the assembly. None of the Travellers could really remember Compton uttering a sentence, though he smiled quite a lot, and said 'Thanks', if you shared some food with him, or passed him a joint. Afterwards, Mo had made Dave laugh by saying, 'Wonder what he's on.' But the general view was that Compton's sudden desire to utter was not provoked by narcotics but by some stranger inner prompting, that capacity given to some individuals, in almost all societies, to be prophets.

'It's not a choice, we gonna have to move on,' he said. Compton's voice projected loud. He spoke in a humming monotone which was suggestive of hierophantic utterance: he might have been a priest intoning in a temple. 'We're goin' to have to move on and we aren't goin' to have any choice 'bout it, and it's goin' to be real bad, and I jus' wish we could get the kids outta here before it happens, 'cause it's terrible to think about. Maybe we should all get out, we can't resist that sort of thing.'

'Compton!' Jay sounded briskly schoolgirlish – the leader of the Guide Company – as she asked, 'Do you know something we don't know?'

'I jus' get *really* bad feelin's: this place is no good for us any more.'

As he spoke, Leila came and nuzzled against Jay for comfort. Jay had come to the conclusion that Leila was the most congenial of all her companions on the convoy. She loved the flat top of her smooth intelligent head, which smelt a little of roast chicken; and the great affectionate glossy eyes, and the featheriness of her black and white fur. Leila, it would seem, had caught the menace of which Compton was the unwilling herald.

When the meeting broke up, and she was sitting in a smaller group which contained Mo, Dave and Leila, Jay stroked the dog while Mo gave them his talk about minerals. Even the dog appeared to yawn.

'No, it'll be OK, actually,' said Mo. 'I mean we could always go back to Wales, I got these – well, I've told you about Richard and Lesley and they'd always let us have their caravan for a bit.'

'Yeah, I know.' Jay remembered that these were the friends who were to have provided her and Mo with a cottage for the winter.

'Then' – Mo affectionately punched Dave in the shoulder – 'you, me, Jay, we could go to Wales and gather minerals. There's this porphyry mine, right. You can get chunks of porphyry that big! Jesus! No fucking about! That big, imagine what you'd get for it. But even small-sized minerals.'

He rehearsed his hundred-times-repeated scheme to collect enough minerals to enable them to set up their own stall in Camden Market in the winter and spend the proceeds on drugs.

Partly through boredom, partly because she felt that her moment had arrived (or at least that she would not find a better moment), Jay asked, 'And what else have you been collecting?'

'How do you mean?'

'I wondered if you'd been collecting anything else lately, apart from minerals.'

'Fook it, the woman's a mystery to me and no mistake' – his stage Irish voice had the effect of making Dave smile good-humouredly, but Jay, who used to be amused by it, persisted with her interrogation.

'I don't like you stealing, Mo. Don't you see it affects me when you do it? Don't you see it affects all these honest people? Geoff says we aren't disliked by people in the village here because we are all honest. How does that make you feel, Mo? They're honest – Geoff is, Compton is, Rosie is. What you've been up to tars them with the same brush.'

'Who said anything 'bout stealing? Look, I'm talking 'bout minerals, right, in the ground that we'd dig out, or find. Jesus, are you so fucking bourgeois, right, with your fucking Macclesfield manners that you think a mountain, a fucking mountain, belongs to someone and, if you dig out a piece of gold or a piece of porphyry, it's like it belongs to someone or something. . . .'

'We aren't talking about minerals in Wales, Mo. We are talking about you stealing things in Ditcham, in this village.'

'Like what?'

'Mo, you've taken me on one of your bloody recces, one of your burglaries. You can't deny that.'

'Yeah, and you came on it willingly enough.'

'Not willingly. We did wrong, Mo. At least that was only petty stuff. This is serious, Mo, robbing a church. You know what I'm talking about, and there's no point in denying it.'

Dave had gone very silent.

'I don't even know what you're talking about, you stupid bitch.'

'I'm talking about a cross you stole from the church, right? Or can't you remember? And, Mo, if you've still got that cross you're going to give it back, right, because there'll be such a stink if you don't.'

'Listen to her!' He stared round at the others, hoping for support. 'What you been doing, going through my things or something?'

'Or talking to the Vicar.' The speaker was Rosie, who had

approached, and overheard their quarrel, and now towered above them, holding a squalling child in her arms.

'What's that?' asked Mo, anxious to justify himself, and willing to seize any advantage in this conversation.

'That vicar she hangs round with,' said Rosie.

'Is this true?' Mo looked murderously angry. 'Have you been talking to a vicar?'

'I can talk to who I like, Mo,' said Jay indignantly.

'So that's it. You've been – what you been doing? God, it makes me sick! It's creepy! You've been hanging round a vicar, a fucking pervert, and he's been telling you to spy on us – Christ, whose side are you on?'

Jay found that the conversation had fizzed out like a firework, as talks with Mo so often did; and she wanted to get away from it.

'Come on, Leila,' she said, and began to stomp away from Mo and Dave.

'You haven't answered me!' Mo shouted. 'You are going off to him now, I suppose.'

'Leave her be, Mo,' said Rosie. 'She's a bad-tempered bitch.'

'I never stole her fucking vicar's cross. I never stole it.'

With an open-mouthed giggle, Mo turned to Rosie, to Dave, perhaps having forgotten temporarily that Dave was the thief. Mo's expression was that of a great orator or public performer, receiving the applause of a vast multitude.

'She's just a selfish cross bitch,' said Rosie, who saw no harm in driving home an advantage, and did not favour subtlety as a conversational ploy. 'You'd be better off without her.'

Palpitating with rage, Jay had gone, with Leila as her companion. She moved away from the encampment and walked along the rough track at the brow of the hill which leads eventually to the Ridgeway. After ten minutes of energetic striding and no less vigorous breathing, her perspective (both visual and emotional) altered, and she was able to take a new view of her condition. From where she stood, it was as if she was on the backbone of a great dragon, with the land sinking beneath her on both sides. To the south, England rolled away: beyond the blue haze of a June morning stretched a hundred miles of land before you reached the

Channel. In that particular bright haze, no conurbations in this direction could be seen. The land swooped and sank and rose in splashes of colour and areas of ever-receding mist, giving a sense that the distance was infinite, limitless. To north and west, human artefacts and buildings could be seen. Here, a cluster of villages, with their churches and roofs and cultivated gardens; there, not unbeautiful in a different way, the cooling towers of Didcot Power Station. Above her head, the sky seemed to lift her spirit. It provided her with no consolation for her sorrows, but it seemed more possible to bear the weight of unhappiness beneath an open sky than in the close confines of a small room.

Jay had been stung by their taunting her with her friendship for the Vicar of Ditcham. It was a friendship which she did not quite know how to understand herself. It was certainly the most peculiar friendship she had ever had in her life. She and the priest had met only a handful of times. She had given him a chunk of edited autobiography, but she did not feel that she had truly been able to make herself, her true self, known to him. And what these encounters had made her wonder was – what that self was. She was disturbed and a little frightened, to find that she was actually turning into a slightly different person as a result of knowing Francis Kreer. Aware that we human beings always present a slightly different self to every new person we meet, not for reasons of hypocrisy, but because human beings are naturally social and chameleon, she had nevertheless become aware that this was something, in the case of her friendship with Francis, over which she had little control. She went on being that 'different person' even when she was not with him. She wanted to become this new person; and this change within herself was what made the company of the Travellers so uncongenial. Until she met Francis, she had been prepared to submerge her own personality, to a very large degree, in that of Mo. She was happy to try to fit in with Dave and Rosie and Compton and the rest, and to put behind her the secret and uncommunicative self which had been hers when she was a student at the Guildhall, or a schoolgirl at Bramhall. But now something different was happening. She was actually emerging from her own youth, and 'finding herself'.

Why this should have happened as a result of meeting the

priest, she could not determine, since after their two great sessions of 'sharing' – she telling him about her life, and he telling her about his grief for his mother – their talk had been stilted. Indeed, on their outing to London, conversation between them had almost dried up to the point where she could think of nothing whatsoever to say to him.

Leila charged ahead of her, and high above her head the clouds raced through the blue sky, as she concentrated in her mind on the unhappy, slightly toothy face of the priest. It had been a shock to her that he had been prepared, so soon, to reveal his grief to her. She thought with disquiet of how little else he had revealed. He had said nothing of his wife, or of his children, or child. Down there in the village, he had a day-to-day life of which she knew nothing, and, by meeting her surreptitiously, he had blatantly shown that he did not wish her to be part of his life.

She found that thoughts of the clergyman had entered into her thoughts of the future. She wanted to part from Mo, and when the convoy moved on she would go in some direction of her own. Perhaps she might even see if she could return to her student life, or look for a job. What was so unexpected was that she now found herself wanting to know whether that unknown future would contain Francis Kreer, or whether they had simply been like strangers who met on a train, or on a ship's voyage, and shared each other's problems precisely because they were strangers, and then parted, never to meet in the future. This idea caused anguish.

When she got to the highest point of the path, and looked down at the stupendous view stretching all around her, the wind blew in her face and she had the first sensations of starting an unpleasant head cold. These physical manifestations came at precisely the moment that she surprised herself by saying aloud to Francis – wherever he might be – 'I'm not going to fall in love with you, you know!'

The phrase had come from nowhere into her brain. She certainly did not want some secret involvement with a married man though, since he never mentioned his wife, it hardly seemed quite real that he was married. Surely her friendship with Francis could do no good to either of them – it was one of those strange fantasies which people sometimes indulge in with persons they have met by chance. It had crept up on her – perhaps it had crept up on both of them – unawares. But he had his own life, she must keep telling herself that: she did not belong to the world of his troublesome parish, or his unimaginable domestic life in the vicarage which she had 'guarded' on the night of Mo and Dave's burglary; and he had his mother's cluttered little flat; and he was twice her age, and they had nothing in common. All these facts she told herself, when the surprising sentence had risen to her lips and been spoken aloud: 'I'm not going to fall in love with you, you know!'

But even as she stood there, looking down on the undulating hills and the distant splashes of light, with the wind on her face, and a sudden blocked nose and sore throat, she had the disconcerting sense that the whole of her previous existence had been a shadow, that reality itself could now begin. How could this be, seeing that she hardly knew the man? She certainly did not want some furtive little affair, and it was impossible to see how their destinies could ever be linked. And yet the wind and the light and the hills, the whole universe itself, seemed, that morning, not so much an indifferent or purely material thing, but rather an enfolding friend which understood her mood and brought with it, even as she felt herself to be ill with a head cold, a deep joy.

2

While Jay was having these thoughts and sensations on the highest point of land outside the village, Sally Kreer had just called out to her husband, 'Will you be in for lunch?'

Francis was standing in the hall. He wore his mufti – his blue seersucker jacket, his light trousers and his sandals, and he was carrying a little satchel which contained a volume of Ovid's *Ars Amatoria* and two apples. On his head was a straw hat which he had not worn for years. He had intended to leave the house without saying anything to his wife, for his most urgent need at this moment was solitude. He no longer felt safe in his own parish. His interview with the Wing-Commander had shaken him, making him feel not merely that old friends such as Ronald Maxwell-Lee were not to be trusted, but also that he could not trust himself:

for, the catalogue of his offences which Gerald Spittle intended to rehearse to the Archdeacon, while being cruelly false, was actually based on a distorted version of reality: he had, quite inadvertently, touched Lindie's bottom; he had told her that he did not mind if she sang 'Eskimo Nell' instead of the Palm Sunday hymn, he had disregarded the Spittles' advice about hymns and heaters. He had been quite unaware, since his mother's death, of the effect which his demeanour was having on other people, and this was what made the Wing-Commander's rebuke so painful; but, much more seriously, he realised that the most important fact of his life, the beginning of his *vita nuova* with Jay Dunbar, was not a secret locked in his heart. It was, rather, something so stupendously obvious that it shone out of him. He had hated hearing the Spittles' version of his tearful encounter with Jay in Reading: it had made them sound as if they were a guilty couple, discovered on some 'dirty weekend'; but, at the same time, he had been thrilled to hear it, because he was not in the least ashamed of his feelings for Jay, and indeed, he was excited that they had not been successfully concealed.

These were his thoughts, and he needed a long solitary walk to get them into some sort of shape. Sally's appearance in the hall with her inquiry about lunch, instead of seeming like the reasonable inquiry any wife might make to her husband at eleven o'clock in the morning, seemed like a prurient intrusion into those much deeper thoughts about Jay, and about his future as the parish priest of Ditcham. So he merely stared at her with cold fury.

'I said, are you going to be in for lunch?'

Francis cast a look of hatred at her and walked out of the house without saying anything. Sally was used to these snubs: for ten years or more, he had had 'off' days, when he hardly seemed able to talk to her.

'They're kids really,' she would say, meaning men.

His absence at least gave her the chance to do something which she had been meaning to do for some time. Jessica was safely at school; Francis was out; she sat at the bottom of the stairs and reached for the telephone. By the intrusive magic of telecommunications, she was soon talking to Father Damian Wells.

'Damian?'

'Speaking.'

'Sally. Sally Kreer.'

Father Wells, who did not have very much to occupy his morning, was lying on his bed. He wore a shirt, but no trousers or underpants, and a copy of a magazine called Zipper rested on the protuberance of his porcine stomach. His thoughts were so distracted by the magazine that he almost found it hard to listen to the cooing voice at the other end of the telephone.

'Listen, if you're very tied up, I'll ring later,' said Sally.

Damian could not be so described, though, as it happened, the young man in the photograph which he had been studying was, in some bizarre fashion, tied up.

'No, no,' he said. Wearily, he closed the magazine and rested it on his bedside table, on top of his comforting E.F. Benson novel, his travelling alarm clock and his photograph of himself wearing a biretta, stole and lace cotta. 'Always a pleasure to hear from you, Sally.'

'I just wondered how you thought Francis was.'

'Francis?'

Damian Wells had barely spoken to Francis Kreer all year, except to discuss arrangements on the occasions when Francis asked him to take services at Ditcham. He had been excited, in a gossipy way, by seeing his friend canoodling in the park with his beautiful, androgynous companion, but also slightly worried by it, wondering whether this meant that Francis had a secret which was going to be revealed, to amuse or embarrass or excite those who knew him. These thoughts were not disconnected from self-interest in the mind of Damian Wells. Francis Kreer was one of the few absolutely 'straight' clergymen he knew, and Damian felt that he earned what he called 'Church of England Brownie points' for helping out with the occasional service at Ditcham. It all helped. One day, Damian wanted to be welcomed back into the fold and offered a parish of his own once more. He felt frustrated by his boring, part-time administrative job in the diocesan offices; it was not what he felt called to do; he longed for his own church, his own altar, and his own people. Being friends with a nice, married country clergyman could do him no harm; but things would start to look very different if he turned out to be the friend of a notorious philanderer.

Hearing Sally's voice on the telephone put Damian on his mettle. Was she ringing up because she had found out about the beautiful little androgyne? He was not in a position to know that, on each of the five occasions when Francis had met Jay Dunbar, he had told his wife that he had been out with Damian.

'I mean, how does he seem to you?' asked Sally.

'I told you on the day of Griselda's funeral,' said Damian carefully, 'he has only to get in touch. I've been very much letting Francis do this in his own time and in his own way.'

'You don't think he's having a breakdown, do you?'

'What makes you say that, Sally?'

'Well, how does he seem when you meet him? Does he talk to you? He can't talk to us any more.'

'Look my dear, you're filling me with the most *hideous* guilt. I know I should have been a better friend to Francis this year. . . .'

'Damian, you're the best friend he's got.'

'It's nice of you to say so.'

'Only, you might see a different side to him.'

'Maybe I should give him a ring, eh, Sally? Suggest one of our lunches. It's been too long.'

'Just if he could have a natter – to someone – to anyone,' said Sally, as she sat there at the bottom of her stairs, talking to the semi-clad Damian. And, as she did so, her stomach heaved, and she felt one of her hot flushes coming on, and she thought that she might be going to cry: because it was all so obvious that Francis had not been seeing Damian at all. Only last week, he had said he had met Damian for lunch in London. And, a little before that, he said that he had been for a walk with Damian. And that he had been to see Damian in Reading: and it was all untrue.

'Everything going well with the preparations for the parish fête?'

'Fine thanks, Damian.' Her voice was faltering.

'Look, Sally, darling, I meant what I said. Anything I can do. I might give Francis a call, maybe come round and see him one evening this week, OK?'

'OK.'

'Thanks for calling, love!'

'Thanks, Damian, you're a treasure.'

And she sat at the bottom of the stairs for ten minutes after that conversation, shocked by what it had revealed. She was so perturbed by the knowledge that Francis had been lying to her that she did not notice that he had left the front door ajar when he went out; so she was still sitting on the stairs, vulnerable to the approach of any stranger, when the door opened and Alison Bill's eager voice said, 'Anyone at home? Mind if I come in?'

3

'Sally?' persisted Miss Bill's mellifluous, musical voice, her only feature which was, by conventional standards, beautiful.

Sally did not exactly dislike Alison Bill, but she was threatened by her intellectual range, and by the friendship which Sally imagined to exist between Francis and Alison. Having just discovered, from Damian Wells, that Francis had some secret life, Sally momentarily wondered whether this life was spent with Miss Bill.

'I'm afraid Francis has gone out,' she said.

Miss Bill's vigorous 'Good!' surprised her. 'This is something I wanted to talk about to you.'

'Has something happened? Why aren't you at school? Jess all right?'

'Jess is alive and well. But it's about Jess that I want to talk. I wouldn't say she was OK, no.'

'Come and have a coffee.'

'That would be lovely.'

Miss Bill deposited her school bag on the hall chair; she never seemed to go anywhere without this great hulking red suede bag, which must have weighed a hundredweight. With stout-legged vigour, she marched behind Sally into the kitchen.

When the electric kettle was humming, Sally asked, 'What's happened?'

'I'm afraid Jessica was rather upset in school this morning. It happened in one of my lessons. I asked her to read aloud from the book we are doing – *To Kill a Mockingbird* – and she just broke down, I'm sorry to say. I asked her what the matter was, and she couldn't say. Well, naturally, after the lesson, I asked one of her best friends if they knew what the matter was. It was Sarah Mackintosh, a nice, sensible girl, and she said that Jessica had been a bit odd all term; well, not so much odd, as different. She said there was a rumour going round the school that everything wasn't happy at home; now, I know that you can't trust rumours. . . .'

Sally's glance at Miss Bill was highly distrustful. This was an intrusion! A parish gossip was fishing for details, and disguising her curiosity as real concern! And yet, despite these unworthy thoughts, Sally was melted by Miss Bill's voice and by her very tender smile.

'We've all been upset since Griselda died – Francis's Mum,' said Sally. 'Of course that takes some getting used to.'

'It's an awful cheek my coming round like this, Sally. . . .'

'No, it isn't.'

'Only, I'm very fond of you all; and it's my job as a teacher to notice whether one of my pupils is firing on all cylinders as it were. And I am worried about Jessica. And – thanks.'

This 'thanks' was for the mug of instant coffee which was held out to Alison Bill as she sat at the kitchen table. As she said the word 'thanks', Miss Bill placed her hand over Sally's hand which held the mug. For a second or two, it was not clear whether she did this simply in order to establish her hold on the mug, or whether she wanted to hold hands with Sally, and it transpired, after a few seconds in which the hand was not withdrawn, that the latter was true.

'I'm very concerned about you, too.'

'Me?'

'Mm.' Alison nodded and sipped coffee at the same time. 'I know it isn't my business,' she said, 'but I think Francis is being a complete bastard to you at the moment.' This sentence, delivered in the usual, well-modulated tones, had a most startling strength. Rather than protest, Sally opened her mouth and found herself smiling. 'I know he is going through some sort of mid-life crisis, such as men often do when their precious mothers die, but for Christ's sake! Can't he see what he is doing to you, doing to Jess – doing to the parish, come to that? It's probably not fair to worry you, but people are starting to *talk* in the parish.'

'About us?'

'No, my dear, they're not; or not in so far as I know. But Ronald and I have had to do a lot of hard work protecting that husband of yours. Not everyone loves him.' Miss Bill seemed to be staring very hard at Sally through her marble-lenses to see whether there was a glimmer of love for the Vicar even in his wife. 'That was lovely,' she said, having gulped down the coffee – it was still too hot for Sally to sip. 'The Spittles have really got it in for Francis. Normally, I'd support him to the hilt; and of course I defend him against *them*. But in some of these allegations – they have got a point. He has been neglecting his duties. If he needs help – I mean psychiatric help – then he should *get* it, instead of leaving old Mabel Norbury unburied, and half the old people in the village unvisited. . . . And obviously, all this is having a shattering effect on his wife and child.'

'It's not been easy,' said Sally cautiously. She was afraid that, if she said one syllable more, she would confess everything. Hitherto, she had been able to contain her frustration and unhappiness by whispering into the ear of the Dog Frumpy and Golly and Teddy. But here was a willing, a sympathetic, human listener. 'He just – doesn't – seem – to – care.' She enunciated these syllables slowly, and (or so it seemed to Alison) with a dazed hatred, as if she no longer minded admitting how unhappy she had been. 'We've had some difficult patches before in our marriage – everyone does.'

'I have never understood how anybody can bear to be married to another person,' said Miss Bill.

'But for the last six months, Alison, it has been hell in this house. Hell.' She put the coffee to her lips, but it was still too hot to drink. She added raffishly, 'Absolute bloody hell.'

It astonished and delighted her to find an appreciative listener in, of all people, Miss Bill, and she began an extended narrative, interrupted sometimes by tears, sometimes by Miss Bill stroking her hands, of the troubles she had endured since Christmas. She told of Francis's persistent domestic coldness, his lack of affection towards her, stretching back over many years, his sarcasm, his emotional meanness and greed (shown in his usually successful attempts to alienate Jessica's affections and make her, Sally, look foolish in front of her own child), his linguistic snobberies ('What's wrong with saying "pardon"?' Miss Bill could have told her, but didn't), his desire on all occasions to exclude her, humiliate her, cut her down to size. But none of this could equal his mysterious behaviour over the last couple of months, and Sally had almost come to the conclusion that her husband was certifiably mad; certainly he was driving her mad; she could feel herself losing her wits, she really could; and she had no one to turn to, no one.

By this point of the narrative, Sally's coffee had passed from being too hot, to being too cold to drink. Miss Bill took charge of replenishing their mugs. She was a skilful listener, and she discerned that there was a final chunk of confession which was waiting to come out. This emerged quite easily, when, having made the coffee and set it before Sally, Alison remained standing up, with one hand on Sally's shoulder, and the other gently massaging the other woman's neck.

'Then, this morning, I rang up Damian Wells.' Unseen by Sally, Alison raised her eyes to the ceiling. 'Alison, I thought that Francis was really good friends with Damian. He's kept telling me that he was going to see Damian, that he went to London with Damian. But it was obvious when I talked to Damian just now that *he has hardly seen Francis all year*. And I know this sounds silly.'

'Nothing you have said sounds silly.'

'But, Alison, I honestly think he might be having,' the sentence wouldn't quite finish itself.

Miss Bill released her hold of Sally's neck and resumed her chair at the kitchen table.

'I can't believe that Francis would have an affair,' said his wife.

'People do,' said the churchwarden.

'Alison – you won't tell anyone about this conversation, will you?'

'Of course not.'

'Only, it isn't really fair on Francis to . . .'

'Look, Sally, Francis hasn't been very fair on you.'

'You don't think he's gay, do you?'

'Would it matter if he was?' Miss Bill asked this question with particular seriousness. How beautiful, at that moment, she was finding the nut-brown squirrelly eyes of the Vicar's wife, and her back-combed, blondish hair and her sweet little Botticelli mouth.

'I've never thought about it,' said Sally truthfully. 'I think it might be completely terrible – I'm not talking about getting diseases. It's years since Francis ever did anything to me which could give me a disease.'

Perhaps there was something just a little too eager about Miss Bill's 'Really?' Or perhaps it was just an inherently embarrassing confession; but Sally had turned very, very red.

'It helps nattering, it really does. But what are we going to do about poor little Jess, Alison?'

'Stand up.'

'Why?'

Both women were about the same height, but Sally seemed smaller partly because she was two thirds the weight, and partly because she was hunched. She allowed Alison Bill to take her in her arms and give her a huge hug. This was so comforting that she luxuriated in it; when Miss Bill's large, woolly, rounded chest was squeezed against her own rather bonier frame, Sally felt tremendously loved, as though she had found what she had been seeking and seeking for years, a lovely, motherly female friend.

'Oh, don't let go,' she said, 'don't let go.'

4

Since his interview with Ronald Maxwell-Lee, Francis Kreer had allowed himself, even more than was usually the case, to become a 'character' inside his own head. This torrent of hostility from his parishioners compelled some such self-protective device. He found himself talking freely, sometimes aloud, and sometimes inwardly, to this 'character', this 'self' whom he alone understood. This strange inner quirk, this ability to talk to himself as if he were someone else, almost to disengage himself from himself, explained in part – at least to his own satisfaction – why he had once enjoyed such a vigorous religious life; but why, once formal religious belief had been abandoned, he still continued with an inner life, a *daimon*. For some years, he had assumed that, roughly speaking, this placed him in the company of those philosophers for whom God, and indeed the whole of experience, was something which was going on inside each individual human head. God was no more than an internalised version of all the inner longings and moral aspirations and spiritual insights of one Francis Kreer. Since losing Griselda and falling in love with Jay, he realised that this was a completely inappropriate way of describing what was going on when he perceived these women that he loved: his mother and his darling. While it was true that he valued them both, not objectively, but as images inside himself, it was not true that he had any control over what he felt about these images; and it made no sort of imaginative sense to say that he had simply dreamed them up. Griselda had died, and he had been shocked and completely broken up by the pain which this caused. In quite a comparable way, he had not chosen to fall in love: it was something which happened. In other words, there were forces and pressures outside him to which he could not respond. And the same went for art, and nature and the beauty of landscape and the interest of literature. These were not things which only had an existence inside him; nor was their existence only a realised existence: that is, something which could not come into meaningful focus until he thought about them. In all these areas, he felt his consciousness invaded, rather than being aware that he could retreat into his own consciousness and select, as a matter of preference, what he would or would not feel.

But in the matter of trouble – trouble such as this tiresome business with the Spittles – it was different. He *was* able to withdraw into his 'self', and talk to himself; and the words which, with shameless materialism, he had repeated since the Wing-Co's visit were, 'Ninety thousand pounds!'

This was the sum which, by Francis's calculations, he could hope to receive after his mother's flat had been sold, and the amount had been divided with Eric Gadney. Of course, it would have been much nicer if he had inherited the entire flat. But, even with £90,000, he would become what he had never been before: an independent man. In the first shock of grief, the implications of all this had been impossible to conceptualise. He had been so stunned, first by his mother's demise itself, and secondly by her apparent lack of love for *him*, that he had not allowed himself to think what his inheritance could mean for him; and this was partly because he had not, until meeting Mr Gadney, even contemplated selling the flat. But, once the idea had formed itself in his head, he was able to spell out his entire scheme. For the twentieth time that day, he spoke out the scheme to himself as he walked along. He passed the top of the village. Dorothy Maxwell-Lee, dead-heading Bourbon roses, watched the Vicar pace past her hedge chuntering to himself and wondered if he was saying his prayers. She felt sad for her husband, who had told her some of the details of his painful conversation with Francis. From the seat of a tractor, two hundred yards up the road, Robin Pimm also saw the Parson, chuntering to himself, and wondered how much truth there was in the stories, which circulated in the village Post Office and the bar of the Rising Sun, that the Vicar, who had never been 'right' since his mother died, had gone 'real peculiar' of late.

'Ninety thousand pounds!' said the Vicar of Ditcham. 'No mean sum!' (He had certainly never possessed such a sum of money before and had absolutely no experience in financial matters.) 'If I place that in a building society at ten per cent, this would bring me in an income of £9,000 per annum – as much as I am paid at the moment!' (He ignored completely the fact that as an Anglican incumbent he was given a free house, assistance with his motoring expenses, and an allowance from the patron of this particular living for the private education of his daughter.) 'I do not need to stay here and be insulted by people like Gerrie Spittle! We could go away!' ('We' in his inner conferences always meant he and Jay.) 'We could take a small house somewhere. I could do translations from the Latin, and take pupils; she could practise her violin. . . .'

All these ideas flooded his brain, not as accurately calculated schemes, but as stories in which he and Jay were characters. He began to think of them in the imagined house. She was at a kitchen table, wearing an open-necked white shirt, and glowing with health, as she peeled potatoes; he was reading aloud to her from his latest version of Ovid.

These reflections, including the imagined speech he had made to the churchwardens when he resigned his living, took him to the brow of the hill, as he entered, with some trepidation, the Travellers' encampment in Potter's Field. Two horses were grazing in one corner of the field. There were some dogs, tied up with ropes, which began to bark at his approach, and a little child, barefoot and somewhat ragged, came trundling up to him.

'Who are you?'

'Hullo!'

'Who *are* you?'

'I'm Francis.'

The child, who was Rosie's daughter Daisy, asked, 'Have you come to see my mummy?'

'I don't think so.'

In a moment of fear, it occurred to him that he had no reason to suppose that Jay did not have a child. She had not mentioned one, but there were a number of things she had not mentioned.

'Mummy's over there!'

Daisy pointed in the general direction of the caravans with a muddy finger.

'Which one is Mummy?'

'She's the one on the steps of the bus.'

The bus was a single-storeyed, old-fashioned bus of the kind which used to convey passengers about country lanes in the days of Francis's childhood. He set off in that direction. It struck him, as he approached the settlement, that it was ill-structured and higgledy-piggledy. Some of the vans and trucks were needlessly close together, others yards apart. It was difficult to see where anyone did any washing, though he assumed that some rather wobbly stakes, draped with torn sheets in one corner of the field, constituted a latrine.

On the seat of the bus, he saw a young woman with piled-up red hair, who was suckling a baby, and two or three young men. He recognised the dark young man whose appearance had struck him so favourably on Palm Sunday and whom he had once seen in Reading emerging from a pub with Jay.

'Mummy, this man is looking for you.'

'What is it?' asked Rosie.

'Good morning.' Francis grinned and tried to assume his most ingratiating manner. It was difficult to know how to ingratiate himself with these people who were so unlike anyone he had met in the normal course of his parochial ministry. 'Lovely day!' he said. 'Thank goodness that rain seems to be holding off!' he exclaimed.

'We get used to rain,' drawled Mo, quite savagely. Mo had not guessed the identity of their visitor until Francis spoke again.

'I was looking for a friend of mine, actually. Jay Dunbar.'

When he said this, his interlocutors agreed afterwards that he looked mad, because his mouth broke into an enormous toothy grin. They could not have guessed the enormous satisfaction it gave Francis to repeat Jay's name in human company. He had now been obsessed with her for the better part of three months and he had not said her name to another soul. To do so on this occasion was an important stage of his relationship with her.

'What do you want her for?'

Simultaneously, Rosie said, 'She's gone for a walk.'

'Well, I might wander up the hill and see if I can find her. She sometimes goes that way.'

'Who shall I say wanted her?' Rosie had to yell this, because Francis was already on the hoof; embarrassed by how different these people were from himself, and wanting to beat a retreat.

Mo shouted, 'Hey, you! Lay off her, right?'

Or Francis thought this was what he said. He turned and waved, and raised his straw hat, almost running away from the camp, and from the hostility which the group had given off. As he ran, he caught in his nostrils the scent of the beautifully sweet tobacco they all seemed to be smoking, not a variety he had ever consciously smelt before.

He walked rapidly for a mile, and was sweating profusely by the time he reached the brow of the hill where, some half-hour before, Jay had stood and said aloud to him in his absence, 'I'm not going to fall in love with you, you know.'

He had to walk another mile before he found her, at a spot where the path sloped down into Robin Pimm's barley fields. The fields were divided at this juncture by hawthorn hedges, and beside the gate there was a clump of large sycamores. Jay was sitting in the shade of one of these trees, with her head on one knee.

'I say! Hullo, there!'

Her reply – 'Oh, hullo' – was bleary.

'How are you?'

'I think I'm developing a really nasty cold.'

'Oh, well, you must watch that.'

'It's just started. I didn't have it when I set out from the camp. Now, I've got a really sore throat.'

'But how *terrible*!'

'It's not terrible.' She laughed a little. 'It's just a cold. But it's a nuisance.'

In his fantasies that morning, Francis had envisaged meeting Jay in just such a spot and openly declaring his love for her. In this particular story, which had unfolded itself to him while he was shaving, she would respond with an equally passionate declaration, and they would fall into one another's arms and kiss: real kisses, sexual kisses, not the comforting hugs which she had given him on the day in Reading when he was weeping for his dead mother. Her truculent concern for her head-cold made an inauspicious prologue to such a conversation.

'It can't be very healthy, where you are,' he said. 'Do you sleep on a damp pillow?'

She seemed displeased by this line of inquiry.

'I'll be all right,' she said. 'I just came out to be on my own.'

Ignoring her unwelcoming tone, he sat beside her and said, 'I've been thinking about you. I've missed you since our visit to London.'

Jay coughed and wiped her nose on the back of her hand.

'It was fun, wasn't it, our trip up to London?'

Jay did not think that this was a very good way of describing it. Not wholly displeased to see him, however, she asked, 'So, how are you?'

'Oh, I'm fed up with the parish! Some of those people make me so angry!'

'Really?' She laughed at this. 'They can't make you as angry as some of *those* people make *me*!' And she waved in the general direction of the camp. 'They're so aimless. They don't seem to want to *do* anything, they don't have anything to talk about.'

'Have you been practising the violin?'

She sighed.

'It's no good,' she said. 'You've been kind.'

'I haven't been kind. I said – if you wanted to use the flat . . .'

'I can't go up to London every time I want to play the fiddle. I haven't any music. I've nowhere to practise. It's hopeless. Actually, I was going to come and see you.'

'You were?'

'I don't think I'll be staying much longer.'

These words made Francis jolt with terror.

'It isn't right for me, that way of life. I think I'll move on somewhere.'

'But – you mustn't – just – go!'

'Why not – I've got nothing to stay for. And I've got a cold.'

He wanted to say, 'You have *me* to stay for,' but the words would not come, and he was afraid of being rejected, or laughed at, if he said them.

'I might even go abroad,' she said.

They sat silently together and watched the field – the breeze blowing the barley, and the flowers in the hedge – Queen Anne's Lace, red campion, rosebay willow herb. An aeroplane passed overhead.

'I'd like to get away, too,' he said. 'I was just having the thought as I walked along. I've decided that I'm going to sell my mother's flat. When the money comes through, I'm going to buy a little place – oh, I don't know where, perhaps by the seaside, and take a bit of breathing space. I might even do some translating.'

'What about your parish, your job?' she asked. 'What about your family?' ('Wife' was a word which she baulked at.)

'I'd go alone,' he said quietly. 'Or anyway not with them.'

'I see.'

But she did not see what this maddening man was saying to her. She was both pleased that he had come, and infuriated by this line of talk. What was he saying to her, what did he want? Was he, in a roundabout way, asking her to run away with him? That was crazy, they hardly knew one another! Or was he saying that he really wanted to be on his own: and, if that *was* what he was saying, why did he torment her by befriending her, and sitting beside her, and seeming to offer, or half-offer, some escape from the unsatisfactory life in which she was entrapped?

'You seem to have all your plans worked out, then,' she said quietly.

'Not really,' he said. 'They are just daydreams; but I do mean to go. I won't stay here and be bossed about by people like the Spittles.'

The moment when he might have made some declaration of his passion had passed once more. He sat and told her instead about the Wing-Commander's visit, omitting all mention this time of the stolen crucifix, and not saying that Gerald Spittle had seen Jay and the Vicar together in Reading. He merely told her of the other allegations. She laughed when he got to the bit about 'Eskimo Nell'. On the whole, however, the narrative displeased her. What if he was just one of these randy vicars you read about in the newspapers?

5

Three trucks left the convoy on the day that Jay developed her cold. They thought that they might reach Stonehenge three days later on Midsummer's Day. The remaining Travellers in Potter's Field (about twenty of them including dogs and children) had vague plans for celebrating the Summer Solstice, but they had not advanced very far by the time they had all drifted off to sleep on Midsummer Eve.

Jay woke before dawn with a high fever. Her head was throbbing, and she had sweated so much that her sleeping bag was quite moist. This made her very cold. Since she had stopped allowing Mo to sleep with her, she generally bedded down with Compton and Leila in their battered Dormobile, and it was there that she woke, staring at the ceiling of the van, unable to breathe through her nose.

In the darkness, Jay's eyes made out the shape of Compton, who slept silently on the other bunk. Above his head was a little shelf, covered with formica. A small figure of the Buddha sat looking down on them, and Jay was surprised by the fact that, when she looked at this figure, it was illuminated by a sudden ray of light.

She saw it in all its detail – it was a cheap little copper figure, but calming, none the less, with its closed eyes and its crossed legs. The flash of light also lit up the rest of the caravan – the small extended table-flap, still covered with the remains of supper; a large saucepan; some empty Guinness cans; a wine bottle serving as a candlestick, the candle all but burnt to its end. Beyond that, the diminutive cooker with its greasy assemblage of cooking vessels. On the string above the cooker, some tiny pairs of trousers, and a little pullover – Compton sometimes did Rosie's washing for her.

Semi-delirious with her fever, Jay only sensed danger with this flash of light when she realised that Leila was frightened. The dog had come to her for protection, nuzzled against her and let out low growls. Stroking Leila's head, Jay could feel that the dog's fur was standing on end. She did not have long to wonder why Leila was frightened, because at that moment the door of the Dormobile roughly slid back and the torchlight shone in her face.

'Get up! We want everyone out of here!' said the voice behind the light.

'What's going on?'

'Hey!' said Compton. 'Hey!'

'There's two of them in here, and a dog!' said the voice behind the light. 'Get on with it! We want you out of here and on the grass. We want to search this place.'

'You can't just come in here . . .' Jay began to say. But she was being dragged out of the Dormobile and made to lie face down on the grass, while two uniformed officers entered the Dormobile, supposedly searching it for drugs.

It was a well-organised raid. There were as many policemen as Travellers, and all the vans had been invaded at roughly speaking the same moment. As she lay on the grass, cold and shaking, Jay could hear upraised voices. Children were crying. Someone (Jay thought it was Rosie) was calling out, 'There are kids in there! Be careful!'

Someone else was yelling, 'These are our homes you're wrecking!'

In Compton's caravan (in which, mercifully, and amazingly,

there was no marijuana discovered) a nineteen-year-old boy in blue uniform was saying, 'It makes you sick to think of people living like this.'

In spite of being told to lie down, Jay turned, because Leila was barking really loudly now, and she wanted if possible to calm the dog down.

'You bloody scum!' said the officer who had completed his rudimentary search of the Dormobile – 'You try to set your dog on me!'

'Come here, Leila! Leila!' called Jay. But she could see the policeman's truncheon come down on Leila's skull, not once, but again and again, and again.

'She tried to set her dog on me!' said one constable.

Another officer had taken Jay by the arm and made her put her hands above her head. Compton was being treated in the same way. With their faces against the outside of the van, they were roughly frisked. Finding some tampons in her top pocket, the constable laughed and threw them away in the darkness.

As light dawned on this violent scene, and as she realised that they had finished with her, Jay went back into the van, fetched a blanket to wrap round her shoulders, and watched with a terrified wonder at what was going on around her. She saw Dave, spreadeagled with his face against the side of Rosie's bus, being kneed in the kidneys by one policeman. When he doubled up with pain, he was given a severe swipe on the side of his head.

Leila's dead body lay at Jay's feet. She was too stunned at first to realise that the dog was dead, and when she did realise it she shook the dog's head in a frenzy and found her hands covered in blood. Dogs who were luckier than Leila were barking. Children were crying. An hysterical Rosie was shouting, 'Bastards! Bastards! Leave my kids alone!'

Abandoning the dead dog, Jay ran towards Rosie to see if she could comfort one of the children and, as she did so, she saw Mo being frogmarched off to a van by two policemen. He did not appear to notice her, but as he passed, in all his vulnerability, Jay thought how beautiful he looked. She had wanted to part from him, but not like this. They were taking her man! The bastards were taking her man.

'Mo! Mo!' she called.

He turned. His attempt to move one shoulder blade in order to look at Jay was interpreted by his police escort as a violent gesture, and he was pushed forward.

'What's happened?' she yelled.

'Get a lawyer!' he yelled back.

'Mo!'

'Get a fucking lawyer!'

They arrested Mo, the boy Geoff, Irma, a girl called Sophie and Dave, all on charges of possessing illegal substances. While these people were being hurled into the backs of vans, a senior police officer came and spoke to them in the first light of summer. He held a megaphone to his mouth.

'Now, we do not want to have any more trouble from you,' he said, 'and I dare say that you do not want any more trouble from us. If you have dispersed by this time tomorrow morning, we shan't trouble you any more. If you want to make life difficult for yourselves . . .'

He paused. He was a heavily-built man, and Jay believed that she detected in his features an expression of pure sadistic pleasure as he turned towards the teepee shared by a dippy pair of Travellers called Rachel and Mike. Two of his officers had decided to take this ramshackle edifice to pieces. The four upright poles which met at the top to form an uneven pyramid came crashing down, upsetting cooking vessels and alarming a goat which was tethered to one of the guy pegs.

'We've endeavoured to search the caravans causing the minimum damage to personal property,' said the man with the megaphone, 'but you must realise that illegal drugs have been found on this camp and that gives us every right to search the place as thoroughly as possible.'

'Please!' Dippy Rachel, frightened and in tears, was struggling with the goat's rope for fear that it would be throttled by the collapsing teepee. 'Please! Oh, God!'

'So we'll trust you to be sensible, and move on.'

'Where?' 'How?' 'Yeah, where to?' and other less polite replies greeted this officer's speech. But by then the Travellers whom they had arrested had been put into the back of police vans and the remaining police cars were churning round and round, making mud circles in Potter's Field, and sounding their sirens loudly.

For an hour or two, or so it seemed, while the sun rose in the sky, the remaining Travellers sat or stood around in collective astonishment. This act of pillage had been an assertion of police power, a reminder to the Travellers of their own powerlessness; and powerless was now exactly what they felt. Some of the women eventually began to stir themselves. Here, someone picked up a saucepan or a child's potty and tried to take it back to the caravan where it belonged. As light rose, it seemed as though the police had thrown objects indiscriminately all over the field. Mattresses, old transistors, cooking implements, children's clothes and toys were scattered about in the dew, looking pathetically valueless. When she eventually found her own little bundle of belongings, Jay found that her violin case had been opened, and her violin lay on the grass. It had been broken in half.

6

It was the Feast of the Nativity of St John Baptist, the beginning of summer. Francis Kreer stood at the Lady Altar celebrating the Holy Communion. Nowadays when he performed this rite, his mind followed such reveries that he frequently missed his place. This morning, he had been thinking: 'God is Love. That is a nonsensical phrase, since God does not exist. But it is not entirely nonsensical to say that Love is God. Love is the deepest, the most important thing which happens to us, and it is not a purely internalised thing: it comes to us from outside, in just the same way that the angel came to Mary in the story of the Annunciation. Falling in love with Jay has changed me, it has revivified me. I had been living in the straitjacket of logic; I had been living in what Paul thinks of as the Law, which can only kill, whereas the Spirit giveth life, the Spirit of love.

'There is no Jehovah. Of course there isn't. But there is something within us which it is not absurd to call divine, and the point is that it reaches out and discovers divinity outside ourselves. It is the Law of Logic which killeth, and the Spirit which giveth life. This, really, is what the New Testament is about. It is all an extraordinary myth about love, about love being able to conquer everything, even death itself. That is why all the words and stories of the New Testament have a capacity to excite us. They are a resource, telling us about Love. Christianity is an organic imaginative growth, not a religion delivered on tablets of stone. It is an extremely exciting discovery about the human heart. Human beings, in all their frailty and weakness, can "come to Jesus" and be lifted up; the only ones who live within closed moral or intellectual systems. I was a Pharisee, and now I am a child of grace, through Jay: not of course that I am "redeemed" in the old Christian sense – but none of that *matters*. What matters is that we have life, and have it more abundantly. Before this year, I would stand at this altar and mouth the words, solely because it was expected of me by Edith Renton and Ronald Maxwell-Lee and others. But now I do it because it all has a renewed meaning, though not the meaning which the compilers of the liturgy intended! If I say, "Lift up your hearts!", I really mean it. I am proclaiming a great *Sursum Corda* from the depth of my being. . . .'

These were his thoughts. Looking down at the altar, he found himself performing the ablutions and wiping the chalice with the purificator. So, presumably, they had all had Holy Communion and he was coming to the end of the service? Nervously, he looked over his shoulder. He had no altar-server, so there was no one that he could ask. What if he was merely wiping the chalice absent-mindedly before filling it with wine? What if he had not got further than the Prayer for the Church Militant? From the place of the altar-missal, he supposed that he had more or less finished. So, he said the final thanksgiving, and then, 'The Peace of God which passeth all understanding . . .'

Would anyone have told him if he had in fact jumped straight from the Prayer of Humble Access to the Blessing and forgotten to give the people Holy Communion at all? Looking at the congregation, he rather thought that they would not have done. The Spittles were there, staring at him accusingly. He rather thought, in the light of his recent conversation with the Wing-Commander, that they might have had the decency to stay away.

With delicate step, Francis returned to the vestry, carrying before him the chalice and paten, draped with veil and burse. Once back in the vestry, he placed the sacred vessels on the table and began to divest himself. It was when he had taken the chasuble from over his head, and lain it neatly on top of the vestment chest, and removed his alb, and was smoothing his hair in front of the small looking-glass, that he heard the agitated female voices.

'Look, you just got to help, please.'

'Please, help.'

The concerned, sensible, mellifluous tones of Miss Bill were heard saying, 'They came this morning? What time was that?'

Several voices answered at once.

'They killed one of our dogs. Can you imagine – in front of the kids, they killed a bloody dog.'

Another voice said, 'There's only us left. The others have driven off and they've arrested about five of us.'

'If you want help' – this was Mrs Renton – 'you really ought to go to the proper authorities. Don't forget, I do know what I'm talking about. I was a social worker in Holborn for over thirty years.'

'Look' – Francis froze, because this voice was that of Jay! His Jay! She said these words to Mrs Renton: 'There are two children here with cut hands and feet. There are two young mothers who have just had their homes wrecked. I'm sorry, but we need help now; it's no good saying, "Go to a social worker".'

'I don't think it's right to let them in the church' – this whining voice was that of Lindie Spittle.

Francis strode into this scene. He was agitated and impassioned, but also very angry. Jay turned to him. Her hands and her face were smeared with blood and her eyes were wide with distress.

'What's happened?' he thundered.

'I still don't think . . .' whined Lindie Spittle.

With the pure and sinless rage of Christ overturning the money-changers' tables, Francis actually swept her aside.

('I've still got the bruise,' she said a week later, 'where he grabbed my shoulders; as hard as *that*; he just shoved me out of the way in order to get – get – to her.')

With many voices being lifted up at the same time, and a considerable confusion in the church porch, it was necessary for one authoritative voice to be heard.

('I have to say, I was rather impressed by the way Francis handled that,' was the Wing-Commander's admission to his wife as they thought about it later over their coffee and biscuits.)

Francis's was that voice.

'You're all to come over to the vicarage,' he said. 'Alison' – Miss Bill had a baby in one arm; with the other she was comforting Rosie who had begun to whimper. 'Alison – can you show them the way?' He turned to Jay and said, 'You look terrible. What happened? Is there anyone left up there? You're sure there are no children left up there on their own?'

In the crisis, the dreamy egoism, which had been the most marked feature of his character in all the time she had known him, had fallen away. His weakness charmed, but irritated Jay. His strength, in that setting, was altogether too much; she almost literally collapsed beneath it.

'Look at that! Look at it!' said Lindie Spittle, as she watched the Vicar put his arm around the urchin-girl. Francis, Alison Bill and the remaining Travellers made a group of about a dozen. At the lych-gate Jay stumbled, and Lindie, from the church porch, watched her pastor lift the young woman into his arms and carry her across the road to the vicarage.

7

In the Diocesan Office, the Archdeacon sat behind a large reproduction-Georgian desk, surveying his desk diary. A satisfying morning of what he termed 'admin' stretched ahead. Plump, genial, neither a good man nor a bad man, he had left his ideals behind him long ago. At fifty-one, he realised that a bishopric was now unlikely, although his wife still nursed hopes. He would have been just as happy had he become a politician or a civil servant, but he knew that, in his present job, he saw a greater variety of human eccentrics and beautiful old buildings than he would have done in any other capacity. He was what is called 'good with people'. Not being given to the habit of thinking, he was inclined to believe that being 'good with people' was 'what the Gospel is all about'.

The desk diary reminded him that he was lunching with the Registrar of the diocese, an old friend. He would punctuate genial inquiries about the Registrar's children and his slipped disc with business: two applications for faculties. One came from an evangelical church which wanted to re-order its sanctuary, remove the High Altar (reredos by Bodley and Garner) and install audio-visual equipment and a movable cinema-screen. They also wanted to move the Victorian font to make way for a sound-proof glass screen and the creation of a narthex which would serve the double purpose of parish room and carpeted play-area, in which children could romp about during sermons without disturbing the concentration of the grown-ups. The other application was for a faculty in a small country church to set up a memorial for a recently-deceased Admiral. A considerable sum of money had been left for this purpose, but there had been some doubt, in these 'weak, piping times of peace', whether it was altogether appropriate to commission a stained-glass window of U-boats being exploded in the North Atlantic. With a little of his famous tact, the Archdeacon had every confidence that he could persuade both parishes to emend their plans.

Then there was the vacant livings file, which he hoped to discuss with the Bishop that afternoon. Poor Aylmer Wallace, the vicar of Lower Shawbridge, was applying, for the third time in five years, for a move! It was that neurotic wife of his. She would not be satisfied anywhere. There was a small, working-class urban parish which had lately fallen vacant, too: old Father Brooks had suddenly turned up his toes in, of all inappropriate places, Marks and Spencer's! The Archdeacon knew that this parish, with its firm Anglo-Catholic tradition, would be just up Damian Wells's street. Damian now came into the diocesan offices for two days each week to help out with 'redundant churches'. The Archdeacon, who derived most of his views from liberal newspapers, took a very lenient view of Damian's proclivities; but one had to be sensible, and think of 'old dears' in the pew, who might be slower than the rest of us to realise that fornication, when practised by homosexuals, was no longer exactly a sin. 'Sin isn't a word we use much nowadays,' the Archdeacon had once said lately, at a dinner-party, and he had not quite been able to see why his company – all lay-folk – had laughed.

His secretary, as well-groomed as she was worldly, made her breezy entrance. She was the wife of a university lecturer and, as he liked to remind people, 'no mean linguist'. He spoke of her accomplishments rather as if they were an extension of his own.

'A few letters I think you ought to see,' said the secretary. She was tall and very handsome, with full expensively-glossed lips and very thick grey hair, elegantly cut. She was about the Archdeacon's age. She was aware that he found her sexually attractive, but there was nothing untoward about their relationship.

'Thanks, Fiona.'

'Ditcham,' she said.

'Ah, yes! Frankie Kreer, what does he want?'

No one in fact called Francis 'Frankie', but it was one of the Archdeacon's beliefs that people liked to be addressed by diminutives of their Christian names.

'It isn't from Mr Kreer, actually. There are two letters, and, as I say, I think you should see them.'

'Dear Mr Archdeacon,' read the Archdeacon. He chuckled. Wholly a man of the late twentieth century, he believed that the Church, like every other institution, had to move with the times; gaiters gave way to grey suits among the senior clergy, just as MPs no longer wore black coats and striped trousers to sit in the Chamber. He rather liked the fact, however, that there were still some people conservative enough to address him as 'Mr Archdeacon'.

Dear Mr Archdeacon,

I hesitate to write to you, but there is a matter which is bothering me, and which must, sooner or later, come to your attention. Since I know that you are a busy man, I wonder if I could make an appointment to see you as soon as possible. Something has cropped up in our parish, and

I am afraid that if I do not have a private word with you,
it will reach your attention in some other way.

Yours sincerely,

Ronald Maxwell-Lee (Wing-Commander Retd)
Churchwarden, St Birinus, Ditcham.

The other letter, which was penned in Lindie Spittle's round-bottomed hand, was much longer. It contained the catalogue of Francis Kreer's supposed sins of which the Wing-Commander had already seen a copy. To this extensive list of clerical misdemeanours there was added a postscript: 'He pushed me so hard that I fell over, and I still have the bruises where he squeezed my arm. There are grounds here for charging him with assault.'

With pudgy fingers which were delicate in their movements (the Archdeacon was an accomplished pianist), he put down Lindie Spittle's letter and rubbed his chin thoughtfully. Then he gently drummed the surface of his desk.

'Have you seen this stuff, Fiona?'

'Yes.'

'I wonder if you could get out the file on Ditcham.'

'I already have. Would you like some coffee?'

'I think I could do with some.'

The Archdeacon hated this sort of thing. He did not know why it should be the case, but Church life, normally blandly agreeable, had the capacity to bring to the surface emanations of terrible malice. No doubt, in the world of business, there were intense rivalries; but the Archdeacon suspected that the secular world could provide few examples of 'motiveless malignity' to match those that erupted in the annals of the church.

Everything about Lindie Spittle's letter inclined the Archdeacon to think that the woman was mad. 'One time in the vestry when I was putting things away in the cupboard, I felt him coming up behind me. He touched me with a broom handle. "Don't forget this," he said. There was a really *salacious* look in his face as he offered me the broom handle . . .'

'Oh, dear, dear,' said the Archdeacon aloud. There were pages of the stuff. The vicar had touched her 'where it was not nice to be touched'; on 'several occasions'. If it wasn't nice, why did she keep going to church, he asked himself with a smile? But it was not a laughing matter, he knew that.

Nothing in the file, either for the parish of Ditcham or for the career of Francis Heriot Kreer, MA, suggested that the Vicar of this parish might be sexually untrustworthy. The Archdeacon did not know Francis very well, but he had every reason to suppose that he was a decent enough fellow. Looking through the file, the Archdeacon saw that Francis was educated at Lancing, Lincoln College, Oxford (2nd cl. Mods and Greats), and Mirfield Theological College. His first curacy had been at a High parish in Willesden, followed by one at St Mary's, Primrose Hill. He had married rather a pretty woman, the Archdeacon remembered – what was she called? Ah, yes, Sarah Edwards. One child. All perfectly middle-class and respectable.

'I think I'd better ring up this Wing-Commander,' said the Archdeacon to his secretary. 'Could you get him for me?'

He sat back, and allowed Fiona to ring the Maxwell-Lees' number and to put him through.

'May I speak to Wing-Commander Maxwell-Lee?'

'Who's that?' – an imperious female voice. In the background, he could hear an old man stammering, 'Who is it?'

'It's the Archdeacon,' said Dorothy Maxwell-Lee. 'He's just coming,' she said into the receiver.

'Ah, Ronnie.'

'Ronald Maxwell-Lee here.'

'Good. Look, I've got your letter. I think I know what it's about. I've also had another letter, you see, from a Mrs Spittle.'

'Ah. Oh dear.'

'Well, quite.'

'Look, we obviously don't want this matter getting out of control, and maybe the best thing to do is if we meet and have a chat.'

'I think maybe we better had.'

'I mean there seem to be three or four things here,' said the Archdeacon. 'There are the church services which Mrs Spittle doesn't like; there is the way Frankie's actually running the parish . . .'

'Frankie?'

'There's the spot of bother with the dear old Travellers.'

'Well, we've got rid of those, th-th-thank God. The police moved them on a few days ago. Francis and his wife were very good about that, actually. There was a gaggle of women and children left behind, but I'm h-h-happy to say they've all been taken care of by a social worker in Reading. So that little episode is behind us.'

All this sounded very hopeful. The Archdeacon began to think that Mrs Spittle's complaints could probably be sorted out by one brisk letter from himself, and everyone else – vicar, churchwardens and diocesan authorities – 'pulling together'.

'And then there are these other matters. Better have a word about them face-to-face rather than discussing them over the telephone.'

'Qu-qu-quite so.'

'How's Sarah coping?'

'What's that?'

'Frankie's wife, how's she bearing up?'

'I think we'd better have that talk,' said the Wing-Commander. And they arranged to meet that evening at the cocktail hour.

8

The Wing-Commander was not quite correct when he told the Archdeacon that 'a social worker from Reading' had taken care of all the remaining women and children from the convoy. It was true that Miss Bill had telephoned a social worker friend of hers, who had driven out to the vicarage and offered Rosie and her children some temporary accommodation, but some of the other women were afraid that their children would be taken into 'care', and they had found their own way down to the main road, where they had hitch-hiked to the motorway. A true dispersal had occurred, some of them drifting westwards in the hope of joining up with other Travellers, others wending towards London. Only Jay had remained.

Sally and Alison Bill, who seemed as thick as thieves, somewhat to Francis's surprise, had insisted that Jay must be put straight to bed. She was very ill, almost delirious with fever, and shivering fits. Alison Bill had offered to take her back to her cottage, an arrangement which Jay and Francis (neither of whom had the chance to offer an opinion) would have much preferred. But Sally had said that there was much more space in the vicarage. Alison Bill had made hot water-bottles, and, when Jay found herself lying in a clean bed for the first time in weeks, clothed in one of Sally's nightgowns, she was dimly aware, through her haze of illness, that Miss Bill was stroking her feet and wondering if it was malaria.

The full significance of what had happened – *that she was lying in bed in Francis's house* – had not quite occurred to her. She was too ill to notice much. She must have fallen asleep, and the next time she was aware of a presence by her bedside it was a doctor. Opening her eyes, she saw a tweedy, paunchy man, probably only in his thirties, but sporting a watch-chain across his ample, waistcoated belly. She did not like his cooing voice.

'Now, I've got to ask you this before I can help you. I'm not prying and, believe me, it will go no further, but you haven't been taking anything – any drugs?'

She had closed her eyes and wriggled about on the pillow. She did not want this man here with his questions, and his bloody *concern*.

'I smoke a bit of dope, yeah.'

'Nothing more serious?'

'No.'

'You can be honest with me. You see, this doesn't seem like 'flu to me. Are you getting night sweats at all?'

'Yes. And day sweats. I'm sweaty – can't you see that?'

'And you haven't been injecting yourself with heroin, or anything?'

Jay had started to cry at this point of the interrogation. How could this man dare to ask her such questions? If one of his 'respectable' patients had developed these symptoms, he would not have sat on their bed and accused them of being a junkie!

'Well, you'll need to drink a lot, to stop yourself getting dehydrated; and take as many aspirin as you can. We want to get that temperature down. How's the tummy?'

'Mmm?' Her incoherent, closed-eyes grunt was vaguely interrogative. What did he mean, how was her tummy? Was he accusing her of being pregnant on top of everything else?

'Have you got any diarrhoea or anything like that?'

Even in her weakness, Jay wondered what, in the doctor's experience, was 'like' diarrhoea.

'I'm fine,' she said.

'Well, you're not very fine, and it's rotten luck, rotten luck,' he said. 'I'll come back tomorrow to see how you are.'

He had no sooner gone than Sally had appeared. She had a habit, which Jay quickly found irritating, of poking her head and neck round the bedroom door. Like the doctor, Sally had a way of cooing at sick persons, old people and young children.

'Still feeling rotten?'

'Rather.'

'Dr Green said you were to have plenty to drink and plenty of aspirin.'

'Mm.'

The head had disappeared. Five minutes later – 'me again!' And she had brought aspirin and a jug of orange squash. The aspirin had a dramatic effect on her fever, which sank to near normal for about three hours. Jay had a very accurate sense of her own temperature, since Sally came in and out to measure it on a thermometer every hour or so. And thus the first day passed. Francis sat in his study for most of this day. He had been shocked to the depth of his being to discover that English policemen were prepared to use violence against harmless women and children. The whole experience had been ugly and frightening, and it would have been so whoever had been involved. The fact that Jay was one of the victims of this violence was simply intolerable, and he felt furiously angry, among the many other confused feelings which gripped him. He also felt afraid that his wife was going to take Jay into the vicarage as some way of punishing him for loving the girl so much. He knew that this was an absurd thing to feel: he knew that Sally was completely oblivious of the fact that he was in love with Jay. She was no actress, and if she had had an inkling of his feelings, she would never have been able to say, 'Aren't you going to go up and see her? I've put her in the spare room, poor lamb, and given her one of my nighties. I hope she's comfy.'

'I dare say she'll want some rest,' Francis had said.

He had walked up the road to Potter's Field, where Robin Pimm and two of his farm hands were tidying up.

'You wouldn't believe the muck those kids have made up here,' said the farmer. 'We found a dead dog and they hadn't even bothered to bury it.'

'The police killed a dog?'

'I wouldn't say that,' said Robin Pimm. 'Anyway, we buried her. Sheepdog. Fine dog. But look at that, I ask you. They've left a bloomin' bus in the middle of the field.'

All the other vehicles had been driven away, but the bus, which had only been propelled up the hill on Palm Sunday by some miraculous power, had finally died. And it remained, rusting quietly in the corner of Potter's Field for several years after that – a not unwelcome refuge for those whom Robin Pimm termed 'honest tramps', who still found their way into the village once in a while.

When he got back to the vicarage, he found his wife fussing with various filthy pieces of luggage.

'They left stuff here, those girls. I don't think it all belongs to her.' Sally's eyes danced aloft to indicate her sleeping beauty in the spare room. 'Some of it's junk.'

'We don't need to keep it,' said Francis. 'Except hers.'

'Funny not knowing her name,' said Sally.

'Yes, it is.'

'I mean, if we knew her name, we could give her mum a tinkle. She's ever so young, and I think she looks such a nice person. Imagine if Jess got into bad company like that when she was a bit older – 'cause she's only a kid, you know' – the eyes went aloft again to show that she was speaking of Jay – 'just a kid.'

There were about four plastic bags of the kind given away with groceries in supermarkets, stuffed with a variety of damp vests, old socks, and other such garments. One contained a Sony Walkman.

'I'll take it up to her,' said Sally – 'unless you'd like to.'

But it got left on the hall table until the next day.

The only interesting item of luggage was a blue cloth bag. It so happened that Francis was the first to look inside it, and, when he did so, he shut it up again at once.

'What's in there?' asked Sally.

'More junk.'

But he took it for safe-keeping into the study. Opening it made his heart pound. There were a handful of small stones – which might have been flint arrow-heads – and there was a larger piece of white stone, perhaps quartz. There was also a much larger object, wrapped in a torn, ribbed turquoise jersey, and he knew at once what it was going to be before he unwrapped it. Mrs Renton's crucifix! At first, he felt a simple lightening of the heart that this precious object had been found. He unwrapped it, and sat down, and put it before him on the desk. One of the ivory hands on the beautifully-carved figure had been snapped off, but it was otherwise unharmed. He felt about in the bag for the lost hand, but could not find it. He emptied the bag on to his blotter, and there came out some screwed-up paper tissues, half a packet of Golden Virginia tobacco, some cigarette papers, some strips of chewing gum, three odd socks, some men's underpants (filthy) and some sweet papers. A final shake of the bag produced the tiny hand, pierced and outstretched.

Francis had stood in front of this crucifix when it was placed on the Lady Altar in church, many times, and he had always seen it as an object of superb craftsmanship – the inlaid black and red wood, the suffering head of Christ falling to one shoulder, the stretched muscle over the collar-bone, and the folds of the loin-cloth, were all carved with profound sympathy. Staring at it now, however, in the purely secular setting of his study, he saw it afresh, this emblem of suffering and sacrificial love. And the words of the Mass came into his mind: 'who made there, by his one oblation of himself once offered, a full, perfect and sufficient sacrifice, oblation and satisfaction, for the sins of the whole world . . .' He felt a deeper sorrow than he had ever felt before that he could no longer pray to the Crucified in this hour of confusion. How many human eyes, for the last thousand years and more, had turned to this emblem, and found consolation in it! It was the most horrible, and the most gruesome and the most sadistic, of all possible spectacles, a young man nailed to the cross; and yet Christians had found it consoling; Francis had found it consoling, in the days when he had been able to believe that this was an emblem of the suffering of God himself.

And then one of those crazy, and almost blasphemous, reveries to which he was subject, allowed itself to play in his brain. He became convinced that Jay had stolen this crucifix. The conviction was infinitely painful, but it did not stop him loving her: the reverse. It occurred to him that great love, such as theirs, was surely destined to be, was always, redemptive: when two people met and fell in love, as opposed to feeling mere attraction, each became to the other a Redeemer. Each held out his arms, as if crucified, to the other. Each bore the sins and carried the reproaches of the other. Francis felt that nothing would ever allow him to let Jay suffer for her sin in stealing this crucifix. He must bear such suffering and punishment, if it were to come: if necessary, he thought wildly, he would even go to prison for her sake!

So intently did he follow these thoughts that he was only half-aware of his wife's voice in the hall, saying, 'Go on through, Gerrie, I think you'll find him there.'

The study door opened, and Gerald Spittle walked in.

Gerald Spittle had just discovered that his wife Lindie had posted their list of grievances to the Archdeacon. This precipitate and decisive action had filled him with panic. Far from being a monster of malice, Gerald was an essentially mild man who, for the sake of a quiet life, went along with most of his wife's opinions and ideas. He quite sincerely deprecated Francis's high church ways, his refusal to use jollier forms of service in church, his habit of hearing Mrs Renton's confession (which both the Spittles considered little better than Roman Catholicism), his friendship with 'that creature' Wells; and he shared her feeling that Francis had been snooty towards them ever since their arrival in the parish. Moreover, there could be no doubt in his mind that Francis had been extremely negligent about the parish since his mother had died: just the sort of occasion where one saw the value of Terry Widger's approach. (How many times had Terry said that the parish ministry was a team effort? It was so true!)

But Gerald Spittle had very mixed views about the sexual accusations in his wife's list of complaints. Sometimes, when she said that Francis had squeezed her bottom, he had felt so angry that he would have liked to go and punch the man's nose! But there were other things on that list where he thought Lindie was getting matters out of proportion. It was unforgivable that Francis should have even known about 'Eskimo Nell', which Gerald had heard more than once when he was doing his National Service; but he honestly did not think that Francis meant Lindie to go and find out what the words were: they had been printed in some filthy book of sex poems she had found in the Public Library. (The things people published nowadays!) Then again, there was the story of the broom handle in the vestry. Gerrie simply did not know what to make of this. If he had had to say anything about his vicar's sexual drive, he might have opined that Francis was a bit of an old woman, really. He had never himself heard the Vicar make so much as a suggestive remark, still less something really obscene about broom handles. Could it be that his wife was fantasising? She was always reading the most vulgar Sunday newspapers, and she seemed to enjoy dwelling on some of the filthiest stories they contained, particularly the stories about clergymen. Gerald himself did not feel able to challenge Lindie about these things. When she talked about them, Gerald tended to blush and did not know exactly what to say. Sex had never been a very big part of his marriage; it was more of a friendship, a partnership, two Spittles against the world, that kind of thing. He had always liked it that way, and assumed that Lindie had too. Her tendency to make wild and priapic accusations against the Vicar was not just embarrassing in itself. Gerald was afraid that if people knew Lindie had said such things they would somehow guess that he himself was impotent.

With these thoughts churning in his head, Gerald Spittle had come to the vicarage, not to make peace with the Vicar exactly, but, in his own phrase, to keep lines of communication open.

Francis, who was still furiously angry with Gerald after the confidences of the Wing-Commander, looked up at the man with unconcealed dislike, and, before any words had been spoken between them, destroyed the good will which Gerald had hoped to create by his visit.

'Hallo, Francis, I'm sorry to disturb you – well, I'll be jiggered.'

Francis could not see that Gerald was genuinely impressed to see the crucifix back again. Gerald did not know that Jay was asleep upstairs. Gerald did not know that Francis believed Jay to be the thief, though Lindie had made the same accusation in her letter to the Archdeacon. Gerald was simply pleased that the crucifix had been returned, and he imagined at first that the vicar had ingeniously found it – perhaps in Potter's Field, perhaps somewhere else. But Francis interpreted Gerald's smile as conspiratorial.

'Where did you find that?' asked Gerald, still smiling.

'I can't say.'

'I was wondering,' said Sally, who almost danced in at the door, 'whether I could tempt Gerald to stay for a coffee.'

'Will you *get out*?' said Francis.

'Isn't that the cross that was stolen? Oh, but that's wonderful! Where did you find it?'

'I was just asking the Vicar that very question, Sally.'

'I'm not going to answer it,' said Francis. 'Now, will you both leave me, please?'

Francis's anger, which was completely incomprehensible to both the other people in the room, and which, indeed, struck Gerald Spittle as insane, had the effect of making Gerald angry too.

'In that case, you wouldn't mind if I took it into safekeeping,' said Gerald, and he advanced towards the desk, and grabbed at the crucifix.

'Do you *mind*! Put that down at once!' said Francis.

'Not unless you say where you got it.'

'Suppose I didn't get it anywhere?'

'What are you saying? You took it yourself? We've put in an insurance claim for this cross in case you've forgotten! Is that your game?'

'How dare you say such things?'

'Oh, please, please, both of you!'

'I'm sorry, Sally, but I'm going to have to take this cross. If you want to know where I'm taking it, I'm taking it to Ronald Maxwell-Lee and if you want to know what I think we oughta do, I think we oughta ring the police and have some people locked up.'

Scarlet-faced, Gerrie Spittle had run from the room, carrying the crucifix, and they had heard the front door slam.

'Oh, love,' said Sally slowly and sadly – 'what's happened to you, love? What's happened?'

'I've asked you once before,' said Francis, 'will you please leave me alone?'

Upstairs, in bed, sleeping by fits and starts, Jay was entirely unaware of these dramas being enacted in the house. She had, in fact, no notion of the crucifix's whereabouts, and assumed that Mo had taken it to the pawn-shop some weeks before. She had been so horrified by the theft, and so frightened of the criminal world which she now saw Mo to inhabit, that it would never have crossed her mind to suppose that anyone, least of all Francis, could have suspected her of taking the precious object.

When evening came, Francis entered her room. At first, she pretended to be asleep.

'How are you?'

'I think my temperature's up again.'

'You should take some aspirin.'

'So your wife keeps saying.'

'Oh, Jay!'

He sat on her bed, and took one of her hot hands in his own. She squeezed it.

'All the others have gone?' she asked.

'Yes.'

'It's so awful. I keep thinking of Leila – you met Leila. She was such a lovely dog, Francis, and those horrible men, they just – they just.'

'I know.'

It was horrible to watch her cry.

'Robin Pimm buried her this afternoon,' he said. 'I thought you'd like to know.'

She did not ask who Robin Pimm was, but she said, 'Thanks.'

In other circumstances, this would have been, for Francis, a dream come true. He was sitting on the bed of the woman he loved, and she was allowing him to hold her hand, and squeezing his fingers affectionately. As it happened, it was all too painful and complicated to give either of them any pleasure.

'I didn't want to stay here. It isn't right.'

'You must stay. At least until you're better. Then we'll go away together.'

'Francis, don't! You know you can't! You can't leave them.'

From downstairs, they heard Jessica murdering a Haydn march. (And he had said his kid was musical!)

'I'm not going to let you go,' he said, and he leaned forward and planted a gentle kiss on her hot, moist forehead.

When he had gone, she could hear his voice, quite different in tone from when he addressed her, brusquely announcing, 'I think she's all right, but she probably needs some more aspirin.'

There were a few more hours before the household composed itself for sleep. Jay received two more visits from Sally, who looked as if she had been crying. She knew, when she looked into Sally's innocent, unhappy face, that this could not continue, this 'thing' between herself and Francis. It was now clearer to her than it had ever been before that Francis was in love with her. She had not asked him to fall in love with her! She had not led him on! It was something which had happened in spite of her. And now she found herself thinking of him so fondly, that she envied his harassed wife, with her scared, rodent-like eyes and teeth. When he sat on her bed, she found him – so beautiful, so simply beautiful! These thoughts were not conducive to a peaceful night.

Sally reappeared in the morning, Francis not. First, Sally brought her a glass of soluble aspirin, and a clean nightgown. She plumped up her pillows and asked what she would have for breakfast. She said that she did not want anything. Then Sally reappeared with the Sony Walkman from the hall table and asked Jay if it belonged to her. Jay said that she did not really want it; it did not belong to her, and she did not have any tapes to play. She put her head back on the pillow, thinking that this would give her half an hour or more's repose, but Sally came back again in five minutes.

'Me again! How are you?'

It seemed rude to say that she was more or less the same as five minutes earlier, so she said nothing.

'I've brought you a tranny,' said Sally. 'Nothing nicer than Radio Four when you're feeling a bit rotten.'

She switched on the 'Today' programme, which was just blending imperceptibly into 'Yesterday in Parliament', and placed the set just out of Jay's reach.

When she had gone, Jay stretched for the set and held it in her hand. For a moment, she thought that she was going to throw it at the back of the door. She hated Radio Four. Almost anything was 'nicer', in her view. From the breezy, middle-aged jokesters who chatted about the news in the early morning, to the pseudo-urgent journalism of the tea-time news programme, the whole jabbering Radio Four day was filled with things which Jay despised: quiz shows, sentimental dramas, programmes specially designed for women, human voices twittering about the problems of the disabled, the problems of single parents, the problems of pensioners, problems bloody problems. This was not what Jay wanted from a radio. When she had recovered from her desire to throw the set across the room, she twiddled the dial, and heard Heifetz in the middle of Beethoven's 'Spring' Sonata – the very same piece which she herself had played to Francis on that fateful day when she wandered into his church. It made her cry. It made her so sad, that she was almost glad when the music stopped and gave way to cricket. Jay quite liked cricket, supporting, in so far as she supported anything, Lancashire.

But Francis, what to do about Francis? The throbbing pains of 'flu had now passed, and the idiot doctor, who called again that day, admitted that his earlier diagnosis had been panicky. She had never spent three days like this in her grown-up life. If she had caught colds before, she had simply had to sniff and bear it. Three days in bed, being looked after by someone else, even in these very painful circumstances, had been quite nice. But it could not go on for ever. She realised this especially, when Sally put her head round the door and said, 'Jay?'

'Yes.'

Hitherto, Jay had been the girl with no name. Sally had

asked her name several times, but she had pretended not to hear or simply not replied. So, how had she heard it? Had Francis told his wife what she was called? There was no particular reason why he should not have done so, but it made Jay feel more vulnerable.

'You're wanted on the telephone, love.'

This was very surprising news. Her legs felt quite wobbly and peculiar as she came downstairs to the hall telephone, and she very much hoped that Francis would not come out into the hall and see her. She had never seen Francis with his wife and she was not sure how she would cope with that.

'Jay?' said the voice on the other end of the line.

'Yes.'

'It's Dave.'

'I know.'

'Jay, it's me.'

'I know, it's you. How did you know where I was?'

'It's norra secret, is it?'

'Of course not.'

'Eh? You living in sin with the Vicar?' His crude laughter disgusted her. She looked around anxiously to see if Sally was listening. She had disappeared. What if she were listening on the telephone extension in another part of the house?

'Eh, hey, listen. You've gorra get Mo bail.'

'What?'

'Can you get Mo bail? I was lerrof with a caution, but the bastards have got Mo. Possession of smack, yeah. They might even do him for supplying, which is just ridiculous.'

'I don't see how I can help,' she said cautiously.

'Get money off the Vicar, can't you?'

'Dave, I'm not – ' Oh, what was the point of trying to explain anything to this child, this silly little child?

'Hey, Jay?'

'What is it?'

'Gorra pencil?'

'Yes,' she lied.

She allowed Dave laboriously to dictate details; the names of solicitors; telephone numbers; an address in Kentish Town where he and some other refugees from the convoy were squatting.

'Oh, and another thing.'

'What?'

'One of the girls musta took me bag, I think. Me blue bag, 'cause I saw one of you holding it when I was dragged off.'

'Oh, God, Dave.' She knew the bag he meant, and she knew what it had contained.

'Hey, look. Gorra pencil, 'cause me money's goin' to run out? It's 071, right . . .'

But she had not rung back. She had gone upstairs, trembling with confusion and resolved on flight.

Later, while Sally was listening to *The Archers* downstairs in the kitchen, Jay had a bath and washed her hair. She felt very weak, but it was wonderful to be clean, and she had just remade her bed when Francis's kid poked her nose round the bedroom door.

Jay said, 'Hallo.'

To Jessica's ear, any manner of pronouncing the English language which did not conform to the standards of her group of friends – south-eastern and middle-class – sounded odd. For a whole term, when a new girl from Derbyshire had arrived at the school, they had mocked her pronunciation, and never hesitated to say 'pass the glass' to her whenever they saw her – since this was how the girl said the words rather than their own 'pahss the glahss'. Jay did not have a strong North Country accent (though she used short 'a's for words such as pass, glass, and bath). By Jessica's standards, her 'hallo' sounded like 'h'loa'. It increased the stranger's strangeness in the girl's eyes.

'Mummy says do you want any supper?'

'How kind! But – I . . .' Jay could not have endured to eat a meal with Francis and his wife, even though she had just started to feel hungry again after three days of consuming nothing but liquids. 'Perhaps I could come down and get an apple or something.'

'I'll get one,' said Jessica.

So far, no one in the household had spoken the mysterious stranger's name to one another. Sally was saving it up as her little surprise for them all at supper, having taken Dave's telephone call. She did not know that her husband was perfectly well acquainted with their guest, nor did she know that Mr Gadney had written to Jessica as 'Dear J': in fact, in spite of all her tender solicitude to her daughter, since Alison Bill had called at the house, no one could get to the bottom of Jessica's evident unhappiness.

Jessica could not get Mr Gadney's letter out of her head. Her father had been in London with another girl, whom he was passing off as his daughter, someone called J. It made her feel as though the foundations of life itself were no longer secure. If you could not depend on Daddy, who could you depend upon? She could not begin to understand her father's motives for this extraordinary deceit. Who 'J' was, Jessica had not the slightest idea. Why had it been so necessary to introduce her to the mysterious 'Uncle Eric' – again, a figure whom no one had explained to her. She felt knocked about by these mysteries, tricked, beguiled. Something was going on, something which they were keeping from her, and she could not endure this knowledge. It made her unable to talk to either of her parents, and she was frightened of talking about it to the worldlier of her friends for fear that they would mock her. There must be some explanation for 'J' and Eric, and it could not be a pleasant one.

She had a certain curiosity about the 'hippy' in the spare bedroom, and had talked quite a lot about it at school. Everyone had been talking about it. The incident with the police, and the break-up of the convoy, had even been on the local television news. Some of the more pretentious children at school said that they thought it was really cool to go on the road, take drugs, and flout the conventions of polite society, but most were still of an age to think it was 'stupid'. But, certainly, it was quite good to be able to boast that the Kreers had one of these strange creatures under their roof.

'Here you are,' she said, when she had returned with the apple. 'Mummy says you are very welcome to join us for supper if you change your mind.'

'Thanks. Did you have a good day at school?'

'It's really boring at the moment.'

There did not seem much future in this line of inquiry. Jessica stood for a disconcertingly long time in silence and stared into Jay's face, as if looking there for the clue to some unspoken puzzle.

'Do you think you're better?' she asked at length.

'Much. You've – all – been so kind to me.'

'Will you go soon?'

'Yes.'

Jessica wondered, as she descended for supper, whether this inquiry had been very rude; but there was surely a limit to the duration of the hippy's stay. Mummy was really over-excited, silly, about having the girl in the house, as if it was having a new puppy or a doll to play with! And it seemed to have cemented the friendship between Mummy and the Old Bill. Jessica did not like this new friendship at all. How *could* parents be so embarrassing? They could not be more embarrassing if they tried.

Supper was macaroni cheese; for palates which found this insufficiently stimulating, a bottle of tomato ketchup had been put on the table, and Jessica silently helped herself to a good dollop. Her father sat on one side of the kitchen table, quite silent and abstracted, while her mother sat on the other.

'How is she?' asked Sally. 'She's a pet.'

'She's very pretty,' said Jessica.

'And I found out her name today.'

Francis looked at his macaroni cheese. Jessica had eaten several mouthfuls.

'Yes,' said Sally brightly. 'She's called Jay. I don't know if it's just the initial J, standing for something else, or whether she's named after the bird Jay. Jay – it's a funny name, isn't it – darling, you have hardly touched that macaroni – darling! What is it?'

Jessica had blushed and risen from the table. By the time her mother asked the last question, she had left the room, slamming the door behind her.

9

'I see,' said the Archdeacon into the telephone. 'Crucifix,' he added, finishing the Wing-Commander's sentence for him. 'Well, Ronnie, what a turn-up for the books. Thank goodness it's been recovered, anyway . . . Yes . . . Yes . . . Well I, too, enjoyed our meeting . . . I quite agree with you, Ronnie. That's the last thing we want. I think I'd better have a word with Frankie, don't you? With Francis. Yup. Well, I'll give him a ring this morning. Well, I think there are several courses of action we could take. What we all need here is a cooling-off period. I think if I could persuade Frank to take let us say three months' sabbatical . . . That's right. Yup. Oh, I agree entirely, Ronnie, no need for publicity of any kind. . . .' The Archdeacon raised his eyes towards the heavens, and with exaggerated nods and smiles thanked his secretary for the coffee which she was bringing to his desk.

'Well, I'll certainly try to get to the parish fête. I think it's the sort of moment . . . quite! J-just what I was going to say . . . Ha, ha! B-b-bye, Ronnie. OK! Yes, I'll tell him that . . . Bye.'

'He's got me stammering now,' said the Archdeacon.

'I don't know if you want biscuits,' said his secretary. This morning, she was wearing a crisp blue and white blouse and a dark blue skirt. Her magnificent legs were shown off to the most alluring effect by 'opaque' lycra black tights. Wriggling further in to the knee-hole of his desk to conceal the effects which his secretary's appearance was having on his own anatomy, the Archdeacon sighed and said, 'Poor old Church of England! We could do without yet *another* scandal!'

'You don't think it's just female hysteria, then?'

The elegant Fiona never commented upon the letters she was required to write unless invited to do so by her employer. The Archdeacon trusted her completely, however, and in delicate cases such as this he liked to use her as a sounding board. How glossy her eyes were, and how much he would have liked to reach up and touch her thick, springy hair, and how *erotic* hair was on some people: how it made one think of the whole naked body, with hair in all its parts – the charming, downy little hairs on Fiona's arms, as well as the pubic hair which the Archdeacon found it so delightfully possible to envisage.

'I'm not sure that it is *just* female hysteria,' said the Archdeacon. 'On the other hand, it would seem from what the old Wing-Commander has been telling me as though Frankie Kreer has run a jolly good show at Ditcham over the last eighteen years.

A bit old-fashioned – but there's a place for that.'

'Of course,' said Fiona doubtfully.

'It'd just be so *sad* if it all got thrown away . . . just because of . . .'

Fiona's eyes nearly melted the Archdeacon when they looked straight into his own in that particular manner.

'Our bodies,' he said, 'play some funny jokes on us, don't they? Not that sex is just a question of the body.'

'I think that letter you wrote back to Mrs Spittle was very well-judged,' said Fiona. 'I think that should pour oil on troubled waters if anything could.'

Lindie Spittle had not, as it happened, been appeased by her typed letter from the Archdeacon. She considered it little less than an outrage that the man had not even suggested meeting her! Nor had he answered her letter point by point. 'I am certainly looking into the matter' was hardly a very reassuring phrase. And as for that paragraph, enjoining her to remember that we were all brothers and sisters in Christ, and not wishing to do anything which would sow discord or scandal in the Church – well! She could see through that one a mile off!

When she had told Gerald about this, he had looked quite blank, and merely gone a bit red.

'I said, I could see through that one a mile off! It's the establishment closing ranks,' she said. 'You see that, don't you, Gerrie?'

'Maybe it was a bit – hasty – to send that letter,' said Gerrie Spittle.

'Whose side are you on, Gerrie Spittle?'

'Do there have to be sides?'

'In this case, yes.'

'Lindie, I just think . . . It's all stirring up . . . I just don't know if you realise what you're doing, how it could rebound on you, on us. . . .'

'So now we know the truth!' said Lindie ominously. As Gerald looked at his wife on the other side of the breakfast table, he read in her features a terrible long-standing anger. He knew, without even wishing to fashion the thought into words, that the anger was really with *him*, and that all this trouble with the Vicar . . . His mind could not even finish the sentence. Just thinking about the subject was like trying to wade through a swamp; only out of that swamp now, like imps or little demons flying from the bowels of Hell itself, came buzzing all Lindie's pent-up sexual frustrations. He'd genuinely supposed that she had not much minded about that side to life! It had never meant much to him – not once he'd come to terms with the accursed fact that he could not function in bed. When you came to think of it, there could be nothing more farcical than the fact that all this anger, and all the potential scandals and horrors which the 'exposure' of the Vicar would cause, went back to the simple fact that Gerald Spittle's penis had not been erect for nearly twenty years. This harmless little piece of flesh, sitting soft as a limp balloon from which nearly all the air had been taken, accounted for so much: for the strange fraternal *solidarity* of the Spittles' marriage; for his craven willingness to defer to Lindie in all other areas, since he could not satisfy her in this; for her perpetual air of brisk crossness, now threatening to erupt into a torrent of crazy and perverted sex-feeling. He felt all this bubbling beneath the surface of her phrase, 'So now we know the truth!' He feared that she was prepared, if necessary, to expose them both to complete ridicule with other people in the village, just for the sake of her revenge; and she could not see that, in pursuing the Vicar with this intense malice, she was in reality punishing *him*, Gerald.

'All the men unite,' she said furiously. 'Well, we'll see about that. I want' – she sipped her coffee and chose a word carefully – 'satisfaction, Gerrie. And I'm not going to be palmed off with soft soap!' She waved the Archdeacon's letter as though it were an order paper and her husband was three hundred MPs listening to her wild speech.

10

'I just wish she'd left a note,' said Sally. 'Or anything. I mean, let's face it, what was she? A kid. Nothing more than a kid. I mean, she wasn't really that much older than you when you come to think of it.'

'She was grown up,' said Jessica.

'Jess, I thought you were supposed to be a sympathetic girl. What was it Miss Bill told me? "Jessica's such a kind person"?'

'Do shut up, Mum.'

'It's just not knowing where she is,' said Sally. 'I mean, supposing she's gone back to the tinkers, Travellers, whatever you call them. I don't think that all the hippies are very nice people.'

A commercial break had occurred in the television soap-opera which the mother and daughter were watching. Jessica liked to sing along with the lyrics of the advertisements, and knew most of them by heart.

'And she still wasn't very well, poor lamb. I wonder what on earth she was thinking of. I still think we should ring the police, in spite of what your Dad says.'

'The menu created for the way we live today,' sang Jessica.

'That's your Dad now.'

Hearing the front door open, Sally bounded to her feet. For the split second that she was blocking Jessica's view of the television, the child said, '*Mum!* You're in the way.'

Francis, who had driven further than Marlborough in one direction, and then back up the motorway, and down towards Salisbury Plain, hoped to slip unobtrusively into his study without a conversation with his wife. He had been out for two consecutive days in his car. Sally did not ask where he had been. She had tried to interest him in the fact that Jay had left the vicarage, without warning, and without so much as a note on the hall table. But he seemed quite impassive when she spoke of these things. It was as though he did not care at all. She was shocked by his indifference. The only time he became animated was when he told her that she was on no account to call the police.

Sally did not quite *want* to know where Francis had been. Since she had developed her friendship with Alison Bill, she had become convinced that 'men' did the most terrible and childish things. Who would have guessed that Alison, who had always struck Sally as such an innocent, would have known about things like that? It both horrified and fascinated Sally. Alison had not spelled anything out, but there was such implied knowledge in her smile.

Sally found it supremely comforting at this difficult time to have a friend like Alison, someone who would not only listen to all her troubles, and seem quite unshocked by them, but who would provide physical comfort. ('Literally', Sally had thought, in a phrase which pleased her, 'a shoulder to cry on.' She loved it when Alison held her in her arms, and stroked her hair.)

'The Archdeacon phoned,' said Sally.

'So I see,' said her husband, who had picked up the pad in the hall where telephone messages were written down.

'He kept ringing – twice this morning, and twice this afternoon.'

'So I see.'

'And the Matron of Gilkes Court rang.'

'I see, and I've forgotten to take them their bloody Communion.'

Francis's visits to this old people's residential home had been regular and unfailing. His use of bad language in this context was quite uncalled for; a sign, however, as Sally now realised, that he needed help. Forcing her face into an imitation of one of Alison's broad smiles, she said, 'Darling, don't you think we ought to talk?'

Francis stared coldly at his wife. He had often seen idiot expressions pass over her features, but this one was the most supremely idiotic that he had ever seen. He ignored her words, and went into his study, slamming the door. As soon as he was there, he reached behind the Lewis and Short Latin Dictionary and poured himself a large slug of whisky.

Francis Kreer throbbed with exhaustion which had possessed his body and his brain for half the week. When Jay had disappeared, he had developed the certainty that she would go to rejoin one or another of the group of Travellers who had set out on the road when their own convoy was broken up by the police. First, he had had some luck. He had found one hippy, Compton by name, who had been very helpful. This Compton had been camping not far from Ditcham in an area known as Pixton Heath, where some of the Travellers had spent the winter. Francis had found him there, sitting on the steps of a gipsy caravan with a goat and a little child who might have been the Christ-child in the legend of St Christopher – or another of the angels not angles in the story of St Gregory.

'Jay, right!' Compton had said – quite unsurprised that anyone might be seeking her.

'But Jay must be with Mo, no, and Mo is arrested?' The sing-song inflexion of the voluptuous Scandinavian girl (Irma) who came out of the Dormobile, parked alongside the gipsy caravan, had been puzzling to Francis. But Compton, who seemed all-knowing, had said, 'No – Mo was arrested. Jay – she went with you, right?'

'She came to stay in my house.'

'That's right. You'll find her!' said the sage, with closed eyes and a bony hand swaying in the rhythm to his curious mode of utterance. 'I know she'd have wanted to go to find herself,' said Compton. And then he had smiled a secretive smile. 'That's a long journey for some people.'

Compton did not tell Francis that Jay was on the road; in fact, at one point, Compton had actually said, 'She might have gone back to London, like to see her old friends. You know the police broke her violin – Jay'll've minded that.'

But he took no heed of this. He became obsessed by the belief that his Papagena – almost his Papageno, warbling her native woodnotes wild – would not have gone back into the city. So, he had begun his crazy search, motoring from encampment to encampment, from convoy to convoy, asking questions and getting nowhere. He did not realise how lucky he had been to come upon Compton; nor did he realise how rare it had been to persuade Compton to talk. He took this first encounter as the herald that there would be many; that, as in a paperchase, diligence would eventually lead him to his darling prey. And, in fact, there had been no other clues. Every mile he drove – and he had now driven for hundreds of miles, until his eyes were tired, and his back ached, and the car engine was hot and dry – had been a journey devoid of purpose.

Once seated at his desk, Francis removed that envelope from his pocket, and read Jay's letter again.

> Dear Francis, I have got to leave this house, and you know why. If you knew me better, you would have an even clearer idea why I must, simply must leave you. I do not think that Rosie and the other girls thanked you and Sally properly for taking us all in at the beginning of this terrible week. I know what risks you and Sally both took in doing this. Thank you both for your Christian courage. Thank you for being our friends. I shall miss you, Francis, but that is why I have to go. XXXX Jay.

This was the letter which he had read repeatedly over the last three days. He had found it on the hall table before he set out to church one morning at 7 a.m. Of course, he had not communicated its contents to his wife, who was not even aware of its existence. She did not even find out that Jay had gone – silly fool – until about a quarter past nine, after Jessica had left for school.

'Jay's sleeping late,' Sally had said, and skipped upstairs, opining that the girl would probably like 'a coffee' to wake her up!

Francis's mind was totally obsessed by the letter. It churned round and round two fixed processes of thought. In the first of these, he focused on the sentence *Thank you both for your Christian courage*. Although the surface meaning of this sentence was to thank Sally and himself for daring to befriend the Travellers when the rest of the village were so hostile to them, Francis read beneath the surface an injunction to uphold the sanctity of Christian marriage. It was literally true that he and Jay must part if his whole world was not to collapse: his marriage, his ministry, his job, his house, his relationship with his daughter. He knew that to pursue this beautiful girl, whom he hardly knew, would spell disaster for everyone in his life, as well as for Jay herself. He also knew, because Francis Kreer had not lost all judgment, that if he were prepared to undergo six or eight weeks of agony, he would probably be able to 'get this girl out of his system'. It was possible to 'get over' people. He no longer wept when someone mentioned his mother. However much he felt that his soul would perish if he did not find Jay, and declare to her undying love, he knew that the virtuous path was to suffer for her. This would be the best thing for Jay, too. What would it be like for her to throw in her lot with an impoverished and disgraced priest very nearly fifty years of age? All her friends would desert her, or mock her. If he truly considered her happiness, he would let her go! But this thought, that by moving in to her life he would drive all the 'others' away, was profoundly beguiling, and set his mind off on its other obsessive track, which was to believe that Jay had written the letter because she loved him. This knowledge filled him with an intensity of joy which made him shake. If she did not love him, there would be no danger in her remaining in the house. The fact that she had written the letter, and left, meant that Jay wanted him to follow her. Although it was such a short communication, he had pondered it to the point where it no longer really made sense unless it was meant to make him 'leave all and follow her'. Christ was the type of absolute love, who made this demand of his followers, to forsake their fishing-nets and their families, and to give up everything, even their own dignity, to follow after him. By the same token, all Love partook of this Christ-like demandingness. *Love so amazing, so divine, demands my soul, my life, my all.*

In this reading of the letter, all the carefully-phrased, scrupulous references to Sally and her kindness had been blotted out. The first few times he had read the letter, it had hurt him that Jay had so written that it would not have compromised him – much – to show the letter to his wife. It did not allude to their secret trysts, their visit to London, their shared confidences and conversations.

'I shall miss you, Francis, but that is why I have to go.'

The neat, rather small italic in which this was penned now told a story to him of a passion which she had been unable to conceal. At first, he had been disappointed in the handwriting. In his earlier musings about Jay, he had made her into a creature of pure nature. The fact that she had been a student, attended a school, passed 'A' levels, did not prevent him from forming this image of her in his head. Now, he re-made her again in a different image; she became a demure, delicate runaway, who needed his protection, needed his money! That was it! She was so delicate, morally, that she was afraid to take his bounty. She had gone, because she knew how willingly he would have run away with her and given her everything, a little house by the sea, a new violin, different clothes.

'Dear Francis, I have got to leave this house, and you know why. . . .'

How could she have penned these words if she had not wanted him to know that she too was seized by the same, terrifying, but deeply joyful madness as his own: by the knowledge that they were in love?

This meditation was interrupted by the telephone. Putting down his whisky glass, he went to answer it in the hall.

It was Jay's voice on the other end.

'Hullo! Hullo! Is that Ditcham 317? Hullo? Is that the vicarage?'

'Jay!'

He shouted her name, so that his wife and daughter, sitting in the lounge, could not avoid hearing it.

'Look, I'm in a call box in London! Francis – Sally?'

'Jay, it's *me*.'

'Hullo? Oh damn!'

It was possibly the most frustrating experience of his life. He could hear her voice, but she could very evidently not hear his. This infernal trick of the telephone could not be overcome by shouting, even though he bellowed her name over and over again.

Just before the telephone rang, Sally and Jessica had been sitting together in front of the television. Francis had been closeted in the study for over two hours.

'You'll be ever so tired,' Sally said. 'Late girl.'

Jessica had been staying up late in the hope that, in spite of his mysterious absences and his air of distraction, her father would put his head round the door and say, 'Game of chess, anyone?', as he had done in the old days before he 'went funny'. Something in his demeanour that evening when he had returned in the car had frightened her, so that she did not dare to intrude on his privacy in the study.

'Like some tea?' persisted Sally.

The daughter's 'Mmmm' – she had a mouthful of hair and was staring impassively at the conjuring tricks on the television – signified a negative.

'Done your homework?'
This 'Mmmm' signified 'yes'.
'Shall I do you a packed lunch for tomorrow?'
'Could you, Mum?'
This packed lunch, a throw-back to primary school days, was a new craze among Jessica's circle of friends, instituted by the tiresome Sarah Mackintosh, who was 'on a diet'. The predictable protest had been raised by all the 'mums' – that a little tub of yoghourt was not sufficiently nourishing in the middle of a school day, that shopping for celery and bits of cheese was a bore, and that washing up the filthy tupperware each evening was more trouble than you'd think – but they had all gone along with the packed lunch thing.
'Oh, and Mum?'
'What, lamb?'
'Can I have crispbread and cream cheese rather than a peanut-butter sandwich?'
'Jay!' They heard Francis calling in the hall. It was not simply that he was shouting. The bellow, the roar, sounded so unlike his normal voice that both his wife and daughter had a moment, as they looked at one another, of fearing that the house had, once more, been invaded by burglars.
'Dad!' It was Sally who called. Jessica was beginning to be embarrassed by her mother's habit of calling her husband 'Dad'. 'Do you think we should go and see?' asked Sally quietly.
'Leave him,' said Jessica. 'He's probably . . .'
After the yelling, an ominous silence. The conjuring tricks had resumed on the television, and Jessica obviously had the gift, denied to her mother, of absorbing herself completely in the drug of television, especially at moments of high tension. Sally had stood up. Her hands flew nervously to her mouth, then down to her waist, then to her breast, as if they were searching for something.
'I'll just go and see,' she said at length. But a good ten minutes had passed, in which mother and daughter had said nothing to one another, and the television had hypnotised Jessica. In fact, the girl hardly noticed that her mother had left the room. She noticed, however, when Sally gasped 'Oh God, oh God!' from the hall.

Going to see what had happened, Jessica found her mother standing with her mouth open, and her cheeks streaming with tears. In her hand was a letter from Francis, but she was incoherent and could not communicate its contents.

'That's Dad! I can hear him – he's moving the car,' said Jessica. They could indeed hear the engine revving in the garage. They themselves left the house by the front door and stood under the carriage lamp in the little porch. They were just in time to see the Maestro reversing out of the garage into the drive. If Francis Kreer saw them, he did not respond to their frantic waves. At the gate of the short drive they stood on the gravel in their stockinged feet and watched the red rear lights roar down the hill, and turn the corner out of sight.

II

The next day was the parish fête.

'Everything all right?' the Wing-Commander called out. He had walked out on to his lawn and found the Spittle man squatting to inspect the guy ropes of the marquee. Surely the lines of demarcation were quite clearly drawn? The marquee was, and always had been, the Wing-Commander's responsibility. He arranged for the hire of the thing, and it was erected on his lawn by professionals. Before Ronald Maxwell-Lee joined the PCC, they had not even *had* a marquee; so, marquees were quite definitely his pigeon. The Spittles had clawed for themselves enough areas of responsibility. It was really rather a pity, considering there were some first-rate gardeners in the village, such as Dorothy Maxwell-Lee and Edith Renton, that Lindie Spittle should have taken upon herself the role of organising what she called 'a garden festival' in the church. Dorothy had been very good about it, as she was good about everything, but she and Ronald had been unable to resist some quiet smiles, in private, in prospect of Lindie's floristry displays. Gerrie Spittle had agreed to man the Tombola, and to oversee the Lucky Dip. All the other stalls and functions had been assigned: home-made cakes, white elephants, plants, each had their organisers; so had the various activities – the tail on the donkey, or the 'stocks' where, very sportingly, the padre had agreed to sit for an hour and be pelted with wet sponges. (Now, poor devil, it seemed all too appropriate that he should be pilloried by the village!) The Wing-Commander took quiet pride in the fact that every sphere had been assigned its appropriate officiant: Edith Renton on cakes; Alison Bill the tail on the donkey, and so forth. Now, along came Spittle, self-appointed tester of guy ropes.

Ronald Maxwell-Lee, who had been over for a glass of sherry with the Archdeacon, felt that they had reached a very satisfactory conclusion. As soon as the fête was over, he would take Francis Kreer aside and urge him to take a three-month sabbatical. The Archdeacon had said that they would arrange a suitable 'locum' to take his place, though he seemed a little downcast that Ronald did *not* believe 'Father' Wells to be a suitable replacement. For his part, Ronald agreed to take the Spittles in hand. Some of their complaints were justifiable. Some were insufferable. Some made you wonder, perfectly honestly, whether the woman was off her trolley. The Archdeacon had been really very amusing about this, and said that the Church of England had more than its fair share of nutty women. Ronald, on his third glass, had amused the Archdeacon with an account of Alison Bill's famous 'crush' on Francis, one of the standing jokes of village life in Ditcham.

'Are you looking for something?' asked Maxwell-Lee as he looked down at Spittle's squatting form.

'Only, I remember Terry Widger telling us' – he gulped in a laugh at the recollection – 'of this parish fête, function, whatever, which was quite literally a flop! Literally! The tent flopped down on all the good ladies in their finery, oh dear me!'

'This marquee has been put up by a firm of professionals,' said Ronald Maxwell-Lee. 'We've been using them for years.'

'Oh, I'm sure it will be fine.' In defiance of his own words, Gerrie stooped once more and tried to force an immovable peg even further into the ground. 'That should fix it,' he said, going rather red as he expended this effort. 'There's only one thing, Ronald, which slightly saddens me about our parish party, Ronald.'

Unkindly, the Wing-Commander did not ask what this 'one thing' was, so Gerrie had to continue unprompted. 'And that's that we haven't made it more of an opportunity for mission.

Now, take Terry Widger. He was perfectly clear in his mind about this. He'd say, "This isn't just any old bring and buy sale, it's a church event, it's an event for God's people. Nothing against them enjoying themselves, but let them enjoy themselves in the Lord." So, we had a group of Gospel Singers on a small stage; we had an information tent where anyone wanting to know more *about* the Bible, or *about* the Church . . .'

'That sort of thing would put people off,' said the Wing-Commander, adding, mysteriously, 'in the country. Sometime, Gerrie, we must have a word about that little matter you discussed with me.'

'Well, it was really that that I'd come to see you about, Ronald. I mean to tell you the honest truth, man to man, I'm *worried*. I'm worried about Lindie. I'd hate this to get out of hand, if you understand me. . . .'

'Perhaps this isn't the best mo-mo-moment, Gerrie. Here comes your g-good lady now.'

'Oh he's *done* it this time!' exclaimed Lindie Spittle. 'Today of all days.'

Later, she would go home and change; now she was in working-gear – a white nylon roll-top jumper and brown slacks. It was slightly too warm an outfit for such a fine summer's morning, and already the nylon top was stimulating perspiration.

'What's Francis done now?'

In spite of feeling very cross with Francis since their quarrel, the Wing-Commander always felt an upsurge of tenderness for the priest when Mrs Spittle was in sight.

'The church is locked, would you believe? On the day of the parish fête. Of course I did!' – this last phrase in answer to an immediate inquiry by both men, whether she had been round to the vicarage for the key.

'Probably overslept,' said Ronald Maxwell-Lee.

'I don't know where he thinks he is; I noticed the car wasn't in the garage.'

'That's odd,' said the Wing-Commander, looking at his watch. It was 8.30 a.m.

'Sally opened the door. Gerrie, I think we should call the police.'

'Oh, *really*, Lindie.'

'Gerrie, that woman's face! Something is going on in that house, and I shouldn't be surprised if it wasn't satanic abuse, I really shouldn't. She looked – oh, she looked awful, I can't describe it.'

'Did she give you the key?' asked the Wing-Commander.

'We searched high, we searched low.'

'Well, look here, I've g-g-got a key to the vestry.'

As the three made haste to the church, Lindie pointed out that this vestry key would not open the church. The public, when they came to see her flower festival, could not squeeze through this narrow and cramped entry; they must approach through the south door of the church. This was the key which had apparently gone missing.

Outside that door, already wilting somewhat in the rising sun, the elements of her floral displays strewed the ground. Three large cardboard trays contained stripy petunias. There was another boxful of French marigolds, and another of bizzie lizzies. Vases which would have looked more at home in Lindie's lounge sprouted their carefully-arranged displays of pinks, gypsophila and maidenhair fern. These strangely dry-looking arrangements seemed as if they might have been fashioned out of sugar-icing.

'We've got to get all those in – and there's the font to decorate properly, and the pulpit, and Miss Norbury is coming to do the window-ledges; and then there's the kiddies' garden. . . .'

'There'll be plenty of time,' said Ronald Maxwell-Lee as he led the way to the back of the church.

'But, I mean, today of all days to choose! Isn't that absolutely typical of that man. I mean, look at all the stuff we've got to get into church.'

As they struggled through the vestry with the pots and the boxes (the Wing-Co could imagine what Dorothy and Edith would make of those zinnias!), the vicar's warden said, 'We could have waited for Francis to come back. He's probably gone to take sick communion to someone.'

For emphasis, Lindie put down her cardboard box, which contained rubber gloves, scissors, green florist's sponge, wire mesh, and several bottles of plant feed.

'I could have cried myself,' she said. 'That woman's face.

Anyway, she just stared at me with these big open – well, you could tell she'd been crying and her mouth was, you know, trembling, and I said, I mean, "It's the day of the fête. Have you forgotten the fête?" Well, I don't know if she's on drugs but nothing would surprise me in that household. But I said to her, "I've got to get into the church, Sally".'

Neither man felt that they needed to hear the narrative of the lost key for a third time, so the Wing-Commander interrupted with, 'I'd better go and see what's up.' When he said 'I', he really meant it, and had not expected Gerald Spittle to accompany him.

Inside the vicarage, where she had been awake for most of the night, Sally was wandering about in tears. She could not stop herself moving – now in the kitchen, now in the hall, now in the drawing-room, now up and down the stairs – she was perpetually on the move. She clutched the Dog Frumpy, but he was little solace. No one could unwrite that cruel, cruel letter of Francis's, no one. Sally wished she was dead.

> Dear Sally, I am leaving you. There is no kind way in which I can tell you this, but this is a letter of farewell. You and I have not been happy together for years. I had assumed that this was an unavoidable position. Now I have discovered a new happiness. You have probably guessed that I can only be happy with Jay . . .

The Dog Frumpy tried to whimper to her that silly Francis would come back, but Sally was a little bit older than Frumpy, and she knew that his letter had been true. She felt very angry with Francis for having written in that way, scaldingly angry: did he really expect her to understand that his happiness was more important than anything – more important than their family life together, more important than Jessica's happiness? Did he? And how did he think it would make her feel to be told that he had not been happy with her? They had their ups and downs like all married couples, but Sally had always thought that, when his funny 'moods' lifted, they knocked along together all right. Then, again, that girl! Oh, Sally felt such a fool, a fool, a fool!

Presumably the 'thing' whatever it was (surely not a full-blown affair? Oh, God!) had been going on for weeks under her very nose. Presumably she was the last person in Ditcham to find out about it. Jess had known. *That* was why Jess was so unhappy, poor little thing! Sally felt humiliated, crushed, hurt. Oh, it was like the sort of thing you read about sometimes in the newspapers: naughty vicar. Oh, she did not want to be married to a naughty vicar, she didn't, she didn't. (It had always slightly hurt Sally that he did not, with her, wish to be a bit more naughty.) Worst of all, she felt wounded, gored, hurt in a way and to an extent which she had never conceived it was possible to be hurt – winded, flattened, destroyed, by the thought that her man, her husband, hers, *hers* had been with *that* girl. And the girl had lain here, bold as brass, in their house. And all the village had known about it. And he had chosen to run away on the day of the parish fête, so that all the village would be coming to the door and asking for keys and wondering where their naughty vicar was and she would have to make excuses and oh! she could kill him, kill him, kill him! And oh! how she longed for him, and if the Dog Frumpy were right, and if she could blink and find it had all been a bad dream, she would welcome Francis back and love him and never have another angry thought again!

Jessica, for the rest of her life, retained the sharpest possible memory of her mother at that moment – an almost demented creature in a candlewick dressing-gown, running from room to room. Jessica herself suffered at that time, and her suffering was to unfold and deepen, becoming, for years, her almost constant companion. But, often, when she heard the word 'suffering', or heard someone discourse on it, she thought of Mummy running to and fro. Human suffering is so seldom revealed to us raw and total, in life. To look at it in its full naked cruelty, human beings have to do so through the glass of art, through the Pietà of Michelangelo, or the grief of Achilles for Patroclus in the *Iliad*, or the tears of Christ in Gethsemane. Jessica knew, as she recalled the morning her father left, that she had seen suffering of this raw and undisguised intensity in her mother's face, a face which was not merely tear-stained, but torn about and distorted by pain.

When suffering forced from her yet more tears, Sally no

longer made an effort to blow her nose or wipe her eyes or stop her mouth from dribbling. Skeins of moisture dripped from her face, as though misery itself was bursting forth in a cruel ectoplasm.

'Door!' Jessica shouted at her mother, for she had an habitual shyness about answering the door-bell, even when it was someone quite unthreatening, such as the postman.

Her mother stood there, gibbering. Her words might have been 'Go, go'; but it was equally possible that she had reverted to babyhood and was saying 'Goo, goo'.

'Yes?' said Jessica, opening the door a crack.

Wing-Commander Maxwell-Lee stood there, with the Spittles.

'Is your mother in?'

'I'm afraid she's a bit busy just at the moment.'

'You see, um . . .' Jessica knew that the Wing-Commander had difficulty remembering her name. She did not help him out. 'Um,' said the Wing-Commander, 'um.'

'There's a flower festival in the church; tell your Mum about that. Isn't your Dad in?' – it was the Spittle woman who shoved her oar in here.

'I'm very sorry, but both my parents are rather busy at the moment.'

'So he *is* in?' Lindie persisted. 'Couldn't you go and remind him that it's the parish fête today – as if he'd forgotten.'

'It's just,' said the Wing-Co in more conciliatory tone, 'um, we just wondered if we could have the key to the ch-ch–'

'Church,' said Gerald Spittle.

'Ch-church, he's – easily d-done – forgotten to unlock the church and – if we could come and . . .'

'We're going to have all the village coming to this festival, and if they can't come into the church through the south porch, it's going to be a disaster.'

'Yes, all right, Lindie' – Gerrie seemed as though he was half-enjoying his wife's agitation. 'But we'll get the key. I'm sure that Jessica will help us find the key.'

'I'm sorry,' said Jessica, 'they are both very busy. They can't come to the door just now.'

The key was found eventually; it was on the hall table where it was always kept. For some reason, it gave Jessica a quiet satisfaction to know that the Spittles and the Wing-Commander had not been allowed into the vicarage to find it. The Old Bill had found it. Whether she had come of her own accord, or as an emissary from the parish, Jessica never determined. Her arrival at the vicarage was as unwelcome to the child as it was needed by the mother. The two women spent hours, closeted together. Jessica wondered how she would ever face *anyone* at school, ever again. It was not that *they* would know: it was that she knew that the Bill had been in the house, heard all her Mum's secrets, held Mum, kissed Mum. So deep were the two women in these sessions of mutual comfort that they did not answer the telephone. After it rang a few times, Jessica answered it. Her father sounded so strained – as if he himself might have been weeping. She did not show him mercy. She rather hated him for ringing up, because it was that telephone call which suddenly made his departure real for her. Because of the shock of her mother's unhappiness, Jessica's own reaction was delayed by a few hours. She knew it was real as he spoke on the telephone: and he had not rung up to ask how she was, even though this was what he had protested: he had rung up to ask her to pass on some message, either to the Bill or to the Wing-Co, about the services on Sunday morning. Damian Wells was to 'cover' for the next few Sundays. That was the message, but Jessica did not feel like passing it on.

12

Mo returned from the nettle-patch, just off the tow-path, where he had just emptied the contents of his stomach. Most of this cleansing had occurred through his mouth, but there had also been a very moist squitter into what served him for underpants. Either his body was passing through a new stage of strange dependency, or the substance which he had injected into his foot (other veins being rather sore from his frequent jabbings) was not all that Martyn had promised.

Martyn was Mo's new friend, his old friend, his master. Martyn had paid for bail, and produced a good junkie's lawyer for Mo at the magistrates' court; the case had been dismissed on insufficient evidence. Martyn knew that Mo needed looking after. If Mo got done for possession, or even for supplying, then it would not take the police long to get Martyn's name out of Mo's strange, pale, sweaty, drug-infested skull! And when they had Martyn's name, and started to do *him* for his range of activities, then they'd start to have a lead on some *really* big operations; and the boys who ran those operations would not thank Martyn if he had proved the weak link in the chain. No-oh. So, better keep young – or not so young – idiots like Mo on a short chain till they kill themselves with the stuff, rather than let them go running off to the filth.

Or so it seemed to Martyn as he sat with Mo and a group of the man's friends at the lock in Camden Town. It was the spot where the canal forms a small basin, between the TV AM studios, the large Sainsbury's Superstore, and a pub called the Devonshire Arms. Many of Mo's friends and acquaintances, some of them known to Martyn, some of them Martyn's customers, sat about on the grass, or dangled from the lock-gate. Some of them had brought over drinks from the pub; others drank out of cans. Some smoked cigarettes, others smoked dope, as they baked themselves in the exceptionally hot June sunshine.

Martyn must have been the hottest of them all, in his lime-green suit, his co-respondent shoes and his large white hat, something between a stetson and a sombrero. It was hard to tell what Martyn was thinking, because he wore impenetrable shades – little round ones which from the outside were looking-glasses.

'I don't sympathise, Mo.' The speaker was Jay, who, perhaps of all those who sat around on the grass, knew the reason why he had just been sick.

'Hey, lady,' said Martyn, 'don't be so hard on your man.'

The display of teeth which followed this injunction could have been mirthful, could have been merely threatening.

To Jay's eyes, Mo looked terrible: deathly pale, and with a cold corpse-like moisture on his face which was especially sinister on so hot a day. His clothes were filthy, and his hair fell down from either side of his face in oily straggles. Jay herself had not fully recovered from the 'flu, and the bright sunshine emphasised her own pallor. She wore, however, a very clean shirt which had been given her that morning by one of the girls in the squat.

'He's not my man,' said Jay.

'Hey, Jay, stop giving Mo a hard time, right?' This speaker was Dave. 'It's tiring just listening to you two.'

'So,' said Mo, 'you split from me, and you gone an' screwed a fuckin' priest and the minute you come up to London you come runnin' after me? Is that it?'

'I didn't come running after you, Mo, right?'

'You're pathetic.'

'Mo, I had nowhere to stay, right? I tried to go back to share with Hilary and Alexander – the people I shared with when I was a student. . . .'

Mo made the rest of the company laugh by putting on a very 'posh' voice and repeating, 'When I was a student.'

'And I bump into, literally bump into, Jane' – this had been one of the women who camped in Potter's Field at Ditcham, but Jay had barely known her – 'and she offered me a room for a few nights, *OK*? A few nights in her place, *OK*? You don't live with her.'

'Look,' said Dave, 'we were in that squat months before Jane ever moved in. I was living there when I first met you.'

'It doesn't matter who was living there when, Dave.' Jay hated sounding so pedantic; what was the point in attempting to have a rational conversation with these *fools*? And yet, even as she made these speeches, she felt an appalling guilt. She heard herself, and she knew how uncharitable it all sounded. It went without saying that her love affair with Mo was over. But he was a pathetic human being whom she had it, perhaps, in her power to help. Jay did not believe in providence, but she had long ago formed in her mind an idea which was not, in fact, original to her: namely that, since there is no personal divinity, we alone have it in our power to exercise 'the love of God' towards our fellow mortals. An indifferent fate would cast rubbish like Mo aside. Jay felt that it was unworthy of her to wish, so deeply, to side with fate over this particular question. She knew that the higher good was to rescue Mo. It was a cursed bit of bad luck that she had ever run into that girl Jane, so shortly after coming back to London. It was an even worse bit of luck to have run into Mo and his gang of cronies, who had turned up at the squat in the middle of the night, while she was asleep, and actually bedded down, some of them, on the floor of the room where she slept. Having met up with him again, she was torn between an unworthy desire to run away and leave them all, and a sense that duty demanded that she give Mo into the hands of some people who could help him. Once he had been handed over to a drug rehabilitation centre, or a social worker, or a nurse, or someone who saw the extent of his problem, then Jay would regard herself as morally free of the man. Until she had overseen this first step on the road to Mo's recovery, she would herself be a passive participant in his downfall. For the sake of what they once had together (even though, perhaps it was not what she would now call love) and for the sake of common human decency, she must deliver Mo out of the hands of Martyn.

One of Jay's 'Buddhist' ideas was that there was not such a person as a 'good' or a 'bad' man. There were only people enslaved to a greater or lesser degree by the chains of desire. In the case of Martyn, Jay considered a wholesale revision of this viewpoint. She had heard of Martyn on a number of occasions before she met him: Mo had usually spoken of him with amusement, first of all alluding to his absurd clothes, his 'funky' tastes in music. In those early allusions, Martyn had been yet another of Mo's dupes – a man who apparently did not know the street value of smack and who was selling stuff at really stupid prices. Little by little, Jay noticed that Mo spoke of Martyn with greater respect. It was Martyn who had given him the name of the pub in Reading where Mo and Dave had gone so regularly. It was Martyn, apparently, who had provided them with a useful 'fence' for odd bits of stolen property which they were able to move his way. Martyn, Jay realised before the convoy broke up, was a man of power. But it was only a reunion with this man, with his strange impassive face, and his invisible eyes hidden behind mirror-shades, that decided Jay that Mo was Martyn's creature. Martyn was running Mo, using him, filling his body with substances, which he craved more and more, and requiring him to be ever more slavish in his attitude to Martyn and Martyn's masters. She herself felt threatened by Martyn. She disliked very strongly his attitude to her sex. Sometimes he called her Mo's 'missus'. Without being melodramatic, Jay did not think it was impossible that Martyn would have inveigled her – if he could have found a way – into some form of slavery herself. She knew that the fact that she did not really use drugs, and that she had shaken free of an emotional involvement from Mo, put her in a position of strength; she knew that she, and perhaps, in that situation, she alone, could challenge the evil which Martyn represented and embodied. But she also felt desperately lonely in this position, which was why, on the pretext of a weak bladder, she had disappeared so many times into the Devonshire Arms in order to telephone Francis. Given the emergency – the surprise meeting with Mo, his desperate physical state – she felt that she must subsume, and so must Francis, whatever emotional crisis had been reached in their own lives. Francis the parish priest was surely in a position to know what to do in this circumstance. He had coped so magnificently when the convoy was broken up. He could cope again. And she missed having a grown-up to consult – it was hell to have fallen in once more with her old friends – and she missed *him*.

'Jay' – Mo had adopted his wheedling tone – 'I feel really thirsty, you'll buy me a drink, won't you?'

'What with?'

'Money. You got money in that purse, I saw. Give me your purse, I'll go, buy the drinks.'

'Mo, you're crazy. I haven't got money. Why do you think I'm staying with Jane if I've got money? Because I'm skint, because after the filth bust up the convoy I've lost all my cards, and I can't get new ones 'cause it's a Saturday afternoon in case you hadn't noticed.'

She heard again in her voice the note of pure, nagging querulousness, which she could not keep down: and all she wanted was a brisk, nurse-like manner towards him – just until she could get him help. God, how she missed Francis!

'I know you got money.'

'Shut up, Mo. I'm sorry you're sick, right. I'm sick too, I've been having fevers, right, I've been in bed all week. But I didn't want to meet you, I didn't follow you here, we aren't together, right. Our meeting like this was just a *coincidence*.'

The canal water into which they all stared was so still, in the small basin above the lock, that it had gathered a layer of dust. It could almost, to look at it, have been set like a jelly. The motionless tin-cans, pieces of rag, food-packets that stood half-submerged on its surface suggested infinitudes of filth in the depth beneath.

'There's dead babies down there,' said Mo, at which everyone laughed except Jay.

'That's a horrid thing to say.'

'It's true. Babies, bits of dead people. They are dredging them up all the time. They found a head down there a few months ago, just a head in a plastic bag.'

Martyn's cackle at this story set off the others into a round of genial merriment, and Dave started up with some grisly anecdotes of his own.

Jay thought to herself how impossible such a tasteless exchange would have been in the vicarage from which she had so lately made her flight. Being very nearly in love with Francis Kreer, she found that her perception of all her old friends and acquaintances had changed completely. After the suburban restrictions of Bramhall, and the earnestness of her fellow students at the Guildhall, Jay had loved this strange Camden scene. Now she felt quite alienated by all these people, sitting around on the grass like Barbary apes: a vaguely Hell's Angel, with a great hairy chest exposed beneath a leather jerkin, and numerous iron crosses and other pieces of Nazi memorabilia hanging as a pendant from his neck, his other biker-friends similarly arrayed; beside the bikers, a whole gang of young people almost uniformly dressed in extra-large tee-shirts (white or black), shorts and Doc Marten boots with or without socks; an almost idiotic denim-clad boy, pock-marked with acne, accompanied by eight Scandinavian girls who conversed in weirdly uneuphonious voices; Dave, who was friends with one of the Scandinavians, perhaps with all of them; and Jane, and Mo. She had agreed to come along for this drink by the lock rather against her better judgement, but chiefly out of concern for Mo, who had turned so abjectly into Martyn's creature. Soon, he would have to steal something more, or beg some money from somewhere, to pay Martyn for his next little bit of oblivion.

Jay watched his head drooping. When he lifted it, he was grinning at her idiotically. She knew that he had not attended to anything she had so primly told him; she knew that Mo still thought she was there, for him. So, in a sense, she was, but not in the sense which Mo believed. Jay was now a much stronger person, or so it seemed to her. She was loved by Francis Kreer. Somehow, this would work for good; on that she was determined.

Mo said, 'I really am thirsty, Jay.' He said it quite urgently, and in a tone of utter seriousness, but she responded as a mother might to a fractious child demanding an ice.

'I've told you, Mo, I don't have any money.'

'Oh, for God's sake!'

It was Jay's friend Jane who at last had pity on Mo. Jane was a muscly girl, who had hitherto taken almost no part in the conversation, and sat there, drinking Newcastle Brown Ale from a can. Jane had shaved the sides of her head. From the top of her head there sprouted some very light dyed hair, almost albino in its whiteness. She had a ring through her nose, and three rings in each ear.

'Get me some Newcastle Brown and buy yourself one,' said Jane, who had got up, and was thrusting a five-pound note into Mo's hands.

Jay wished to remonstrate. She wanted to call the whole assembly to witness that it would be almost inconceivably unlikely that Mo would return with Jane's drink. He would go to another part of the pub, scrounge more money off another fool, and buy his next fix from Martyn. By 'taking pity' on him, Jane was in fact doing him great harm – and this made Jay so angry.

'So it's a Newcastle Brown for Jane – anyone else want a drink while I'm going?' he asked.

'Rum an' coke,' said Martyn, grinning at his protégé.

'How 'bout you, sweetheart?' Mo asked Jay.

Thinking quickly, she said, 'I'll have half of bitter if you're going to the pub. But, Mo, why don't I come and help you carry the drinks?'

'No need,' he said.

'I'll come all the same,' she said.

The gate of the canal lock provided a precarious bridge over which the more agile of the Barbary apes could prance and scamper. Mo, quite predictably, had leapt up, at the prospect of

Jay intercepting his theft of the five-pound note, and was halfway across the lock by the time she shouted, 'Careful.'

Mo turned to amuse the company by doing a fake wobble. It made Jane and Dave and Martyn whoop with merriment. Mo gave a jokey wave of his hand, and then, as Dave split his sides laughing, Jay could see the fake wobble had turned into a real wobble. Jay watched as Mo fell, like a broken doll, into the dark waters of the canal lock.

13

The two strange men in Lincoln's Inn Fields had Jay locked up inside a wooden packing-case. One of the men was a bald Irishman with red eyes. He wore a mackintosh belted with string, and when he smiled you could see that he had hardly any teeth. The other man, much younger, was white-faced, but he had enormous dark-brown dreadlocks, reaching almost to his waist. He was sitting on the packing-case and drumming it with his heels, which made the imprisoned Jay scream out: 'It's the parish fête! You must let me out, because today is the parish fête!' When her dreadlocked tormentor continued to bang the box with his feet, she cried, 'Miss Bill! Miss Bill!'

Francis was on his knees in front of this small packing-case. It was of supreme horror to him that the two men were torturing Jay, but, even so, he could not get up from this kneeling position, because the box was a holy object, like the Ark of the Covenant, or the Tabernacle containing the Blessed Sacrament. Jay, and the Blessed Sacrament of the Altar were in fact one and the same, infinitely sacred, wholly divine. If, however, he could reach the box with his hands, and open it with the Tabernacle key which he kept on the Lady Altar, he would be able to release her. Through the slits of the packing-case, it was impossible to see Jay, but, by putting his nose very close to the slits, he could smell her. It was a smell which, having lived a life of married celibacy for so long, he had almost forgotten, but it was the most enticing odour which his nostrils knew, the smell of female genitalia in a state of readiness and arousal.

The closer he crawled towards the box, the smaller the box became; and the likelier it seemed that, before he opened the box, he would himself ejaculate. And he needed to open the box because, inside it, the telephone was ringing.

When he woke up, the telephone had just stopped ringing. The sexual arousal caused by the dream had reached an almost-climactic stage, but his consciousness that he had just missed the telephone was, in his waking mind, anaphrodisiac, and he soon calmed down. He was in his mother's flat, lying on his mother's bed. The sensation of falling asleep during the day always produced in Francis Kreer a heaviness in the head to equal a hangover.

The two men in the dream had been seen by Francis several hours earlier. Ever since the frustrating experience of hearing Jay's voice on the telephone, and being unable to make his own voice heard at her end, he had conceived the irrational certainty that she was sleeping rough on the streets of London. True, the weather had never been warmer, and Jay was a young woman; but she was still barely recovered from 'flu and he was sure that, if she risked exposure to the elements, Jay would develop pneumonia.

He had spent the night in the environs of Waterloo station, where, as he had read in the newspapers, vagrants are to be found sleeping in cardboard boxes. It was shocking to go there and see this phenomenon for himself. Poor Tom on the blasted heath, curled up in a sleeping bag in the middle of the most prosperous city in Europe – and multiplied hundreds of times. As he stepped among these cowering, recumbent men and women, lying on the concrete, he imagined that each one of them could be Jay. Each one of them could have been the person he loved. In sleep, they were totally vulnerable, their few belongings bursting out of plastic bags, or piled in little heaps at their side.

Kneeling down beside one of them, who might have been Jay, but wasn't, Francis found himself in a state of mind which was more like prayer than any which had taken hold of him for years. In this strange state of spiritual abstraction, he thought of the stable at Bethlehem. The books which he had read at theological college had informed him that it was highly unlikely that the Christ-child had been born in Bethlehem; and he had since discarded the mythology of the Virgin Birth. Kneeling beside a young person in a sleeping bag, and peering at him (for it turned out to be a sixteen-year-old boy, and not Jay), Francis thought how trivial he had been to discard his belief in Bethlehem, on the grounds that it was 'only a myth'. Was not the 'myth' created by the most magnificent idea of the Godhead which had ever been conceived by the human race? It was a myth of God, so yearning with love for every human being, even for the outcasts and the social misfits, that He had chosen to strip Himself of the Godhead. Perhaps He had not even chosen to do so. Perhaps His love was so intense that He had, as it were, overspilled into humanity, becoming human, because there could be no other channel for His grace to find. Francis knew that what he was allowing to pass through his mind was not thought; it was nonsense. He wondered, however, whether God, in becoming incarnate in the person of Jesus Christ, had ceased to exist. Henceforth, all the qualities of divine compassion were to be contained in human hearts, and all the potentialities of divine love, if they were allowed to survive, would be in the hands of men and women. 'I have loved this much,' God said to Francis as he knelt beside the sleeping boy in Waterloo, 'but, since I became even as these outcasts, I have no more love left to give, and no more power. Now, it is for the human race to possess itself of my power and of my love.'

Francis returned to Waterloo in the morning. In his head was ringing the passage from Saint Paul: 'Let this mind be in you which was also in Christ Jesus; Who, being in the form of God, thought it not mockery to be equal with God: But made himself of no reputation, and took upon him the form of a servant, and was made in the likeness of men: and being found in fashion as a man, he humbled himself, and became obedient unto death, even the death of the Cross.'

The shanty-town underneath the arches near Waterloo had been cleared away by the time he got there next morning. Municipal cleaners with hose-pipes were sluicing the scene. Where had they all gone, the Poor Toms with their sleeping-bags and their bundles of belongings? Francis found some of them standing on Waterloo Bridge.

'Are you a journalist?' he was asked by one young man, who seemed rather hopeful that he might have been.

'No,' said Francis. 'I'm looking for a friend of mine. I think she might have spent last night down here. She has short blonde hair, a very animated face' – how could he describe Jay to these people without sounding like either a lunatic or a lecher? 'She's called Jay.'

'Do you know a Jay?' this young man asked among his friends.

Joy? Jay? None of them did. It was the bald old Irishman with a string belt who said, 'But then she might be up Lincoln's Inn Fields. Have you tried up there?'

This simple inquiry immediately persuaded Francis's fevered brain that Jay was, indeed, camping in Lincoln's Inn. Having accepted directions from the men on the bridge, he set off to find her.

Francis was not a Londoner, in spite of the fact that his mother was. Throughout his childhood, his parents had lived in Gerrard's Cross, and he had hardly ever spent more than two or three consecutive nights in the capital city. His sorties to London in the last decade had almost always been family 'jaunts' or short visits to his mother in Cornwall Gardens. He had very little instinctive sense of where one familiar area ended and another could be found. Without the instructions of the men on Waterloo Bridge, he would have had no idea where to find Lincoln's Inn Fields, although he had visited it about half a dozen times in his life, either to take Jessica to the Sir John Soane Museum, or to call on Sandiman, the family solicitor. The walk, therefore, though not a long one, was interrupted by many pauses, and inquiries of policemen or newspaper vendors to ascertain that he was going in the right direction, up Aldwych and Kingsway.

As he walked, he wondered whether he and Jay, as a bargain with the universe, should agree to shed abroad the love in their hearts helping the homeless, the 'poor naked wretches whereso'er they are'; even as he had the thought he recognised it as one of those fantasies which had always been appealing to him, like the fantasy of himself as the Reverend John Keble, sweeping snow from the church path so that hobblers could attend Morning Prayer: it was the love of an idea of virtue rather than a realised virtue which he had been able to practise: and yet such fantasies did enable us to do good. In all his punctilious observances of parochial duty which, until this year, he had maintained, in all his visits to the sick and the old, and in all his counsellings of the unhappy, he had been guided by the Victorian saint's example.

As he approached Lincoln's Inn Fields, other fantastic projections were thrown up by his brain. The weather matched his magniloquent mood – exaggerated, puffy clouds of gunmetal grey hurtled across a wide blue sky. Lincoln's Inn Fields is a very large square, bordered on three sides by fine old houses, and on the fourth by the west wall of Lincoln's Inn – one of the Inns of Court, where the Lord Chancellor regularly dines, and where the Court of Chancery sits.

In the middle of the square there were well-planted gardens, paths and walks. Francis walked down the central path which divides the square, gradually becoming aware that this garden was highly populated. One of his favourite books as a child had concerned a hedgehog who was a tramp. Some other hedgehogs, the milkman-hedgehog and his little child, befriended this 'gentleman of the road', as did a kind rabbit. Francis could remember the illustrations of this story (his first remembered pleasure in literature) and the wandering hedgehog's ragged old coat and hat, and his briar pipe in which he smoked dried leaves, his cooking-pots and few modest possessions. It was of this story that Francis thought as he saw the bushes on either side of him, where people had established residence. There were a number of tents, but, for the most part, the shelters were makeshift, with pieces of plastic sheeting suspended from the branches of shrubs. Some of these shrub-encampments had a touchingly domestic air. Beside one, there was a pair of trainers, an alarm clock, and a paperback copy of Thomas Mann's *The Magic Mountain*, making him realise that those who found themselves in these indigent circumstances were not a sub-species, but people with minds and feelings and the need for home.

In the slightly deranged mental condition which his love for Jay had created, he felt even more certain that one of these little bush-houses would contain her, and he plunged into the shrubbery, looking at each tent and hovel in turn with the expectation that he would eventually find her. It was while he was conducting this search that he came face to face with the young man of the dreadlocks.

'I'm looking for a friend of mine,' he said.

The dreadlocked one was sitting cross-legged outside a tent, listening to music on a Sony Walkman. His head moved gently from side to side in rhythm. Francis repeated his statement.

'What?'

'I'm looking for a friend of mine. I think she's camping out here. You haven't seen her – she's a young woman.'

'She could be anywhere,' said the young man dreamily. 'Have you tried over there? There's more tents and stuff over by the tennis courts.'

The tennis courts were on the opposite side of the square, near Lincoln's Inn itself. As he approached them, Francis remembered an afternoon which he had completely forgotten. He had been a young curate at the time, in his late twenties. He was in love with Sally, who was a nurse at Bart's Hospital. He had agreed to meet her after a game of tennis which she had been playing with some friends. As he came up to the courts, she was just finishing her game, and he remembered the beauty (as it had seemed to him at the time) of her thin, innocent face. He remembered how ecstatically pleased to see her he had felt, and how happily she had smiled at him. Later that day, he had proposed marriage and been accepted. How could he have blotted this memory out? In his current version of his own emotional history, he had never much liked Sally; indeed, it was something of a mystery why he had married her. He had grudgingly supposed that they must once have been fond of one another. Now he knew that it was all much sadder than that: they had loved one another, and that love had died. This powerful and involuntary memory did not stop him loving Jay, but it disturbed him, and made him acknowledge that happiness and goodness were of their essence fragile, and that, if he had taken the trouble to nurture the one, he might have learnt how to practise the other.

He had not found Jay in the camp near the tennis courts. After much aimless walking round the square and its environs, he had gone back down Chancery Lane towards the Strand, and then to the Temple, where he had caught an underground train for Gloucester Road. Physically and emotionally exhausted, he had fallen into the stupor from which the telephone now aroused him.

And now, for the second time in five minutes, the telephone rang again. Francis weighed in his mind the possibilities of who might be trying to reach him. Obviously not Jay. The Wing-Co? Miss Bill? He dreaded the idea of speaking to anyone from the parish; and he was glad that he had had the presence of mind to telephone Damian Wells and arrange for the next two Sunday services to be taken care of. (He had invented a lie about visiting sick relatives.) He felt guilty about having cut the parish fête, and guilt made it intolerable to contemplate exchanging so much as ten words with the likes of the Spittles. Lest the trilling telephone were they, he let it trill.

Jay returned from the payphone to the waiting-room of the Casualty Department of the Royal Free Hospital. It was her fifth attempt to telephone Francis. She had tried Ditcham rectory; on one occasion, she recognised the child's voice, distant and hostile; on another, it was a mellow, rather beautiful female voice, not Sally's, which answered. 'Who is that?' this voice had asked. And then, after a pause, the voice had said, 'That's Jay, isn't it?' Jay had hung up in a panic. How had the possessor of the well-modulated tones known her name? There was something commanding about the voice, in spite of (perhaps because of?) its quietness. She had then started to ring the number of Francis's flat, but she was not getting any reply. Having failed to reach him, she had rung some other numbers in desperation – her old flat-mates; and a couple of fellow-students from the Guildhall, whose numbers were scribbled in her diary. Perhaps it was not surprising that, on a hot Saturday in June, these people were not all sitting beside their telephones in London.

At this juncture, however, she simply could not face having to deal with Mo on her own. She desperately wished to speak to Francis. She missed Francis. She believed that he would have a solution to the problem. Surely, being a vicar, he would know where to *put* Mo. There must be a place where men like Mo were put, young men who could not look after themselves, who had developed dangerous drug habits, fallen into canals, from which they had to be rescued by two passers-by.

Then a doctor came from the X-ray department to speak

to Jay. This young houseman told Jay something which she had already observed for herself, namely that Mo had a very nasty gash in his forehead. There was some possibility, said the doctor, that Mo might be suffering from concussion; the surprising thing was that he had broken no bones.

'Have you examined him?'

'Yes. No need to look so anxious!'

'You've really examined him, given him a general examination?'

'Yes. We're just doing a couple more tests and then you can take him home.'

Had the doctors and nurses failed to notice that Mo had been sticking needles into his arms, his ankles, his genitals, in the attempt to find a vein which was not already punctured and sore? Or did that sort of thing not 'count', if all they were looking for were broken bones?

It dismayed and horrified Jay that the hospital authorities could consider discharging Mo, and it was then that she decided she must find Francis to help her. Having inwardly accepted that Mo was partially her responsibility, even before he fell in the canal, she had assumed that this responsibility would end when she had placed him in the hands of a doctor. It so surprised her, that she was dumbstruck by it, and found herself unable to say to the young houseman, 'My friend is a heroin addict; he needs help, can you please *do* something?'

The further tests on Mo took two hours. In this time, Jay sat and watched the coming and going of a whole parade of calamities. There were two lunatics, separate rather than attached, who approached the desk on average every quarter of an hour to ask for an aspirin, only to be turned away in the politest terms by the duty nurse. There was a great hulking Frenchman, bearded, half-naked, who was accompanied by an infuriating young woman (or Jay found her infuriating) – self-consciously 'sexy', with blonde hair and large breasts – who giggled suggestively about the injuries sustained to the hairy hulk's right leg. He emerged, the hulk, after about an hour with the doctors, with this leg in plaster. When they had gone, Jay recognised that there was a large measure of envy in her anger with the 'sexy' woman: envy of a couple so much at ease with themselves that even a distressing matter like breaking a leg could be made the subject of erotic play and laughter. Then a drunk had come in with a black eye, followed by another drunk who had cut himself with a tin opener, and a third who had splinters of broken glass stuck in his cheeks. Then, again, there were the children who came and went: the one who had something stuck up its nose, and another with its head wedged between the bars of a cast-iron gate. The boy's father and mother had carried the gate into the waiting room, with their offspring walking awkwardly beneath it, hollering, a sight ludicrously redolent of Roman slaves or captives being marched in triumph through the streets of some eastern Mediterranean town. Jay had sat, and sat, watching this bizarre procession of individuals enter the waiting-room, and thought how easily human life descends into chaos: sad chaos for those involved, but, for those observing it, grotesque or even comic. And she and Mo were just such a pair of human accidents, who probably seemed as absurd, to the others, as the hairy hulk or the little boy with a gate stuck round his head, did to her.

Alison Bill, who answered the telephone when Jay rang from the hospital, decided not to tell Sally that the girl had been on the line. She had passed an emotional two hours, calming Sally down. She had read Francis's letter, and she had struggled with a variety of emotions while she did so: pity for the man who could be so foolish as to have written it; sadness for the Church that one of its priests could so grievously step aside from the path of virtue; anger with Francis for treating his wife so cruelly; and deep joy that nothing now stood in her path. She could hold and pet and love Sally as much as she liked. Sally was now *hers*.

She had come over to the vicarage at once when Ronald Maxwell-Lee had told her what had taken place. She had found Jessica, pale, embarrassed, speechless in the hall, and, after preliminary searches for Sally in the kitchen and the drawing-room, she had thumped upstairs to find Sally in the bedroom, half-kneeling, half-crawling on the floor, surrounded (how odd) by a family of stuffed toy animals. She had knelt beside Sally and taken her in her arms, and for half an hour or so she had done nothing but hug her, nursing her quivering, sobbing body in her large arms. Then she had taken Sally into the bathroom, and removed her candlewick dressing-gown and her nightdress. Sally had been like a whimpering, docile child, allowing herself to be undressed, to be led into the bath, to be soaped and caressed, and stroked and sponged by Alison Bill. Then Miss Bill had taken her out of the bath and dried her and powdered her, dabbing each part of her body with the palms of her hands.

Jessica would not eat with the two women when Alison had, at length, persuaded Sally to have some tinned tomato soup. The child claimed to have eaten a piece of toast.

'And there's nothing in the fridge,' Sally said quietly.

'That doesn't matter,' said Alison Bill, 'because you are both coming home with me.'

When the telephone in the flat had rung twice more, Francis began to feel besieged. He decided that he should go out again, and continue his quest for Jay among London's destitute. He was in the lavatory when he heard the key turn in his front door, and a female voice call out, 'Anyone at home?' After a pause, during which Francis did not answer, this voice added, 'I think the coast is clear. Now, as I told you, you've got yourself a *real* bargain.'

Francis flushed the lavatory with as much ostentation as he could command in order to announce his presence.

When he opened the lavatory door, he found that quite a party was assembled. There was an Australian couple and a rather leathery-faced woman of late middle-age, who had sunglasses pushed back into her platinum blonde hair, and, taking up the rear, Eric Gadney.

'Hallo! Zenda de Freitas!' The leathery blonde extended a jangling wrist to Francis. 'You must be Mr Kreer.'

'Yes, I am. Excuse me for asking, but . . .'

'I'm from Pepperdine Gallows,' said Mrs de Freitas – a South African, Francis guessed, from the twang of her intonation.

'The estate agents,' glossed Eric Gadney a little unnecessarily.

'And let me introduce your purchasers –' gushed Zenda enthusiastically. Her teeth, particularly the molars, had been so filled with mercury that they had turned grey. Everything about her, Francis thought, had a metallic quality – tinny voice, jingly-jangly wrists and ears; even her make-up, the pale blue smeared on to the sunburnt eyelids, the dull pink on her lips, were more the colours you would spray a car than paint a face.

'I'm Rodney Carter,' said the Australian man.

'And I'm Merry,' said his wife. 'Isn't it great?' said Merry.

'We did try to contact you,' said Zenda de Freitas, 'but you've been a little bit incommunicado.'

'Obviously,' said Merry, 'we wouldn't want much of this stuff, but Zenda said we could come and give it the once-over and make you an offer. The beds, for instance, would you be wanting to keep the beds?'

Francis understood immediately the purpose of this invasion, but he was slow to absorb its emotional significance. Mrs de Freitas of Pepperdine Gallows had now all but sold his mother's flat to these strangers; and now the strangers were nosing about, wondering whether they would make an 'offer' on the very bed where Francis's mother slept the last night of her life.

'The kitchen's a right old mess!' Merry called out cheerfully. She had stridden into this room and was calling out to her husband who stood shyly with the others in the drawing-room. 'Hey! Come and look at this fridge, Rodney!'

While he did so, Francis asked brutally, 'How much have they offered?'

'Seventy,' said Zenda.

'Seventy thousand pounds?'

This was at least £100,000 less than Francis had been hoping for. How could it be in the interest of a house agent to allow the place to go for a ludicrous sum like this? He realised that, in his conversations with his lawyer about the sale of the flat, he had paid no attention whatsoever, and that there were several letters from Sandiman which he had not even bothered to open. Francis was eventually to discover that the lease on the flat, which he had assumed was a long one, was only thirty-five years.

'I think given the short lease and the very dicey condition of the flat,' said Zenda, 'it's a fair offer. I mean, I've been showing some really beautiful flats in this square – Smallbone of Devizes kitchens, the nicest bathrooms, air-conditioning, all the paintwork tip-top, clean fitted carpets – and they've been going for a hundred and eighty, whereas eighteen months ago – I mean, you could hope for at least two hundred, two hundred and twenty. That is the reality of the situation.'

'I think you've done splendidly, I really do.' It was Eric who spoke. He combined an obsequious deference to the woman with a smile of pure lechery. What right had he to be there at all? Only the right of having been mentioned in Griselda Kreer's will. The likely reason for Eric being remembered by Griselda was not something upon which Francis had ever allowed his mind to dwell; but in this smile, which spread across his peculiarly ugly, injured mask of a face, Francis sensed sex. He could not prevent his mind from painting a picture of this blemished, stretched face, with its very moist lips, pressing down on his own mother's face: of Griselda's pretty little mouth being swallowed in this man's slobbering chops. This image did not drive out the thought of the money. The two dismaying ideas presented themselves simultaneously: that Eric Gadney had indeed and in flesh been Griselda's lover, and that he, Francis, was not to be the possessor of his 'ninety thousand pounds'. If they were to divide the spoils equally, Francis would barely have enough to buy a small cottage in the country.

'We could smash all that wall down there,' he heard Merry informing her husband. 'Then there might be room for a really nice bathroom.'

Rodney added, whether or not in jest, Francis found it hard to tell, 'We could even fit ourselves up with a nice jacuzzi.'

'No,' said Eric approvingly, 'I think it's a fantastic stroke of luck that we've had such an efficient, and such a *lovely*, agent. One hears of flats and houses hanging fire for months in this recession. Years.'

'That's right,' Zenda confirmed. She launched into a relentless narrative about a particularly desirable Knightsbridge property which had been on the market for eighteen months.

'Now that place,' she said, nodding her equine skull to emphasise each word, 'would have gone for four hundred and fifty no *probs* four years ago. No probs at all. Nowaways . . .'

'Shall I answer that?' proposed Eric. The telephone was trilling once more.

Francis heard him say, 'Yes. Who's that? Jay! How lovely to hear you. No, Eric, your unc– no, super! Really super to hear you!'

Francis wanted to grab the receiver from this slightly doddery, lopsided old man, but before he did so he felt he would have liked to seize some heavy object, such as a table lamp, and pound it into the grey head of his mother's lover.

'It's Jay' – said Eric Gadney, holding the receiver with a convivial air. You could almost have supposed, from his manner, that it was he, rather than Francis, to whom Jay had wished to speak.

'Look,' said Jay's voice, 'I'm running out of cash. Could you ring me back?'

While she dictated the number, Eric was talking.

'But don't youngsters speak indistinctly these days?' he boomed. 'I could have sworn she said she wanted to speak to Fancy. I nearly said – "*Who?* Fancy *who?*"'

'Please be quiet,' said Francis. 'Yes, I've got that. I'll ring you back. Where are you?'

'I'm at the Royal Free Hospital.'

But the line went dead.

He rapidly dialled the number which Jay had given him. A female voice, but not of this world, clipped, sounding like a message from a space ship, said, 'Sorry. The number you have dialled is not available.'

He dialled again. Once again, the inter-galactic disembodied female expressed her apologies.

'Royal Free Hospital,' said Francis desperately. 'Where's that?'

'It's in Hampstead,' said Zenda de Freitas.

'How do I get there?'

'Look here, I'm awfully sorry. Poor Jay!' The over-courtly 'concern' in Eric Gadney's voice sounded entirely phoney.

The telephone rang again.

'Francis?'

'Jay, thank God!'

'I don't think you can ring in on this telephone. One of the nurses has just told me. Someone just lent me 50p.'

'What's the matter? Are you all right?'

'I'm fine.'

'But what are you doing in a hospital?'

'Listen, Francis. I've got a tremendous favour to ask you.'

'Shall I come and fetch you?'

'That would be really, really kind. Look, Francis. I've got this friend who's had a bit of bad luck; fallen in the canal. They seem to think my friend's OK, but I really think we ought to get some help, and I was wondering . . .'

'Look, darling!' How it pleased him to use this word when addressing her. 'I'll come. She can rest in the flat if she'd like.'

'She?'

'Your friend.'

'We'll be waiting in the Casualty department. It's really awful, they keep you waiting such ages . . .'

'Jay, it is so wonderful to hear you. I've been missing you so much.'

'Is she all right?' The intrusive voice of Eric Gadney drowned Jay's reply. 'I mean, if there's anything *I* can do – anything at all?'

'Well, this is all great!' said Merry. 'We're not going to need those curtains, are we, Rodney? Look at those!' She pointed contemptuously at Mrs Kreer's faded chintz.

'And of course,' said Zenda de Freitas, 'you can always come back again and measure up properly when you've exchanged. I can let you in and out.'

'Jay!' said Francis. 'Jay! Can you hear me?' But, once more, the line had gone dead. The inter-galactic messenger quickly returned to say, 'Please replace the handset and try again. Please replace the handset and try again.'

Seeing that Francis was about to leave, Zenda de Freitas said, 'Well, Mr Kreer, we'll lock up after us. I'm glad you've had the chance to meet Mr and Mrs Carter.'

There were many things about this sale which Francis found unsatisfactory, but this was not the moment to discuss them.

'We'll lock up,' said Zenda, 'and I hope you find your friend all right!'

She was still talking when he was downstairs.

14

'It's the most terrible thing when a parish blows up in a man's face,' said the Archdeacon. 'Everyone in Ditcham seemed pleasant enough yesterday at the fête. But I don't feel good about it. This woman Lindie Spittle. Dear old Lindie.'

He chuckled somewhat lecherously.

The Archdeacon was in the passenger seat of Damian Wells's secondhand Peugeot 205, in which the atmosphere of Xeryus de Givenchy stung his sinuses. Damian had already been over to the village once to celebrate the eight o'clock Mass. It was the third Sunday in the month, and so, in deference to Wing-Commander Maxwell-Lee's liturgical preferences, the later service was to be Mattins. Damian had hoped to enliven this rather stolid dose of Mrs Cranmer with his sermon on the Seven Dolours of Our Lady – Our Lady on Seven Dolours a Day, as he had once waggishly described this florid piece of prose. The Archdeacon had shoved his oar in, however, and had telephoned that he would be visiting the parish himself, and haranguing them on the virtues of tolerance and all pulling together, and restraining the tongue of the backbiter.

This instruction made Damian feel that he was being spied upon; but, since that was the situation, he was determined not to put a foot wrong. His future career could depend on this. After the early service, he had hoped to be given breakfast at the vicarage by Sally, but there had been no answer, either to her telephone or to her doorbell. So – it had been a dash back to his flat for a bowl of Sugar Puffs and a cup of instant coffee, and then a further dash to the station to meet the Archdeacon's train. Now, yet another car journey.

'You're close to Frankie Kreer, aren't you?'

'We were at Mirfield together, we've been in touch ever since,' said Damian cautiously.

'You've heard what Lindie has been saying?'

'Only what you told me.'

'She seems reasonable enough – but, with women, you can't tell.'

'No.' Why, in that case, thought Damian with a sudden spurt of rage, do liberals like you want to ordain the cows? But he kept his counsel.

'I perhaps should have been clearer in what I said. Lindie's made various sexual allegations against Frankie.' The Archdeacon rubbed his chin thoughtfully.

'How do you mean?' This was news to Damian. All he had heard was that the Spittles had drawn up a list of complaints against Frankie, alleging laziness and incompetence of one sort or another.

'Well, I wouldn't want you to betray any confidences,' said the Archdeacon. 'But had you any idea that Francis was . . .'

'There was a day in London,' said Damian. 'I'd rather not tell tales out of school, but I just – I just happened to see him with a girl.'

'In what circumstances?'

'I'd rather not talk about it, as I say. They were –' He hesitated to state that they were in the park, lest the Archdeacon should wonder what Damian himself was doing there. 'I just happened to be coming out of church – I'd nipped in to light a candle at the Annunciation, Bryanston Street, and I saw him with a girl – that's all.'

'Not a prostitute?'

'I couldn't say,' said Damian.

Through the open window of the car, as they drove past Robin Pimm's farmyard, he thought he heard the crowing of a cock.

Mattins was a popular service, and there were already about eight cars parked on the verge outside the church.

'I think old Frankie gets a number of Prayer Book recusants coming in from other parishes for this service,' said the Archdeacon with a tolerant smile. 'Not the sort of religion you and I go in for,' he added tolerantly, somehow wishing at that moment to show Anglo-Catholic solidarity with Damian (he was longing to hear more about Francis and the tart), 'but it has its place. Natural religion, old Father Curatin used to call it.'

The Archdeacon's cassock, surplice, scarf and MA hood were in a small holdall on the back seat of the Peugeot. Damian was already wearing his cassock and relied on Francis's collection of Anglican regalia, to be found hanging on coat-hangers in the vestry. (Had he been taking the service himself, without the Archdeacon's prying eyes upon him, he would probably have worn one of his chaste Belgian cottas.)

'Good heavens,' said the Archdeacon, 'you don't think we're late, do you?'

'It's only ten past,' said Damian, consulting his wrist-watch. 'We've got five minutes.'

But, as they consulted the notice-board in the churchyard, the two men saw that Morning Prayer was not, as they had understood, at 11.15, but 11 a.m.

They hurried through the vestry door and, as they did so, they were aware that some form of musical diversion had already started without them. A guitar was playing, and two or three voices were singing:

O come, Lord Jesus, yes, come, Lord Jesus!
Come quickly – into my heart.
We love you Jesus, we love you Jesus,
We love you – so, set our hearts on fire!

'What on earth?' asked the Archdeacon.

They opened the vestry door a crack and peeped through. Three young people, in their early twenties, were standing on the chancel steps, where they had just finished their song. They wore open-necked shirts, jeans and sneakers, and their well-scrubbed faces gleamed with vacant self-righteousness.

A man in a blazer, tie and grey flannels advanced to a microphone which had been set up a little to their right and said, 'Thanks, Pam, Richard and Malcolm. What a splendid sound. And you might like to know that Malcolm wrote that song himself.' Then he tapped the microphone with his fingers and said, 'Is this thing working? Testing, testing!'

A banshee shriek was released by the electrical equipment and Gerald Spittle, blushing a little, came forward to adjust it.

'Sorry, Terry,' he said, 'is that all right for you?'

'Friend Widger,' the Archdeacon quietly explained to Damian Wells. 'What on earth's he doing here?'

'Come quickly, Lord Jesus – wonderful words – very nearly the last words of our Bible. If you've got Bibles, you'll find those words in Revelation 22:20 – that's the twenty-second chapter of Revelation, and the twentieth verse.'

The congregation, which was largely made up of elderly and middle-aged people who had, as the Archdeacon surmised, driven some distance in order to partake of a traditional Anglican Mattins, did not have Bibles. They had come, hoping to hear Wing-Commander Maxwell-Lee read from the eagle lectern, stammering his way through a piece of prophecy or military history in the incomparable version of King James. The Reverend Terry Widger's performance was not what they had expected at all.

'Now, if Lindie would like to bring up her three volunteers from the Sunday School – thanks, Lindie – that's splendid! What are your names?'

The children – who were called Wayne, Melanie and Mary – were told to climb into the pulpit and hold up some balloons on strings. On one of the balloons there was a large letter S, on another the letter I, and on another N.

'What does that spell? Anyone?'

'SNI,' whispered the Archdeacon, rather childishly, but truthfully, since the children were standing in the wrong order.

'Should we go in?' whispered Damian, but his superior, who had begun to enjoy himself, shook his head.

'Anyone?' asked Terry Widger once more. 'You!' he pointed to Mrs Renton in the front row, whose expression would have given new meaning to the expression, 'looking daggers'. 'Or anyone?'

Lindie supplied, 'Sin!'

The Reverend Terry Widger was a smooth-faced, smooth-haired man with spectacles. His voice was not in the least euphonious; there was a harsh timbre to it, and he could easily have made himself heard, in that comparatively small church, without a microphone.

'Now when I ask the children to burst those balloons, they're going to burst them one by one,' said Mr Widger. 'But first we are going to see what they spell. S.I.N. Sin. And S is the first letter and it's for self. Putting self before others, self before God – that's the beginning of sin. And that's what the Galatians were doing, and that's why Paul had to give them a jolly good talking to, a jolly good ticking off! "Oh, you idiots!" He actually uses those words and you'll find them in his letter to the Galatians, in the third chapter and the first verse. Because that's what we are if we think we can rely in this life on ourselves, rely on our own initiative, our own virtue, our own ideas. God wants to shake us out of all that, and so when he sends Jesus into our lives to take away our sin he wants to get rid of that letter S, that Self. Okay, Melanie.'

Lindie had considered it unsafe to supply the children with pins, so Melanie had a certain amount of difficulty in bursting her balloon; when she did so, with a pencil lent by Wayne, there was some giggling.

'I' turned out to be for Indifference, and after that Terry thought it was time for a song before they all heard what N was for. The trio came back into the centre of the chancel steps and sang a different song about Jesus coming into their lives.

'So now we've realised two things about Sin,' said Terry. 'We've realised that Sin is putting ourselves first, and in order to break down that barrier we have to ask Jesus to puncture our very selves. And then we have to ask Jesus to overcome our indifference, and we've seen what damage that indifferent attitude has produced in the society of today, with all its unhappy people drifting along with no fixed beliefs, no ideology, and their lives in a mess. Now I wonder if anyone can guess what N stands for? No, not Naughty, though that's a good try!' (This suggestion had come from one of the Watson twins.) 'Not Nothing . . .'

No one got it. N was for Need.

Jessica Kreer sat at the back of the church with the Old Bill, who had insisted on taking her to the service. Sally was still lying in bed in the Bill's house. Jessica, who felt numb with shock after the experiences of the previous twenty-four hours, was simply wondering who would deliver her from the intolerable situation in which she found herself. Ever since she had come into the church, she had been praying, simply, fervently, earnestly, for Francis's return. She did not know if she was praying to God or praying to

Francis himself, but she just wanted him back; she wanted things to go on as normal; she wanted the pain in her own heart to stop; she wanted to get out of the Old Bill's sphere of influence.

This sort of preaching, so strange to many of the congregation, was quite familiar to Jessica. Whenever the C.U. addressed school assemblies, they employed devices such as mnemonics, or drama, or catch-phrases to get across their message of salvation. Guided by her friends, Jessica had always really despised the Christian Union, and those girls who fell for its tricks. But this morning she was impressed by the speaker – some clergyman the Spittles had got hold of, apparently, when they had heard that Daddy was not returning that day to take the service.

'N is for Need. Oh, we can go along very cheerfully when life is happy and smooth, can't we? Putting S for Self first and being I for Indifferent to the things of God. But deep down inside each one of us there is N for Need. We can express this need in many ways. We can say that we need to be loved, and that is true. We can say that we need to be fed, and this is true. But there is a deeper need in each one of us, and it is there in the hearts of all of us today. Jesus was once sitting by a well, wasn't he, and he asked a woman for a drink; but he told her that, if she drank the water from the well, she'd get thirsty again. He offered her a drink which would satisfy her forever – living water! He sensed that woman's need. He met that woman's need. And in the Gospels we read of countless people, bringing their need to Jesus, and he alone can supply it. Sometimes they think they are just bringing some ailment to be cured – it may be blindness or deafness or palsy. But Jesus says to them, I know your need. Your need is to have your sins forgiven you, and that is what I am going to do for you. And that is what he is saying to us, now, to you and me in this very church today. He is calling out to you and he is saying, I know your need. I know how much you need me. Come and drink my living water. And, in another place, it's in Matthew – Matthew 11:29, if you've got your Bibles open – he says, Come and learn how to do it from me. Take my yoke on your shoulders. Now the yoke, for carrying water or milk, is a wooden cross-bar, isn't it? I expect you have all seen pictures of yokes, and some of you might even have seen old yokes in some agricultural museums. . . . And you'll see it's a wooden cross-bar across the shoulders. And that is what Jesus is saying. Lay down your needs. Jesus knows your need. And that's why we're going to sing a hymn about that, and as you sing it I want you to pray, and I want you to say, "Come, Lord Jesus. You know my deep need of you today. Come and take away my Sin. Come, Lord." '

For the first time in this service, the organ struck up, and the congregation rose to sing 'Just as I am'.

The words of Mr Widger's address had already begun to work their effect upon Jessica Kreer's heart. The music completed the work. When they reached the verse which sang of 'fightings within, and fears without', Jessica could feel God himself reaching out to her in all her need and perplexity.

Just as I am – thy love unknown
Hath broken every barrier down –
Now to be Thine – yea, Thine alone!

Jessica, singing these words, felt a great burden lift from her heart. A warm glow suffused her, and she knew, quite certainly, that she was being visited by Jesus himself. His presence was as real to her, and as palpable, as if she had turned and seen him standing beside her, instead of Miss Bill.

It seemed to Jessica nothing short of a miracle that, when the hymn stopped, Terry Widger said, 'Dear Lord Jesus, you have come down into our hearts this morning in Ditcham. In this very place, Lord, even now, you have entered the hearts of some of your people in this church. And we thank you, Lord, for coming here this morning.'

'If we'd known He was coming,' whispered the Archdeacon to Damian Wells, 'we needn't have come all this way ourselves.'

15

After the heatwave, it was something of a relief that the weather broke. London, in this moist, grey, rather blowy cold, took on a seasidey air. Gulls cried in the cloudy skies of Cornwall Gardens.

The trees outside the flat soughed and rustled. Mo slept on.

'So you do see, don't you, why we *must* get him help?'

'Oh, Jay! You are so beautiful! And so good!'

Francis was holding Jay's cheeks gently in his palms, and staring into her eyes, like one on whom an enchantment had been cast. She let him kiss her once more on the lips.

It was late in the morning, but Mo, in the spare bedroom, slept on. Francis had insisted on Jay sleeping in his mother's bed, while he slept on the put-you-up in the sitting-room. With three people sleeping in it, the flat felt quite crowded.

Having kissed, and held one another, and kissed some more, they were now sitting upright on the bed, stroking one another's faces.

'You are beautiful,' she said.

'No I'm not.'

'You are! And you should learn to take a compliment.'

'That's so true.'

With gentle bossiness, she stopped his words by touching his lips with her finger tips. She found him, this morning, both the most delightful and the most exasperating male companion she had ever known. He was so gentle in his approaches, so courteous, so embarrassingly effusive, and she liked all that. Most of the other men she had ever met would have been crawling all over her by now, and she would have let Francis do that if he had wanted to; but this was so nice, this gentleness, this stroking, this kissing. There would be time for the other stuff, later; when they were alone together, really alone; when they had solved the problem of Mo.

Jay had given Francis an 'edited' version of her friendship with Mo. She had said that he was one of the more raffish and amusing members of the convoy and that they had 'gone about together for a bit'. She hoped this phrase 'covered' the situation without the necessity of entering the realm of detail. She had not expected to meet Mo again when she came up to London; her meeting with him had been entirely fortuitous. She found him a menace and a bore, but she felt that she must find him help.

'There must be places,' said Francis.

'Only if you go to them willingly,' said Jay. 'Mo doesn't even admit he has a problem! Half the time, he's kidding himself, pretending he's not doing it.'

'He is all right here for the time being,' said Francis. Only love for Jay called forth this lie. He had actually been horrified by Mo's appearance, both by the young man seeming so ill, but also by his clothes, hair, earrings. Admittedly, few of us look at our best when we have just been lifted out of a filthy canal, but Francis (who remembered glimpsing Mo in Ditcham and being arrested by his louche handsomeness) somehow felt cautious about having 'a person like that' in the flat.

Mo now lay in the spare bedroom, naked. Francis had placed at his disposal some underpants, socks, trousers and a shirt. He did not expect that the young man would be very happy wearing such clothes which were not in the least 'fashionable'. Jay had washed Mo's own pants, jeans, and T-shirt and they were hanging up in the bathroom to dry.

'I really think we should do something about Mo today – before . . .'

Before, what? They had formed no plans, but their reunion had been joyful. The unspoken assumption on both sides was that, whatever happened in the next few weeks, they would be together. Jay, when she had the chance to tell Francis about her ideas, hoped that they would go somewhere by the sea. There was so much to share, so much to tell! She wanted Francis to tell her everything which had happened in Ditcham since she left. His blurted-out, gabbled story of leaving home, his resolution never to go back, both alarmed and delighted her. It was terrifying that two people who knew one another as little as they did could contemplate being together (*living* together? at least, running away together). But because of his gentleness, and his beauty, and because she had almost come to admit to herself that she loved this man, Francis Kreer, it was also tremendously exciting! Jay did not remember a time in her life when she felt so happy, so childishly excited by anything, as by the love of this owlish, wonderfully handsome, angelically clever and delicate man.

The only barrier between themselves and complete happiness seemed, at that time, to be Mo. And, as they spoke about the problem, it emerged that this was something which they were simply obliged to do.

They had talked until late last night. Francis had needed to talk a lot about his mother, and Jay was very willing to hear about this fascinating subject; for she now wanted to know everything about Francis – about his childhood, his parents, his spiritual pilgrimage, his religious beliefs.

She had expressed her 'Buddhist' idea of impersonal goodness: that each individual was sometimes 'given' a particular task, or test, to perform by the fates; that, in a world without God, the Good could not survive unless we responded to these challenges by behaving with the 'love of God'. Francis had agreed with her! She was somewhat shocked by this – surely he was *meant* to think that God was personal and intervened in human affairs if they only turned to Him through faith in Jesus? But Francis had said it was all the most fantastic coincidence because he had been having thoughts very similar to her own only recently, and these thoughts must have been occurring to each of them separately but almost simultaneously; and yes, of course, he agreed that the 'task' imposed on them at the moment was the duty of finding a suitable place for Mo.

Speaking as quietly as she could into the telephone receiver, Jay had rung up a couple of clinics which were found in the Yellow Pages telephone directory under Hospitals. These all turned out to be private rehabilitation centres which would only take fee-paying patients. The second person she spoke to was kind, and gave her the numbers of various 'centres' run by charitable organisations, or local authorities.

'Look,' said Francis, 'we're not going to solve this immediately. Let's go for a walk; have some lunch.'

'I'd rather we had some name, number, *anything*, something concrete which we could offer Mo. You don't know Mo. He'll slither through our hands like an eel.'

'On Sunday afternoon? Where will he find on Sunday afternoon?'

'Oh, all right then.' And she leaned forward to kiss his pyjama-clad thin form. Was this going to be it? She was in a T-shirt and shorts, but they would come off easily enough if he wanted it;

but, instead, he held her very, very tightly for about five minutes. Within a quarter of an hour, he was dressed, and the letter to Mo had been composed and left, propped up on the chair beside the front door.

Mo heard them go, and then he got up himself. He had heard the last bit of their conversation, and it made him very angry that they should consider 'helping' him, from their great moral height. Here was a priest, a fucking priest, fucking his fucking woman, and they had the cheek to sit down and think of ways of locking him up in some loony bin! Their capacity for moral self-delusion made Mo quite determined that he must get away from them. At the same time, he did not want to leave the flat without taking away a few souvenirs.

The lord of all he surveyed, he strode about the rooms, wrapped in the pants the priest had left for him. It was great, this place! He wandered into the bedroom. There was this real, like, fascist guy in a silver fucking frame by the bed! Mo picked up the frame and whistled lightly. That would pawn for twenty quid at least. And there were so many other bits of silver lying round! In the sitting-room, there was a whole mantelpiece of silver boxes, silver ashtrays, silver frames.

He had built up a few debts over the last few weeks, particularly with Martyn. In fact, Martyn said Mo owed him £500, which was ridiculous! All the same, this place should show them! The silver alone would fetch a fortune; and there were antiques all over.

It was a triumph of memory to remember the number in Acton at which Martyn could be reached.

'Well,' said Mo, 'could you put me through to him.' He spoke to a young female ear. Her voice, breathless and excited, suggested that she was very close indeed to Martyn as she spoke.

'He says, what that fucker want?' She giggled and slightly moaned, as she said it.

This was the ultimate in power! Mo was both nauseated and impressed that Martyn could make women answer the telephone while he *had* them.

'Tell him it's something big,' said Mo.

This provoked the inevitable ribaldry at the other end of the line, followed by a great orgasmic scream, which made Mo wonder whether the woman really had noted down the telephone number, and the address of where Mo was staying.

Dressing himself in his still-damp jeans, but deciding he would borrow the priest's shirt, Mo looked in the hall mirror. In case Martyn wasn't coming, he thought he would take a few silver ashtrays, and see what money he could make from them. He gave a self-satisfied little chuckle when he found that the Vicar had been considerate enough to leave a front-door key on the chair in the hall.

16

All those who took part in the raid on the flat were under the influence of drugs. Martyn and his friend Wesley (who was driving the van) had taken a strong dose of cocaine. They had brought some of Mo's favourite, and he was now in a state where he both did and did not observe their swift, efficient action. Another man was with them, whom Mo had not met before. Mo was not sure whether the wardrobe was flying through the room or whether the unnamed man and Wesley had it beneath their shoulders.

Martyn was sifting through the clothes. Griselda Kreer's neat little cocktail dresses, her slips and stays, her suits, her summer frocks, danced in the air before Mo's gaze.

'Let's see some action here!' Martyn boomed, and then doubled up with laughter.

The davenport, and all the nicer pieces of furniture, were already downstairs in the van. Jewels, cutlery, silver candlesticks and photograph frames, such as had remained from Mo's initial raid, had been hoarded in hold-alls in a corner. It had all happened with dazzling speed. Mo hardly knew what was happening.

'Action, I said!' Martyn repeated. 'Get those chairs downstairs.'

Mo found himself on the staircase with an armchair on his back, like the shell on the back of a tortoise. It was much heavier than he had bargained for, and when he returned, having stowed the chair in the van, he was sweating and needed to sit down. But the rooms were empty of furniture. Almost everything had gone downstairs: beds, tables, pictures.

It seemed both funny and natural that Martyn should have unzipped his flies, and should be watering the heap of clothes on the floor. But when Martyn said, 'Let's see some shit!', Mo almost came to himself, and tried the good-humoured laugh which usually got him out of doing anything which he did not want to do.

The other men, who had come back for the last few bags of valuables, were obediently squatting, one in the sitting-room, and one in Mrs Kreer's bedroom.

'Pick it up!' ordered Martyn.

'No, no.'

One man held Mo by the back of the neck, and the other forced the excrement into his fingers. Mo blearily complied, wiping it down walls and doors.

'Piss on the floor,' said Martyn, and Mo did so.

It was not unlike the sensation, very shortly before waking, when you dream that you are emptying bowels or bladder because you so much want to do so. Martyn was wiping his hands clean on the curtains, and he threw over one of Mrs Kreer's blouses so that Mo could clean himself up.

'Now we go,' said Martyn. 'You been a good boy. We may reward you.'

The others laughed at this.

'I can't stay here,' said Mo.

'You can't come with us,' said Martyn.

They were down on the first floor landing. The world was swaying about for Mo. He did not like moving, still less indulging in all this energetic activity, while the effect of the drug was at its height. He made no effort to join them in the van, since they did not want him. They had screeched off down Cornwall Gardens, leaving the front door of the house wide open.

Mo walked like a drunkard. Above him, the opalescent sky seemed intolerably bright. He just wanted to lie, to lie down. He might have been walking ten minutes, he might have been walking half an hour, when he found a doorway, and lay down, sinking for an hour into oblivion. When he recovered himself, dimly aware that he had been involved in a disgusting scene, but unable to recall exactly what had happened, he felt in his pockets. They were empty. Stirring himself, he walked as far as High Street Kensington station and sat by the entrance, holding up a dirty palm, and uttering the repeated question, 'Got any change please?' He said it so often that the words had no meaning to his brain.

'Gotney chinge please, gotney chinge please.' It was like the recitation of a mantra. In this way, he collected eleven pounds in an hour and then crossed the street and caught a 31 to Camden.

St Bartholomew

I

Some letters

Dear Daddy,

Please come back. We do not know where you are, but I am sending this to Granny's flat. Darling Daddy, we love you, and Jesus loves you. Please, please come home. Jessica.

Dear Daddy,

I am sending this letter to Granny's flat. I do not know where you are, but I hope that it reaches you. Today, Mummy, Miss Bill and I all drove over to Oxford. It was very pleasant. We had tea in a café which had a piano! Miss Bill introduced us to someone she used to know when she was a student. Life in the village continues much as normal. Mrs Spittle has got a new car!! (A Volkswagen Polo). I miss you dreadfully. It makes me so sad that you aren't with us. With love from Jessica.

Dear Daddy,

Thank you for the postcard from the seaside. It looks nice. Did you get my letters? This card is of Jane Austen's house, where Miss Bill took us the other day. With love from Jessica.

Dear Jessica,

I am so glad that you found the Bible Notes helpful. Read

the Scriptures every day. Remember that Jesus said that, if we laid all our burdens on him, he would give us rest for our souls (Matthew 11:29). I am praying for you, and offering up thanks to God that you have come to know the Lord Jesus and to have a relationship with the living God through him.

Yours ever,
Terry Widger.

Dear Archdeacon,

I have delayed answering your letter for some time. May I say that I consider it something of a pity that you wrote it, and, in particular, that you chose to adopt that particular tone? It might interest you to know that there has been a harvest of souls in Ditcham since my visit and that I have been in correspondence with folk there who have been called to a living relationship with Jesus through my words.

Naturally, I am sorry that you had a wasted journey, when you thought you were going to take the service that morning, but you would have been only too welcome to join in our act of worship. You question my authority to take services in a parish without the permission of the vicar. Since it is you who raised the matter, I should perhaps point out to you that the Vicar of Ditcham has left his parish in highly unusual circumstances. Two of the good people of Ditcham, who used, as it happens, to belong to my own congregation at Immanuel, asked me to take that service. It was very recognisably a cry for help from those two individuals. They tell me that they have written to you about their worries and that they have not received very satisfactory replies.

Surely it is more important to preach the Gospel of Jesus Christ than to follow the exact letter of protocol about who is, or who is not, entitled to take services? A real case, here, I think, of the letter killing, but the spirit giving life?

Terry Widger.

Dear Mr Kreer,

I am glad to have an address for you at last! Your disappearance has caused considerable worry in a number of quarters, and it would be helpful, in future, if you could always keep me informed of your whereabouts. There are basically three important areas which we need to discuss.

(1) The enclosed correspondence from your wife's solicitors. I have no idea, since you and I have never discussed your private affairs, whether this will come as a shock to you or not. May I say how very sad I feel for both of you? I know how distressing such things always are, and for a man in your profession this must be doubly upsetting. Notice that your wife would appear to be asking for a legal separation, rather than, at this stage, a divorce. It would seem as though she is proposing that you get divorced, if mutually acceptable, after two years, on the grounds of separation. If, for religious or other reasons, you contest this, she will be entitled to divorce you after a period of five years.

This is certainly much better news than if she were suing you for divorce on any other grounds. We shall, however, need to discuss the proposals in her solicitors' letter. You might feel that the access offered to your daughter is insufficient. The sum of £5,000 per annum for maintenance seems reasonable, in the light of your own financial circumstances, and the fact that Jessica's school fees, and some of her expenses, can be dealt with by the terms of your mother's will. If you could spare the time to come up to London for a morning, it would be much easier to discuss these matters face to face.

(2) Your letter to the Archdeacon and your letter to the Bishop. I think that the opening paragraphs, in which you ask for a period of six months' sabbatical leave from your parish, are perfectly reasonable. As you point out, you have been the vicar of the parish for sixteen years without a break, and there is no reason why your friend the Reverend Damian Wells, who knows the place well, should not be asked to run it for six months. I think the second half of each letter – particularly the letter to the Archdeacon – is a little ill-judged, though I did not see the original correspondence, to which he alludes, between himself and Mrs Spittle. Here again, I wish you would come into the office to discuss this matter with me. If you accuse someone of criminal slander, which is what in effect you are saying, that is a very serious matter and I think it is important that you have your case very well prepared. This sounds

a most distressing matter, and I should be only too willing to help with it in any way that I can.
(3) Your mother's flat. It seems as though the police have no 'leads' whatsoever in the case. Such burglaries are, I am afraid, happening all the time, all over London. We can only be grateful that Mr and Mrs Carter have decided to go ahead with the purchase. In view of the redecorating and cleaning involved, I think it is reasonable to drop the price by £7,000, as suggested by their solicitor. I am sorry for the various delays, but it does now look as if they have completed their searches, and we should be ready to exchange contracts some time next week, and complete in about a month's time. I am glad that you and Mr Gadney are agreed on the price of £63,000. Because of the extra time and effort in selling this flat by Pepperdine Gallows, and their representative Mrs de Freitas, I have agreed that they should have a fee of 2% of the purchase price. I hope this is acceptable to yourself and to Mr Gadney. I will, of course, be communicating these details to Mr Gadney's solicitors.

Perhaps you could telephone my secretary to make an appointment for a further discussion of all these matters.

Yours sincerely,
Doreen Moore.
Dictated by Mr Sandiman and signed in his absence.

Dear Sirs,
I am writing to you as a CHRISTIAN woman who is DISGUSTED by the treatment she has received at the hands of her church and her pastors. Hopefully I shall receive more SATISFACTION from you than from the church authorities. I inclose [sic] my original letter to the Archdeacon, and the COMPLETELY HOPELESS letter he sent back to me. This is a COVER-UP by the Establishment of a sex scandal and an exploitation of women. I am a comited [sic] CHRISTIAN, and so is my husband and we are both utterly SICKENED by the way we have been treated by our church.

Yours faithfully,
Linda Spittle (Mrs.)

Copies to: His Grace The Archbishop of Canterbury.
Sir Alexander Carew MP.
Rev. Terry Widger.
HM the Queen.

Dear Francis,

You can hardly expect me to sympathise with you. You say that you were surprised and hurt to hear of my decision through a solicitor rather than from me direct. Francis, I did not even know *where you were*. You deserted your wife and daughter, and you did not even answer Jessica's letters. (Admittedly, since what you told me had happened in the flat, those letters might have gone astray. I am truly sorry to hear about the burglary, and I know how upsetting you must have found that.)

Francis, we have both been torturing one another for at least ten years. I have tried to get you to talk your problems through, and you have refused. I could not go on living like this. Life is for living. Our marriage had become Hell for me, and I suspect for you too, though that was not something you ever seemed willing to discuss. The best we can both do is to try to find happiness apart, and to do our best for Jessica. She is all right, but Alison and I are both worried about her. She seems to have become almost morbidly religious. For the time being, Jess and I are staying with Alison.

Francis, Jessica and I are having to stay in this village because we have nowhere else to go to. I can't leave the district without uprooting Jessica from school, and the child needs some stability in her life. It is you who started all this. I did not ask you to stop speaking to me. I did not ask you to torture me for ten years. I did not ask you to scandalise the village by running off like that. You say that it is cruel of me to allow you such restricted access to Jess, and you ask if I have contemplated what that is doing to the child. Francis, have you considered what it would do to her to visit you in your present *ménage*? I am not being judgemental, but I do not consider the hippies in that commune suitable companions for our daughter.

Sally.

PS I have shown this letter to Alison and she agrees with me. She sends her regards.

*From the Bishop of ****** to the Archdeacon of ******

Dear George, I think we should have a word about the enclosed. I have also had a very disturbing telephone call from a journalist on the *Sunday Mercury*. Yrs. Harry.

Dear Daddy,

I knew you wouldn't have just ignored my letters. How terrible about Granny's flat. It must have been really frightening for you. I am writing this from a cottage which has been lent to us by Miss Bill's sister. There's a terrific beach, where we have been bathing. Yesterday, Miss Bill took us to where Coleridge wrote 'In Xanadu, did Kubla Khan': it was really nice. Tomorrow we are going to see the grave of (forgotten his name!!) a man that Lord Tennyson wrote a poem about. Miss Bill *makes* Mummy read: at the moment, she is reading a Jane Austen book.

I miss you so much, too. Why can't you just come home? I told you in my letters that got lost that we all love you, and most important of all, JESUS LOVES YOU! Jessica.

*From the Archdeacon of ****** to the Bishop of ******

Too late! See enclosed – I don't imagine you normally read the *Mercury*! I think we can probably 'contain' this one. I've shown it to our lawyers. Almost every word of it is inaccurate, needless to say. We must do something, though, and just hope that it is not taken up by the other papers.

Dear Francis,

The Archdeacon showed me the unpleasant article in the *Mercury*, and let me first assure you that you and your wife and daughter are all in my prayers.

I slightly wish you had come to see me before taking matters into your own hands. Although your solicitor is obviously right, and the article contains much that is damaging (to me and to the Archdeacon as well as to yourself), I think there is a danger of playing into the journalists' hands. There is nothing they would like more than to lure a clergyman into the libel courts and stir up trouble.

I would like you to come and see me at your earliest convenience. Before proceeding any further with the matter, I think that it is necessary for me to have your absolute assurance that every word of this article is untrue. If you and your wife have been having difficulties, I can assure you that you will find a sympathetic ear in Graham, the new Bishop of Didcot, and in me. That is what a bishop is here for.

With every blessing and my love,

Harry.

To the Editor of the *Sunday Mercury*

Sir,

Article in the *Sunday Mercury*,
16th July 1992,
'RANDY REV AND ESKIMO NELL'.

We are instructed by our client, the Reverend Francis Kreer, to act for him in the matter of the article which appears on page 5 of your issue of 16th July 1992. In this article it is stated that:

(1) Mr Kreer proposed substituting an obscene song for a hymn during divine worship, and that he encouraged a female member of his congregation to learn the words of this song.

(2) That on a number of occasions he made overt sexual advances to the same, unnamed, female member of his congregation; that he sent her flowers, fondled her bottom, and made a comparison between a broom handle and his erect male member.

(3) That he was discovered indulging in a sexual act with another woman in a remote side street of Reading.

(4) In the fourth paragraph of your article, you state: 'This Randy Rev has also been on the fiddle. When a priceless jewelled cross disappeared from the church, Rev Kreer claimed the

insurance money for the "stolen property". It was subsequently discovered hidden under his desk in the vicarage.'

(5) That he has been persistently negligent in his conduct of parochial duties, forgetting the times of church services, and even, on one occasion, refusing to bury a much-respected member of the congregation because he wanted to watch television instead.

We wish to state on behalf of our client that every one of these allegations is completely false. He never, at any time, proposed singing obscene songs in church. He has never made sexual advances to any member of his parish. He did not indulge in a sexual act on a public street with a strange woman. He has not been party to an 'insurance fiddle', nor, as your article implicitly states, has he been dishonest in his management of church property or moneys. Nor has he been negligent in pursuit of his duties.

We therefore propose that you print an apology and retraction in full, giving as much prominence in your newspaper to this apology as to the original damaging allegations. We also ask that you should compensate our client for this profoundly damaging personal and professional defamation by substantial financial settlements, and by paying his costs in full.

Yours faithfully,
W.J. Sandiman.

Dear Francis,

How *could* you? I suppose you think it is funny to have this disgusting story printed all over the Sunday newspapers. Alison and I brought Jessica back from a lovely holiday in North Somerset and found the whole village talking about it. And with Lindie Spittle! How *could* you? Sally.

Dear Daddy,

Jesus said, 'Neither do I condemn you. Go and sin no more.' Love from Jessica.

2

On the feast of St Bartholomew August sun lit up, and intensified, the heaviness of summer heat in the Thames Valley. The Bishop's windows were open, but this neither cooled nor refreshed his room.

On the Bishop's desk were several files and folders. They contained the humdrum records of Francis Kreer's parochial ministry, of parish visitations and letters to the Diocesan Finance Committee about his quota. Then, quite different in tone, there were photocopies of Lindie Spittle's letters; of the article in the *Sunday Mercury*; notes from the Archdeacon; photocopies of letters from Wing-Commander Maxwell-Lee. The suffragan Bishop, comparatively new to the job, had never met Francis before. He found it impossible to gauge whether there was any truth in Mrs Spittle's allegations or not. The Archdeacon had hinted that Father Kreer had been seen in London, with a prostitute, by one of his fellow-clergy! The rumour in the parish was that Francis had run off to the seaside with some floozy, and that Francis's wife was conducting a lesbian affair with one of the churchwardens. It all began to look as if the Archdeacon's policy of 'containment' was not going to work. The Archdeacon had advocated playing for time; he had been in favour of allowing Francis a six-month period of sabbatical. The Registrar of the diocese, a solicitor who the Bishop had already decided was a friend, had cautioned against this. There was a danger, said the Registrar, that, if any of these rumours were true, they would merely come back to haunt them all when the six months were up. And, anyway, how were these six months to be spent? If rumour was to be believed, these six months were to be spent with some young woman in a cottage by the sea! It was hardly what one normally thought of as an appropriate sabbatical leave for a clergyman.

The Registrar had therefore drafted a letter which he advised the Bishop to get Francis to sign.

My Lord Bishop,

I am writing to resign the living of St Birinus, Ditcham, taking effect from the 1st August 1992. This is for personal reasons which have nothing whatsoever to do with the rumours at present circulating about me in the newspapers; my resignation in no way endorses these damaging and inaccurate reports.

The Archdeacon said that any man who was wily enough to employ a solicitor in Lincoln's Inn Fields, as Francis did, would be highly unlikely to sign such a document, but the Registrar said that it was worth a try; the great thing being that it would let them off the hook. Let the man stew in his own juice with the newspapers, and with his marital troubles; but, if he had once been persuaded to resign, it ceased to be the church's problem.

'We read your letter, Francis,' said the Bishop of Didcot gently, 'and, basically, Harry and I are very much in favour of this sort of thing – priests taking time off to recharge the batteries. If you *were* to take six months off from the parish, I do not know where you would think of spending it.'

'Some of it in London, some of it in the country,' said Francis Kreer curtly.

The Bishop was not an intimidating man, but in his presence Francis felt distinctly uncomfortable. The Bishop, who was probably Francis's age or a little younger, seemed genial enough, but there was no doubt, in this conversation between two men, seated in armchairs on either side of a fireplace, who was in charge.

'Well, I've got to be honest with you, Francis,' said the Bishop, 'and ask – "How much of all this is true?" '

The words 'All what?' did not come to Francis's lips as confidently as he had hoped. It was not until he entered the Bishop's study, and sat down, and sipped with trembling hand his tea, that Francis became aware that, in this interview, his entire life was being judged: his career and reputation, and all his future security, were at stake. If he had known the Bishop well enough, he might have been able to tell the truth about his life; or at least to spell out what seemed to be true to him at that minute. He wished that he possessed any friend in the world to whom he could talk about these things; but he did not. He had half-wondered, since leaving the parish, whether Ronald Maxwell-Lee would not have provided such friendship, but it was too late now; after all the accusations and counter-accusations and rumours, it would have been impossible to resuscitate his friendship with the Wing-Co.

If the Bishop had been a sympathetic ear, and if Francis had trusted him totally, he would have wished to make him a speech which went a little bit like this:

'I am a man of forty-seven years old whose entire life fell to pieces on the death of his mother last January. Since I was fond of my mother, but not aware of any excessive fondness for her, this intense grief, which very nearly amounted to a nervous breakdown, took me completely by surprise. During this period, I also had to come to terms with the fact that my mother left an extraordinary will, in which I only inherited half her London flat. The other half was inherited by Eric Gadney, a man whom I had never so much as heard of, and who I assume, but have never been told, must have been my mother's lover. The more I know of this man, the more extraordinary and disturbing and disgusting this thought becomes to me: so much so that, on some days, I think that I am going to be unable to think about anything else.

'In the course of my bereavement, breakdown, call it what you will, I undoubtedly neglected my work as a parish priest; I became absent-minded in areas where no caring and pastorally-responsible person has a business to be absent-minded: I failed to visit the sick and, on a few occasions, I forgot to attend church services, or I was late in turning up for them. The worst such instance of this is when I forgot to take the funeral of an old and dear parishioner, Mrs Norbury.

'All these things are symptoms of the fact that I need a period of rest and refreshment. During that time, if I were allowed it, I should be able to reflect on the very strange things which have happened in my inner and emotional life this year.

'I should be able to reflect upon my relationship with Linda and Gerald Spittle. The catalogue of malicious and erotically-charged accusations levelled at me by Lindie Spittle suggests that she is seriously deranged. I never, at any stage, felt the slightest desire to make love to Lindie; I feel no such desire now. As it happens, I have a rather prudish attitude towards "bawdry" and I am not very highly sexed. At no stage in my whole life would I have felt tempted to squeeze the bottoms of strangers, or make Chaucerian remarks about broom-handles. Mrs Spittle should obviously see a psychiatrist, who would perhaps be able to explain to her and her husband why she had felt compelled to make these accusations. Meanwhile, my lawyer in London – with whom I was corresponding over other matters, and whom I had to visit to discuss the final stages of selling my mother's flat – has urged me to sue the *Sunday Mercury* for printing Lindie Spittle's fantasies. This is not because I feel vindictive towards Lindie or towards the newspaper, but because what they have printed is *not true* and I owe it to my own good name, and to the church, and to my daughter, to clear my name.'

All this, Francis would have wanted to say to a sympathetic confidant, and as he sat with his Bishop he almost wondered whether he dared. But he knew that there would have been no point in making half a confession. He would have needed to say everything, and it was this everything which he could not bring himself to say. For, in addition to all these other thoughts, Francis would be obliged to say, 'I am one of the many priests in the Church of England who does not believe in God. I do not consider myself a "hypocrite" for continuing to practise my parochial ministry while not believing the creeds. I am convinced that I was able to do positive good to people in the parish of Ditcham; and what convinces me of this fact was their evident distress when I stopped being efficient, stopped for the reasons which I have given. Even in the late twentieth century, there is a place for the sort of 'ministry' which good parsons have exercised in their parishes since the Middle Ages. Hitherto, I have taken the view that this ministry is worth doing *in itself*, regardless of the religious opinions of the parson. I have now come to revise this view, and to fear that there is something fundamentally dishonest in it; and for that reason I have asked to have six months' leave. If, at the end of that six months' period, I decide that by exercising a priestly life I am "living a lie", then I intend to resign my parish.'

These thoughts had been with Francis for days, ever since the Bishop had summoned him to this interview; and now, when the Bishop smiled and asked Francis how many of the rumours about him were true, a truncated, and infinitely speeded-up, version of these thoughts replayed in his brain. He also wondered how much he could trust the Bishop with the truth about his emotional life. Again, had he been able to tell the truth, he would have said, 'I have been married for nearly twenty years to a person whom I do not respect, and whom I regard, not altogether unfairly, as a fool. I have been cold and impatient to my wife Sally so often, and for so long, that minor domestic cruelty to her has become an ingrained habit. As an experienced parish priest, I know that this is very usual, and that by the standards of many households ours was quite happy. We were not actually hitting one another, and we were both, in our very different ways, devoted to our only daughter Jessica. Nevertheless, in emotional and sexual terms, I was in a marriage which popular newspapers or romances would have described as "loveless".

'About five months ago, I fell in love with a young woman called Jay Dunbar. Again, having watched many marriages over the years, and received many confidences from unhappy people, I am fully aware that it is not in the least unusual for middle-aged men to fall in love with young women. She also loves me, though whether she is "in love" with me I do not know yet. It is not true to say that we were "thrown together" at first. I pursued her. Nevertheless, because of a series of accidents – accidents over which neither of us have or had control – we were "thrown together" by events. First as a result of police violence in Ditcham (of a kind which I never expected to see in England in my lifetime) and then as a result of a number of very sad events in London, we found ourselves together. It would probably sound very improbable to the village gossips and the newspaper reporters, but we have never, in fact, indulged in sexual intercourse, although we have hugged one another, and stroked one another, and held hands as we walked by the sea-shore. We are sharing a small house, "Tudun-Teku", which has been rented to us, for a very modest rate, by Mr Gadney, my co-heir. It was not my ambition to become Mr Gadney's tenant, but after the complete wreckage of our London flat by burglars there was no obvious refuge, and he was kind enough to make the cottage available to Jay Dunbar and to myself.

'I assume that my marriage with Sally is over. She has moved into Alison Bill's house, and has asked, through her lawyer, for a formal marital separation, with a view to divorce in two years' time. I am not in the least sure how I regard this request. On the one hand, I find it exciting to think that, at our age, we can both, separately, make fresh starts. I do not know what the nature of Sally's relationship with Alison Bill might be, but I hope it can make her happy. On the other hand, I am extremely alarmed by the effect that all this will have on our daughter, and I am also irrationally angered by Sally, just by the thought of her. I hate her for having set up house with Miss Bill, and I also hate her for seeming to believe all the crudest and silliest rumours about me, including the newspaper account. I also hate her for instituting legal proceedings against me before telling me that this was what she intended to do, and for making very greedy demands of me – a cash settlement of £20,000 was mentioned in her solicitors' last letter.'

All these thoughts were in the heart of Francis Kreer, and he knew, from a professional point of view, if from no other, that the Bishop could not make a sensible decision, either about Ditcham or about Francis himself, unless he knew them. And yet, Francis discovered that, when the prospect of actual dismissal from Ditcham arose, he did not want to go! It was partly the force of nearly twenty years' habit; partly a sentimental attachment to the job, and the place and the people; partly a cussedness, which made him think, 'I maybe ought to resign, because I don't believe in God, and because my wife wants a divorce, and because I am in love with Jay Dunbar: but I'm damned if I shall resign because Lindie Spittle has taken leave of her senses.'

'Father,' said Francis, 'I should not be suing the *Sunday Mercury* if what they said were true.'

'We need not worry ourselves unduly about the newspaper,' said the Bishop with an insouciance which did not come entirely naturally to him. He spoke, as unworldly people sometimes do, with an air of unconvincing cynicism. 'If we all believed things written about us in the press, I think we'd never get up in the mornings!'

Apart from his own appointment as Bishop of Didcot (which had appeared in the *Daily Telegraph* and the Church newspapers, with photographs of himself standing outside the cathedral with the Archbishop at his consecration), the Bishop had not appeared very often in the newspapers. A number of his speeches had been reported in the local papers, and in those free newspapers which get posted through everyone's front door there had once been a photograph of the Bishop visiting a local primary school. But he spoke with the genial air of a cabinet minister who regularly has to tolerate pictures of himself on the front page of every daily paper. In fact, and in spite of his better nature, the Bishop belonged to the 'no smoke without fire' school of newspaper readership, without whom many editors could not function. He thought that if any paper, even one as tenth-rate as the *Sunday Mercury*, should have printed such a story about Father Kreer, there must be something about it which was true.

'Let me make my position clear,' said the Bishop, pressing his palms together and smiling at Francis. 'I'm your father in God, and I support you utterly. At the same time – and this is important – I'm also the father in God to the people of God in Ditcham.'

Francis did not feel particularly in need of this rather basic Sunday School lecture on the functions of a suffragan bishop.

'Mrs Spittle is a pathetic woman who has been telling lies – to herself, to her husband, to the Archdeacon and now to the newspapers. That is all there is to it,' said Francis, wishing he did not sound so defensive and 'huffy'.

'Now, I'm not saying you have done anything wrong, but there is no doubt a scandal, a stone of stumbling – well, it's a snare, really, isn't it, *scandal* in Greek?'

Francis had immediately summed up the Bishop as one of those modern clergymen who do not know Greek, but who have about a dozen Greek words (they would probably call them buzz-words) in their heads, and which they repeat when talking to the clergy – *koinonia, metanoia, eucharist* . . .

'I do not think there has been any scandal in Ditcham,' said Francis, 'however you define the term.'

'How's Sally bearing up?'

'I'm not sure it's a question of her bearing up,' said Francis. 'As you probably know, my wife and I are living apart at the moment.'

'I'm sorry,' said the Bishop.

'It has nothing to do with the article which appeared in the *Sunday Mercury*; nor with Mrs Spittle.'

The Bishop crossed and then recrossed his legs. He wore a lightweight summer suit which his wife had purchased at Marks and Spencer's. His bright purple shirt seemed very new, as did his episcopal ring and his pectoral cross, which was wooden. The Bishop was hating this stiff little interview with Father Kreer as much as Francis was. But he was not a 'career clergyman' for nothing, this Bishop, and he knew that he could not allow Father Kreer to leave his study until the matter of Ditcham had been settled one way or the other.

'Francis, if you want to talk about any of the difficulties you've been having . . . I mean, we *all* have difficulties in our marriages.'

Once again, this cliché on the Bishop's lips was untrue. He had had a singularly uneventful marriage, which had never caused him a day's anxiety; as far as could be discerned, his wife was perfectly happy too and they had been together for nearly twenty years. As for Francis Kreer unburdening himself to his 'father in God', the Bishop was not in the least sure that he wanted to hear all the sordid details of this 'rum cove's' life.

A distinct lack of sympathy existed between the two men. Francis fell back on thinking that the Bishop was a fool, and the Bishop began to think that Francis was an intellectual snob, and rather 'creepy'. He very much disliked the cold way in which Francis described his wife.

'I don't know if you have considered my application for sabbatical leave,' said Francis, 'but I think it is the solution.'

'We have some problems here, Francis,' said the Bishop. 'There is, for example, the question of who is to run the parish in your absence. And there does remain, and I'm sorry I shall have to say this to you, Francis, there remains the question of scandal.

I must ask you, for instance – this house you are living in at the moment, the one in Sussex.'

'It's in Kent,' said Francis.

'I mean, I take it you aren't alone down there?'

Francis had resolved not to lie to the Bishop. The thought, however, that his relationship with Jay should be classified as something 'naughty', something which he had to justify to his employer, made him feel stubborn about his interrogation.

'They say in the village that you are living with a young woman down there. Is that true?' Francis burned with silent rage. 'Whether this is the same young lady you were seen with in London – where was it – Hyde Park Corner?'

'What?' There was unconcealed anger in Francis's voice. 'Who said that?'

'If you are in our profession,' said the Bishop, 'you can't wander around and not be noticed. I am quite prepared to believe that many of Mrs Spittle's accusations are exaggerated, or even plain wrong. But we are not simply talking about Mrs Spittle, are we, Francis? There is your young lady friend in Kent, there is the fact that you have split up with Sally. Now I'm not being judgmental . . .'

'But you are,' said Francis. 'I thought I'd come here to discuss matters reasonably. I see that you just want me to go! I have the freehold of that parish . . .'

The Bishop did know this; it had been explained to him most painstakingly by the Registrar that the only easy way to 'get rid' of the Vicar of Ditcham was to persuade him to sign a letter of resignation. To give him the sack, it would be necessary to undertake an elaborate and painful procedure in the Consistory Court of the Diocese, proving gross professional misconduct on the part of a clergyman. This everyone, from the diocesan Bishop downwards, was most anxious to avoid, since, apart from anything else, these very rare cases of trials in the Consistory Courts provide a 'field day' for newspapers and always show the Church in an unfavourable light.

'Of course, you have the freehold,' said the Bishop. 'But I think what you and I have to do is to work out, very gently and sensibly, what is best for the parish.'

Francis Kreer felt, at that moment, a tremendous weariness. He thought of Jay, whom he had left that morning in the cottage outside Deal, sitting at the kitchen table, wearing shorts and a dark blue cable-knit jersey which they had bought together at a charity shop. They had enjoyed some very happy days together, but their life was in a state of suspension. It was obviously highly unsatisfactory that they should be living in Mr Gadney's cottage. They were simply refugees from life at the moment, rather than participants in it, and the future was obscure. Everything which had happened since the breaking up of the convoy had been violently disturbing, and when they finally reached the cottage they had both been in a state of shock from which they had not emerged.

The next stage of life, whatever it might be, could not be reached unless he resigned the living of Ditcham. He knew that. By pursuing Jay, he had wanted to leave his old life behind him, and to set out with her on a new journey. Neither of them had been able to do this. The plundering of his mother's flat – presumably her ghastly friend Mo had been responsible for this – had been a terrible emotional experience from which neither of them had yet recovered. He had repeatedly told her that he did not blame her for what had happened, but she was unable to absolve herself from blame, and he was unable to blot out from his mind the sight of the flat when they had returned to it – the empty rooms, the carpets spattered with filth, and his mother's bedroom, stripped of all its furniture, but with her clothes strewn on the floor and reeking with urine and excrement.

The sorrow caused by all this would have taken much time and love to heal. Instead, they had spent this period in a spot which neither of them would have chosen, merely because they could not think, at that moment, where to go, and Mr Gadney had provided them with the bungalow, 'Tudun-Teku'. It was Mr Gadney, too, who had shown Francis the article in the *Sunday Mercury*.

Francis had never had the slightest desire to be famous. It had never been his ambition to see his name in a newspaper. This article, supposedly about himself, had such a powerful effect on him that when he read it he had rushed to the lavatory and retched. This pantomime joke, this 'Randy Rev' who supposedly went around his parish making advances to women, was meant to be him! There was his photograph, and a picture of his vicarage, and the church of St Birinus.

The two events, the attack on the flat and the newspaper article, had reduced Francis Kreer to a state of gibbering fear. The world had taken on the atmosphere of an evil jungle populated by unseen, malicious forces, hostile to himself. Nothing was safe, nothing was secure any more. He had tried to fix in his mind the point when his life had begun to slither out of control. It did not seem so very long ago that he used to feel sorry for himself because his life was so humdrum, and so boring! He knew that he had been good at his parish duties, but the performance of these duties sometimes had made him numb with tedium. But there were high spots – 'fetching time' at school, his easy, innocent little talks with Jessica, his Latin lessons and secret whisky-drinking with the Wing-Co. This stable and largely virtuous way of life, only really marred by the fact that he did not get on very well with his wife, could have gone on forever; and now there was nothing stable. He had at least assumed, with his frequently repeated mantra of 'ninety thousand pounds!', that when the sale of the flat went through he would be financially secure. By the latest count, having divided his share with Mr Gadney, he would receive about £30,000; and already Sally's lawyers (who could have put her up to this? her family? She was neither aggressive nor intelligent enough to have thought of it for herself) were asking him for settlements of up to £20,000 and assurances that he would give money towards Jessica's keep.

Life, fortune, security, happiness itself had all drained away from him with his mother's demise. He had hoped that he was to be the one who could rescue Jay. At present, it was the girl who had the task of shoring *him* up. And they had no sooner begun to cohabit at 'Tudun-Teku' than Francis, habitual doubter of everything, had begun to wonder how two people, however much they might be in love, could live together without a common purpose or a sense of the future.

These problems were not ones with which he could burden the Bishop. But as Francis Kreer sat before his Right Reverend Father in God, and sensed the man's lack of sympathy, he became aware of something more than personal dislike. There was a great unbridgeable metaphysical gulf between them. Ever since January, Francis Kreer had been exposed to suffering. The cruelty of individual events – the loss of his mother, her foolish last will and testament, the misery of his marriage, the violence of the police towards Jay, the breaking-up of the flat, the crazed malice of the Spittles – were in a way no more than he would expect, having come to inhabit the shadow side of the world, the tragedy-view, which sees life as essentially dark and painful and 'happiness as but the occasional episode in a general drama of pain'. And the man on the other side of the fireplace did not inhabit the world of shadows. He lived in the sunshine. It was faint, English sunshine, but you could see from the Bishop's face that he had never really suffered and, indeed, never really thought about anything. The Bishop was presumably what is normally thought of as a good man. He had never swindled or fornicated. He had been kind to his parents, and to his wife and to his children. King's College, London (2cl. Theol. – how Francis and Damian had enjoyed the entries of their fellow-clergy in Crockford in the old days of their friendship, and how much they had enjoyed guessing and reconstructing which university or theological college the clergy of their acquaintance had attended!). Westcott House. Made deacon by the Bishop of Rochester, and priest by the same Bishop. Safe little suburban curacy, followed by a tutorship at Cuddesdon. Canonry of Ely. Principalship of another theological college, and now, at forty-five or so, the suffragan bishop in charge of Francis's neck of the woods. And never once in all those forty-five years had this bland, faintly ridiculous man been compelled to confront the terrible truth about human life on this planet, the truth with which, in their crudely fantastical way, the Biblical authors had wrestled: the fact of death, the fact of evil, the difficulty of virtue, the fickleness of one's own heart. Religion – especially the gentle Anglicanism which the Bishop and Francis had been cheerfully peddling all their professional lives – was designed precisely to disguise from the customers the horrible facts contained in the Biblical myths. When had the Bishop ever known what it was like to be excluded from the Garden of Eden, burdened with the knowledge of death and the consciousness of irrecoverable lost innocence? When had the Bishop ever felt, as the Psalmist did, that God was afar off, and that human depravity and our own feebleness made it impossible to speak to Him, or of Him? When had the Bishop ever known the horrors of Job, or the sufferings of the Hebrew exiles as, by the waters of Babylon, they sat down and wept? But Francis Kreer had known these things. In the year when he had finally given up any pretence at believing in the Bible, he had lived the Bible, and now, like the Chief Representative of those who dwell in the shadow side of the earth, he had come forth, bearing his crown of thorns, to stand before Pilate's judgement seat.

'We owe it to the good folk of Ditcham – who all love you, Francis – to make a decision.'

When the Bishop said 'who all love you', Francis leaned forward and wept. It was not a silent weeping. From the bottom of his chest a deep howl was let forth, followed by moans which shook his shoulders and his diaphragm.

'You doooon't understand!' he moaned. 'You don't understand!'

'I think we understand more than you realise,' said the Bishop. 'We're here as shoulders to cry on, as well as just ecclesiastical bureaucrats.'

It was very difficult for the Bishop to calculate whether, in this gibbering state, the Vicar of Ditcham would be more or less likely to sign his letter of resignation, but he thought that it would be worth the risk. As he reported back to the diocesan by telephone later that day, it was clear that the man was under very great strain, and somebody (not that this was the Church's responsibility) should try to persuade the poor chap to get help. To tell the truth, the Bishop of Didcot thought that Francis Kreer was *mad*.

'Francis,' he said, with the gentle tone which he would have adopted if trying to persuade a lunatic to release his hold on a dangerous gun, 'I am going to ask you to sign a letter of resignation from your living. If you do so, I give you my word that the Church will do all in its power to support you and your wife and family in the coming months.'

'You don't – oh, oh, oh.' Still Francis shook and moaned and gibbered.

'I mean, I think we would both hate it, wouldn't we, if we had to have recourse to the law. That isn't the way we, as Christians – here, Francis.'

He had laid the letter of resignation on the coffee-table at the Vicar of Ditcham's knees. He placed a uni-ball micro deluxe pen in the man's fingers and, to his enormous relief, watched Francis sign.

Later that evening, when they were discussing the matter, the Bishop of the diocese and the Archdeacon weighed up the results of the interview, and of the part played in it by the new suffragan, whose name was Graham.

'I'm afraid that Damian Wells has raised his hopes and thinks that we shall offer Ditcham to him, but it would be entirely unsuitable,' said the Archdeacon.

'It's the last thing we need,' laughed the Bishop. 'I'm sure Damian has mended his ways, but that parish needs a nice *married* man.'

'I'm very glad that Graham persuaded Frankie to resign though,' said the Archdeacon. 'Poor old Frankie.'

'Oh, he's a marvellous man, Graham,' said the Bishop. 'Marvellous with people.'

3

'Well, I call that a really good tea,' said Ena Gadney, who had consumed the last potato chip from her plate, and was now dabbing the corner of her mouth with a paper napkin.

'It was lovely,' said Jay.

'You can never go wrong with the Lobster Pot,' said Eric.

In Jay's experience, this was true. It was an old-fashioned teashop on the sea-front at Deal. One of its rooms was occupied by working men and youths, who consumed huge fried meals at all hours of the day. The other, slightly more genteel room, where the three of them sat, was set aside for families, single ladies, and old age pensioners.

'Go on,' said Ena. 'Have another slice of cake.'

'Do!' urged Eric.

'I couldn't!' exclaimed Jay.

Ena Gadney was a stout party. Owing to her disability, she could not get much exercise. She had a large, mottled face, and her chin had been sketched by a caricaturist in the middle of a great jowly expanse where cheeks wobbled indiscriminately down to neck. Grey eyes darted about her, taking in people at the tables around them – holiday-making families mingling with the regulars.

'Well, if you're not having a cake, I'll have a good old fag,' she announced, and unclasped her large handbag in search of St Moritz menthols. When she had lit up, she said, 'I'm looking forward to hearing you play when we get home.'

'So am I!' said Eric.

'It really was incredibly kind of you. I didn't know how much I was missing my violin until you said you'd buy me a new one.'

Since Francis Kreer was occupied on his mysterious business in Reading for the day, Eric and Ena had elected to take Jay to a music shop in Canterbury to buy her a violin. She had protested at such extravagant generosity – they could not possibly know what violins cost! – but Ena had won her round.

'Learning how to receive is as generous as learning how to give,' she had said. 'Let old Uncle Eric buy you a fiddle. We don't have many youngsters to give presents to. We never had kids, see?'

Jay understood, or felt she understood, why Francis had such very ambivalent feelings about the Gadneys, but she sometimes wished that he could be more gracious to, and about, them. It was inevitable, given Francis's obsession with his mother, that he should have strong feelings about his mother's lover – for such he must assume Eric to have been. But Francis's perpetually sarcastic tone when talking to the old dears really embarrassed Jay, and she hated the way, when they were alone together in 'Tudun-Teku', he railed against Eric.

('If that old man had had a grain of decency, he would never have claimed his share in Mummy's flat. She only made the will about three weeks before she died. I never once heard her mention him. Not once! I think we could easily have proved that the balance of her mind was disturbed. What does *he* need her money for? They are perfectly comfortably off. They have their sheds, and their pelargoniums.'

'Oh, Francis, don't be mean-spirited. I don't like it when you show that side to your nature. We shall be all right. Who needs money?')

Perhaps some strong feeling of awkwardness about Griselda Kreer's will made Eric wish to make his extravagant gesture, and buy Jay a violin. Jay saw that it would be ungenerous in her to refuse the gift, and besides, she could not refuse; she did not merely want a new fiddle, she needed one. So, the expedition to Canterbury had been made; and the three of them had trundled round the Cathedral, as best they might with the wheelchair; and they had stopped at their beloved Lobster Pot before going home.

Jay *liked* the Gadneys. She thought that they were some of the nicest people she had ever met. Poor Eric had his face half burnt off, and Ena was old and fat and by some standards ugly, but they both possessed an exuberant zest for life which Jay found wonderfully helpful at that juncture in her existence.

The day when the flat was burgled was one which would take more than time to recover from. Jay had become slowly and dispiritingly aware, during her association with Mo – not that *he* was evil (she refused to believe that persons, individuals, could be evil) – but that there did occur in human lives certain conjunctions which were conducive to evil; rather in the way that certain chemicals, harmless when left to themselves, turn into dangerous explosives when mixed. Mo's arrival at the convoy on his journey from Wales, his association with her, his particular narcotic dependency, had all led inexorably to that scene: to Francis holding up one hand to his right cheek as though that part of his face had been burnt, wandering like a stretcher-bearer through a battle-field. 'Mummy's clothes,' he had said quietly. 'Why have they done this to Mummy's clothes?'

And Jay could not answer this question, but she felt responsible. She did not consider herself morally culpable for what Mo and his friends had done to Mrs Kreer's flat. She was, however, aware that she had been the link in the chain which made such an act of evil possible. She had been an enabler of evil. Now, for her own spiritual health, and for that of others, she deeply wanted to be an enabler of good things: a vessel or channel of grace. Her association with Francis Kreer could be of such a quality, and so could their friendship with the Gadneys, she felt sure. Perhaps there were things reaching far back into Francis's past, and into his mother's past, and into Eric Gadney's past, which needed to be blessed or hallowed or absolved? Francis was bitter about the will and angry that his mother should have left money to a man whom she had 'never so much as mentioned, not once'. But was he not angry at some much deeper level with his mother? Did Mr Gadney not represent those semi-forgotten, or wholly forgotten, years of Francis's childhood when his mother was not providing her 'Little Boy' with the love he so fervently desired?

How many hours had Jay spent hearing about his mother? Already the time was immeasurable. He would, presumably, have to find therapy of a professional kind; for there were some days when he could speak of nothing else, and the thoughts and memories would tumble from his lips so rapidly that he would jabber, without breath, for hours. Sometimes it would be a specific thought – 'That blouse that was so very filthy.'

'Don't think about those clothes, Little Boy.'

'It's odd. It just came back to me. She bought it in Jaeger, and I remember her wearing it when she came to lunch for the first time at Ditcham. "Darling, are you sure there are going to be enough of *our sort* in this parish? Some of these places are *different worlds*. . . ." I must make her sound so snobbish, which she wasn't, she wasn't at all.'

He did, indeed, make her sound snobbish, coquettish, negligent in important areas of emotional need, probably unfaithful to her husband, improvident with money, capricious, not without cruelty, beautiful, beguiling, intellectually limited, far less intelligent than some of her remarks (mere parrot memories of things Daddy said) would have indicated, odious. Almost every speech which Little Boy made about Mummy was a speech for the Prosecution, but the alarming thing about these speeches was that Francis, normally sharp and intelligent, seemed entirely unaware of this. He spoke of this woman, whom he had obviously detested, and had every reason to detest, as if she were a saint.

'I hope you won't get the impression that Mummy drank too much, but she didn't . . .' And there would follow a string of memories, stretching back to the point where memory faded into instinct, of Mummy getting tight at parties, losing her temper, saying humiliating things to Daddy, or embarrassing her Little Boy by flirting. But, when the indictment was complete, he would add some little formula like 'Bless her', and Jay would see that he missed her, and wanted her to be as beguiled as Little Boy by the memory of Mummy, half-sloshed on dry martinis, dropping names or failing to cook a decent meal. 'You mustn't think Mummy and Daddy didn't get on . . .' and there would follow chapter and verse accounts of Daddy eating supper on a tray, while she entertained her supposedly 'smart' friends. The night James Agate (who was staying with some neighbours) was inveigled into coming over for dinner in Gerrard's Cross! Jay thought that Little Boy himself was a little too impressed by the grandeur of the guest (whoever James Agate was – Jay had never heard of him!) to see how appallingly his mother had behaved. Or – staying in some modest seaside hotel – 'Little Boy and I are going out to dinner; you can stay here and eat high tea and do the crossword if you like!'

When he remembered his father, his tone was like that of a man remembering a favourite schoolmaster, or perhaps an uncle. He spoke of him solely as a good classicist who had passed on his passion to his son, or a man who could do the crossword, or recite the whole of *Lycidas*. (Jay had said nothing during the memory because she was not completely sure what *Lycidas* was.) His father seemed just like a walk-on part (messenger or spear-carrier) in the great Mummy-drama. Everything Jay heard about the father made her think she would have liked him; everything she heard about the old woman made her know she would have loathed her. But – there she was, lying between them when they lay together at night, dancing in and out of their thoughts whether they woke or slept. Jay wondered how Ena came to terms with the thought of Griselda? It was not something which Jay had ever spoken about. Had Ena always known about Eric's 'past' with Griselda? It was an unfathomable question. Had the legacy sweetened the pill of jealousy, or re-opened old wounds?

'Thank you, my old love,' said Ena, who had a hand on each of Jay's shoulders. This operation, of heaving Ena from a sitting to a standing position, was quite hefty work. Jay did not understand how Eric had managed before her arrival. (If Jay had a fault, she recognised, it was the desire to be thought indispensable.) 'And where's old Eric?'

'He's gone to get the wheelchair.'

'Well, that's good. It'd be nice to have a little turn on the front before we go back to Sunnymede.'

The car, with its orange disabled stickers, was parked just outside, so that Eric was soon at the door of the Lobster Pot with the wheelchair.

'No, I'm fine, old love, if you just – oof, pff! oo! No, that's lovely!'

Lifting her extraordinary ankles – almost as collapsed and fleshy as her neck, almost as wide – on to the foot-rests of the wheelchair was the final stage before what Eric called 'take off', the releasing of the brakes and then they were away.

The warmth had left the day. Ena remarked that she was glad of her cardie. Wind was coming in off the choppy sea, and gulls on the wing were being blown off course. Families on the beach either huddled yet more closely behind their wind-shields or started for home.

'I love the little front at Deal,' said Ena. 'Nice little shops. Hullo, dear!' she saluted passing dogs, children, with uncomplicated and unfeigned benignity. Jay pushed the chair, and Eric waddled along at her side, with his arm lightly round her waist.

'I wonder what those boys are catching,' said Jay, when they passed the small pier where a group of anglers hurled their lines against the winds.

'Cold, I shouldn't wonder,' offered Ena, which they all thought very funny.

'I shouldn't mind getting one of them to teach me to fish,' said Jay.

'Old Eric could teach you,' said Ena, 'couldn't you, love? You've got some rods.'

'That's right,' said Eric. 'You might get a bass or two off there if the tides were right.' He spoke in what Francis cruelly dubbed his pompous, know-all tone, but which Jay found rather sweet. She half-liked it when men, like little boys, could not bear to be considered inadequate in any of life's areas. Where she admitted that she knew nothing of fishing, but would like to learn, Eric had to be something of an expert; Mo had been like this, and she had wearied of it in him; but she had never really *liked* Mo, she now believed, whereas she liked the Gadneys, both of them, very much indeed.

'We're both looking forward to our concert,' said Eric, whose hand had strayed from Jay's wrist and was gently massaging her buttocks.

'Have we bought her enough music?'

'It's fine, really, to start with,' said Jay. 'The Dvorak is lovely, and quite difficult: it will keep me going for weeks; and all those Beethoven pieces are wonderful.'

'And don't forget *Ruddigore*,' said Ena.

Jay smiled. She realised that she must be growing up. A year ago, her detestation of Gilbert and Sullivan would have made her stand out, on principle, against the purchase of these absurd airs. Now she saw that Ena and Eric were buying her a violin, it was a very small price to pay to entertain them with 'A highly susceptible Chancellor'. Nor did she even mind, though she was not quite sure, either what it signified, or how far she should allow it to go, that the old man's hands, expertly and gently, were stroking her in a far from paternal manner.

4

While the wind got up at Deal, a thunderstorm had broken over Berkshire. The thunderbolt cracked almost instantaneously with the lightning, giving reason to suppose that the storm itself was located almost directly above St Birinus's Church, Ditcham. These violent lights and sounds were accompanied by a downpour of rain which had the solid intensity of a monsoon. Anyone who stepped out in it would be instantly drenched. Roses, hydrangeas, lupins and delphiniums were being flattened in gardens all over the village. Footpaths were being transformed into clayey mud-pits. Ditches were filling with puddles; puddles were turning to small ponds. Robin Pimm, driving over the brow of the hill in a tractor, his cloth cap soaked and clinging to his skull, his cigarette not merely extinguished but bent by the rain, thought for a nasty moment that his back wheel was stuck in a mud hole, but by judicious revving he got it out again. Bowling along the road, he nearly collided with an idiot who was driving at far too great a speed for such weather conditions. Since he was wet and cross, and wanted to get home for his tea (the storm was happening at about the time Ena Gadney was finishing her cod in batter with chipped potatoes), Robin Pimm saw no reason why he should reverse his tractor for the sake of this impatient car. If the driver wanted to reverse, let him: if he wanted to pass at that patch of road, let him risk sinking his axle in two or three feet of muddy water.

'And blow me,' said Robin Pimm half an hour later, when he was relating the incident to his wife, 'if it wasn't the parson!'

'Driving like the lunatic he is!' said Mrs Pimm. 'You know, Mrs Renton was telling me the other day that she always thought there was –'

'Something funny in the man's eyes,' Robin completed the sentence for her. 'You keep saying that.'

'Was the woman with him?' asked Mrs Pimm.

'What woman?'

'The woman he's gone off with.'

'I couldn't see who he was with; but I tell you one thing, he was driving like the devil himself, like a lunatic.'

The weather had, indeed, been so violent, that Francis had wondered, at the bottom of the road coming out of Streatley, whether he should attempt the journey. At one point, the road had turned into a shallow, fast-moving rivulet. It was some time since he had checked the tyres on his car, and he slipped back a lot as he roared into the village, too fast and in too high a gear.

After his interview with the Bishop, Francis turned back to Ditcham as if by instinct. Once there, he knew that he must try to see Jessica, and have a talk to his daughter about what had happened. It was insufferable that Sally, and Miss Bill of all people, should be preventing him from seeing his own child! He also wished to pick up a few boxes full of books from the vicarage, and perhaps some clothes. He had driven away more than six weeks ago, and he was desperately hungry for reading-matter, and rather less desperately in need of something to wear.

His first port of call, then, was at the vicarage. It was strange to enter that house as a revenant. It both welcomed him and shut him out. When he was in the study, packing books into boxes, he was at home; the room embraced him, and everything which had happened since he left it buzzed in his mind like a cruel nightmare from which he had awoken. He could return to all this, surely? It was his! This was his natural habitat.

Francis both did and did not know that he had resigned the living of Ditcham. We shall never know the truth about the state of his mother's mind when she changed her will, but in this matter of the resignation, here was a real case of the balance of his mind being disturbed. He knew that he had done so, but, even *while* he knew it, he could not accept it; and there were to be some days, and even extended periods in the coming months, when he actually forgot that he had resigned the living. It was one of the points where Francis's mind, and his entire imaginative consciousness, took leave of empiricism or what could be called reality. There was an absolute divergence between what he perceived and what was the case. Many people did not fully understand this, and there were many, the majority, who found it easier to explain the mental dislocation which I am describing, by saying that Francis had 'gone mad'.

With tremendous, over-excited energy, and a tumbler of whisky at his side, Francis packed his dearest old friends into cardboard cartons: Virgil, Horace, Statius, Homer, Sophocles, Aeschylus, E.R. Dodds on *The Greeks and the Irrational*. His Baedekers for Southern Italy: that was it! He and Jay could go down to Pompeii, and Herculaneum. Then they would need Pliny! His long agitated fingers held the volume, and could not resist, before flinging it into the box, flicking back to Pliny's letter to the Emperor Trajan, describing the activities of the Early Christians.

'A terrible thing, the persecution of the Early Christians,' Francis remembered his Ancient History tutor once saying to him, 'not *nearly* severe enough.'

How shocked priggish, Puseyite young Francis Kreer had been by this hardened Gibbonian cynic, who had also once said to him, 'Do you want to know my definition of a religious maniac? Someone who believes in God!'

How completely Francis had absorbed this man's world-picture without knowing that he had done so! Of course! That was the explanation for why he had so-called lost his faith! Francis, kneeling before his books on his study floor, swigged more whisky. He saw that now! His mind had been completely possessed at the age of nineteen by this formative influence, that of his Ancient History tutor – Harris of Balliol. But it had taken his soul, and his imagination, about twenty years to catch up: so, while being a pure creature of Harris when he was in his study, Francis had gone on trying to be a loyal High churchman for the rest of his time; and it did not square up.

'Why do you need to go to church? Religion's for buggers and women,' Harris had opined. Francis had often thought of it, during twenty years of parochial ministry. It was now an opinion with which he agreed.

Gibbon himself, the seven small volumes of his pocket edition, must go into the boxes, and the Loeb Thucydides and Herodotus, and some of the English poets – Cowper, Pope, Keats.

Upstairs in his dressing-room he packed a suitcase at random, shoving in shirts, a suit, a cassock (one never knew if this might not one day be needed), a couple of jerseys. Francis possessed few clothes and, when he looked at the ones he was leaving behind, he realised that it would be no grief if he never saw them again. There had been several moments in his life when Francis had been caught off guard by an event. A small example of it had been when he first drove a car: no one had told him that you propelled a car by removing your foot from the clutch. He had assumed that in order to make it go forward, you pressed the accelerator. The 'driving lesson' had therefore got underway seconds before he had intended, and he and his mother had hurtled off before his brain had adjusted. Something of the same sensation had occurred at many of the turning-points of his existence – the train pulling out of Gerrard's Cross to take him off to National Service; the processional hymn starting up at his ordination service, slightly before he had anticipated it. And there would be this 'down the chute, here we go' feeling. In his over-excited, and by now slightly inebriated condition, Francis Kreer knew that some such 'new phase of existence' was about to start; and it was different in kind from everything else which had ever happened to him: all these other 'down the chute' experiences had been predictable, and the end was known. He had known that he would be sent away to boarding-school, and that he would have to do his military service, and that he would attend university; he had decided to be ordained, and he knew that he would one day be married, so that even these great emotional milestones had about them an inevitability, when the moment of decision had been reached. And, although he had this sensation in the pit of his stomach which was a mixture of panic and excitement, it had always been accompanied by the knowledge of what he would be doing next. 'In an hour's time I shall be enlisted in the army, by the end of this hymn I shall be a priest, by the time the clock strikes three I shall be married.' Such thoughts could create heavings of stomach, bowels, nerves, but they did so because they sprang from a determinist certitude that his future could not now be changed. In the present case, the excitement and fear were generated by the knowledge that nothing was certain. He was going out, like one of the patriarchs in *Genesis*, with no certainty of where he was going, nor of what he was going to do. He was going as Love's pilgrim, because he worshipped, venerated and adored Jay Dunbar. This was his vocation. The previous forty-seven years had been what most human lives are, a following of tramlines of other people's devising. For what doth it profit a man if he gain the whole world and lose his own soul? Or what shall a man give in exchange for his soul? Were not the Biblical writings, at their core, a whole series of myths about men and women who dared to be independent of conventions, or religious stereotypes, or social groupings? Biblical man, or woman, was on the move, despised and rejected of men, a very outcast. This is true of Adam excluded from Paradise; it is true of Abraham leaving the security of Ur of the Chaldees, it is true of Ruth refusing to turn back to her own people, the Moabites, but following Naomi out of pure affection, wishing that her people and her God might be the same.

Ruth's prayer to Naomi was Francis Kreer's to Jay Dunbar: 'Entreat me not to leave thee, or to return from following thee: for whither thou goest, I will go, and where thou lodgest, I will lodge: thy people shall be my people, and thy God, my God.'

When he recited these words to himself, in the vicarage, he was imbibing his third, quite stiff glass of whisky. It was several hours since he had eaten anything, and he found that he was slightly drunk as he closed the vicarage door for the last time, and walked out into the storm. The car was now loaded with books and clothes, and the easy part of his journey to Ditcham was complete.

He decided to walk down to Miss Bill's cottage to visit his daughter. It would give him time to form his thoughts into words: for it was essential, he understood this, to say nothing to Jessica which was unnecessarily hurtful; at the same time, it was imperative that he should tell his child the truth. God knew what 'those women' had been saying to Jessica. She deserved to know that her parents were no longer to live together, but he had no wish to desert his child. When the future, the wholly unthought-out and undecided future, became clearer, it should be possible for him and Jess to live together. The little girl would surely understand that, just at the moment, he could not be seeing her all the time? Jessica's residence with 'those women' need only be temporary, and this was one of the facts that he must get across to her. The other thing which he knew must always be emphasised on these occasions was that he still loved her. There had never been any question of the truth of this statement, but he knew that he must be very explicit about it. Jessica must realise that her father loved her, and the fact of his having gone away in no way diminished this. The third thing which Francis believed that he must share with Jess was the extraordinary joy which had come into his own heart since meeting Jay. Neither depth nor height, nor angels, nor principalities, nor powers, nor things present nor things to come could separate him from this love, which was, as far as Francis was concerned, of a redemptive character. He had not been 'saved' yet, but, having abandoned all to follow his new goddess, he was walking in the way of salvation, and this was something which he wished he could find words to express to his child; for he was sure that, if he presented it all to Jess as a positive thing, she would understand why it all *had to be*.

As this confused jumble of thoughts tried to make themselves into consoling sentences in his mind, sentences which could be uttered to Jessica, Francis – who wore only a light raincoat and no hat – was becoming completely drenched by the pelting of the pitiless storm. Rain spattered his face, which was lit, every few minutes, by flashes of lightning, followed by instantaneous cracks of thunder.

In Alison Bill's small house, Jessica was in the spare bedroom. She had opened a copy of *Good News according to Luke* and had come upon the words, 'Ask, and you will get what you want; look, and you will find what you want; knock, and the door will be opened.' She closed her eyes and called up the presence of Jesus into the room. Within a minute or two, she felt the 'warm glow' which signalled His arrival, and she spoke to Jesus in prayer, 'Lord, I ask that Daddy should come home. Look after him, Lord, and, wherever he is, bring him to me.'

As always when she spoke to Jesus, Jessica found that He was very close, and very real. She felt as warm and comfortable in His presence as if He had His arms around her; in fact, if she closed her eyes and gave herself completely to Jesus, she could actually feel Him touching her. Knowing Him to be so near, she quietly hummed to Him the tune of one of the numbers on the tape which Terry Widger had sent to her, 'Saviour mine'. It was good to do this during the storm, which lashed the tree outside her window, and rattled the window-panes, because it reminded her that Jesus, who once stilled just such a storm when he was in Galilee, was stronger than the thunder, brighter than the lightning, and in charge of the whole Universe.

The storm was so loud that at first she did not hear the knocking at the door, but when she heard Miss Bill opening the door, and heard her father's voice, Jessica was not surprised: Jesus had said that, if we ask the Heavenly Father for anything in His name, he would grant our request. Anything at all! A little matter like bringing Daddy home might have sounded difficult to other people: but, for Jesus, it was easy! What had Terry Widger said in that tape-recorded sermon which had been sent to her from the Immanuel Church? 'Jesus is the Original Superman; only he is so much more powerful than Clark Kent because he's for real!'

Alison Bill opened her front door to the accompaniment of

a thunderburst and saw her former vicar standing outside her porch, dripping with water. His hair was matted to the side of his skull, and his clothes were dark and heavy with moisture.

'You can't come in,' said Alison Bill.

'I have come to see Jessica.'

'I'm sorry, but you can't come in.'

Alison and Sally had discussed repeatedly what they would do in the inevitable event of Francis's reappearing. Alison knew that Sally would 'weaken' when she found herself face to face with her husband; and Alison was quite confident in her mind that it would do Sally no good at all to be reunited with Francis. The only hope for Sally, as Alison saw it, was to separate herself from the ignominious role of being despised, humiliated, crushed by daily life with the man. Sally must break *free*; this was what Alison Bill had told her, and Sally had, of course, meekly complied with this. Sally agreed that, if Francis ever did come to the door, Alison must answer it. Sally would be kept out of the way until he had been persuaded to go.

'I have come to see my daughter,' said Francis once again.

'And I am very sorry, but I can't let you in.'

The pleading tone in Francis's voice, the implied appeal to old friendship, struck quite the wrong note. Francis had been blind to all that had happened between his wife and Miss Bill this year. He had failed to see that Alison Bill loved Sally with a possessive mania, and that this had turned Alison from being one of the Vicar's allies in the parish to being one of his bitterest enemies.

'Please. Alison.'

The former Vicar's appearance counted against him. Had it been a dry day, and had he been dressed with the cleanliness and neatness which usually characterised him, Alison Bill might have been more inclined to treat him like a reasonable being; since he looked like a wild thing, she treated him like one.

'If you want to talk to Sally, you must do it through her lawyers,' said Alison firmly.

'Jessica! Jessica!' he called desperately.

'Daddy! Daddy!'

'I told you that you mustn't . . .' began Miss Bill.

In this moment, Miss Bill did not seem merely plain, she seemed ugly and terrible. Her large mouth with its sprouts of moustache on the upper lip appeared particularly aggressive; the marble-eyes behind thick glasses seemed inhuman and sinister.

'Go back upstairs, Jess,' she commanded authoritatively.

'Daddy!'

Jessica ran through the front door into the rain and hugged, clawed, adored her father. It was like the reunion of lovers.

'Daddy, I knew you'd come!'

'Of course I'd come.'

'Daddy, we can go straight home. I'll get Mummy. I'll get my things. Wait a quarter of an hour, twenty minutes, less. I'll pack. You can come and sit with me while I pack.'

'I'm sorry, Jessica, but your father isn't coming into the house.'

Jess very conspicuously ignored the Old Bill.

'I'll get Mummy.'

'Darling, I haven't come to take you and Mummy back to the vicarage. . . .'

'But I don't understand.'

'Jess, I've come to have a talk with you. If the weather wasn't so bad, I'd say we ought to have a walk.'

'But you are coming back? I mean, we will all be together again? Miss Bill kept telling Mummy that you wouldn't be back, that it was all for the best – that your marriage, oh Daddy, I'm so glad to see you, it's been terrible, terrible.'

To the top of her head, which pressed against his bosom, Francis said, 'Darling, I'm afraid I'm not . . .'

'Oh, Daddy!'

She looked up at him.

'Don't go – not now you've come back. Don't go, Daddy.'

'Jessica, I've *got* to. I hope that soon, very soon, we shall have a new place to live, you and I.'

'You are lying,' said Miss Bill. 'Jessica, come back indoors. Do not listen to your father, he is lying to you.'

'You!' The anger of Jesus Christ cleansing the Temple, which had seized Francis on the morning of the police raid on the convoy, seized him now, and he flew at Miss Bill. He took her turquoise mohair cardigan in his fists and grabbed at it, until she too was out in the rain, becoming wet.

'Leave me alone,' she protested.

'What lies have you been telling Sally and Jessica? Just who do you think you are?' he said, the hatred for this being almost spewing out of him.

'Do you want me to call – let me *go*, let me go – do you want me to call – Jessica, call the police!'

'Oh, stop fighting, both of you.'

'You aren't going to stop me seeing my own daughter. Do you hear? You are an evil woman!'

These words were partially stopped by Alison Bill putting out a palm to cover Francis's face and pushing him very hard. He staggered backwards slightly and, when he regained his balance, he struck out with a fist at her.

'Stop it! Stop it!' called Jessica.

'You!' Miss Bill now came at Francis with her nails clenched, and scratched at his eyes and cheek. She seized some of his wet hair. He responded by landing a hefty punch on the side of her head, and, when he fell in the muddy puddles of her garden path, he brought Alison Bill down with him.

Jessica screamed and ran into the house.

Francis was by now in a madness of rage where he only wished to beat Alison Bill, and if necessary kill her. Not only was she massive, however, but she was also extremely strong, and she easily managed to hold her own in the fight with the willowy and far from muscular priest. Her spectacles had flown off in the scuffle. Both of them were still rolling and writhing on the path when Ronald Maxwell-Lee stood over them with an umbrella.

'Stop it! B-both of you, s-stop it!'

When they clambered to their feet, they were both drenched. Both had scratched and bleeding faces.

'This is d-disgraceful,' he said. He was holding Jessica's hand. 'Are you going to be all right?' he asked the child.

'I'm all right.'

'If your mother and you want to come over to us. . . .'

'We'll be all right.'

Jessica seemed quite numbed by the experience of watching

her father and her schoolmistress fighting on the ground like rough schoolboys.

'Just go, go!' said Alison Bill.

'I think you'd better do as she says,' said the Wing-Commander.

Francis, who had not worked out the manic rage which he felt against Miss Bill, could not believe that the Wing-Commander, *his friend*, was taking Miss Bill's side against him. He hovered uneasily for a few seconds between leaving the scene, as requested, and making one lunge against Miss Bill, tearing at her hair or smashing her nose.

'Jessica!' he called out.

'Haven't you caused enough t-trouble for one day?' the Wing-Commander asked him. The old man's tone was so withering that Francis turned back through the rain, and went out again in the road. Beyond the garden gate and the hedge, he looked up at the upstairs windows. He thought he saw Jessica peep down from one of these windows and then disappear behind a curtain. Then he broke into a run and made his way in haste through the parish and back to the vicarage.

They did not know it was their priest, the Spittles, as they stood by the metal-framed picture-windows of 'Gleneagles' and looked out at the storm.

'Come away from the sockets, Gerrie,' Lindie enjoined; she was of the view that, during a thunderstorm, electricity could come and 'get' you via the holes of electric sockets in the wainscotting.

'I've told you, that's impossible.'

'I hate storms.'

'It'll pass.'

Since writing to the *Mercury* Lindie had quietened down, Gerrie was glad to say. She must have realised, when she saw that newspaper story, that she had just gone too far. Their lawyers had been on to her about ten times since, collecting evidence: for Francis was going to sue. The idea of the trial filled Gerrie with horror. Would he be called as a witness?

'Is your wife in any way unbalanced, Mr Spittle?'

'No, your honour.'

'I mean, she is a perfectly healthy, reasonably attractive woman.'

'Yes, your honour.'

'Sexually normal, well-satisfied, and so on? . . . Well, come on, man, tell us! Can you *give* it to her? Women don't go round having fantasies about broom handles if they are getting it often enough from their men! The Clerk of the Court will now establish your virility by removing your trousers and showing you off to the ladies and gentlemen of the jury.'

'There's someone out jogging,' said Lindie, as the figure of Francis Kreer scuttled past the front gate.

So much of their *business*, their buried, unmentioned lives, seemed in danger of exposure as these lawyers asked Lindie questions: who else in the village had been molested by the 'Randy Rev'? What were his favourite places for doing it? Which female types was the 'Randy Rev' said to 'go for' – the lawyers meant, was he a legs man, a tits man? Yes, these were serious questions because they would use them to humiliate him if it ever came to court. Any damaging anecdotes about him, or his wife or his friends might be useful to their purposes.

'Aren't you going to tell them – it's all out of proportion?' Gerrie had said. 'I mean – Francis.' There was something rustic and boyish, blushing, about Gerrie's laugh. He had laughed like that when, the first time Lindie made him kiss her, in a bus shelter in Caversham, he had gone 'all shy'.

Lindie knew that she had overshot her bolt. She had to answer the questions by the lawyers, but she made up for it by being especially kind to Gerrie, cooking his favourite meals and so forth. The thunderstorm was a shame because it was taking place during one of Gerrie's favourite television programmes. Having the set switched on during a storm, was, of course, out of the question.

Unaware of the Spittles' eyes upon him, Francis ran on. By the time he reached the car, parked outside the vicarage, his clothes were completely sodden. He was very dirty and his cheeks had begun to sting. He wondered whether to change his clothes, or to bathe his wounds before the car journey, or whether to eat something. In the event, he could not bring himself to waste any more time. He ran back into the house for one last visit to the lavatory, and took, as he ran out again, the bottle of whisky which he had left on the hall table. He could swig that as he went, but he must be back with Jay, for where she goeth, he must go;

her people would be his people and her no-God, his no-God.

Normally a cautious and rather timorous driver, Francis when drunk became Toad of Toad Hall, a bold jumper of red lights, an intrepid and skilful overtaker, and a master of getting the car straight on the road when the back wheels skidded on corners. The rain continued to fall so profusely that the wipers could never quite wipe the windscreen clear. The road ahead, as the darkness of the storm was swallowed in the greater darkness of dusk, became less and less distinct, but still Francis forced the car onwards, his foot firmly pressed against the accelerator, the nose of the bonnet thrusting forward through the darkness, and the wet, and the haze of pearly falling raindrops, each dazzling with the orange reflection of passing headlights. It was more like flying than driving by land. And all the time, over his head, the storm followed him southwards and eastwards, rumbling its bellyful, spitting fire and spouting rain from the heights of the clouds above the bleak outer suburbs of London, orange with light and lacerated by arterial roads, where Surrey imperceptibly turns into Kent in a huge sprawl of fast lanes and tower-blocks and houses.

'You all right?' asked the man at the service station, when Francis paid him for the refill of the petrol tank. (This was somewhere outside Canterbury.)

'Yes.'

'You shouldn't be driving, mate,' said the cash clerk, taking a careful note of Francis's wet, dirty hair, cut and muddy face and whisky-red eyes, sure that he would sooner or later be summoned to give evidence, and would need an accurate memory of Francis's appearance.

Francis signed his credit card chit without a word.

'You are Reverend?' asked the clerk.

A queue was forming behind Francis. Did he really look so strange that a clerk in a petrol station would not believe him to be sufficiently creditworthy to have a Barclaycard? Unsatisfied, the clerk rang a number and checked that the card was still valid, had not been stolen or cancelled by the owner. Then he peered very closely at the two signatures, the one on the card.

'You don't look like a Reverend,' said the clerk.

'I am the Vicar of . . .' For the first time in seventeen years,

Francis found himself unable to say with truth that he was the Vicar of Ditcham; or was he still the Vicar of Ditcham? Through the dizziness caused by two hours on the road, the blinding of undipped headlights, the pangs of an empty stomach, the glow of whisky, he murmured, 'I am the Vicar of Sorrows,' and shuffled out into the rain.

Thereafter, Francis made this phrase his secret description of himself. On a full tank, the Maestro gathered speed, and through the wet haze of the windscreen and the side-windows, the Vicar of Sorrows, acquainted with grief, hurtled past the old walls of the city towards his goal. At some lights, he had to slow from fifty-five to nought in a few hundred yards. He did so with much squealing of brakes but with remarkably little skid. He was developing a taste for this sort of driving, and before red turned to amber he unscrewed the bottle at his side and gulped back a further mouthful of Famous Grouse. He had seldom been at the perfect level of inebriation for long: the level where the world had not yet started to spin, and where he felt no degree of nausea, but where the old slang phrase perfectly fitted his mood: lit up. He was now without inhibition. As the car climbed from forty, fifty, seventy, eighty, miles per hour, the priest roared out hymns – the *Vexilla regis* and *O salutaris hostia* – with tears running down his blood-stained, muddy face. At twenty to eleven, having passed Deal, he turned off the Walmer Road and screeched to a halt outside 'Tudun-Teku'.

5

Francis could hear the violin music – the Beethoven Sonata – coming from the bungalow before he rat-a-tat-tatted on the stiff old door-knocker. Whether or not Jay possessed a violin was not, at that moment, uppermost in his mind. He did not ask himself how she came to possess the instrument. It seemed quite natural, as he approached her, that there should be music. When it continued, he wondered if the sonata was coming from a radio, but the fact that she stopped, started, replayed certain phrases, made it clear that she was in.

'I'm sorry, I just wanted to get to the end of that – oh my God! What's happened to you?' were her words as she opened the door.

In the light of the little hall, she looked very clean, Francis very dirty. She wore a crisply-ironed, short-sleeved blouse, decorated with a motif of yellow yachts sailing on a calm blue sea (another Oxfam purchase); she also wore carefully-ironed black trousers. Her feet were bare.

'Poor Francis!' Her small, cool hands reached up to his face and for the first time he was aware of how much pain he was in.

She closed the door behind him. He dropped his baggage on the carpet, and she led him into the living-room.

'What happened?'

'Jay, Jay! Hold me.'

'Oh, you poor man. You poor, poor man!'

'I love you, Jay.'

'Oh, poor Francis. You're soaked. Who's been attacking you?'

'Alison Bill.'

'Not the nice schoolmistress?'

'She is not a nice schoolmistress. She is an evil woman.'

'You must get those clothes off. You are completely sodden.'

Jay the former Girl Guide (First Aid had been one of her badges) made Francis sit down. She untied his dripping shoelaces, and removed his shoes and socks.

'Wait a minute. I'll be back.'

Dazed, he sat, hearing her rummage in the bedroom, and running a bath in the tiny bathroom which abutted on to the kitchen. She returned with a blanket. He raised his hands aloft, as he had done when a very young child, allowing her to remove his jersey, and his shirt. Then she took off his trousers and pants, and wrapped the blanket round his shoulders. She ran from the room with the bundle of filthy clothes, and switched off the bath. She came back with a warm wet face-cloth and a towel.

'Sit still while I bathe your face.'

'I love you. She's got Jessica there as a prisoner. She is a madwoman, an evil madwoman. I went to see the Bishop. The Bishop of Didcot. He is a fool, but he sees that they are all mad. They can't just get rid of me.'

'But you don't want to stay. You don't want to stay at Ditcham.'

'I won't be driven out by mad, evil people. Lindie Spittle is mad, Alison Bill is mad. Sally is mad. She did not even come to the door to see me, but I knew she was there. The Bishop talked the usual rubbish about . . . And then Ronald Maxwell-Lee came. He had a gun, I think. Or an umbrella anyway. Oh, Jay, I love you. I need you.'

'There! That's my brave Little Boy. Some of these cuts are rather nasty. I might put a sticking plaster on when you've had your bath.'

'I fought her. I fought Alison Bill. I wouldn't let her keep Jessica as a prisoner.'

In the bathroom, Jay removed the blanket from his shoulders and helped Francis to climb into the bath. His naked body, which she had never seen before, was elongated, angular; not angels but angles. She gently sponged his shoulders, legs and stomach, while he continued to talk.

'There was such a storm – has it been raining here? – it was pouring down, pouring, all the way, the windscreen wipers never stopped, and of course, if it hadn't been raining so hard, I could have taken Jessica out for a walk, but they would not let me in, those women, they would not let me in to see my own child. It will be a different story when I have won my libel suit. That will prove that Lindie Spittle is a maniac – a lunatic! The Bishop sees that at least, fool that he is in other respects; the typical career clergyman. I can't tell you how bland he is. I don't really know why he bothered to see me. Oh, this is nice, nice! My own, darlingest, most beautiful Jay!'

'Quiet, Little Boy.'

In addition to the dismay which Jay felt at Francis's condition, she was very much alarmed to discern that he appeared to believe his visit to Ditcham had been for the purpose of returning there as the Vicar! She thought that he had in some senses of the word run away with her. If he wanted to remain as the Vicar of Ditcham, then what was he doing in a bungalow near Deal with her?

'I had a nice day with Eric and Ena,' she said. 'And guess what! They have bought me a violin.'

'But I could have bought you a violin.'

'They wanted to buy it. I think they believe it is a small

consolation for all your bad luck. They feel awkward about your mother's will.'

'Feeling awkward did not stop them pocketing all my money and putting it in their bank account.'

'We don't need to worry about money.'

'Everyone needs to worry about money.'

'We are all right. Lie back and let me sponge your front.'

'Eric's a greedy old goat. I don't like Eric.'

She started a little at this word, goat. Did Francis suspect their old friend of having designs on *her*, or was he still harping on about his mother?

'We are not going to stay here much longer. I want us to go to Italy. I want to show you Pompeii. I've brought the guide books from Ditcham. We can drive down. God, I drove well this evening. I flew here. I could not have got here faster if I'd come on a magic carpet. And we must go to Cumae, go to Cumae and consult the sybil. It's fantastic, you go down this long corridor towards the mouth of the cave, and when you get there it is dark, dark. Help me out, my sybil, I want to make love to you.'

Skinny, priapic, mad, he stood up in the bath, and clasped her to himself.

'I love you.'

'Maybe you're not such a little boy after all.'

'Say you love me.'

'Francis, that hurts.'

'Say you love me.'

'I love you, I love you.'

He pressed her against the bathroom wall, and tore roughly at her blouse and trousers.

An hour or two later, when they were both dressed in pyjamas and lying beside one another in the uncomfortable double bed, Jay said, 'It doesn't matter. You were in a bit too much of a hurry, that's all.'

'Of course it bloody matters.'

'We've got plenty of time.'

He sighed deeply.

Francis allowed her to hold, and to stroke, his hand. From the heights of his manic mood when he arrived back at 'Tudun-Teku', he had plunged into a pit of melancholy and self-pity.

'We've both tired, too; that makes a difference,' she said gently.

'Just shut up about it, will you?'

6
Some more letters

Dear Mr Kreer,

Thank you for your various letters, one of 2nd September, and two dated 3rd September 1992. First, the matter of your libel suit against the *Sunday Mercury*. As I think counsel explained to you during our interview in August, you do, indeed, have a very strong case against the newspaper, but various considerations have to be borne in mind.

A newspaper such as the *Mercury* has almost limitless funds at its disposal. A few libel cases from private individuals such as yourself would be regarded as mere 'expenses' in the business of running a newspaper. Their damages would in any case be paid for by insurance; and there is a danger that they would decide to make your trial as entertaining for their readers as possible. Their counsel would be perfectly entitled to subpoena as many witnesses as they liked, however unsubstantiated their allegations against you. It is particularly unfortunate at this time that you should be separated from your wife. Had your wife been able to appear in your defence, and make a show of marital solidarity, that would have counted for much with a jury. As it is, there is a danger that the *Mercury* could drag out the court proceedings for as much as a week or a fortnight. During this period, they will be quite entitled to parade every detail of your private life, however painful, for the entertainment and amusement of the public. Even matters which you do not consider relevant to the case, such as your relations with your wife, could be brought into open court and made a subject for witty speculations by a clever counsel.

All this time, as I have explained to you on more than one occasion, the *Mercury* will have been fighting a war of costs. In order to conduct a case on this scale, you have to consider paying for a fortnight in court, and that, together with all the preparatory work by myself and my assistants, and by counsel, will, as I say, be very costly. You have already entailed very considerable costs. As I have emphasised in all my previous communications with you about this matter, even if you do win the case, and receive damages from the court, there is no guarantee that you will reclaim all your costs (allowing for tax being paid, etc). There is then the near-certainty that the *Mercury* would take you to the Court of Appeal, where you would have the whole battle to fight again. I should not, therefore, advise you to continue with this action.

Yours sincerely,
W.J. Sandiman

Dear Miss Dunbar,

Thank you for your note. I will of course treat it with the strictest confidence. I have written to Mr Kreer, putting to him as forcefully as I can the arguments for withdrawing from this action. I do not, candidly, see how he could afford to proceed with it in any case, but from what you say about his present state of mind, it would not be a good idea for him to appear in court. So much, in a libel case, depends on the demeanour of the plaintiff in the witness box.

With all good wishes, W.J. Sandiman

Dear Francis,

If you attempt to come near us again, we shall be forced to take out an injunction to prevent you from seeing Jessica, or Alison, or myself. You are sick, and you should get help. Leave us alone.

Sally.

Dear Francis,

Thank you for your letter. I must confess to being a little confused by it, since I understood from the Archdeacon that you had now resigned as Vicar of Ditcham. It will not be necessary to ask Damian Wells to take the services. The

Bishop of Didcot has arranged for a retired priest, a Canon Barlass, to look after the parish in the interregnum. I gather that they are thinking of appointing a new man as soon as possible.

You can gather the sadness which Dorothy and I felt when we saw the furniture vans earlier this week outside the vicarage. You and Sally have been good friends to us for so many years, and, in spite of the troubles of the last few months, old friendship still counts for much. I shall personally very much miss our little Virgil sessions! Goodbye, my dear, *Heu, miserande puer, si qua fata aspera rumpas*. R.M–L

Dear Mr Kreer,

Thank you for your letters of 4th September (I believe I answered most of the points raised in this letter in mine of the 3rd which clashed with yours), and 5th September.

I think I have already given you the reasons, during one of our many telephone conversations, why I think you should accept your wife's lawyer's request for a payment of a lump sum of £20,000. You do not know what your future circumstances will be, and you could very well find that, if you agreed now to paying your wife an allowance, it would be difficult to keep up the payments on a regular, monthly basis.

You said on the telephone, and you repeat it in your letter, that if the barrister's fees are beyond your means you could always represent yourself in court. I must reiterate that this course of action would be most unwise. The *Sunday Mercury* would be sure to hire a clever QC who would, to be candid, have fun at your expense (and I mean the last phrase literally).

You have already run up considerable legal costs. Your interview with counsel alone cost £1,500. The subsequent correspondence between our firm and the solicitors representing the *Sunday Mercury*, and the investigations which we have already undertaken on your behalf, already exceed £9,000. My advice to you would be to withdraw from this action now, and attempt to put the whole matter behind you.

May I express my deep personal sympathy for you at this time? I know that you have been going through a difficult patch, and I think that the best that you can do is to try to rebuild your life in quietness.

With all good wishes.
Yours sincerely,
W.J. Sandiman

Dear Daddy,

Jesus said, 'My peace I leave with you.' With love from Jessica.

Dear Francis,

Thanks for your note. I was a bit puzzled by it, because I had understood that you had resigned as Vicar of Ditcham. In any case, the Archdeacon has asked old 'Barking' Barlass to look after the parish in the interregnum. I dare say that the congregation will enjoy his interminable reflections on life in South India! The wonderful news is that I have been offered a parish of my own! St Agatha's, Hoxton. The institution and induction will be at 7.30 p.m. on 28th October. A concelebrated mass, and of course I'd be delighted if you could attend.

Love and prayers, Damian.

Dear Francis,

Thank you for your very long letter. May I say at once how sorry I am that you feel aggrieved. I am extremely sorry that your life has passed through a dark period, and let me say at once that, when I accepted your resignation, I did not in any way mean to suggest that I endorsed or accepted the things which were written about you in the *Sunday Mercury*. Nevertheless, resign you did, and Canon Barlass is looking after the parish in the interregnum. We considered that it was in everyone's best interests to make an appointment to the parish as soon as possible, and a young priest, James McDadd, will be instituted to the living on the Feast of SS. Simon and Jude,

28th October. (You might like to know that, to our great joy, Damian Wells has got a parish in Hoxton, and will be instituted to that living on the same day. I know how pleased you will be for him.)

You and Sally are both in my prayers, and I wish you well for the future.

Yours in Christ,
Derek Didcot.

Dear Mr Bridges,

The Reverend Francis Kreer

Thank you for your letter. I had not, in fact, heard that Mr Kreer was asking me to act for him in this matter. I shall write to him to say that we do not feel able to do so. Strictly between ourselves, I do not think that any lawyer would be prepared to take on this case, and if he were to apply for example to the Citizens' Advice Bureau, I am sure that they would advise him not to pursue a Wrongful Dismissal Case. I quite understand that, as Registrar of the diocese, you felt obliged to write as you did. On a lighter note, I believe that your young colleague, Simon Munnion, was at Sidney Sussex with my daughter!

All good wishes.
W.J. Sandiman

Dear Mr Kreer,

The money has at last come through from the sale of the flat, and I am writing to enclose a cheque for £4,379.56p. This is the sum of £35,000, less £20,000 which we have forwarded to your wife's solicitors, and the legal costs arising out of the three transactions – the flat sale, our correspondence with your wife's solicitors, and the solicitors for the *Sunday Mercury*. The accounts are enclosed.

I have received a letter from the Registrar of the diocese, concerning your desire to sue for wrongful dismissal. I am afraid that I have replied to him that I am not willing to act for you in this case. The truth is, you do not have a case. You were not dismissed. You resigned the living in a written letter to the Bishop of Didcot. As I have said to you before, it really would be better to look forward to the future, and not to rake over these old grievances.

Yours sincerely,
W.J. Sandiman.

Dear Francis,

Sally has shown me your letters. They are sick, Francis. She has begged you not to write, or visit, or telephone. You simply must *leave her alone*. You chose to run out on her, and I make no comment upon that, but her relationship with me is absolutely none of your business.

You might like to know that Lindie Spittle deeply regrets having written as she did to that awful Sunday paper. It has been a hard time for her and I think even more for Gerrie, but they have bravely decided to put all that behind them. You really ought to try to do the same. No doubt, at some future date, when you have sorted yourself out, Jessica will want to see you again, but at the moment it is simply disturbing for the child to receive letters implying that you and she are going to live together. *This is just not going to happen*. I hope that you will one day find some peace of mind. We are all praying for you.

Yours,
Alison Bill.

Dear Sir,

We write to remind you that the credit limit on your Barclaycard is £500. At present, the balance of your account stands at £1619.23p. It is some months since any repayment reached us. The minimum repayment for this month is £60.51p. We must insist that minimum payment reaches us before the end of the month, and that, until your credit balance is reduced to £500, you cease using your Barclaycard.

Yours faithfully,
Curly-wurly squiggle. Area Manager.

Lady Mary de Mandeville School, Reading. From the Bursary.
30th September 1992
Dear Mr Kreer,

We note from our records that your daughter Jessica's termly fees, payable in advance, have still not been paid. Please forward a cheque for £1910.54p as soon as possible.

Yours sincerely,
Alexander Mack (Commander R.N. Retd.)
School Bursar.

Lady Mary de Mandeville School, Reading. From the Bursary.
4th October 1992
Dear Mr Kreer,

Thank you for your cheque for £1910.54p, which I am returning to you because you have inadvertently signed it 'Lazarus'! If you could let us have it back as soon as possible, with your own signature, I should be most grateful.

Yours sincerely,
Alexander Mack (Commander R.N. Retd.)
School Bursar.

Lady Mary de Mandeville School, Reading. From the Bursary.
8th October 1992
Dear Mr Kreer,

I think that the fact that your mother was born in 1910, and that our bill for Jessica's fees is £1910.54p is purely coincidental. There must be some confusion – you appear to believe, from your letter, that I was a friend of your mother's. I never had that pleasure.

Thank you for the cheque.

Yours sincerely,
Alexander Mack (Commander R.N. Retd.)
School Bursar.

Dear Francis,

I went into the School Bursary today on some other business, and happened to overhear them talking about your letters. I also gather that the cheque you sent to pay for Jessica's school fees this term has bounced. Can you not realise how humiliating it would be for the child to know that her own father could not even collect together the school fees for his daughter's education?

Yrs
Alison

Dear Mr Kreer,

I had in fact already heard from your wife's solicitors. In the circumstances, I think that it is perfectly in order for me to continue paying Jessica's fees as the trustee of her own estate. The terms of your mother's will made it clear that Jessica's money could be spent on her own education.

I had no idea that you were in quite such straitened financial circumstances. I hope things improve for you. I do not think it is worth pursuing the significance of the numbering of the school invoice from the school. The fact that your mother was born in 1910 and the cheque was for £1910 must, surely, be regarded as coincidental. I also think you are wrong to read much significance into Commander Mack's phrase, 'you appear to believe that I was a friend of your mother . . . I never had that pleasure.' It simply means that he did not know your mother. I am sure that he did not imply (as you state in your letter) that, to quote your own words, 'he was one of the few men in the world who had not enjoyed her sexual favours'. The 54p in the school bill was clearly arrived at by computing the normal school bill and the various 'extras' such as a theatre expedition, and music lessons. I do not believe that it is intended as the Commander's way of 'confessing' to you that your mother was 54 years old when she went to bed with the Commander. Indeed, it is hardly necessary to repeat that your mother never *met* the Commander.

Yours sincerely,
W.J. Sandiman.

SS. Simon and Jude

I

A cold wind blew off the Channel by the grey light of an autumn evening. Heaving, pitiless, grey, the sea raked the shingle. Gulls sobbed overhead. Waking that dawn, Jay Dunbar could hear the wind rattle the peeling, ill-fitting windows of 'Tudun-Teku'. When they had first come down to live in the bungalow, Ena had told them that you could not get tenants for it during the winter because it was too cold. After her nine months of caravans and tents and squats, Jay had thought 'Tudun-Teku' looked comfortable enough. But on this, the first really cold day since the spring, she began to see why no one chose to live here after November. When Ena had said – 'No, it needs double glazing, nice bit o' double glazing, new windows, metal-frames, and a few radiators before you'd get me sleeping in there!' – Jay had heard this as no more than the bleating of modern man: our ancestors, after all, lived without these luxuries. But, then, our ancestors probably wore more clothes in bed.

Her skimpy pyjamas and the light duvet did not provide much warmth or comfort. These had to be sought from the recumbent form at her side. Francis Kreer had become so thin, and his face was so anguished, that Jay in bed sometimes had the fantasy that she was lying in one of those medieval tombs, where the deceased personage is depicted in all his mortal decay, with the flesh rotted off the bones. Certainly, the skeleton in pyjamas who lay beside her provided very little warmth. She slipped an arm over his waist, nevertheless, because she needed him, and he needed her. Her Little Boy.

It had turned out, none of it, as she had intended. She

had not meant to provoke a marital crisis when she arrived that morning at the vicarage, dazed from the death of Leila, scared out of her wits by the police raid. She certainly had not meant to meet up with Mo again; and, having met up with him, all she had intended was to help him; when Francis spoke of her going away with him, she had been excited by the idea, but she had not exactly imagined that it would be 'Tudun-Teku', and the Gadneys. Yet, in the event – what a mercy! Francis grumbled about the Gadneys, but where would he, or Jay, now be without them? It was true that the Gadneys had inherited half the money for the London flat – and, obviously, it was difficult for Francis to banish bitterness about that. But at least, when they saw the plight of Francis and Jay, the Gadneys had offered them 'Tudun-Teku' – 'until something else crops up.'

Something very like a routine of life had established itself. In the mornings, Francis went into the Public Library at Deal where he was doing some sort of research. In spite of having given up the parish, he still appeared to have an enormous amount of correspondence. Jay was amazed by the number of letters which sometimes came by the morning post. She knew that some of these letters were to do with money, and she did wish that Francis would confide in her a bit more about this worrying side of life. When they had first met, he had given her the impression of being rather rich – in fact, loaded! But there had been some terrible fuss over paying the kid's school-fees, and a cheque had bounced, and the Barclaycard people did not let him have credit any more.

Her 'Buddhist' nature thought that all this was probably a good thing. Francis appeared to agree with her.

'I don't want us to own anything,' he had said a few days earlier. 'I think our way of life in this house is very nearly perfect. I even regret bringing the books with me from Ditcham. I don't need the books. I've got the library, though my research is going to take me forever.'

'Poor Francis.'

'A bit less of the bloody poor,' and he had slapped her hand from his brow.

But this resistance from her Little Boy, these displays of irritation, were all good; or so they appeared to Jay. They were a sign that he was growing up a bit; growing through the worst of his troubles. Jay had been so full of her own troubles when she first met Francis that she had naturally supposed that he, a grown-up, old enough to be her dad, would provide her with support. And he had done this to a certain extent. She had simply failed to recognise, for a long time, that their first really intimate meeting – the one in Reading, when he had cried and cried for his mother – was not, as she had supposed at the time, an aberration. It was to set the tone of their whole relationship.

She could not remember when she had fallen into the habit of calling him Little Boy, but he said he liked it. In his own way, he probably provided her with a bit of a father-figure. It was all too pat, wasn't it, to say she was his mum, and he was her lost dad? But there was a bit of truth in it; a bit of that underlay their strange inter-dependence.

Jay Dunbar found in herself a great longing to make Francis Kreer happy, and a wish that she could do something to assuage his sorrows. There had been times when she thought that she could not endure to hear any more about his mother, and she had made an excuse, and gone to have a bath, or to sit on the lavatory, simply in order to get away from this presence, this Other Woman. But, even then, Little Boy would come to the door –

'. . . and when we got back to the hotel, Daddy and I, we'd find she had gone off to play golf with the Sidgwicks – that's the family I told you about, the other family staying in the hotel. And Daddy and I had come all the way back from the beach, thinking she'd be lonely without us! That was absolutely *typical* of Mummy; you see, I think she really had that rare gift, charm. People really wished to be with her, so of course, she responded, how could she not . . .'

'With you in a minute, Little Boy,' Jay had called from the throne. Plop, plop, plop.

'But the funny thing was, that although she knew she was beautiful, she was not really vain about it. I think you're like that.'

'Just leave me until I've finished in here, darling.'

'OK. But if she was sitting at her looking-glass; and I remember that I was allowed to come in and be with her when she was dressing in the morning, and I remember coming up, I can't have been more than three because my head hardly reached up to the seat of that stool by the dressing-table, do you remember it – she had it in the bedroom in the flat. They even took Mummy's stool, the brutes.'

'Just one minute. Just leave me for a few minutes.'

But he could not stop speaking of his mother, when these fits were on him. They were rarer. Of that, Jay Dunbar was sure. The poor man was, undoubtedly, working something through. Probably, it helped, having an academic project on hand. She was surprised, but glad, to find that he had all the books he needed in Deal Public Library.

While Little Boy was in the Library, Jay would go to work at the Sunnymede Garden Centre for three or four days each week. (On the other mornings, she practised her violin.) There had been much work to do recently, bringing all the pelargoniums and geraniums back into the hot-houses. Ena particularly liked a bloom named Grand Slam, a vivid red. The care of these plants, and the propagation of the cuttings, would be part of Jay's task for the months of winter. She, Little Boy and the other two assistants at the Sunnymede had also been hard at work dismantling the 'display' garden sheds, and carrying the component parts back into the large warehouse, where the teak benches and the reconstituted-stone garden-ornaments were stored.

As the Boss remarked every few hours, there was always something to do at Sunnymede. The turnover in bulbs that autumn had been 'truly amazing, super'. The Boss's large, moist mouth had been in a permanent grin at the sight of the customers, queuing up at the till with their brown paper bags bursting with tulips, crocuses, daffodils, narcissi, snowdrops.

'It gives you hope, doesn't it, planting out the bulbs?' This was Ena's view, often expressed, on the days when she was wheeled to the check-out till in the indoor-plant house. She liked to have the odd word with customers, as did the Boss.

Jay had wondered, when she became accustomed to the Gadneys' superabundant self-assurance, whether either of them had made a calculation that customers would spend more money by virtue of their disabilities? No logic here, Jay knew that. She just *felt* that the sight of Ena in the wheelchair, or of the Boss's burnt-out old face, made people scoop an extra shovel-full of W.P. Milners or Spellbinders into their brown paper bags, and even to add the occasional 'indoor' extravagance to their loads: here an African violet, there a poinsettia: well, as the Boss said, every little helps.

Certainly it was not what Jay had planned, any of this – not the particular turn of her relationship with Little Boy; nor her relationship with the Boss; nor the work at the Sunnymede, and the help with Ena. It was all a far cry from her romantic idyll with the Cornish potter and the little skiff moored at the end of the jetty. What surprised her was how much, having given herself over to it all, she found it made her – well, if happy is too strong a word, she was at least at peace, at least happier than she had been when racked with the frustrations and anger of her life with Mo.

Her 'Buddhism' enabled her to give herself up to what fate had decreed. There were some situations in life, she had decided, where it was inappropriate to follow too delicate a moral course; indeed, where the truly moral thing to do was to be, by conventional standards, 'immoral'. Anyone would tell her that what she was doing with these two men, with Little Boy and the Boss, was immoral, deceiving the one with the other. There were times when you had to forgive yourself, and when, in friendship to that strange companion, your own body, you had to be humble – to allow it to have its life. Jay had been tormented at first not so much by Little Boy's poor performance as by his self-reproach and anger about it all. But there was anger and frustration in her, too; much more than she had feared, and the first time she had allowed the Boss to do this to her, she acknowledged to herself that there was an element of revenge in her motive. 'If Little Boy can't satisfy me, then he *deserves* it if I go after someone who can.'

Since that first time, she had realised that all resentments of this kind, which tie us to the earth and to our own petty selves, must be got rid of. The mind can be cleared of such feelings by an act of will. She was able, now, to be a very tender 'lover', after their own strange fashion, with Little Boy. Sometimes the act itself was achieved, but not very often. She had learnt not even to *say* that it did not matter. But he needed her, of that she was sure. He needed her to hug him, and hold him, and stroke him. Sometimes, she knew that he only wanted her to wank him off – that was all that little boys really enjoyed, not fucking. And she did not mind this in the least. She knew that her satisfaction would come later in the morning, among the pelargoniums, where the Boss would be waiting for her. The age, the face, the character of the Boss during these delicious sessions did not trouble her in the least. He was, quite simply, the best lover she had ever had, or could ever hope to have.

Jay the Buddhist knew that a better arrangement than the present one could not be found. It could well be that, in future months, they would all have to reconsider their positions. At present, 'Tudun-Teku' was the best berth that either she or Little Boy could hope for. Little Boy *needed* her; he did not realise, or refused to acknowledge openly, how much he now depended upon Eric and Ena. But Eric really was 'the Boss' now; he was housing them for nothing; he was giving them pocket-money for their work at Sunnymede. Jay did not really object to the old man's exercise of *droit de seigneur*, not least because it was performed with such energy, such fervour, such joy. He was seventy-five years old; whatever had happened to the rest of his body, he still had the cock of a young man.

When she had recognised what interest the Boss took in her, Jay had felt it was right to resist. Her reasons for doing so, when they came to be examined, all seemed to her fallacious. She must not fuck the Boss because she 'belonged' to Little Boy. Well, that was untrue. She and Little Boy would have to see how they went. They were certainly very far indeed from being a married couple. The Boss and Ena were a married couple, it was true, but Jay saw no reason to suppose that Ena would object very much if she knew that her magnificent stud of a man was providing rapture for another woman among the musty-smelling Sweet Sues, Chelsea Gems, Cherry Glows and Grand Slams. Our bodies, surely, only start to rebel or to play strange tricks in our minds when we deny them what they need. Jay's body, and that of the Boss, would only nag to be satisfied, like a cat wanting to be fed, until they *were* satisfied. It was a case, here, where Oscar Wilde's remark about temptation was perfectly true. Why not just be humble enough to recognise that, at the moment, she and the Boss really fancied one another, really liked doing it? (How the delicious and slightly sweaty smell of the geraniums blended into, and resembled, her smell when she had been satisfied by the Boss.) This put everyone in a good mood – her, the Boss, and even Little Boy and Ena, who, in their happy ignorance of what was going on, were the unwitting beneficiaries of it: for their partners were in a better humour; more than that, while the Boss was happy, the position of Jay and 'Tudun-Teku' was secure. She was not in love with the Boss as perhaps she was with Little Boy. Sex was just something the Boss liked doing, and she enjoyed it also. If the Boss had wanted her to play backgammon or to watch television with him and 'the missus', as he called Ena, she would have been as happy to comply with his demands. If that sounded like whoredom, then it was only humble, and realistic, to recognise that many human transactions – and not merely transactions between the sexes – came down to a form of barter which could, if one chose to label it thus, be described as prostitution. It was better just to recognise these things and, having recognised them, put them beneath one's consciousness; to continue loving, and tolerating oneself, and not allowing trivia of this kind to clutter the consciousness. This, very largely, Jay had achieved.

It meant, this detachment from the emotional predicament, that she possessed a greater power to concentrate on her music than she had known since her early teens.

Turning in the bed, partly for warmth, partly out of desire, she folded herself into Little Boy's back, bottom, nuzzled against his shoulder, and placed her hand inside his pyjama-trousers. Poor Little Boy never had any difficulties when he was still asleep. In the early mornings, she could usually have some such game, either bringing him to a climax in her hand or inside herself. This morning was too cold for undressing and she opted for the former alternative. It meant that he would wake up in a good mood, and she liked the feeling of this glue-of-life as it spurted over her palms.

She kissed his neck and said, 'Good morning, Little Boy.'

'What time is it?'

'Look what you've done all over me.'

'That was so nice. Thank you. I love you.'

'Now I suppose you expect me to make you tea?'

'That would be nice.'

'Well, it's your turn.'

While he boiled the kettle – it was ten to seven – she went to the bathroom, and by the time he returned with the tray, Rich Tea biscuits, a tea-pot, milk and mugs, she was lying back on the pillows, with a thick blue fisherman's jumper over her pyjama-top.

'Where had we got to?' he asked.

'Emma has just persuaded Harriet Smith to refuse Mr Martin's offer of marriage, and Mr Knightley has got really cross with her.'

'Oh, yes.'

It had been beyond belief that Jay had never read Jane Austen – not a word. They had taken to reading her aloud. Having finished *Pride and Prejudice* and *Sense and Sensibility*, they had moved on to Little Boy's favourite.

'Emma's a prat,' said Jay, 'but I like Mr Knightley.'

Francis assumed a particularly owlish appearance when he put on his horn-rimmed spectacles. Since abandoning the habit of a grown-up lifetime – the daily recitation of the divine office first thing in the morning – it seemed strange to wake up and not to have anything to read aloud. So, this did very well as a substitute. This morning it was his turn to read.

'Mr Knightley might quarrel with her, but Emma could not quarrel with herself . . .'

For some half-hour he read, while Jay nuzzled against him. She was absorbed in the story, but it did not prevent her from having her own thoughts. She found herself wondering about Mo, not with love, but with a distant anguish. She had wasted a year looking after him, and failing to change him, and merely hurting herself. She had never meant to get involved with another 'lame duck': why couldn't she find a man who could look after *her*? Why must it always be the other way about? And yet, the unaccountable thing was, she felt reasonably happy. This was a far from satisfactory arrangement. Many would think it was positively improper – her going to bed with a married clergyman and making love to the Boss, a man old enough to be her grandfather. But it all felt perfectly all right. . . . Having laughed at Mr Woodhouse's willingness on all occasions to defer to Mr Perry, they got up.

Little Boy boiled the eggs and made the toast, Jay laid the table with last night's side-plates – to which only a few bits of butter and crumbs still adhered – and some clean knives and spoons. With the aid of an ancient toaster, Little Boy incinerated four slices of bread.

'We've got to move a lot of pots about in the geranium house today. There are more plants than we thought,' she said.

'And I have to decide whether to go to London.'

'To your friend's service?'

'Damian's being inducted at St Agatha's, Hoxton this evening. He told me I'd be welcome.'

'Don't upset yourself.'

'I shan't; but if I go to Damian's do, it might help me to forget what's happening in Ditcham today.'

'I don't like your minding it so much. If you *mind* about their forcing you out of the parish, then what are you doing here with me?'

'I can mind the way they did it; I can mind the Spittles.'

'Put them behind you.'

'Mummy always said, if you feel a grudge, admit it, don't bury it; much worse to bury it.'

'But better not to feel it.'

'You're a perfectionist.'

'There is no point in having morality at all unless you are a perfectionist.'

'The perfect egg! It so rarely is quite perfect. Usually too soft, because I am so impatient. You are wrong; it is precisely because we can't be perfectionist that we need moral standards to which we can aspire. Perhaps, after all, I am *au fond* a Christian, and you are a Buddhist.'

'But neither of us believes in God,' she said cautiously, just to make sure that this had not changed during the night.

'No,' he said with a laugh. 'We've seen off that old fraud. But that's all the more reason for wanting to get the serious business of life *right*. Seeing that religious language is all mythological is only the first stage; we still recognise the importance of living by myths; and therefore it matters, which myths you choose.'

'What myth do you think Ena lives by?' asked Jay.

'Many myths: the myth of her husband's chastity' – Jay coloured but it was hard to see whether Francis noticed – 'the myth of the Battle of Britain. I hated that thing in Mummy, you know – she had an absolute obsession with the war: anyone who had fought in the war was a hero in her eyes. Hence – we must assume – our present delightful domain!' He swept his hand in the air to indicate 'Tudun-Teku' and its inadequacies. 'I have so much work to do,' added Francis. 'Since I left the parish in the hands of someone else, there has been a deluge of work: more than I ever had in my life.

'I think the theory is revolutionary,' said Francis, 'and it is incontrovertible. I am not telling you about it yet, because I want to have absolute proof.'

'And again you can really find all the books you need in that small public library?'

'Oh, easily. So' – he rose to run washing-up water – 'shall we try to meet back here at midday for a meal? And then I shall let you know whether I am catching a train up to London in the afternoon, or giving the whole occasion a miss.'

So it was that, three-quarters of an hour later, Jay was in the plant-rooms with Eric Gadney, her naked buttocks pressed against the slightly muddy slats where, later, the pots would be stored in rows, with the Boss, trouserless energetic old badger-body thrusting and pushing, while Francis Kreer, with his notebook and pencils had arrived at the Deal Public Library.

An essential research-tool was a pocket-calculator, which he had purchased remarkably cheaply shortly after he made his discovery. He now spent hours, with a Bible and a copy of *Who's Who* open on the table in front of him, making computations with the calculator and noting the results in an exercise book. The more he pursued it, the simpler and truer his idea had become, and the stranger it was that he, and he alone, in the entire human race, had been able to make the connection between the two volumes. Francis's discovery was that the Bible and *Who's Who* were parallel texts. Each verse of the Bible corresponded to an entry in *Who's Who*. For example, the 170th verse of the Bible (Genesis, Chapter 7, verse 11) read, 'In the six hundredth year of Noah's life, in the second month, on the seventeenth day of the month, on the same day were all the fountains of the great deep broken up, and the windows of heaven were opened.'

The 170th entry in *Who's Who*, which corresponded to this Biblical text, was the biography of Prince Sadruddin Aga Khan, who, as he read in the reference book, lived in the city of Geneva (hence, 'the fountains of the great deep', a reference to the fountains in Lake Geneva). Field Marshal Lord Carver, Chief of the British Defence Staff, had a Biblical parallel text which was so overt that it was not even in code: Exodus 15:3, 'The Lord is a man of War'. Elizabeth Taylor, the film actress, had John 14:18. 'Thou hast had five husbands, and the man whom thou now hast is not thy husband.' If any so-called Biblical scholar wished to dismiss this fact as a 'coincidence', then there was clearly going to be no point in arguing with him. It all absolutely fitted, as tight as a glove, providing that one missed out the Apocryphal books. Rather oddly, the Bible, whose last words were 'The Grace of the Lord Jesus be with the saints, Amen' (Revelation 11.11), gave out in the middle of the W's in *Who's Who* with no less a person than the Duke of Wellington.

There was no easy explanation for this, for one would have assumed that the number of entries in *Who's Who* was, in fact, exactly the same as the number of verses in the Bible. Part of each morning's research consisted in an eager perusal of the Deaths columns and the obituaries in the reading room to see whether one explanation was that the 'saints' – i.e. those whose names appeared in *Who's Who* – were in fact diminishing in number; but, if one went through *Who's Who* each day deleting the names of those who had died, this grossly upset the 'grid' by which the original calculation had been made. For instance, it only needed three A's to die, and the Prince Sadruddin Aga Khan was moved from his 'fountains of the great deep' in Lake Geneva to verse 8 of Genesis 7: i.e., 'Of clean beasts and of beasts that are not clean' which rather 'fitted' a professor of cell physiology at Cambridge, Lord Adrian. Another explanation could be, of course, that once the W's ran out it was permissible to start measuring the grid from the Apocrypha, and this was something which he intended to investigate by a process of trial and error.

Together with his copious correspondence, this occupied him

until the time of the midday meal, and already, after his quite short residence in the seaside town, the Vicar of Sorrows had become a familiar sight in the library – his bespectacled scrawny face fixed attentively on the large volumes before him on the table, his eyes darting from one book to another, as he collated and collected his references. Mummy, he knew, would have been proud of him for his discoveries, and proud of him for having 'won' Jay, whose beauty and kindness had done so much to salve the wounds in his heart. When he went back to the parish – in triumph! – he looked forward to driving up to the vicarage with Jay in the front seat of the car. There would be no more subterfuge.

It troubled him, what they were doing in Ditcham today. He both knew, and did not know, that it spelt defeat. He had looked up his successor in the parish, the Reverend James McDadd, in Crockford's *Clerical Directory*. For a moment, he had been seized by a *new* idea – which, when the life's work on the Bible and *Who's Who* was complete, would be worth investigation: viz, that there was some analogous grid-relationship between Crockford and Virgil's *Aeneid*. How fascinated dear old Ronald Maxwell-Lee would be to know that this was a possibility. Measuring James McDadd's name on the Virgilian grid-method, for example, got you, '*Ecqua tamen puero est amissae cura parentis*?': 'has the boy nevertheless some love for his lost mother?' – clearly a reference not to McDadd but to *him*, Francis! (But perhaps this was a sign that McDadd should not be the Vicar of Ditcham. The Vicar of Ditcham was – if Virgil and the grid were accurate – one still grieving for his mother – i.e. Francis Kreer.)

James McDadd was only ordained in 1983: a mere chicken. Before that he was at Durham University, and Ripon College, Cuddesdon. He had served a couple of curacies, one in Swindon, another in Oxford, and he was also, concurrently, the chaplain of an Oxford college. It all seemed quite suitable, but it was obviously a mistake. Although, clearly, it was far too early to 'go public' with the Crockford/Virgil theory, it was surely worth pointing out that this particular line in the *Aeneid* (Bk III. line 342) could not possibly refer to McDadd? Francis wrote a rapid letter to the Archdeacon on this subject. He also wrote one of his abusive letters to Sally, describing in graphic detail what it felt like to ejaculate in Jay's hand. He also wrote his daily letter to Mr Sandiman – no harm in keeping these thieving lawyers busy! He posted these letters on his way back to the bungalow. He enjoyed his walks by the sea-front and today – blowy, moist, cold and, it seemed to Francis, the sort of weather that an English body and English lungs were built for. Before he turned into 'Tudun-Teku', he stood on the sea-front and looked towards Walmer, and thought of the old Duke of Wellington, pacing about there in his old age when he was the Warden of the Cinque Ports, the ancestor of the present Duke who, as Francis alone knew, rounded off the entire Bible – the grace of the Lord be with the saints, Amen. Or, if you prefer, 'His grace' – the very word 'grace' puts us at once in the presence of a Duke. What could be clearer than that?

2

Sally had wondered whether it might not be more tactful to stay away from the induction of Francis's successor, The Reverend James McDadd, but Alison had said that Sally and Jessica must attend. Not only was Alison a churchwarden who counted on their support, it was also important to establish that Sally and Jessica had nothing with which they could reproach themselves. They should feel neither embarrassed nor ashamed. None of the misfortunes of this year had been their fault. It would be psychologically mistaken, Miss Bill averred, to hide away – just as it would have been a mistake to leave the village. Sally had said that she wanted to get right away. She had spoken of going to live near a sister in Brighton. Alison had said, 'And when you came back to Ditcham?'

'I might never come back.'

'And when you came back you'd be too shy to look a woman like Edith Renton or Dorothy Maxwell-Lee in the face. No, Sally, it won't do to bury this. You've got to face it, you've got to admit it's happened and walk tall.'

Sally knew that Alison was trying to be kind – and had been amazingly kind. Where would Jessica and Sally have been if it had not been for Alison's extraordinary hospitality and generosity? All the same, she was *married* to Francis. Sally was not at all sure that it was a good idea to have brought the lawyers into the situation so promptly and so fast. Alison had insisted that Sally get a formal legal separation, with papers and signatures and, eventually, that lovely cheque from Mr Sandiman. And yes, old Francis had been awful to her – tortured her by his coldness and his snobbishness and his petulance, but he was her husband. This was something that Alison did not appear to grasp, at the imagined level, at the level of the emotions. And Francis was Jessica's Dad. And, from the few signs that Sally had read, Francis was *not* in a good way. Sally now reproached herself with not seeing how upset Francis was made by his mother's death. She now realised that he must have suffered what is called a nervous breakdown – that many of his silences or eruptions of anger were *not his fault*. Sally was sad to admit the fact to herself but she had never really liked Griselda! She was such a very *superior* sort of person, she always had to remind you who was boss, with her memories of semi-famous people known, or moved among, and her snobbish air of *chic*. She had always *condescended* to Sally. It was hard for the daughter-in-law to grieve when Griselda died, particularly since the death had been (apparently) sudden, painless – and the more so because Sally assumed that now they would at last be able to buy that holiday home! Sally had for a long time been aware that all was not well with her marriage. We all knew that many relationships lacked, after ten or twelve years, the ardour of their early days, but in the Kreers' marriage there were too many tell-tale symptoms that something was amiss: their inability to have a good old *natter* about things (she made no apology for using the word!) was one symptom, and the dwindling into nothingness of their sex life was another, and Francis's mean trick of luring Jess into the study for chess after supper was another. Sally had often supposed that if only they had been able to *get away more* – either to the seaside or the country, or up to London, they would have been able to refresh themselves, as a couple, as a family, to – she searched for a metaphor and discovered, to recharge their batteries. It was not just greed which made her rejoice at Griselda's demise. It was the thought that *at last* and, as a family, the Kreers could go away and be like other families, and not have this horrible feeling, which you got all the time in the vicarage, of all eyes in the village upon you, watching you and seeing how you behave.

And now, Sally thought, this burden was passing to pretty Mrs McDadd, who was sitting loyally in her pew with a couple of young children watching the institution and induction of her husband to Francis's old job.

There was a large congregation for the service. About fifty residents of Ditcham (together with Mattins 'recusants' from neighbouring villages) had been joined by an equal number of James McDadd's friends and supporters from Oxford. In addition, some twenty-five clergymen filled the sanctuary, all wearing cassocks, surplices, scarves and academical hoods as they boomed out Evensong for St Simon and St Jude, and then watched the Archdeacon perform the ceremony of leading Mr McDadd to the font, the reading desk, the pulpit and the altar. Then the new parson went to the back of the church and rang the bell; it was said that the number of times he pulled the bell-rope corresponded to the number of years the new incumbent intended to stay in the parish. And then the Registrar of the diocese, wearing a wig and gown, effected the legal part of the proceedings, and, when Mr McDadd had sworn to his belief in the Thirty-Nine Articles and his commitment to use no form of liturgy other than the Book of Common Prayer or other authorised services, the business was done.

The Archdeacon, fumbling for his sermon notes, reflected ruefully that 'poor old' Francis Kreer had been one of the few clergymen in the entire diocese who had taken these promises seriously. With friend Widger on the one hand with his balloons and his extempore prayers, and the likes of Father Wells at the other extreme with their Missa Normativa, there were few enough parsons who really appreciated the Church of England for what it was. During the second verse of 'Christ is made the sure foundation', the Archdeacon sank to his knees. This was supposedly to pray for inspiration during the sermon, but the sermon, though freshly typed that week by the adorable Fiona, was in fact the sermon which he always preached at inductions. Also, although the Archdeacon was not an atheist, it was years since he had really prayed, that is to say spoken to God directly, or believed that God had spoken to him, either silently or in the more mysterious way He used to speak, by filling his mind with pious thoughts or good desires. During the third verse of the hymn the Archdeacon waddled towards the dark oak Laudian pulpit and heaved himself up the steps. When the music stopped he made the sign of the cross and boomed – 'Behold, I make all things new! . . .' As he declaimed the oration – it must have been the twentieth time he had used it – he wondered whether the analogy about buying a new car on the first page had not gone on a trifle long: but they all laughed at the joke about the new broom: and he thought he got good mileage out of the two sayings – the new broom sweeps clean and you can't teach an old dog new tricks – and how well 'any archdeacon could tell you that *that* is true'. The polite laughter which always accompanied this aside might, the Archdeacon realised, spring from the audience, or rather, congregation, thinking the Archdeacon himself was an old dog, rather than realising that he was making a gentle dig at the recalcitrant conservatism of some of the minor clergy. Still, as he shifted the sermon back in his pocket and descended the pulpit steps to the tune of 'O Jesus I have promised', he felt he had given the crowd their money's worth.

Sally noted that Jessica sang the hymn not merely lustily but almost hysterically. There was something wild-eyed and pale about the girl. She had lost all her rather alarming satirical nature and the mother had found this reassuring at first. Now she thought that it was not healthy. The girl still treated her mother as a stranger. In the old days she had been walled up with her dad the minute supper was over. Now she had her sermon-tapes, her Youth Fellowship meetings and all the other activities run by the C.U. at her school. Sally was happy for the girl if it was her way of working through the difficult business of Francis – but Sally did wish that Jessica would treat her as a friend.

'O Jesus!' shrieked Jessica, 'thou hast promised
To all who follow Thee,
That where thou art in glory
There shall Thy servant be . . .'

He had promised, but what were *His* promises worth? What her mother mistook for pious fervour in her daughter was actually

Promethean rage. Like all other grown-ups in whom she had put her trust, Jesus had let her down. Jessica's life had become a journey across hidden quagmires. What appeared to be solid ground (family life, her parents' love for her) dissolved at every pace she took. It did not particularly interest Jessica whether her parents loved each other. It was one of those questions you didn't ask, but, having asked it, she would have assumed that Daddy found Mummy pretty irritating and Mummy found Daddy cold and lacking in affection. This was all their business: but that the grown-ups should choose on these or other grounds to punish *her*, Jessica, not only by breaking up the home but by withdrawing affection from her – this hurt. Jessica hated the fact that Daddy had gone away without explanation to her – did all their years together, their shared jokes and books, their games of chess, their holidays, count for nothing? His absence was not just a grief but an insult. And as for Mummy's domestic arrangements: of all the people in the village, in the world, with whom she might have stayed, she had chosen the Old Bill. Jessica knew that when she met her mother's wild mad sorrowful eyes, on the day Daddy left, she had looked at Pain Itself, Sorrow Itself. They had all believed they might cast the burden of this Sorrow on another pair of shoulders – Mummy had cast her cares on Miss Bill: Daddy was having his absurd idyll with the hippy. Jessica had found a friend in Jesus. But what if this was just making a scapegoat for our troubles? When she was little, Jessica had an Imaginary Friend. No one else knew whether this imaginary figure was in the room or not. Only Jessica knew. She would sometimes set places at table for this Friend and her conversations with her were ceaseless. What if Jesus were just another Imaginary Friend? Wasn't that all that Terry Widger had to offer – an Imaginary Friend who would bear our griefs and carry our afflictions? No wonder she'd found it tempting, and no wonder Sarah Mackintosh and the others thought she was a baby for falling for it.

At the 'bun-fight', which was held in the primary school, the village had the chance to take a closer look at their new priest. There they all were again – Miss Norbury, Mrs Renton, the Spittles, the Maxwell-Lees. Over a hundred people squeezed together, clutching in their one hand a small glass of German white wine or Bulgarian red, and in their other a paper plate, on which was dolloped a spoonful of coleslaw and a spoonful of potato salad, a thin slice of ham rolled into a cylinder, a slice of quiche, some tomatoes. Nobody in the room liked this food and they all knew that it had been chosen because it was 'easy' and supposedly no trouble to serve or prepare: yet in the general conversation, and in the various speeches, everyone repeated their amazement that 'the ladies' of the parish had taken so much trouble to prepare such a 'wonderful repast'.

Mrs McDadd, a thirty-year-old D.Phil student, writing a thesis on eighteenth-century travel writers, and by no means certain that she wished to take on the role of a country vicar's wife, smiled so hard that the corners of her mouth ached. She did not know who her interlocutor was, a child of twelve.

'So where do you live?' she asked Jessica.

Jessica wished this question had not been asked. She was finding this evening difficult and the one thing she found so hard was, why had Jesus not answered her prayer? He had said so clearly that He would be able to grant any request made in His name! Jessica had asked for Daddy to return, and he *had* come back, but he had been drunk, and frightening; the strange madman fighting in the mud with the Old Bill had not been her Daddy, not Daddy as Jessica remembered him. Jessica felt sadly tricked by Jesus. It was as if He were a cruel joker who had turned on her and said, 'What are you complaining about? You asked for your father to come back and he *came* back, didn't he? Oh, you wanted him sober, and you wanted him to take you and your mother to live with him at the vicarage, and you wanted everything to be like the old days? Well, you should have *said*.'

'We don't live anywhere just at the moment,' said Jessica, in answer to Mrs McDadd's question. 'We're staying with Miss Bill,' Jessica added.

'Oh, right. The churchwarden? I'm finding it difficult to remember who everyone is, to tell you the truth. That's Miss Bill over there?'

Yes, that was the Bill, wolfing sausage rolls and talking animatedly to the Archdeacon about the ordination of women. Jessica hated her. She knew that it was wrong to hate another human being, but she hated the Bill. She slightly hated her mother for having fallen into the Bill's clutches, and she hated her father for having deserted them and caused all this pain and behaved so very irresponsibly. But she could not hate either of her parents completely. Sally was a baby who could not be blamed for her foolish behaviour and Daddy was going through a 'mid-life crisis'. Emily Roberts's dad had gone through one when he was made redundant by Southern Electricity: he had had an affair with the woman who was his secretary, and then come back to his family and now they were all OK again, Emily said. Jessica had found her talks with Emily – easily her best friend this term (Sarah Mackintosh was a thing of the past, having mocked Jessica's religious conversion and all but undone it) – really, really helpful. Jessica felt that Mummy and Daddy would have got together again if they had only had the chance and if only the Bill had not weighed in. Mummy kept telling Jessica how grateful they must be to the Bill!

'Oh, g-good, you two have met!' said the Wing-Commander, who thought that the new vicar's wife needed to be rescued from the former vicar's peculiar child. 'You were telling me before the service about your work,' he said to Mrs McDadd. 'The G-grand Tour and all that. F-fascinating. H-h-how's your Latin?'

Mrs McDadd, who held the usual view in Oxford that anyone who was not a member of the university must be stupid, explained, 'I'm writing about eighteenth-century travellers, not ancient Romans.'

Worth a try, mused the Wing-Commander, allowing himself the unpardonable generalisation that no woman ever gets the point of what one *says*. He had merely thought that, if she liked the connoisseurs who had visited Rome, Naples, Paestum, Cumae, she might have a smattering of Latin, and that if she did, she might like to read with him . . . When he had done the *Aeneid* he thought of moving on to Ovid; but here he had drawn a blank.

Lindie Spittle in another corner of the mêlée had buttonholed the new parson, James McDadd, a vaguely porcine young man with wire-framed spectacles balanced on a nose like a piece of putty. He shared his wife's view of the world outside university. During the weeks before the induction they had both suffered from cold feet about the whole enterprise. Would he not have been better off hanging on for one more year of the college chaplaincy and then, when this temporary post came to an end, trying to obtain a lectureship in Theology at some other university? Ditcham had been made to sound so tempting by the Archdeacon – the lightest of parochial duties, time for research ('old Frankie Kreer was by way of being a bit of a scholar'), within easy reach of Oxford and of London. The reality of things came as a shock – the 'bun-fight', the horde of well-meaning but uneducated people like the Spittles.

'Only I do hope you'll be keeping the Sunday School going. Terry Widger liked to tell us that the kiddies *are* the church!'

James McDadd's attempt at humour came out as a donnish put-down.

'I'm not sure whether Irenæus or Athanasius would be happy with this definition.' Then, seeing the baffled distaste in Lindie's eyes – oh hell, he was going to have to live among people who had not even *heard* of Irenæus, still less read him – he lurched into a wholly uncharacteristic attempt at demotic earthiness. 'But, fundamentally, you're right. The church wouldn't have got very far without encouraging people to be faithful and multiply. That basically means – if we want what the Archbishop of Canterbury calls "bums on pews" – we need more babies and – er –'

He regretted beginning this sentence. Only nervousness had prompted it, and now it was hard to see how it could end.

'More babies –?' asked Lindie.

'Only one way to get those,' he said, gulping his Blue Nun hotly and feeling himself come out in a childish flush.

Lindie's eyes and ears were not deceiving her. Gerrie could say what he liked afterwards when they were at home. He could claim that she was exaggerating, but within *seconds* of engaging her in conversation that young man was talking about *how babies were born*.

'How about you?' Mr McDadd asked – his flush showing no signs of vanishing. Men did not just *go red* – as she told Gerrie over and over again for the rest of the evening – unless their minds were brimming over with a certain subject. That was what he said to her – first, bums; then the very coarse suggestion that everyone in church should be especially, well, active; then the blatant invitation, 'How about you?' He tried to cover it up with,

'How many children do you have?', but Lindie knew she was not that easily fooled. That man wanted her body. What else could he have meant, when he made a sudden nervous grab for a plate of 'eats' at his side, and thrust it towards her with the words, 'How are you off for sausage?'

3

The induction at St Agatha's, Hoxton was a more ambitious affair from the liturgical viewpoint. With the help of a friend who traded in vestments and *bondieuserie*, Damian Wells had been able to borrow fifty scarlet fiddle-back chasubles for the evening, and the visiting clergy, like a swarm of vermilion beetles, were all arrayed in these garments to concelebrate the Mass of the Holy Spirit. The area Bishop, who had a taste for this sort of thing, had dressed up in full Roman pontificals with a lace alb and a purple zucchetto on the back of his head. A ten-year-old black boy, decorative in red cassock and pie-crust cotta, carried the Bishop's mitre in a silk scarf draped around his skinny little shoulders. A counter-tenor, hired for the occasion, sang Mozart's *Ave Verum Corpus* as a Communion Motet, and the hymns included 'Faith of our Fathers', 'I'll sing a hymn to Mary' and 'Sweet Sacrament Divine'. It was only sad that there were so few members of the laity to enjoy these exuberant expressions of piety. Not counting the servers, of whom there were eight, there were only twelve people in the congregation. Six of these had driven over from Reading to give Father Wells their support, and one was his old friend Father Francis Kreer, who did not feel equal to concelebrating the Eucharist. When they all adjoined to the parish hall, it was discovered that the 'good women' of the parish had catered for twice the numbers. The trestle tables were laden with paper plates, plastic bowls of potato crisps, soft white miniature bread rolls, cut in half and coated with a range of 'spreads' – fish paste, meat paste, egg and salad dressing, St Ivel. Little mountains of fairy cakes, heaps of paper napkins, pints of ready-mixed orange squash, lay about, untouched. The tiny handful of regular congregation kept to themselves during this joyless repast, and made no efforts to interrupt the esoteric conversation of the priests who had left their liturgical vestments in church and now milled about, in their soutanes or black suits, greedily piling their plates high with egg rolls and crisps but making only small in-roads into the vast amounts of uneaten cheap comestibles.

The parish hall was a gloomy venue for so joyful an event as an induction. Unshaded sixty-watt bulbs dangled from cross-beams of a very late Victorian Gothic barn. The gloss crimson paint peeled and puckered from the wainscotting which was warped and swollen with damp. Above the wainscotting at a height of about seven feet, the walls were plastered. The cream emulsion must have been slapped on forty years since. Grey and black damp patches sprawled across its surface like maps. One of the upper windows was smashed. One of the walls was sprayed with graffiti – a relic from the days when a former incumbent was sufficiently trusting to allow the hall to be used for dancing (a so-called Youth Club which had been closed down by the police). On one wall, ghoulishly large, one and a half times life size, was a painted crucifix. Even on this, the paint was crumbling, giving the impression that, in addition to all the torments of the Sacred Passion, the crucified figure was suffering from some appalling skin complaint. Great peels of paint, the colour of Max Factor, curled from the thorn-crowned brow, the pierced hands and feet. Above it, on the cross-beam, in ill-executed pseudo-Gothic lettering, was the legend SO GOD LOVED THE WORLD.

Francis found himself being addressed by an old priest with ill-fitting false teeth and a biretta on the back of his head, who, from the desperate way in which he was pushing fish paste rolls into his mouth, might well have been observing a liturgical fast of some duration in readiness for the evening's solemnities.

'Of course,' he said with his mouth full, and spattering Francis with bits of half-chewed fish paste and margarine, 'St Agatha's always was what we called Full Faith. Oh yes, father, very much so. Your parish, father?'

'It's in the country. I'm the Vicar of a small parish in the country. I'm the Vicar of . . .'

The ancient priest did not really care what parish Francis came from. 'Big six, of course, very firm on reservation even in the earliest days. And a missal-church, oh yes. None of your Prayer Book twaddle. Very lucky in the war – most of the houses near here got a direct hit but this lovely hall was spared, and though they lost glass in the Blitz, the church was never actually hit.'

A group of clergymen of various ages had congregated around Francis. It was hardly socially demanding because none of them really wished so much to converse, as to talk. Sometimes their monologues converged in a peculiar shared hoard of myths, images and stories about the heroes and exploits of the extreme Anglo-Catholic wing of the Church of England, or about its beleaguered condition today: sometimes they merely wished to talk about themselves.

'Of course I was in Bethnal Green all through the Blitz, wonderful people, wonderful . . .'

'I'm very happy to say that I have never even allowed a woman in the sanctuary, let alone to read the sacred Scriptures aloud at the holy mysteries.'

'Dear old Father Brush-Tankerville used to say – "I will not have Jezebels, sweeping the sanctuary of God with their Wack-u-um cleaners".'

The whole company roared in appreciative laughter.

'And do you remember when one of the parents in his parish school objected to her child being made to go to confession . . .'

This was such an old chestnut that the circle of black-clad men almost said it in unison. A concelebrated joke.

'Madam, I trust you would not send your son to school in filthy clothes. I would undertake not to send him home with a filthy soul. . . .'

Francis wondered whether the famous 'monsters' of Anglo-Catholic legend, such as Archibald Pelham Brush-Tankerville (Vicar of St Agatha's from 1917–1949, one of the last bigots to be sent to prison for offences against the Public Worship Regulation Act of 1874) could really have been as rude, and as blustering, and as affected as their admirers made them sound. Strangely, Francis did not nurse a comparable scepticism about the sanctity of those good men, like old Father Wainwright in the Docks, who gave their lives to the poor. But there seemed to be no Father Wainwrights nowadays. Anglo-Catholicism, which must always have been a rather fantastical dream (entertained at one time by about a third of the Church of England), but a dream which translated itself into lives of heroic virtue, buildings of mysterious beauty, now seemed to have shrunk and diminished to the point where it was the preserve of a handful of deeply warped bachelor clerics.

Francis felt glad that he had come. He possessed enough self-knowledge to know that he had himself become 'odd': but his oddness was so much at variance with the oddness of these priests that he could no longer deceive himself into thinking that he belonged to them. He was the Vicar of Sorrows now, and his future was not in parish halls but in waste places. He was no longer required to hold fast to 'the Faith of Our Fathers' in which it was impossible to believe: on the contrary he felt a profound inner compulsion to spread doubt. Uncertainty was the only safe state of mind in a century which had produced the Nazis. That was why Francis would be performing such a useful purpose when he proved that the Bible was no more than a code-book for explaining *Who's Who*! Even before he had made this discovery, however, he had realised that what explained the particular oddness of so many Christians was their (in some ways rather heroic) need to hold fast to untruth, to mouth gibberish as if it were not merely true, but verifiable, as logical as physics or maths. These old men in birettas, as if the doctrines of the creeds, of the Primitive Church and of the Scriptures were not enough to swallow, wanted to add yet more rubbish to the lumber-rooms of their brains – the bodily Assumption of Our Lady, the Infallibility of the Holy Father, the validity and lawfulness of their own orders, in spite of the fact that the same infallible Holy Father had declared them to be absolutely null and void! Christianity was very largely a Lewis Carroll wonderland of nonsense: its dialectic was surreal: witness the discussions in progress up and down this trestle table, about the admissibility or otherwise of women to Holy Orders.

'Ena's not going to desert us,' said Damian Wells, who had lit up a cigarette. Ena, or Ena the Cruel, was the sobriquet employed by the younger clergy for the Bishop of London. The older men who recalled the palmy days of the Movement – the Anglo-Catholic

Congresses in the Albert Hall, the flourishing sisterhoods, the frock-coated ancient Tractarians who could almost remember Dr Pusey – did not like this strand of King's Road camp which had crept in since the 1960s. 'But I'm absolutely firm, Father. St Agatha's will not accept the authority of any bishop who ordains women.'

'No thanks,' said Francis in reply to the offer of a cigarette.

'So, Francis, how are you?' asked Damian who was actually rather embarrassed that his old friend had turned up at the induction – and looking such a wreck! Francis used to be so neat. Now he was not properly shaven, his finger nails were black (he said it was gardening but Damian had never thought of Francis as much of a gardener), and he was dressed like a ragamuffin. Beneath his Sarum cassock (fancy wearing one of those old maternity dresses to a 'do' like this instead of a nice buttoned soutane!) he wore a filthy, very thick dark-blue fisherman's jumper, whose cuffs and collar burst from the robe at neck and wrists. The cassock was rather short and did not hide his pale khaki army-surplus trousers, pale grey, very thick socks and dark blue yachting plimsolls. Damian also thought that, while not everyone would insist on men exuding the sweetness, as he did himself, of lotions and unguents, there was no excuse for smelling, as Francis did, of B.O. He never used to stink when he lived in Ditcham!

The débâcle in Francis's life had struck Damian as almost incomprehensible. This was chiefly because Damian, though obsessed from his boyhood by 'religion', had no interest in metaphysics, world-views, personal mythologies, or other people's inner lives. He had never entertained 'doubts' of the sort which had once tormented Francis before his final parting of the ways with theism. He had never considered whether his religious beliefs presupposed or suggested a fundamentally tragic view of the world, as Francis did. For Damian religion was a system into which you fitted yourself with greater or less difficulty. Once in, to start questioning or spiritual wrestling was a sort of madness in itself: for, once inside the household of faith, the only things which could interest Damian were the colour of the furnishings and 'family squabbles' among the faithful. It had therefore never occurred to Damian quite how profound a change had come upon his friend. He thought Francis had become odd, perhaps because of his mother's death. The marriage had broken up: since Damian could not really understand why people got married in the first place, he saw no point in trying to understand why they got divorced. The idea that Francis was an atheist would have frightened and surprised Damian Wells. The idea that Francis, who had long been a notional atheist, had only recently come to terms with the implications of his world-outlook is one that had never occurred to the newly installed vicar of St Agatha's, Hoxton. Damian's own career had fallen so easily into an abyss the last time he disgraced himself. He knew that the Church was giving him a second chance, but they would not give him a third. If he got into another scrape they would drop him in the *shit*. He was determined not to blot his copy-book again.

The arrival of Francis Kreer at the induction, wild-eyed and oddly dressed, had not gone unnoticed.

('Father!'

'Yes, Father?'

'Who's that rather *strange*-looking Father who has just come in? The one in the plimsolls?')

Damian had noticed how people shrank from *him* after he had been arrested. Francis Kreer had been alone among his local clergy in continuing to be on terms with Damian, even after the hearing in the magistrates' court had been reported in the local newspapers. (Thank God, thought Damian, his own cottaging activities had never made it into the pages of the *Sunday Mercury*.) All this should have made Damian wish to show his gratitude to Francis when he was down on his luck, but he was afraid to touch pitch and be defiled. To Damian's way of looking at things, his own bit of bad luck had been a misfortune beyond his control – whereas Francis's martyrdom at the hands of the *Sunday Mercury* had really been *his own fault*. Had not Damian, with his own eyes, seen the Vicar of Ditcham and a young woman in Hyde Park? If men did such things, they were almost asking to be called 'Randy Rev'. And Fr Damian Wells did not want to be seen associating with men whose sexual antics had been paraded all over the cheaper newspapers.

The Bishop had come over to join them. To check up on them more like. Oh, why wouldn't Francis just *go*?

'And you are?'

'Francis Kreer.'

'Is your parish in London?'

Damian exhaled smoke thoughtfully, unable to decide whether this was a trick question, or whether it showed that the Bishop had no idea 'who Francis was'.

'Damian and I were at Mirfield together,' said Francis.

'Splendid!'

'Was it?' laughed Francis joylessly. 'I don't remember it as all that splendid. On the other hand Damian has been a terribly kind friend to me. . . .'

Even if Francis had not been smelly, the Bishop would have been on the move. He had merely intended briefly to salute everyone in the hall before leaving; but the Vicar of Sorrows, ancient mariner-like, had seized his elbow and fixed him with a wild eye.

'. . . He took my mother's funeral, you know.'

'Ah, bless you,' said the Bishop.

'I don't know if your own mother is still alive. . . .'

'I'm happy to say she *is*!' said the Bishop. 'Eighty-two and with more energy than I have myself. . . .'

'I suppose there must, for some men and women, be a deep tie with their mothers – the umbilical cord itself – to whose severance they can never accustom themselves. I believed myself to be bereaved – and of course I was: but the mistake I made was in imagining that I should, or would, ever "get over" this event. . . .'

'The process of healing,' said the Bishop, who was better with people than Damian and prepared for five minutes to confront Francis's unhappiness. His willingness to listen produced a torrent of words.

'. . . The reason is – or this is what I'm beginning to suspect – the reason her death caused me such pain was because it was just a reminder of that thing which I never wanted to happen, with which I could never come to terms. The cutting of the cord. I believe it's just a thinnish piece of tubing like a sausage skin! Strange to think one's whole outlook on life could be coloured by it. You see, if you'd asked me in Mummy's lifetime, I should have said that we weren't really very close to one another: I think I always rather *resented* being cut off from her at birth if you want to know the truth!' Francis harrumphed, a loud slightly halitoid laugh in the Bishop's face. 'I mean, people blame parents, they think parents should bond with their children, but some children can *arrive* feeling resentful. I'm much more of a nihilist than Ivan Karamazov. . . .'

'Ah,' said the Bishop, who had never read Dostoyevsky but had heard frequent allusions, in sermons and retreat-conferences, to the legend of the Grand Inquisitor, 'what a wonderful novel that is.'

'At least he wanted to hand his entrance ticket *back*,' said Francis with another embarrassing horse-like whinny, 'whereas some of us really are more like Job – we never wanted the entrance ticket. We never wanted to be born. But here we are – and we find ourselves with the impression – is it an illusion? – that we are *moral beings*. . . .'

Damian was moving from sensations of embarrassment to ones of desperation. While Francis gabbled – and there was no shutting him up – Damian just wanted to get the Bishop out of the way.

'Father,' he said, squeezing the Bishop's purple sleeve, 'I think it's time for us to meet the churchwardens.' He tried to lead the Bishop in the direction of a silver-haired Jamaican in the opposite corner of the hall.

'So the cord's cut – we've been marooned here, and we never wanted to arrive, but we find ourselves with this peculiar sense of *responsibility* towards the other survivors of the shipwreck,' said Francis, 'and how that feeling arises – where it comes from, this sense of right and wrong, God knows – or that's what God would know if he existed. That's really what *The Grammar of Assent*'s all about – you find Newman at the end of his life having been through all this rubbish –' Francis gestured wildly first towards the peeling crucifix and then towards the crowd of black-clad priests – 'this *crap*! The Arians of the fourth century! Why St Augustine condemned the Donatists! Are the Catholic claims of the Church of England valid, should he join the Church of Rome, all those extraordinary arcane problems which obsessed him in the *Apologia* – he puts them all behind him and he asks where do we get our sense of right and wrong from? And it's an extraordinarily bold book because he admits there *aren't* any proofs for the existence of God. It's a book which could have been written by an atheist and in some moods I think it might have been, except that he seems to be saying that the existence of *conscience* is such a mysterious thing, that the impenetrable mind of God – if it existed – big if' – another crazed whinnying sound – 'could be the only thing which could encompass such a thing as Good and Evil – that scale of value outside ourselves which we all recognise. Now it's a false argument. . . .'

He was still talking of Cardinal Newman's religious ideas when Damian led the Bishop away. Some speeches followed. The white-haired Jamaican read from the back of two postcards an address of welcome to Father Wells, and Father Wells in a booming and rather insensitive voice (when he shouted the South London vowels crept through the plummy artificiality of his usual tones) expressed the appreciation of all those present for the really splendid refreshments which had been so lavishly supplied. With rather a violent metaphysical leap, Damian in one sentence praised the egg rolls and in the next said that to be a priest was the greatest privilege in life, and he hoped he would be worthy of the great task of being the parish priest of St Agatha's.

'These are very hard times for us Catholics in the church,' he boomed. 'The hymn we sang in church wasn't just a form of words. We have had the faith of our Fathers entrusted to us by Almighty God and though some people, even the bishops of our own church, might call that faith into question, we stand firm.'

The audience liked this. The black-clad priests, and the tiny congregation stamped and clapped and there were cries of 'hear, hear!'

'We stand firm on doctrine – we believe in the Virginity of Our Most Blessed Lady!'

(Cheers)

'We believe in the threefold ministry of the Catholic Church. You don't make a priest merely by putting a liberal – or a woman – in vestments. Only God can make a priest and He makes priests in His own way. . . .'

(Louder cheers)

'And any synods or northern ecclesiastics, whom I shall not name – we are supposed to be enjoying ourselves . . .'
(Laughter)
'. . . who might think that they can overthrow these things will find that they have us at St Agatha's to contend with.'

The handful of old ladies and Jamaicans cheered, and Damian's fellow-priests gave him thunderous applause as he called out, through the roar, 'Faith of our fathers! Holy Faith! We will be true to thee till death!'

It was now about twenty past nine in the evening, and the discernible restlessness of the company could perhaps be explained by the desire of many of those present for alcohol. Francis Kreer was largely oblivious to this. During the speeches, his face had been lit up with a curious smirk, and at some points he was scarcely able to prevent himself from laughing. This was not because he considered everything Damian Wells had said to be ridiculous. It was because the *Who's Who* Biblical Parallels secret had come buzzing back into his brain, and it suddenly struck him as so funny. Jesus on the Cross had cried aloud and said, 'My God, My God, why hast thou forsaken me?' This was Matthew 27:46. On the other hand, Jesus was not using his own words, but quoting from Psalm 22, verse 1. This was one of the most extraordinarily blatant of all the clues left by the Biblical 'hoaxers' who compiled *Who's Who*. For the Psalm 22:1 reference gave you HUME, His Eminence Cardinal (George) Basil; see Westminster, Archbishop of, (RC). If you looked up the grid-equivalent of Matthew 27:46, you got, WESTMINSTER, Archbishop of, (RC) since 1976. It could not conceivably be a matter of chance that the two occurrences of the words 'My God, my God, why hast thou forsaken me?' *both* turned up the Roman Catholic Primate on the grid. It followed that the Roman Catholics were more or less publicly admitting that God had forsaken the world, that the whole elaborate structure of Christendom, and the great Catholic myth which Damian Wells was expounding in his speech, was a carefully-constructed con-trick.

So, Francis had smirked; but the amusement was caused by a curious dislocation in his mind. Since his brain had begun to race along these lines, and he had 'discovered' the Great *Who's*

Who Biblical Conspiracy, Francis had become, in his conception of himself, two beings. The old Gibbonian Oxford man, trained in the ways of common sense and scepticism by Harris of Balliol, knew that such 'theories' were always bosh. They occurred to clever, deranged minds, who seized on totally false first premises and then pursued them with relentless logic. By such means, it had been 'discovered' that Queen Elizabeth, or the Society of Jesus, had written the plays of Shakespeare, that Homer was a woman, that the Gospels concealed the mysteries of a hidden and forgotten orgiastic cult, or that everything in English political life was organised by the Freemasons. Rational Francis looked at Francis the propounder of the *Who's Who* Conspiracy with the callous amusement of an eighteenth-century reveller who had gone to Bedlam to laugh at the lunatics through the bars of their cages. He could almost envisage himself as a separate physical being, hunched, grinning, fanatic. When he propounded the theory to himself, he did not do so for effect; no one else, after all, so much as knew about the theory. But it was as if he were on parade, and the performance by the clownish maniac Francis afforded the cool, sceptical and pessimistic Francis such amusement that the mania 'acted up' for his sane self's amusement. It was as if a species of mental pantomime was being permanently enacted inside his skull. Which of the two beings – the sceptic or the madman – was in control, Francis did not know, and that was one of the reasons that he was afraid about launching his 'theories' on the world. If he had gone up to the Bishop – who at this moment was taking his farewells of Damian – and expounded the theories, he would not have known which of the two beings was speaking. The lofty sceptic would have been hurt if the Bishop did not laugh at his ingenuity. The crouching, grinning propounder of the theories, however, would have been murderously angry if the Bishop did not take these ideas seriously. Already, this figure, who seemed in his mind's eye a little like Quasimodo, a little like Eric Gadney, was known to sane Francis as a person of furious energy. During moments of mental vacancy in Deal Public Library, sane Francis had caught the Mad Genius pausing from his work on the *Who's Who* entries and planning acts of retaliation against those scholars and public figures who did not accept his ideas. He had considered, for example, a campaign of fire-bombs in all the major churches, not dissimilar from the terrorist campaigns of the Irish Republican Army. And this idea in itself had caused the body of Francis, which contained these two very disparate beings, to convulse itself in the reading room and let out such yelps of amusement that various heads had turned until he quietened down.

When sane Francis had conquered his amusement at his mad inner companion's intellectual gymnastics, he made another of his resolutions: he must find ways of keeping the mad friend at bay. It was all right for mad Francis to expound his theories when they were alone together; in fact, sane Francis positively enjoyed it. He even felt tempted to believe the theory – when they were alone. It was certainly no less implausible than other techniques of Biblical exegesis which he had studied, such as the widespread medieval view that every word of the Old Testament prefigured the New Testament, and that figures such as Noah, Moses and Samson were 'types' of Christ. But the mad theorist was not a man to take about with you at parties such as this. He would interrupt, and talk about his work among the 'M's or 'N's of *Who's Who* when other people were wishing to make small-talk. He would be a freak. It was rather like having a badly-behaved dog; there were occasions when such a creature must be left at home or locked in the back of the car.

Sane Francis actually said aloud 'Down, down' to his mad companion, somewhat to the surprise of the clergyman standing at his side, and he squeezed through the clerical throng to Damian, who had edged away from him most conspicuously. Francis had become desperately bored, as well as alienated, by this induction crowd. He had begun to think of Jay, and to imagine her lovely long smooth legs in their denim shorts, and her springy blonde hair which was growing longer once more over her ears (he wanted her to grow it really long again, as it was when he first saw her), and her short-sleeved blouse with sailing-ships, open to the breast.

Damian looked glowing with relief when Francis eventually found him and said he was going.

'Look,' he said, 'any time, dear. You only have to call me up, and there's a bed in the presbytery. Really.'

'That is really kind,' said Francis. 'And I'm so glad for you, Damian. I do hope that everything will work out.'

'Thanks,' said Damian. For a split second they were for one another, these two middle-aged wrecks, the young friends which they had been more than twenty years earlier at theological college, and waves of real affection passed between them. But then absence of sympathy descended once more like a curtain. The few priests who went down to Old Street station with Francis kept their distance from him on the platform. They still paced about in twos or threes, continuing the rarefied Anglo-Catholic conversations which had enlivened the evening in the parish hall. Francis heard the word 'Walsingham' at one point, and from another group 'Ecclesia'. In Francis, these men saw only a wild creature, with food dribbling down the front of his cassock, muttering to himself and smiling oddly.

4

Jay had passed an evening of such contentment that she did not notice the time passing. At about half-past six – the time of day when she felt hungriest – she had eaten a delicious meal, which consisted of baked beans on toast, followed by tinned pear halves in syrup with Nestlé Condensed Milk. Having balanced her dirty plates on the mountain of congealed and unwashed dishes and pans in the sink, she had washed her hands thoroughly, returned to the sitting-room, and sat on the upright chair near the one-bar electric fire. She really needed a music-stand. The Beethoven sonata which she was practising was balanced precariously on a pile of books which had been placed on another upright chair. With each hour that passed, Jay realised how badly she had fallen behind. Not only did she make many mistakes, but, ever since buying the violin (and the violin, Chinese, was very poor, she *must* get a good one), she had begun to fear that her interpretative gift, her musicality, was lost. Even at an early age, when she was doing Grade 5, a teacher had remarked on the sensitive way in which she brought out the 'soul' of the great composers. Few children of that age, apparently, see that it is not simply a question of getting the notes right;

that playing, say, Haydn requires a completely different technique from playing Brahms. Her musical career had dawned from this point, but it really blossomed during her last year at school when, with something very like mystical telepathy, she had seen into the life of Beethoven. There was no point in trying to put this into words. Had she been able to put it into words, neither she nor Beethoven would have needed to put it into music. But it was as if, when she had played his work, she had made a joint statement in perfect harmony with his own; and that the curious combination of messages in the late Beethoven works, particularly the String Quartets – their infinite sorrow, but their dogged, almost perky determination to struggle on and to find hope in the bleakest of landscapes – this was something which she, Jay Dunbar, had seen into, and been able to grasp. It was like going down into a pit with Beethoven in his sorrow, and coming up again with him into the light. And it was not like Brahms, or even much Schumann, which were 'easy' in a way to interpret because you could ham it up and be 'schmaltzy': this was really difficult, academic, hard-edged music, as 'difficult' as the sort of atonal modern stuff which some of her contemporaries at the Guildhall were struggling to compose, but at the same time rich and always jerking poignantly between heartbreak and mellowness. And this was the voice, the quality, the Beethoven magic which, that evening in 'Tudun-Teku', she felt herself at last recapturing; so she sawed away for hours at her fiddle, and did not miss Francis and did not notice the time when there was a knock at the front door and it opened.

There was a small hall, but so small that in effect the front door opened into the sitting-room.

'Only me!' called Eric Gadney. 'Wondered if you'd like some logs. Ena's anxious you'll both be cold. But, please! Don't let me interrupt!'

Jay Dunbar was not pleased to see the Boss. She knew that he was her landlord and that he was entitled to enter 'Tudun-Teku' because it was his property; but, since she began to allow him to indulge himself in the potting sheds, she considered that it would be more tactful for him to stay away from the house which she shared with Francis. She did not want the Boss here; but he was making his way towards her. With his strange slightly sideways walk, his one 'funny' arm dangling at his side and his tight-stretched shiny mask of a face, he was more like a crustacean than a human being; in the dimly lamp-lit room, it could have been a giant lobster crawling its way towards her.

Apart from the moral proprieties, and her quasi-marital sense of loyalty to Francis Kreer when on the 'home territory' of 'Tudun-Teku', Jay did not wish her musical evening to be interrupted. Within the last half-hour, she had advanced; she was indeed beginning to recapture that Beethoven technique, that combination of precision and feeling, that sheer brutal energy of Beethoven's genius; she was beginning to hear his voice again; and she did not want to be made to think about logs.

'I'll carry a bag or two in – no, please, please.' Always that pseudo-courtesy, that exaggerated gallantry in his intrusiveness. The lobster-invasion had managed within two minutes to create an atmosphere of flustered chaos in the room. When she stood, the pile of books which had been serving as a music-stand teetered and fell.

'Let me.'

'There's no need! I can do it.'

She stooped. He stooped. He was slow and shakily clumsy at such operations, and, in picking up the two books, he managed to knock to the ground the three which had remained on the chair.

The activity, however, as she realised a moment too late, provided him with the chance to place his grinning stretched mask very close to her own face. Her startled eyes and pouting, very full lips would have been tempting even to a less insatiably libidinous man than Eric Gadney.

'Please.' She moved back from his kiss, and spoke very closely to the stretched mask. 'There are some things I think we should agree.'

'He's away,' said Eric Gadney. With his 'good arm' he stretched out to her and held her shoulder. It was an ambiguous gesture, which could have been the movement any old man would have made in order that another person could help him to his feet, or could have been the grab of a predator. It had the effect of making them both roll together on the carpet, and soon she was pinioned beneath the lobster on the hearth-rug. 'He said he was going to London. You told me this afternoon in the potting-shed that he might be away for the night.'

Jay remembered this. Why had she allowed such an indiscretion to fly from her lips? As she recalled the exchange, it must have seemed to the Boss as if she were giving him an open invitation to visit her in 'Tudun-Teku' while Francis was in London.

'But he might be back.'

'He won't, Jay, he won't.' And his moist grin smothered her mouth with another kiss.

'Please don't. Not here.'

'I've bedded the missus down. She's had her last jimmy-riddle.'

'I don't care if she's – please – no, please don't.'

The heavy shoulders of the wonky arm pinioned her to the floor while the 'good' arm fumbled with the buttons of her shorts. Gnarled arthritic fingers pushed down into her knickers.

'No!'

She said it loudly and firmly and was able to push him to one side and sit up.

He paused in his assault, but it was not over. One of the fascinations of his face, when in the early days of their acquaintanceship she had found pity for him turning to fascination, had been its absence of expression. The very moist smile was the only thing about it which moved. The rest was fixed. She wanted to use his name, but she realised that she had never called him 'Eric' and that 'Mr Gadney' in these circumstances would not be appropriate.

On her knees, she edged away from him backwards, and she darted out of his reach as she got to her feet. The 'good' hand was reaching for her ankles. His trousers must have been open already when he came through the door, and the determined old crustacean was crawling along the floor towards her.

'Please stop this,' she said. 'I want to talk to you. You don't understand how difficult all this is for me. I'm not saying it hasn't all been very nice – between you and me. But Francis and I . . . Francis needs me. We must . . . If you can't limit it to what we do when we are in the Garden Centre, then it's got to stop. Francis and I . . .'

'God, you're like your grandmother when you're cross,' he said, with an appreciative leer.

'How do you mean?'

'She was like that. When I wanted her to marry me and she told me her first loyalty was to her old man and,' he smacked his lips as he brought out the knowing phrase, 'and Little Boy.'

Jay was thankful enough that this, to her, impenetrable remark had brought a halt for the time being to his libidinous quest. He had become once more a pathetic old man, staggering on all fours on the carpet. She felt almost callous allowing him to wrench himself into an upright position and to stand up. When he had done so, he sat down at once on the arm of the lumpy sofa which was splashed with red and white floral designs.

'What do you know about my grandmother?'

'You don't think she left me all that money for nothing?' He seemed affronted by the idea that he might have been admired for his character rather than his sexual prowess.

'But – Francis's mother . . . You didn't think that Francis was – my father?'

The smile disappeared from the stretched mask, and the blotched face darkened.

'You *told* me he was your father.' The wet lower lip was thrust forward now almost to the point where the lower plate of his false teeth jutted up, and he sucked at them angrily. 'I wrote to you as his daughter. You've never denied it! I thought you were Griselda's grand-daughter. If you aren't then who the hell are you?'

Jay looked at the little alarm clock on the mantelpiece. It said five past eleven. She felt nauseated. She had not tried to trick the Boss. She had never received letters from him and did not know what he meant when he said he had written to her. Everything had happened so quickly after Mo and his friends had raided the flat. Francis had said that they had nowhere to go. The Boss had struck up a friendship with her (and at that stage she had genuinely believed it to be nothing more than a friendship). She had never at any time said that she was Francis's daughter. She hated the thought that her chief attraction for the Boss was the false notion of her being the grand-daughter of Griselda Kreer. Had she been, it would surely have been almost incestuous to have allowed him his *droit de seigneur*.

'You filthy, scheming bitch,' he said, 'you little whore. You mean to say you've been two-timing me with this – wimp!'

'Francis loves me. I didn't think I needed to explain.'

'You didn't think. Well, you'll have to think now. He's in this too, I suppose. Is he your pimp as well as your wimp? Does he know what's been going on between us?'

'Of course not! It would hurt him terribly if he knew.'

'We'll see about that when we tell him in the morning.'

'You'd never do that, you'd never do such a cruel thing as that; not when he's so unhappy, mad with unhappiness sometimes.'

'He must be mad if he thinks he can get away with this! He must be mad if he wants to live with a whore like you!'

'That's a horrible thing to say! Oh, you *horrible* man!'

'We'll see about that!'

He was on his feet once more, and he advanced so quickly that he was able to drive her back against the fireplace wall.

'Oh, please don't, please not! Please! Ow! That hurt! Look, Eric!' – at last she came out with the name! 'If I let you, if I let you make love to me just once – ow! I shall scream, why are you being so rough with me, please, please!'

The 'good' hand had got her by the cheeks and he was squeezing, as he held her head against the wall. The rest of his barrel-like body had her imprisoned firmly against the wall.

'Is the little whore trying to make a bargain?'

'Look! Eric!' She was crying and breathless. 'If I let you just one more time, just once, will you promise me, promise me faithfully, that you will never, ever tell Francis? Look, we've both been deceived, and we've both done wrong, OK. I see that now. I admit it. But please don't commit the much worse evil of telling him. Because that would be really cruel.'

'Why do you mind about being cruel? You don't love him. If you'd loved him, you wouldn't have let me roger you.'

This horrible phrase provoked her to say, 'I do love Francis! I love him.'

It was sad, since Francis Kreer had to come in and find them together, that he did not come in just at that moment and hear her make this declaration, for it might have mitigated the situation for him. As it was, he came in about three minutes later, when she had consented to lie down on the carpet with the Boss. When Francis entered the front door, wearing a duffle coat over his cassock and a beret on his head, he did not find the pair *in flagrante delicto*, but they were lying together. Eric was almost on top of Jay, and his good hand was thrust into her blue blouse with the yachts on it, and his trousers were unbuttoned at the top. It seemed rather lame, when they looked up and saw him, that all Jay found to say was, 'Francis, what a good thing you've come. Eric has come round to see if we want any logs.'

Advent

I

As winter set in the Thames exuded dank mists, so that the river-villages such as Molesey, Streatley and Goring lay beneath a perpetual foggy blanket. The hills around did not rise above the fog so much as penetrate deeper into its milky obscurities; by the time you had mounted as high as Ditcham, you could have been inside some great mythological cloud, the theophany on Sinai or Parnassus.

By late morning, these thick mists would sometimes be penetrated by the sun which suffused the palest of yellow lights through the trees at the top of Potter's Field and made of the village a fantastical domain which appeared to float on clouds.

On other days, when mist was light and frost was hard, you could see all the views which had been visible in summer, though now bereft of leaves. Grass, in the distance, appeared as a silver smudge. These were the views which Robin Pimm saw as he came back to the farmhouse for breakfast; he would push back the tweed cap from his brow and meditate silently on the mystery of things.

There was snow in November, but it melted away, and not long after that a nasty virus 'went round' the village, a sort of 'flu with diarrhoea, some sufferers also complaining of ear-ache. Poor Mrs McDadd, the new Vicar's wife, whom no one in the village yet liked very much ('stuck up', 'too clever by half', 'snooty', were epithets which had been applied to her) went down with it, so that her husband had to do the 'school run' with the children. Gerrie Spittle also had it, and the Watson children, and Dorothy Maxwell-Lee thought she had a touch of it, though her disorders might have been caused by a glass too many of the Wing-Commander's Madeira. (The Maxwell-Lees had 'taken on a new lease of life' by purchasing a fox-terrier bitch called Calypso. Even more than usually, both Maxwell-Lees now observed and appreciated the passing seasons, as they took Calypso for walks around the village and the surrounding countryside. Calypso was a friendly dog, but she had formed a particular tendresse for the new Vicar's black Labrador, Jake. Mrs McDadd had not laughed when Dorothy Maxwell-Lee said, after church one day, 'That's one way of them finding out about the facts of life.')

People noticed that the congregation of St Birinus was very slightly smaller than in Francis Kreer's day. Not dramatically so, but noticeably. James McDadd had abandoned the monthly Mattins, and it was not known where the 'Mattins recusants' now went on a Sunday morning. He had introduced the Alternative Service Book, Rite A. Poor Ronald Maxwell-Lee hated this! A keen reader of *Private Eye*, he referred to the new liturgy as 'The Rocky Horror Service Book', but he did his best to be polite, and to read lessons, take prayers and so forth as before. Miss Bill was the only person in the village who seemed to have made friends with the new parson, and she said that she 'backed him to the hilt' in his decision to introduce a more up-to-date form of worship at St Birinus. Not only did Alison Bill take a much bigger part in the service – conducting the readings and prayers almost as often as the Vicar – she even assisted with Holy Communion by distributing the chalice. Lindie Spittle, who was not so privileged, said that the Vicar had 'favouritised' Miss Bill, and they both enjoyed being 'uppity' together and talking about theology, articles in *The Independent* and such, leaving the 'likes of Lindie' out of it. Lindie told Gerrie (and he was just beginning to tire of this refrain) that things had been so much more dignified under the last Vicar; it was an old church and it was surely appropriate to keep alive some of the older, more traditional forms of worship, particularly since older people liked it. (Mrs Renton was even rumoured to have become a Roman Catholic because she did not like the new dispensation at Ditcham; this was quite untrue, but she had taken herself off to a convent at Burnham – C of E – where a priest would hear her confession and she sometimes stayed for Mass; so she was far less regular in her support of St Birinus than she had been in Francis Kreer's time.) Lindie also thought it was extraordinary (and Mrs Pimm agreed with her on this one) that the new Vicar's wife, without so much as a by your leave, had completely re-organised the flower rota.

Sally Kreer watched all these developments in the village with an increasingly mature eye. It was an enriching experience, discovering at forty-three that one could still grow. Her marriage to Francis had frozen her. Her counsellor had helped her to see this. Apparently, it was quite normal for grown-up people to have dolls, and to talk to them, but what a statement about modern marriage! Teddy, Golly, and the Dog Frumpy now lay in a drawer in Sally and Alison's bedroom, and she had not spoken to them since Francis went away. All her thoughts about herself, the whole addictive adventure of self-discovery, now had more than a chance to be aired, either with the counsellor or with Alison herself. There was so much about herself, her body, her childhood, her feelings about men, her feelings about her child, that Sally had never understood before. Out it gushed, sometimes with tears, sometimes angrily, sometimes with exultation, in her weekly sharing sessions with the counsellor. She had gone back to her work with the Samaritans, and she found that her own experiments in self-examination helped her enormously when she was on the line, allowing all those unhappy anonymous callers to pour it all out and have a good old natter. So much of the unhappiness in life was caused by bottling it all up. Sally also had a part-time job, doing light secretarial duties three days a week for Relate, the marriage guidance charity which had an office in Reading. The work was interesting, and it provided her with a bit of cash. She and Alison were thinking of moving to a bigger place, and they had more or less decided on a lovely four-bedroomed property not far from Jessica's school. With the £20,000 she had received from Francis and a nest-egg of Alison's, they would easily be able to afford this larger house, where Jessica would not be so much 'under their heels' and where they could put Ditcham and its sad memories behind them.

Ten days before Christmas, Jessica and her mother sat at Miss Bill's kitchen table. The three of them had just eaten their early supper, a rather slimy mushroom risotto, followed by stewed apricots and yoghurt.

'You didn't eat much,' said Sally.

'I ate enough,' said Jessica. She very much disliked the Old Bill's taste in food, which was fibre-rich and more or less meat- (and flavour-) free. The Old Bill and Sally were in the habit of heaping their plates with these nutritious meals, and the size of their portions, and the sight of the seemingly insatiable manner in which the women forked the stuff into their mouths, was not conducive to appetite.

'You really do need to eat more, Jessica. Your mother's right.'

'I said, I ate enough.'

'Well, I'm feeling rather pleased with myself,' said Alison, dabbing the corners of her moustache with a napkin. 'I've done all my Christmas cards.'

'It was nice doing so many of them together,' said Sally, a remark whose purport Jessica tried to overlook.

'And we're all agreed that nothing could be more ghastly than spending Christmas eating battery turkey,' said Miss Bill, 'so there really are hardly any more arrangements to make.'

Jessica remembered that her mother had, in all previous years, taken a harmless delight in buying food for the Christmas holiday. In spite of the oddness of her parents' marriage, there had been some happy Christmases – her mother's childish glee in the 'trimmings' round the turkey; the crackers, the paper hats, the pudding. Was it really only as recently as last Christmas that Daddy had come in from the kitchen with the pudding alight, and they had all clapped and laughed – Granny and Mummy and Jessica? Granny could be a bitch, but she always knew how to make parties seem festive, however small the numbers.

'I'm very glad we've settled on a baked-potato Christmas,' said Miss Bill. 'It will give us all time to read, and walk, and listen to some music.'

'I think I'm going upstairs', said Jessica. She ignored her mother's rather timorous question, 'Aren't you going to help with the washing-up?' She heard, as she slammed the door, the Old Bill saying, 'Leave her. There's still a lot she's got to come to terms with.'

What neither of these women realised was that Jessica had decided that she would not 'come to terms' with any of the present arrangements. She did not like Miss Bill. The woman was her teacher, not her aunt or her mother; why should she be made to live with her?

Sometimes unhappiness overwhelms us with a moody fog, so that we are lost in it, and cannot see our way through. Sometimes, like the clear light which can precede heavy rain, it makes the world much sharper. Jessica was in this clear-sighted condition. She saw that her existence had become intolerable. They had petted her and nagged her and bossed her and, in a clumsy way, loved her, her parents; and they had congratulated themselves on how much money they had spent on her education. And when it suited either of them, or they were cross with one another, they had made of their daughter a special little friend. But, when it actually came down to it, they put themselves first. They had both contracted liaisons (of how great permanence in either case, Jessica could not determine) with no thought of their daughter. Jessica would just have to 'come to terms' with it, in Miss Bill's heavy phrase.

Well, perhaps it was time that they came to terms with certain things also, such as that, even if you are thirteen years old, you have feelings, you are a person in your own right, you can't just be shunted about as if you were a pet dog!

The Christmas discussions only heightened a generalised unease which Jessica felt in the presence of the two women. When they talked of the new house – they were going to put the Old Bill's cottage up for sale, and buy a new place – they threw into the conversation the occasional sop to Jessica – 'You'll be able to have a lovely big room – and although you'd think Arnold Close sounds very urban, being on a housing estate, it really does feel almost rural, leafy anyway, doesn't it, Alison?'

They had decided on this house without even taking Jessica to see it! Jessica, during such long-term plans, felt a very clear-edged, naked hatred for both women. Sometimes, she said that it would have been better if they had only seen fit to ask her, 'Do you want to live with us on a housing-estate on the outskirts of Reading?' She realised that this would only have been a courteous way of telling her that this was the scheme; but courtesy, though it would not have changed the situation, might have gone a small way towards easing its painfulness.

Jessica felt that, since her parents cared so little for her as to be able to put her through such misery, it was as if her life had ceased to have any worth. When she got to her bedroom, she threw herself on the small divan and stared at the darkness. She did not wish to read, so there was no point in switching on the light. She hated the room, which was a quarter the size of her old bedroom in the vicarage and which was full of reminders of the Bill – a college photograph of the Bill and her contemporaries at Homerton (she'd been as plain at twenty as she was at forty-five); incy-wincy little pictures of Swiss flowers, mementoes of the Bill's walking-holidays near Lausanne. It was better to be in the dark and not to see such horrors.

To die would be the most effective way out of the situation, providing release for herself and punishment for the grown-ups. Jessica had been thinking about it for weeks. She had studied the newspapers for accounts of suicides. Not long ago, a man had put his head on the railway line at Goring and been decapitated by an Intercity 125. People threw themselves under cars, jumped off bridges, overdosed on aspirin. All these methods had been coolly considered by Jessica Kreer. And she had also been inspired by a television documentary about overcrowding in British prisons and remand homes, in which half a dozen teenagers had killed themselves in the space of a few weeks: two by cutting their wrists and the other four by up-ending the beds in their cells and hanging themselves with sheets.

Since having her perception that Terry Widger's Jesus was no more than an Imaginary Friend (hence His universal power and appeal) Jessica had become aware of how infinitely painful human life was. She no longer allowed herself soppy consolations in which God, or another person, takes upon himself our sorrows and sins. She felt with acute keenness that we must carry our own imperfections, and endure our own misfortunes; no one else would do it for us, even though, as it said in the prayer, 'the burden of them is intolerable'. The only television programme she watched these days was the six o'clock news. Night after night, images of the utmost terror and ugliness were beamed into the Old Bill's sitting-room through the cathode ray tube. Civil wars in the Lebanon and the Balkans, in which, each day, parents lost their children, wives their husbands, families their homes and all their livelihoods; refugee camps in Ethiopia and Gaza, swarming with tens of thousands of miserable people whose lives could never be happy. That evening, Sally and the Bill had talked gaily to one another, slicing mushrooms for the risotto, while the newscaster had told them that a young man's head had been shot off in a snooker club in West Belfast, that a hurricane was sweeping through the West Indies destroying crops, houses and human lives; that scientists believed that pollution in European cities was now responsible for as many chest illnesses as smoking. . . .

All things wise and wonderful,
The Lord God made them all.

It was some hours later that Alison Bill put down her gros-point (she was making a tapestry cushion cover based on a medieval design from the Musée Cluny) and said, 'Well, dear, let me make you a herbal infusion.'

'That would be lovely.'

Alison affectionately touched Sally's shoulder as she passed her, and caressed the back of her neck. Sally brought up a hand to clasp Alison's. While the kettle boiled, Alison hummed advent hymns. It was her favourite season of the Church's year. When she brought back the infusions, she said, 'You know, it's funny, but in spite of all the terrible things you've been through I think this has been a good year!'

Sally put down her book on marriage guidance counselling, and said, 'So do I! I think it's been the best year of my life!'

'Shall I take a cup of something to . . .' Alison did not use Jessica's name: she pointed, merely, towards the ceiling.

'That would be kind. You're so good with her. It's nice to see you making friends.'

'Do you think so? I worry sometimes that she might – not resent me, exactly, that's too strong a word . . .'

'She doesn't resent you! How could she, after all you've done for us? Obviously it must take some getting used to, when your mum sets up house with a teacher at your school, but she's coping. All girls of her age get a bit sulky.'

'I wish she wasn't so thick with that Emily Roberts,' said Alison. 'I was worried enough when she seemed to be best friends with Sarah Mackintosh, who's a real little minx. But Emily's so negative. Anyway, I'll take up a mug of Sleepy-Time.'

Alison Bill was gone from the room for a surprisingly long time, considering how small her house was. Sally assumed that she had fallen into chat with her daughter, and she felt that this was good; she so wanted them all to love one another.

When she came back, Alison was still holding the mug of Sleepy-Time.

'Now, you're not to get upset,' she said, 'but Jessica seems to have disappeared.'

2

It was a little over a week before Christmas, and from the unpitying sky a delicate drizzle fell upon London, on the huge sprawl of its motorways and circular roads, and its suburban outer reaches, and its elegant streets and crescents and squares, and its areas of wasteland, and its winding, dark, evil unlit alleys and corners, all of it lying beneath the orange glow of a large wet sky. A Christmas angel, descending on London at Advent for the miraculous birth, would have looked down on an area densely packed with human souls. Before completing his descent, the angelic messenger could have hovered just high enough, and flown just far enough, to see the actors in our drama as it draws to its close. Such a visitant could have seen Mr Sandiman, the lawyer, with a small glass of excellent dry sherry in his hand, gazing down through the long Georgian windows of his first-floor office, at the bare wet branches of the trees in Lincoln's Inn Fields. The encampments beneath the trees and shrubs were, from this angle, all but invisible. Mr Sandiman felt pleased that the local residents in Lincoln's Inn Fields had made so much progress this year towards 'cleaning the square up'; it should not be too difficult, in the coming winter months, when the population of campers was inevitably reduced, to find some excuse to move them all on. The Advent angel, flitting on his way, would have seen Mr Sandiman's sherry-moist smile, and seen his eyes, twinkling beneath his half-moon spectacles. Mr Sandiman was not a bad man – he could not see the figures, slumped beneath the shrubbery, nor feel their sorrow.

Swooping like a London pigeon, now here, now there in the night air, the angel might have flown over Soho, and passed a little incident happening at the doors of Centrepoint – not the great gleaming empty office building by Tottenham Court Road station, but a hostel further buried in Soho, in Berwick Street. In this place young homeless people can find soup, warmth, and a refuge from the night. Many of those in greatest need of help are dependent on narcotics of one sort or another. The particular incident was happening outside Centrepoint on the pavement. Dave, our friend from the convoy, was standing there crying, and Suzanne was shouting, 'Don't stand there – go in and get *help*, can't you?' Suzanne, whom we have not encountered before, was a girl who had met Mo six weeks ago in a squat in Lambeth. For the first three weeks, before she found out the extent of his addiction, she had found him delightful, a really nice guy with whom to make love and share drugs. For the next three weeks, Suzanne had found herself in the position of being Mo's minder, Mo's helper. She had to keep a terrified *qui vive* while he performed his acts of petty larceny; she had had to spend some frightening evenings with Martyn and Wesley and their friends; she had had to hug Mo, and mother him, when the fears and the sweats and the shakings came upon him. But they would come upon him no more. She did not think they'd o.d.'d, any of them; they'd taken quite a modest dose, sharing a needle (but it was safe with someone you knew as well as Mo, right?) and finding a few unpierced veins – in her inexperienced case, somewhere near her elbow, and in Mo's between the toes of his right foot. And when they'd recovered they'd been to this pub – it was somewhere near Cambridge Circus, and they'd had a few drinks. (Suzanne did not know that Mo had injected himself once again in the gents' lavatory of this pub.) Now they were outside and this was, like, serious. Suzanne could not, herself, fully concentrate on what was happening; they had only had a few drinks, but the world was a dead place for her;

so no wonder Mo was falling down on the pavement, mouthing strange ravings, and leaning back with that weird, toothless laugh and wet-faced pallor, so white, so white, as the vomit came up through his throat, his nostrils, and was inhaled, back again into his lungs. In a London street, with his rolling eyes staring at the opaque sky, Mo died by drowning.

'It's OK,' one of the helpers from Centrepoint was saying to Dave. They were being kind to Dave and Suzanne, and putting their arms around them; and someone else was trying to resuscitate Mo, without success.

Less than quarter of a mile away, and wholly unaware of the fact that her former lover was at that moment dying, Jay Dunbar heard the distant strains of the ambulance sirens and the police sirens wailing their requiem for Mo. They slightly annoyed her since they cut in upon the edge of her music.

People could say that London was in the grip of a recession, or that the crowds were staying away from the West End for fear of terrorist bombs, but Jay had never done better business as a busker. In the underpass at Tottenham Court Road, where the acoustics were crude, you could even find something pleasing in the strains of the cheap Chinese violin. Paganini, Bach, Brahms, Haydn wafted through the underpass, and could even be heard far away down the corridors, where you bought tickets for the trains. Almost everyone who passed threw money into Jay's violin case. The previous day she had made eighty pounds, and it looked, by the time she finished tonight, as though she was going to improve on that figure today.

She had decided that there was no point in pretending to herself that people did not enjoy her beauty. So, she wore thick black tights, slightly fluffy on her long beautiful legs, and very short denim shorts, cut off to make a chaotic fringe four inches below the top of her legs. She also wore a black mohair jumper, tightly waisted with a thick leather belt covered in studs; it emphasised the charms of her breasts and her waist. She had started to grow her hair again, and it was already at shoulder-length. Her eyelashes were black with mascara and her thick, strangely uneven lips were glossy red. On her head, she wore a peaked baseball cap. On days when she dressed like this, she found that she made twice as much money as when she wore baggy jumpers and jeans.

For the first time in a year, Jay was in funds. She had reapplied at the Guildhall. To her surprise and relief, her old teachers there had been very accommodating, and she was going to return to full-time studies after Christmas. The difficult matters of money and grants were in the process of being sorted out. She had met some of her old student-acquaintances and they had been quite friendly to her. One of them had told her of a flat where a room could be rented for forty pounds a week. It was in Clapham, and she had taken up the offer. She practised each day, and she made money in the afternoons and evenings by busking. The extreme painfulness of the previous weeks had allowed her mind to clear, and she was at last aware of what she wanted to do with her life. She wanted to be a teacher like her mother.

Francis Kreer and Jay Dunbar had left 'Tudun-Teku' the morning after he had found her lying on the carpet with Eric. She now wondered whether she had accepted the Boss's advances, not because she enjoyed his lovemaking (though she had done so, she acknowledged that) but because she wanted to bring her association with Little Boy to an end.

When Eric Gadney had shuffled off, buttoning the tops of his trousers, Francis had said nothing for about an hour. He had sat, far apart from her, staring at the electric fire; then he had said, 'I would like to kill him.'

'Francis, it wasn't what you thought. Some men – darling Little Boy – some men just are . . .'

'Some men have to have their wicked way, and there's nothing a woman can do to stop them, is that it?'

'No, no.'

After another agonising silence, he asked, not looking at her, 'Has this happened often?'

There was so much pain, that she did not want to add to it. He was her Little Boy! She was supposed to be looking after him! She must protect him from the knowledge of what had been happening among the geraniums and pelargoniums. And yet, she found it was impossible to lie. She loved him now; but she loved him enough to know that she could not help him, that their association could never bring happiness to either of them; and she loved him enough to wish to respect him. He wasn't a little boy: he was a married man, in a desperately unhappy plight. She did not want to exacerbate the pain but nor did she wish to molly-coddle him any longer.

'Eric has never been here before. I told him I did not want to make love to him. I told him that I loved you.'

'But he has made love to you?'

'Francis, don't let's torture ourselves.'

'Why? Why him? Couldn't you just have been – a little kinder to me?'

When he began to weep, she came over to comfort him, but he shook her off. 'Please don't,' he said.

In the morning, they had loaded the car – his final asset – and driven away to London. Jay wished that she could have said goodbye to Ena. She liked Ena, and she wondered how the Boss would explain the sudden departure of their tenants at 'Tudun-Teku'. It was a chilling drive. Francis was unable to speak to her. She sensed enough of his pain to know that he was not being deliberately stand-offish in order to hurt her or to score points. By an appalling accident – or so it seemed to her – she had managed to do what she least wanted: to inflict pain on a man whom she loved. As the car reached the morning rush-hour in the Mile End Road, she said, 'Francis, I don't want us to part as enemies. Let's say something to one another.'

He did not reply.

'I've really liked being with you. You've helped me, you really have. And you've been so gentle, and so kind. I really hope things work out for you, Francis. God, I'm not putting this well, but you've been the first lover I really liked. It's true! You've been my friend.'

No reply.

'And I really want to know how *Emma* ends!'

They had stopped at some traffic lights about two hundred yards south of London Bridge.

He spoke at last.

'Where would you like me to drop you off?'

He asked it as vacantly and as casually as if she had been a hitch-hiker whom he did not know.

'Francis, are you going to be all right?'

This question was so ridiculous – she knew that as she was asking it. Of course, Francis was not going to be all right! Who would look after her Little Boy? She could not do so, and he could not go back to his wife, and he had no money. He had a wild, strange look in his eyes.

'Francis, I think I'd better come with you – do you know where you are going? Have you got somewhere to go?'

The lights had changed to green, and the cars behind were hooting.

'I think you'd better get out here,' he said. 'Goodbye.'

And she had got out, and watched the Maestro lurch forward over London Bridge until it was lost in the traffic.

She was not Francis Kreer's keeper. But, as well as feeling anxious about him, she missed him, as she stood in the underpass at Tottenham Court Road and played her cheap Chinese violin.

'Thank you,' she said, when a middle-aged man in a tweed suit and an old-fashioned mackintosh threw a five pound note into her violin case.

'Merry Christmas,' said the man. He was looking at her in the way that all men looked at her. 'That was lovely. Play something else.'

She waited for the stranger to walk away towards his train, and then, abandoning Paganini, she struck up the tune of 'The Jolly Miller', and sang softly to herself as she played.

I care for nobody, no, not I
And nobody cares for me.

3

Flitting eastward, the recording angel might have found Jessica, shaking with fear, somewhere in Bethnal Green. She had last heard from her father ten days ago. He had sent her a postcard to say that he had left Deal, and was seeking accommodation in London. Letters, he said, would reach him, if she wrote to c/o The Reverend Damian Wells, St Agatha's, Hoxton.

Jessica had decided that she could not endure 'a baked-potato Christmas' with her mother and Miss Bill. She did not plan to escape that very night; it was something which she did on impulse, throwing a few belongings into a plastic carrier bag, and slipping out of the Bill's cottage while the two women were engrossed in conversation downstairs. She had hitch-hiked to Didcot because there was no bus, and she had caught the first train up to Paddington.

It was frightening being out on her own, and she now wished that she had gone home, and made her runaway the next day, during the daylight hours. The man who gave her the lift had said that it was dangerous for young girls to hang about on their own at night, and this had made her all the more scared. He had asked her what she was doing out so late at night, and when he left her at the station she had run on to the train for fear that he would follow or attack her. Everyone on the train seemed like a predator, and she did not wish to be seen to be vulnerable. Most of the journey was spent locked in the lavatory, where she studied her small A to Z map of London and tried to find Hoxton. After a number of false starts, she had found herself on a Central Line train and had leapt off at Bethnal Green. It was eleven o'clock at night by the time she got there, and the streets near the station were full of drunks. She did not dare to approach any of them for advice, and she hoped that, if she walked briskly enough, no one would follow her.

She did dare to stop an old woman, who was walking a dog, and ask her of the whereabouts of St Agatha's church. This old woman gave her quite specific directions, so hard to follow that she forgot half of them, and now found herself lost completely. Panic threatened to set in. If a taxi were to come along, she thought of hailing that (she had eight pounds in her purse), but she was afraid of standing beside the kerb to wait for a taxi in case of being picked up by 'someone funny'. A car did come to a halt by the kerb and an Arab with a thick moustache got out, calling, 'Hey! Young lady! You want a lift? I'm a taxi! I'm a mini-cab!' at which she broke into a run, and sprinted the length of a dark, narrow street, one side of which was a large, gloomy Victorian school. She no longer hoped to find Hoxton, she was now running away, not running to. She wanted to find light. She wanted to find a policeman. In the larger, brighter street into which she turned, a police car did drive past at some speed, and she waved at it, but it did not stop.

This street was lined with brightly-lit shops: video shops, betting shops, a shop selling mountain bikes. There was a group of young people waiting at a bus stop about fifty yards ahead of her, and this made Jessica's heart beat all the faster. She was sure that these people would attack her, or at the very least shout abuse. On the other hand, she was also frightened of crossing the road, where some of the passers-by looked just as threatening.

At this point, she realised that she had been walking round in a circle and that Bethnal Green Station, which she had left half an hour before, was now up ahead, beyond the bus stop, on her left.

'Hi! You lost or something?' One of the boys at the bus stop was calling to her.

This made her step into the kerb, thinking that it was worth risking being run over rather than falling in with this young man, a very lanky youth with his presumably abundant hair contained in a multi-coloured, crocheted cushion-cover.

'Hey, girl, you're lost!' he had taken her by the elbow. 'You nearly walked under a car, there!'

'Let me go!'

'Where are you going?'

The three companions of the tall youth were divided. One of them was saying, 'Leave her alone,' while another was countering the tall youth's questions, 'Where you from? What were you doing, walking out in front of that car? Don't you know it's dangerous? What have you been taking, girl?'

Jessica was so frightened that she did not really understand the purport of these inquiries. She found herself weakening, and allowing herself to be taken in hand by the boys.

'Please help me! Please take me to St Agatha's.'

This made two of the boys laugh, while the tall lanky one said, 'Shut up, man. You tell us where you're going, and we'll take you there.'

Jessica told them again. She was going to St Agatha's, Hoxton, where her father was staying.

'We don't know where that is,' said Lanky. 'But you're coming along with us.'

4

If in the earlier part of the evening the Christmas angel had flitted until he hovered over the vicarage – or, as the incumbent preferred to call it, the presbytery – of St Agatha's, Hoxton, he would have found a scene of considerable pathos. Damian Wells knew that he had offered accommodation at 'any time' to Francis Kreer, but he had not really expected his friend to pursue the invitation. Even a week of Francis's presence in the house had reduced Damian's nerves to a frazzle, and what was so alarming was that Francis had given no indication of when he intended to leave.

The physical discomfort of sharing a small house with such an untidy person was not the least of Father Wells's causes for complaint. Damian had always believed that Francis Kreer was neat, and clean. It was true that – filthy habit – he smoked a pipe. But the vicarage at Ditcham, though not furnished in a style which excited Father Wells, was always spotlessly dusted and hoovered. Francis himself, likewise, had always been punctiliously washed, shaven, manicured, trimmed. This time was past. He had turned into a sordid ragamuffin, wearing the most extraordinary combination of clothes bought from charity shops, and not seeming to notice that they stank. Damian had even felt moved to tell Francis to have a bath, the smell was so bad, and the poor man had obeyed; but although Damian had added, 'and if you put all your clothes in the laundry basket, I'll get Mrs Carver to put them through the Hotpoint,' Francis had simply climbed out of the bath (still unshaven with what looked like a week's scrubby growth of beard appearing on chin and cheeks) and revested himself in his reeking pants, socks, jerseys – and those awful plimsolls, now permanently damp from this spell of wet weather: and that cassock. The towel – as always when Francis went to the bathroom – had been just thrown down, any old how, and puddles of water and footprints had been left on the beige fitted carpet. This was the sort of thing which other people could probably tolerate, or at least 'get over' quickly; but the sight of a dirty crumpled towel on his bathroom floor upset Damian for hours. It left him shaking, not just with anger but with the sensation of 'things fall apart, the centre cannot hold'.

As a human being, as a Christian, as a priest, Damian knew that he ought to pity Francis. Something had gone terribly wrong. But the way that Damian put it to himself was, 'I'm not the right person to help in this situation.' Take the example of Francis's Maestro. Damian understood that Francis was financially ruined. Barclaycard had recalled his credit facilities; the bank had refused to allow him to sign cheques. He seemed incapable of organising himself into attendance at the local DSS offices, where someone would surely explain to him his rights and entitlements. But Francis refused to concentrate on important matters like this. He had even begun to talk differently, a much higher pitch than his usual tone, and an unstoppable gabble of words.

'I really think you should go down to the Unemployment Offices,' Damian said pointedly. 'I mean, they could help you get fixed up with a place to live – if you really think there's no chance of your going back to Sally.'

You could not get a more blatant hint than this that Damian wanted him out of the house and *off his hands*, but Francis had said, 'You see, I don't suppose I'm entitled to benefit, resigned, resigned. I resigned the living of Ditcham, that was the trouble, if they'd sacked me it would be a different story because then the state would have to put me on the Civil List – give me the pension, the right word escapes me exactly. No, I think my best bet would be to sell the car, I can't afford to run it and I hate cars. Hate them. Always have, and this one has such painful associations. One day I'll tell you, Damian, but it's too sad, too sad.'

Damian guessed that Francis had been ditched by his girl: it was no surprise.

'Well, don't go and get ripped off. I mean that's a C-registration car, it's probably worth three or four thousand pounds.'

But this advice had not been heeded. When Damian returned to the presbytery that afternoon, he found an exultant Francis.

Some man in a garage had given him £900 in cash. Enough to last him for months, he said, with his simple tastes.

A religious squabble had threatened to flare that evening. Damian had insisted on preparing the sausages, mashed potatoes and brown sauce himself: Francis had 'helped' in the kitchen on the day of his arrival, but Damian could not afford to have *all* his pans burned, nor the non-stick scraped off with a metal fish-slice. When they were settled at the table with their food, which Francis ate with great speed and greedy, slurping noises, Damian had said, 'I'm not sure how I'll get through this week – we've got the church to decorate, we've got the trees to order; the shepherds in the crib are really naff, and one of them's lost its head – I must get a better crib for next year. Then I'm going to be in the confessional three days running. Not that any of them go to confession any more.'

'I don't blame them.'

Damian ignored this. 'Then there's a rehearsal for the Midnight Mass – I expect we'll get a lot coming to that, and another big mass on Christmas morning, and sermons to prepare.'

'I could give you a good sermon – pass the bread, please, thank you – I could give you a good Christmas sermon.'

'You're tired, dear.'

'There should be a moratorium on Christmas,' said Francis. 'Every single New Testament scholar realises that the Infancy narratives in the gospels are pure mythology. Even the orthodox ones who accept the bodily resurrection realise that there's not the slightest reason for supposing Jesus ever went to Bethlehem, let alone being born there.' He hurrumphed and whinnied. It was a mad-sounding laugh. 'And yet, year after year, we feed out more opium for the people – Baby Jesus in the crib; it doesn't even say in the Gospels that he was born in a stable, or that his parents were staying in an inn. As for the universal census at the time of Quirinius – well, we all know that Quirinius and Herod were not even contemporaries . . .'

'Don't let's talk about it, dear. If you don't mind.'

'Oh, no. Don't let's talk about it. Let's go on pretending that we all believe in fairy tales. Very useful, very edifying.'

'Look, Francis, I don't know what's been passing through

your head, and if you're having difficulties with the faith I'm sorry for you . . .'

'Difficulties! No difficulties at all. There's nothing difficult about recognising a fairy story as a fairy story. You're the ones who are having difficulties, the ones who go on peddling this stuff.'

'I'd rather you didn't . . .'

'What's so frightening about telling the truth? Well, quite a lot of things now I come to think about it. Thinking is the bravest human activity – just as brave as fighting in a battle; the church has been in business for two thousand years because people are too frightened to think.'

'You know that I believe in it, Francis, let's just drop the subject, can we? I'd no idea you'd lost your faith. As I say, I'm sorry for you.'

'I don't want you to be sorry for me. I'm in a mess, mess, mess, yes? Just 'cause I'm going mad, it doesn't mean that I can't see that I'm going mad! Ha! Ha!' The laugh was like a little dog yapping. 'Have you ever seen a woman's cunt, Damian? You may think this is a disgusting thing to say, but they are the most beautiful parts of their anatomy. And when you've seen one, and really *known* one –'

'Please!'

'You wouldn't want to make a cult of virginity if you had. All the cult of virginity stuff – I remember Harris of Balliol telling me this years ago – it was all invented by queers. Plato was a queer, Plotinus was a queer, St Paul was a queer. They'd never got their noses into a cunt – let alone their cocks. It was as simple as that. So they spun all these fairy stories about the *Parthenos*, the Virgin-Goddess. Now Our Lady – nothing against Our Lady, wonderful woman no doubt.'

Damian felt himself becoming uncontrollably angry; it was far worse than the irritation over his untidy bathroom or burnt frying-pan.

'Francis, you are my guest. This is my house. I won't have you insulting Our Lady! Do you hear? I won't have it!'

Francis's voice, which had risen by an octave and was jabbering, said, 'As you will, as you will. I didn't mean to be offensive!' Then another crazy laugh. 'But I did, really. I want to drink some gin, Damian. I bought some gin with the money I got for the car. Did I tell you about that? I got a huge amount of money for the car.'

'You got £900. You were swindled.'

'I don't need money. Money is an illusion. Money is shit. All our thoughts about money derive from our thoughts about shit, has that ever occurred to you? So do our thoughts about religion, come to that. But Mummy must have been very good about that – you would think from the way she brought me up that I would be an anal retentive type, but I'm not. I might have seemed like one. Potty training must have been relaxed. I've no fears of poverty. Do you think Mummy wanted me to go through all this; do you think she realised what she was doing when she altered her will? She must have done it just under a year ago, because I remember she came for Christmas and she seemed perfectly well, her usual charming self. Mummy always had this great gift of charm.'

'You don't need to have money if you sponge off your friends all the time.'

'Is that what I'm doing?'

'I'm sorry, Francis. I shouldn't have said that. But look – dear – you can't stay here forever. It just wouldn't work. We'd get on each other's nerves.' The telephone interrupted this.

'Yes. Sally! How are you? What – oh my God, how awful!'

Francis leapt from the table – 'What is it? What is it? What's happened to Jessica? What have they done to Jessica?'

5

Francis Kreer sat in the Good Morning! Café at twenty to eight next morning, smoking a cigarette over his plate of bacon and eggs. It was a crowded little café, and the windows were steamy. Outside, it was still dark. Damian was in church saying Mass. Francis had come down to the café for breakfast less because he was hungry than because he could not stay still. Also, he dreaded being on his own in the presbytery when the telephone rang. He now assumed that Jessica was dead. He just did not feel strong enough to hear the details from the police; nor could he endure to have a telephone conversation with Sally. The sleepless night, when worry about Jessica had deepened into despair, and into the certainty that she must be dead, had sharpened Francis's hatred for his wife. Many sentences beginning 'if' had started in his head. If Sally had not *let* the girl *out*; if Sally was not such a *fool*; if Sally were not living with Alison Bill . . . The rational part of Francis's mind, the side of the mind which had been nurtured and taught by Harris of Balliol, tried to introduce a note of calm. None of them knew for certain what had happened to Jessica. It would be unwise to hope too brightly, but there was even the chance that she might still be alive somewhere. Whether Jessica was dead or alive, the blame could not be laid at the door of Sally, who – to judge from Damian's conversation with her on the telephone, had not so much as known that Jessica was gone, until it was too late.

She could be anywhere – she could have been abducted in Berkshire, she could have committed suicide, she could have been trying to come up to London. The police had no 'leads' though a girl answering Jessica's description had been seen catching a late train at Didcot the previous evening.

Francis squashed the cigarette into the yolk of his fried egg and sipped the acrid strong tea from his mug. The Management, the Fates, however one liked to term it – No-God – had taken everything else away. Taken his money. Taken his mother. Taken his wife. Taken his job. Taken his reputation. It would have been surprising if they had left him the chance of happiness through his daughter. Francis thought there were no further boundaries of pain to be passed. Jay had appeared like an angel to soothe the pain of Mummy's death, to be his friend and his lover, in the world of No-God when the parish became impossible. And she, his kindest friend, his most erotic of lovers, cared for him so little that she was prepared to do *that*. The sight of her on the carpet with Eric Gadney was in its way just as painful as the knowledge that his mother was dead.

And now, in addition to this knowledge, he had to force his mind to the knowledge that Jess was dead – his own darling daughter. From a very early age, almost before she could talk, Francis had recognised Jessica as an ally, someone who would make life bearable again at Ditcham vicarage. As well as being father and daughter, they were secret allies, clever fifth columnists in the realm of the stupid. How much he had loved her physically when she was a tiny child – how happy they had been snuggling in bed together when she was three or four, and he had begun to awaken her mind to the pleasures of literature: Beatrix Potter (entire), the better Blytons (of which there are many), Dr Seuss, Roald Dahl, E. Nesbit, Conan Doyle – as the years unfolded, this reading aloud together and cuddling had been such a good part of life; as had the chess-playing.

Jay had not been a substitute for a wife so much as the substitute for a daughter. True? What did it matter now? He had lost them both.

He had been *kept* from Jess by the events of this year. Almost as if he had been prevented from seeing the child because of illness or a prison-sentence. He had every confidence that when life calmed down (and life always did calm down, didn't it? – you couldn't *live* at the emotional fever-pitch of the last six months), then he would somehow be able to reconstruct his life with Jessica. Perhaps she would begin to understand, a little, some of the fires and tempests through which he had passed; and, having understood, pardon. No chance of that now, and no chance that he would ever find another human being on this planet who was even remotely sympathetic.

If only there had been a Christmas angel hovering at that moment! He could have announced to Francis Kreer glad tidings of great joy. He could have told Francis that Jessica was not dead, but that within an hour she would be taken to Hoxton in a bus by Lawrence, the lanky boy in the woolly hat, and by Lawrence's mother, Mrs Maycock, a well-dressed woman who looked too young to have a son as large as Lawrence.

Jessica had been taken home by Lawrence Maycock because he thought she did not look safe. He had watched her walk round the block – self-evidently lost – twice, and he had watched her step into the kerb and very nearly be killed. He and his friends had instinctively decided to befriend Jessica. Because she was so frightened of them, they at first wondered if she was mad, or on drugs, and they had kept asking her what she was 'on'. It had taken the common sense of Mrs Maycock to realise that any girl or young woman, accosted late at night by a crowd of boys whom she didn't know, would be frightened.

'Still, you're safe now,' said Mrs Maycock, blocking her ears as she spoke because Lawrence put his rap tapes on the stereo.

So, Jessica spent that night *chez* Maycock. It was in a tower block poetically named Tintern House, but actually resembling one of the bleaker socio-architectural experiments of Eastern Germany or provincial Russia in the days of the Stalinist terrors. Mrs Maycock had provided Jessica with malt bread and butter, cake, tea, and a comfortable place to sleep on the sofa, which converted into a put-me-up. There appeared to be no Mr Maycock, but Lawrence had two younger brothers. Jessica had slept the night through, and at the moment when her father was singing her sad requiem inside his head in the Good Morning! Café she was still asleep. Only when she woke did Mrs Maycock set about discovering the whereabouts of St Agatha's, Hoxton, which she did by applying to the vicar of the church which she attended herself. By mid-morning the parents of Jessica Kreer knew that she was still alive.

But there was no Christmas angel hovering over Hoxton, and so Francis Kreer knew none of this, and continued to smoke and to think his sad thoughts, and to order another large mug of tea when his waitress took away his breakfast almost uneaten, and to watch the workmen in the café come and go, and to see the grey dawn break through the steamy condensation on the café windows.

He did not know how long he sat there, but it was long enough for Stella, the fat Italian waitress who never smiled, to hover beside his table, and say, 'Are you all right, darling?'

'No,' said Francis Kreer simply. 'I've broken my heart.'

And he arose, and walked down the two or three blocks to the presbytery – a nasty, two-up two-down little building, thrown up in the 1960s. Luckily, Francis walked everywhere stealthily these days, or he would have gone right up to Damian's front door, and walked slap into his enemy. For there was Alison Bill's Astra parked beside the kerb, and that lady was getting out of one door, while Sally, standing with Damian beside the open front-door of the house, shouted, 'There he is!'

There was no logical explanation of why it should have turned, instantaneously, into a chase, but Francis was in too much of a hurry to be logical. He did not wish to speak to these women. He dreaded them. He ran to the main road, jumped on board the first bus which came along, not seeing its number or direction, and began to think about this urgent matter of bus numbers as he took his seat. A 38 bus would have signified 3 plus 8 equals 11 – the number of the apostles after the traitor Judas had hanged himself ('And his bowels gushed forth . . . and the lot fell upon Matthias'). A 15 would have taken him westward, down Fleet Street, through the West End, and all the way to Ladbroke Grove via Paddington.

Fifteen could have been 10 commandments plus the Famous Five, but he could not give a final judgement of this question until he had looked it up in the book of Revelations (alias the W section of *Who's Who*). And meanwhile, with unhurrying chase, and unperturbed pace, Miss Bill was coming along behind, flapping her huge bat-like wings. Better change bus. It was an old-fashioned bus with a conductor, who called out – 'Ere! You haven't paid your fare!'

This man was amazed when the dirty clergyman placed in his hand a £50 note and hurried off the bus into Lombard Street.

Francis still had over £500 in his cassock pocket, left over from the sale of his Maestro. It would be pleasing to him when he had spent the last penny of Mummy's fortune, and when he could live as the fowls of the air and the lilies of the field.

Francis Kreer looked about him. He knew that he was somewhere in the City of London, but he did not know exactly where. The pavements were thronged with people going to work in banks, insurance offices, the Stock Exchange, or smart lawyers' firms. They all wore a sort of uniform. The men had blue overcoats and, beneath that, double-breasted dark grey suits. The women had slightly more variation of colour, but gave off the same air of uniformity, so that the Vicar of Sorrows made a particularly conspicuous figure in that busy scene. He was bare-headed, having left his beret on the bus, and he had a little over a week's growth of beard. His eyes were bloodshot and his cheeks were gaunt. His teeth were now turning from yellow to brown, and his hands were developing that amber patina of the chain-smoker who never washes. Delicate as the morning sunlight was in that pale winter, it was still strong enough to catch the surface of his cassock and make it shine as it fell on the slimy congealed substances which clung there.

'Must get away from Miss Bill, Jessica dead, heart broken.' These were the three great imperatives in the mind of Francis Kreer as he leapt along the street, diving on and off the pavement, and dodging the traffic when he came too near the kerb.

At length, he came to a church with an open door. It was one of the old City churches which had escaped both the bombing of the Luftwaffe and, late in the century, the bulldozers of the developers. Outside it, there were a number of placards. One announced that it was collecting money for a charity for the homeless called Crisis at Christmas. Singers were gathered there to sing a 'carol marathon' and there were trestle tables set up at the back of the church laden with Christmas cards, profits from whose sale were to help the homeless.

Some of the homeless had taken refuge in the church. A smell of urine was inescapable as one pushed open the great leather-covered doors and beheld the Wren interior – the vast carved Baroque reredos, the slightly crumbling Corinthian columns, the polished box-pews. It was in these pews that various men and women were sitting or lying. There were probably fifty or sixty of them in the church, so that it was, perhaps, unsurprising that Francis, upon seeing this 'congregation', formed the impression that they were all awaiting his arrival.

It was really a good turn-out, more than he would get at Ditcham, even on the days when the 'Mattins recusants' drove over for their 'fix' of 1662. And this congregation, unlike the congregation at Ditcham, *looked* like Christians. Here were some people who had, for whatever reason, decided that it was blessed to be poor. They had denied themselves the comforts of this world in order to become like Christ and to lie down in destitution. Foxes have holes and the birds of the air have their nests but the Son of Man hath nowhere to lay his head – that gentle text well could they understand.

Odd the way human beings look when they've been deprived of their fitted bathrooms and their company cars for a week or two. Francis wondered if these people, snoozing and pissing and mumbling at different corners of this church, were not in fact the

Mattins recusants who had fallen on hard times. That maroon-faced woman, with the holes in her stockings, and the cider-bottle in her hand – she was surely Dorothy Maxwell-Lee? And the pair in the box-pew behind her – the man with the string-belt and the trilby hat on – weren't they those rather smart people from Aldworth? That man looking for something in his plastic bag – wasn't that the Bishop? What was he looking for? The secret of the universe, probably. Well, in that case, Francis had better tell him what it was.

The level of noise and activity in the church was all of a controlled nature. There was not silence. Nor was there riot. Some of the 'homeless' were wandering about muttering to themselves, and some of the 'helpers' were calling out thoughts – who wanted some coffee, where a particular carton of Christmas cards were to be found – and some of the 'public' were rootling through these piles of cards, while outside, in the porch, the little choir sang, 'In the bleak mid-winter, long ago.'

Francis walked with dignity up the aisle. Nobody stopped him – he would have been astonished and affronted if they had done so – when he reached the bottom of the pulpit steps and began his dignified spiral ascent. Once there, he leaned against the crimson cushion which served as a lectern and gave out his text.

'Psalm 53, verse one, The fool hath said in his heart there is No-God – and I speak to you in the name of No-God, No-Father, No-Son and No-Holy Ghost. Get out a calculator and, if you haven't got a calculator, I'll do your work for you. This verse – "The fool hath said in his heart, there is No-God" – is the 19,612th verse in the Old Testament. And I expect that you have often asked yourself who is this fool in the text? After all, there is nothing foolish about saying there is no God, is there? What is foolish about telling the truth? The matter becomes clearer when, with our calculators to the ready, we turn to the appropriate entry in *Who's Who*. There you will find the answer. The 19,612th entry in *Who's Who* is, as you might have expected, Professor Meynard Harris of Balliol College, Oxford, the retired Barnes Professor of Roman History. In other words, this text points us in the direction of Harris, and all he has stood for. Harris is the fool. You, my friends, are not fools if, in your desperation and nakedness and despair, you shake your fists at the empty sky and say, "There is no God!" You have every right to say that, just as Jesus had every right to cry aloud on the cross, "My God, my God, why hast thou forsaken me?" For you and I are those who wander through this world, crying and wailing and mourning and muttering for our lost God. And we try to find him in all the most unlikely places – in ourselves, and in the faces of the poor and the sick, and in all the places he has most refused to dwell, we look for him. But you see, the fool – Harris – got there before us. He's been telling us there is no God ever since 1789! And, unfortunately, it is the one piece of knowledge which is completely useless to the human race. It's an irrelevance! You see, Harris wants to tell us that we don't need God as an *explanation* for things: and what we want to tell Harris is that we didn't go to God as an explanation for things. Harris went to God because he wanted to explain how the universe came into being. So, when he was a child and thought as a child and spoke as a child, Harris assumed that the universe was an artefact, a thing which someone had made, and that this someone was God! And when Harris became a man he saw that there was no need to posit a Creator, that things, matter, the universe itself could simply be, without the supposed 'mad inventor' who was sitting above the cherubim, making the world and the stars, and cancer and the angels. So, out goes God as the maker: and the fool in his heart said, "There is no God", because Jesus could never have thought he was God. So out goes the idea that Christianity must in some way derive from the experience of the Resurrection or the conviction that the apostles really knew God through Jesus. Because Christianity cannot be explained by our feeble speculations about the historical Jesus – if he even existed – and if he did exist he certainly was not divine and did not think he was divine, and so Harris has to tell us. And we need this fool, telling us there is no God, just as old kings in medieval courts needed fools: because only fools dared to tell them the truth, only fools dared to puncture their vanity . . .'

'That's very nice!' One of the 'helpers', a kind-faced young man in jeans, was standing beneath the pulpit and was calling up to Francis. 'But perhaps you can come down now?'

Outside, the carol-singers had reached the verse –

What can I give him
Poor as I am?
If I were a Shepherd,
I would bring a lamb . . .

'But what so maddens the Harrises of Balliol, the fools, is that human beings will always go on *finding* God. Their hearts are restless until they find him: and it really does suggest that we are much odder beings than Harris would want us to be, much more beautiful beings, really! Look at the places we find him – in the non-existent stable at Bethlehem, in the slums, and the Gulag and the leper colonies. Oh, I'm not betraying my old Damoetas, my Harris, my fool. I know he's *right*.' Francis really bellowed this.

'Please come down!' said the helper. 'We could give you a nice cup of coffee.'

Some of the 'homeless' were amused by the performance and had sat up to listen to Francis as he preached to them from the pulpit. Some of the card-buyers were listening, too, and there was an agitated conference happening by the font between the Vicar of the church and some of his helpers.

If I were a wise man,
I would do my part!

from the singers in the street.

'You and your cleverness! That was something Mummy used to say when Daddy sat there with one of his puzzles, but the world isn't just puzzles and cleverness. I'm the Vicar of Sorrows, despised and rejected of women! Mummy didn't understand *The Times* crossword, let alone ENIGMA!'

Francis was now shouting at the top of his voice. The great weight of sorrow which seemed to be tugging inside his chest, pulling at his rib-cage, filling his oesophagus and lungs with the sting of heartburn, wringing his very vitals, was not lifted by shouting, but it seemed as though for the first time he was strong enough to stare the darkness in the face and to shout at it. He could look at the most painful snapshots in his mind – Mummy's empty bedroom or Jay, wriggling on the carpet beneath Eric Gadney, or Jessica, raped and strangled, and corpse-pale, lying in some municipal rubbish heap, and he could defy this horror with the last shriek of the dying Christ as he upbraided God for forsaking him!

And Francis knew now that he was hallucinating, probably something they had put in his tea at the Good Morning! Café, for the church was crowds, all looking up at him, and through the crowds came a man in uniform, an ambulance man, hand in hand with Jessica, and behind them, terrible and anxious, Sally and Alison Bill.